In the Absence of Honor

a novel

Jim Proebstle

EMERALD
BOOK CO.
A Division of Greenleaf Book Group LLC

Published by Emerald Book Company
4425 South Mo Pac Expwy., Suite 600
Austin, TX 78735

For ordering information or special discounts for bulk purchases, please contact Emerald Book Company at: 4425 South Mo Pac Expwy., Suite 600, Austin, TX 78735, (512) 891-6100.

Design and composition by Greenleaf Book Group LLC

Publisher's Cataloging-In-Publication Data
(Prepared by The Donohue Group, Inc.)

Proebstle, Jim.
  In the absence of honor : a novel / Jim Proebstle. -- 1st ed.

  p. ; cm.

  ISBN: 978-1-934572-04-7

  1. Casinos--Minnesota--Fiction. 2. Ojibwe Indians--Minnesota--Fiction. 3. Organized crime--Minnesota--Fiction. 4. Murder--Minnesota--Fiction. 5. Minnesota--Fiction. I. Title.

PS3616.R64 I5 2008
813/.6   2008927640

Printed in the United States of America on acid-free paper

12 11 10 09 08   10 9 8 7 6 5 4 3 2 1

First Edition

For Leonard and Helen Proebstle

part 1

one

AN EXHILARATING FEELING took hold of Jake as he and KC, his ten-year-old golden retriever, wound down the curving, forest-canopied entrance to his cabin at Sandy Cove in the Minnesota North Woods. Large, mature oak and maple trees, still holding their fall leaves, lined the grassy half-mile access road with an occasional spruce tree accent. The final light of day barely captured the brilliant fall colors in the crisp air. His anticipation of arrival was like no other as the comfort of childhood memories created the familiar sense of well-being.

With his first glimpse of the cabin, however, Jake immediately knew something was wrong. The back door to the three-season porch stood wide open. It appeared stuck or jammed, allowing anything to come or go as it pleased. In thirty years, this had never happened. Oh, there had been the time when someone used the cabin to escape a winter storm for a few days, but for the door to be open like this—it made no sense.

The hair on the nape of KC's neck bristled, and as soon as Jake opened the back gate, the dog jumped from the Yukon and barked aggressively while moving toward the cabin. His hips were lowered and his front legs braced in a ready stance. His eyes focused suspiciously in anticipation of a hidden menace.

"KC, stay." The years of training showed as KC immediately became motionless.

"Good boy," Jake reinforced as he quickly clipped on the dog's leash. Jake didn't know what to expect, but he sure didn't want KC running headlong into the cabin and trouble he couldn't handle.

Jake pulled his shotgun from its case in the back of the truck and chambered three shells. Rather than approach the cabin directly, however, he circled. The cabin was situated one hundred feet from the lake on a two-acre clearing in the forest, giving Jake plenty of room to observe, but he was losing light rapidly.

He moved slowly.

KC continued to bark and tug at the leash.

Rounding the corner of the cabin, Jake saw that the front, lakeside door was open as well. He'd been meticulous in closing up when he left in September, just two months ago. Besides, the Millers would have called if something serious had occurred—and if not them, then someone else. The few people who lived on Arrowhead Peninsula were always looking out for each other, making sure that damage from weather or vandalism didn't get worse by going unchecked.

As Jake and KC approached the open lakeside door, a big gray squirrel ran from inside the cabin across the wooden deck.

"Terrific!" he murmured under his breath. While squirrels were the least of his worries, he knew this was not a good sign.

Moving closer to the elevated cedar deck, Jake called out, "Is anybody here?"

No answer.

By now it was almost dark and the shadows of an emerging moon low on the horizon made it difficult to see inside the cabin.

Jake decided to take KC back to the truck, which would free him to approach the cabin with both hands on the shotgun. An open cabin in the deep forest could mean a lot of things—none of them good.

As he returned to the Yukon, Jake instinctively checked for fresh vehicle tracks in the soft dirt of the driveway. He saw nothing in the truck's headlights that would indicate another car or truck.

"KC, kennel!" The dog responded immediately and jumped back into the cargo area of the truck.

"I'll be back in a minute, boy. I want to check this out by myself. You'll be okay."

New batteries for his big flashlight were on tomorrow's shopping list. He tried anyway. Click. Dead, just as he thought.

Jake walked back around to the lake side of the cabin under the remaining light from the water's reflections. Visibility was marginal.

Quietly, he moved closer. He detected a rotten aroma but could not clearly identify the smell. Stale garbage, maybe? The screen door hung on one hinge, in pieces, as if someone or something had ripped through it.

This is not good, he thought.

Once he was on the deck, the stench became overwhelming. Peering inside, Jake saw the living area in total shambles. The place had been ravaged, but there was more. The sickening smell came from rotting parts of a deer carcass, partially eaten and strewn across the floor.

"Aw, shit!" He repositioned himself to get a better look.

"How could this happen?"

His heart left him when he heard bobcat-like growls from the upstairs loft. Two large raccoons lurked in the deep shadows at the top edge of the stairs leading to the bedrooms. Jake knew they were harmless so long as he stayed out of reach. But raccoons would attack and do severe damage to a dog, even one KC's size. He regarded his decision to kennel KC as a good one.

Jake backed away and reached for the wall switch. Everything became clear with a flick. He gasped in horror. The raccoons and squirrels might account for some of the damage, but not for the chaos that lay before him. The deer carcass and its grotesquely disjointed parts looked like an insane massacre had taken place.

Staying clear of the raccoons, Jake cautiously checked the rest of the cabin, praying for no more surprises. He found none.

He knew the raccoons must be evicted tonight. Locking the doors with them inside would only create panic and inevitably more damage. Leaving the doors open in the hope they would leave would be just plain stupid. He had to get them out now, he thought, and tackle the bulk of the cleanup tomorrow. Other than removing the remains of the deer carcass, there was little else he wanted to do tonight.

He remembered a trick using gasoline, rags, and a pole and started toward the garage. He would gas the rag, stick it on a long pole, and jam the pole into the raccoons' faces—a sure formula for sending them on their way.

Detached from the cabin by about forty feet, the garage stood in the darkest shadows of the yard near the forest. Jake laid down the shotgun and tried the door handle. It was locked, a good sign. He pushed inward after unlocking the door, but it was impossible to see anything. The garage had never been wired for electricity, and Jake had become used to fumbling for things he needed in the dark. The noticeable smell of mice droppings permeated the air. Mice seemed to prefer the garage to the cabin for their winter stay.

Jake knew the gas can sat in the far-right corner of the garage just as he knew his socks were in his bedroom chest of drawers, second drawer on the left. Things had their place in his world. The rags lay on the workbench to his left. Several long poles were propped near the side garage door. Jake groped his way across the garage in a Pin-the-Tail-on-the-Donkey fashion, both hands straight out in front of him. The garage was home to piles of stored summer items—boat stuff, boxes of household items infrequently used, various tools and equipment and a disassembled Hobie Cat. Airtight containers for food and bedding were on several metal tables out of reach of the mice. Better go slow, he thought, don't want more of a mess.

Extending electricity to the garage was one of those projects that never got done. Minnesota summer nights never got really dark until about ten o'clock or so. Late fall and winter were different. It was barely six o'clock and completely dark in the garage. The priority of this project would have to be moved up, he thought.

With his mind and extended hands focused on successfully navigating to the gasoline can, his face ran straight into something heavy and soft.

"What the hell," he said, as his hands instinctively rose to protect himself.

Surprise escalated to horror in an instant when his hands felt the legs of a body—a human body! He stumbled backward, nearly losing his balance, knocking tables and summer supplies over in his panicked retreat.

Once outside, he ran to the cabin to get the kerosene lantern off the fireplace mantel, his mind whirling from the chain of events. He avoided the raccoons, retrieved the lantern and matches, and returned quickly to the garage. He struck match after match, trying to light the lantern with shaking hands. Finally the mantels lit and a cascade of light flooded the garage.

"Oh my God!" Jake cried out as he saw the man, an Indian, hanging from the rafters. Stunned, he cautiously moved closer.

He did not recognize the corpse. Was this a murder or a suicide? Whatever it was, it had to be recent. The body had no smell of decay. He remembered only the scent of the mouse droppings when he opened the garage. What is going on? Who is responsible for this? Questions raced through Jake's head.

Reaching for the man's wrist, Jake tried to get a pulse; there was none. The deep purple color of the man's face and neck offered further proof that he was dead. Jake touched nothing else as he got the gasoline, rags, and poles from the garage. He would call the police from the cabin and then deal with the raccoons.

* * *

After several rings, an officer answered. "Chippewa Lake Police Station."

"Officer, my name is Jake Lorenz and I want to report a dead man in my cabin." Jake's voice shook.

"This is Sheriff Betts you're talking to. Slow down. Tell me first, are you in any immediate danger?"

"No, I'm not."

"As near as you can tell me, do you expect to be in any danger?"

"No, I don't think so, but I really don't know. I do have a loaded shotgun if I need it." He recognized the potential consequences of the sheriff's comment.

"Is there anyone else there with you?" Sheriff Betts was purposely measured in his speech, encouraging Jake by example to slow down.

"No, I'm here alone with my dog. We just arrived at my cabin and found this guy hanging from my garage rafters."

"Did you say *hanging?*"

"Yes."

"We'll have a car there as fast as we can. What's the fire ID number?"

"84B."

Without an address or a mailbox, the fire code was required on all driveways for emergencies. It would be easy to spot with only one road leading onto the peninsula. The sheriff said he would be there in less than thirty minutes.

While waiting, Jake went about the task of evicting the raccoons. The first left quickly, but the second was cornered under a chest of drawers in the upstairs bedroom. It hissed viciously as Jake approached. The room was small, making the long pole awkward to handle. Finally, he was able to position the gasoline rag with a wire hanger from the closet. The raccoon's coat bristled in defense as it flashed its razor-sharp teeth. Jake was closer than he wanted, but thankfully the raccoon chose to oblige his efforts by leaving. Deciding that it would be wise not to move anything in the cabin, Jake closed the lakeside door, opened some windows for ventilation, and left everything else the way he had found it.

As he walked around the cabin to the open windows on the three-season porch, he noticed something completely out of order. The hold-open washer on the pneumatic door-closing mechanism had been set to keep the screen door open.

"Why would someone do this?"

Jake had no enemies, but this destruction and the death of that poor Indian were certainly premeditated. He was beyond bewilderment.

* * *

"This is no suicide," Sheriff Betts said after taking his time to survey the scene. "Our local Indians can be very self-destructive, but they never commit suicide like this. Drugs, alcohol, and guns, yes; but hanging, never. Besides, this man was clubbed from behind," he said, pointing to the blood and matted hair on the man's skull. "Nope, this man was murdered."

two

JAKE DECIDED TO head back to Chippewa Lake once the body was removed and Sheriff Betts had completed his initial investigation. The police work had done little more than confirm what Jake already knew and darkness had prevented a detailed search of the crime scene. The sheriff posted a deputy until they could get a better look in the morning.

Jake's thought was to stay at the small motel on the bypass of Chippewa Lake. It was a bit of a dump and as far as he knew it did a better hourly business with locals than overnight business with travelers. Considering the circumstances, it would have to do; there were no other choices. He needed to collect himself. The stress of the events and concern for that poor Indian had him pretty unraveled. He remembered the sheriff had mentioned a daughter. *How does a daughter cope with something like this?* His heart ached.

On his way to the motel, Jake decided he'd better stop at Bud and Helen Miller's. Bud and Helen had lived on Arrowhead for thirty-five years, moving from Chicago after Bud's liquor store was robbed and he was beaten for the third time. Bud earned a living as an electrical contractor and handyman for the area, and Helen was a part-time cook at the Cedar Lodge and Fishing Resort nearby. Their longstanding friendship with Jake's parents led them to becoming informal care-takers of Sandy Cove over the years. Bud opened and closed the cabin in the spring and fall and handled some of the small projects Jake couldn't quite get to. Helen looked after the few renters the cabin occasionally had. She checked them in, making sure they had what they needed, and cleaned the cabin for the next arrival after they left. Bud and Helen generally made it a point to look in on the cabin from time to time for potential problems. Maybe they would know something. In any case, he felt the need to alert them to what had happened.

The area floodlight at the peak of the garage provided a shadowed image of their weathered, log-sided home as he entered their driveway. KC started moving around, sensing that they were stopping again.

"Go on, boy, but don't run off," Jake said, letting KC out to snoop. KC was familiar with the Miller's house and yard and would likely find Blackie, the Miller's dog, outside. Jake walked the twenty feet to the front door and knocked.

"Well, if it isn't Jake Lorenz. This is a surprise," Helen said, smiling as she opened the door. "I heard your car in the driveway, but didn't expect you so soon."

"Buddy," she called out. There was no answer. "Buddy," she called out even louder, "Look who's here."

Buddy's response was somewhat muffled. "For Christ's sake, Helen, I'm in the bathroom. I'll be out in a minute." Helen's persistence in calling her husband "Buddy" added to Jake's amusement. He knew that Bud hated the nickname because of the way Helen accented the second syllable.

"You know, Jake, it seems like men have some kind of spiritual relationship with the bathroom. If it wasn't for that bathroom I don't think Buddy would read at all. But why am I bothering you with all this? Come in and sit down while I get you some coffee. Do you still drink it black?"

"Thanks, Helen, I do." But before she could turn around, Jake gave her a big hug, just like he always did when he saw her. Her stout, overweight physique was quite a handful. In reality, he hadn't known

Helen and Bud well for very long, but they were friends nonetheless. Maybe it was the closeness they had with his parents that made his bond so real.

"It's good to see you too." Helen adjusted her thick, gray wig from the shift made by Jake's embrace and smiled a crooked half-grin in a self-conscious response.

"You said you were coming for the winter, but I'm still a little surprised. Come to think of it, this is the first time anyone from your family will stay at the cabin after October. Your mom and dad sure didn't."

Bud entered the kitchen from the hallway while still tucking in his washed-out flannel shirt. His wiry build demonstrated his attention to his health and the bounce in his walk spoke of a positive attitude.

He and Jake shook hands heartily.

Jake respected Bud for being able to pick up stakes after the problems in Chicago and start a new life on the peninsula. Even though the early 1960s weren't like the days of real homesteading, Arrowhead was still off the beaten path and much less settled then. Only the Stenway family had owned property on the peninsula longer than the Millers.

"We're really looking forward to your stay here this winter, Jake," Bud said. "You're going to find out that the winter is completely different—more so than you'll ever imagine. It's my bet that you'll like it a lot."

"I think you're right, Bud, but I've got to tell you it's starting off on a real downer. I want you to listen to something unbelievable." His sober expression was very noticeable as he sat down at the kitchen table with his cup of coffee.

"A man's been murdered at the cabin . . ."

"What!"

"An Indian—the sheriff said his name was Smith. Beaten and hanged by a rope from the garage rafters."

"Oh my God."

Looks of disbelief registered their horror as the details unfolded. Jake was thorough by nature and left out nothing in his step-by-step description of the sequence of his events upon arriving. Helen was the peninsula's living version of an Internet bulletin board and first to comment. It would be impossible for her not to want every detail.

"Did Sheriff Betts say the Indian's first name, Jake?"

"Someone by the name of Two Fingers Smith. Do you know him?"

"Why, I do know who he is. Buddy, you know him, too. I'll bet you've seen him in Chippewa Lake. Two Fingers is the caretaker of the Indian cemeteries on the reservation. He's been there for at least ten years, right after his mink farm failed."

Bud nodded. "You're right. I used to see him mostly at the hardware store. He pretty much kept to himself. What the hell could he be mixed up in that would lead to something like this?"

"From what I've heard, this poor man had nothing but bad luck his entire life," Helen said. "Timing hasn't been good for him, his family, or his business. Rumors had it that the market for his furs dried up and his business failed. I heard it forced him into bankruptcy. To make matters worse, he was a bit slow handling those little critters. That's how he got the name 'Two Fingers' in the first place. He told me himself. He said that those high-priced cuddly animals were vicious with teeth as sharp as razors.

"And that's not the worst of it. Within months of the bankruptcy, his wife died; people said it was cancer. And the following summer, his son was murdered in Bemidji. The police labeled it a hate crime, but the evidence I read in the *Bronson Times* was pretty sketchy. Nobody was ever arrested."

"My God, that's unbelievable." Jake shook his head in disbelief.

Despite this family's terrible circumstances, the evidence kept tugging at Jake's mind. "You know, Bud, the more I think about it, I'm not sure the damage to the cabin and the murder are actually connected."

"Why not?" Helen said, preempting Bud's response.

He thought for a minute before he replied, "Let me try to explain. First, my instincts tell me the cabin was broken into some time ago. The deer carcass was very ripe. I'll bet it had been there for at least a week, if not more. Plus, why would someone call attention to a murder with such a bizarre act of destruction?"

"Wait a second," Bud interrupted. "Are you saying that the cabin was a setup for a different crime?"

"I don't know how else to explain it. The screen-door latch was set to keep the door open. But the sheriff estimates the time of death as late yesterday. If I'm right about the timing of the deer carcass, something's missing."

Jake paused in his recollection as if the truth had just been made clear, or at least clear to him. He continued slowly. "To me, it seems logical the murderer would have known that the cabin destruction would be discovered sooner, rather than later, and ultimately lead to the discovery of the body. As I think about it, there's no question in my mind that the murderer wanted someone to find that body, and soon."

"What's really got me curious," Buddy said after taking his last swig of coffee, "is the way the cabin was trashed. The use of the deer carcass and parts almost sounds like it was placed there as bait, you know, the way you 'bait' a bear during hunting season."

"What do you mean?"

"You see, a hunter will bait a bear to build up a feeding pattern to lead the animal to the same spot so he can make the kill on the first day of hunting season. Did you notice any food other than the deer carcass?"

"I'm not sure. What would I be looking for?"

"Bears are usually more attracted to fruits, cornmeal, vegetables— stuff like that. While meat is a part of their diet, it's only a small part. What I'm trying to say is that if you're the average hunter and you're going to bait a bear, you'll use those foods over meat."

"I didn't think to look that closely. I'll check tomorrow."

"For the life of me, though, I can't figure out why someone would attract a bear to the inside of any cabin, let alone yours. If that were the case, though, the condition you found your cabin in would pretty much be the result.

"And there's another thing I can't quite understand. Bear season was over in September. What you may have is a bear that, for some reason, hasn't been able to gorge enough food, you know, calories, proteins, and carbohydrates, to go into hibernation. Time is running out now. A bear that hasn't eaten enough runs the risk of getting caught in the first blizzards. At this stage, they'll eat anything to complete their feeding preparation."

"That's the last thing I need. We need to make sure tomorrow that the cabin is cleaned as soon as possible to discourage it from returning."

"I'm trying to remember exactly when we were at your cabin last," Bud said. After a moment of concentrated thought, he looked to Helen for assistance.

"It's been at least a month, Buddy."

Bud's expression revealed how upset he was with himself. He usually checked on things more frequently.

"I knew you were coming and after everything was put in order for your arrival I didn't think to check again, the way I usually do when I close the cabin for the winter."

Knowing that a month would have easily given whomever it was the time, he looked at Jake to apologize. "Time gets away from you in the fall with the preparation for winter. I should've paid more attention."

"You're not to blame. This was no accident, and besides, insurance will cover the damage," he said, while reminding himself to notify the agent first thing in the morning to get the paperwork moving. "Anyway, your absence may have been your lucky star. Whoever did this would not have looked kindly on the interruption."

While they continued to talk, Helen warmed up some dinner leftovers for Jake. She was a wonderful cook, and even her most basic meals tasted like a banquet. The meatloaf he saw out of the corner of his eye would be no exception.

After eating and speculating more about the murder and break-in, Jake said, "It's getting late and I've imposed on you enough. I need to get checked in at the motel in town."

"You're not doing anything until you've had dessert," Helen insisted. "And besides, you're not staying in that rattrap. Our extra bedroom is all made up and I won't have it any other way."

Suddenly, the side door from the garage leading into the kitchen opened, startling Jake. He wasn't expecting anyone to just walk in. Helen and Bud had lived alone for years. Jake was even more surprised to see a pretty young lady, about nineteen, with a great smile, walk into the kitchen. KC and Blackie followed, with the storm door catching KC on the butt as it closed.

"Hi, Michelle," Helen called out. "How was school?"

"Really good, Grandma," she answered in an upbeat tone, her pleasant smile capturing Jake's attention.

"Honey, I'd like you to meet Jake Lorenz. He owns the cabin down on the peninsula, you know, the one we told you about. Jake, this is our granddaughter, Michelle Collins. She's living with us while she finishes her last two years of college at BSU."

Jake stood up to shake her hand. "I'm very pleased to meet you, Michelle." Her firm clasp and solid eye contact gave Jake a good first impression.

Helen extended the introduction, explaining that Bemidji State University was a better in-state choice than the out-of-state tuition at Iowa. "Besides," she said, "we're thrilled to have her here with us." As Michelle looked at Helen, Jake easily saw the feeling was mutual.

Michelle joined the trio at the table with Jake recapping his shocking discoveries. Within the hour Jake's exhaustion took over. They decided to call it a night and committed to help Jake with the cleanup at the cabin as soon as the sheriff would let them begin.

He thanked them profusely, knowing he was lucky to have such good friends.

three

Jake's sleep was fitful. He couldn't stop thinking about this poor man's daughter. Under the circumstances, it's hard to find a protocol of how to respond, he thought. Regardless, he decided to pay his condolences the next day when she was likely to need them most and before he was consumed in dialogue with neighbors. I can pick up some things in town while I'm there, he thought, reviewing his shopping list as he drifted off.

He woke up the next morning feeling surprisingly refreshed. It was still early, but he could hear Helen in the kitchen and smell the special aroma of bacon sizzling in the frying pan. Jake recalled that exact smell as a child returning from early-morning fishing trips with his dad. To this day, the bacon smell held center stage as one of his memories differentiating the cabin from the Twin Cities house.

"Yes, Laura, you won't believe it," Jake overheard Helen saying on the phone while he came down the hallway. Laura and her husband Ken lived on the peninsula year-round. Their home was about a half mile from Jake's, across the peninsula's dirt road on the main lake side of Arrowhead.

"Jake stayed with us last night, but if you ask me, I think he's a few cards short of a full deck if he still thinks that staying in that cabin for the winter is a good idea. This is more than just bad luck," she said, banging the frying pan for emphasis as Jake entered the kitchen.

Bud stood by the refrigerator shaking his head. "You know your business isn't really your business here on the peninsula. What's happened down at the cabin is real news, the kind Helen has been waiting for all of her life. I don't think Dan Rather himself would be able to describe what's going on better than Helen. Hell, she'll not only report the facts, she'll invent the facts, and within a few days people will know things about you that you don't even know about yourself."

Jake laughed. "That's okay. It's going to save me a lot of time not having to tell a story that's already been told. Besides, she might find out something that Sheriff Betts might not think to uncover." That, Jake thought, left Helen with a whole lot of territory to work, since his impression of the sheriff's police work left much to be desired.

"I'm going to head into town to do a few things while the cabin's sealed off," Jake said to no one in particular. "Would it be too much trouble to leave KC here? I feel bad putting him back in the truck again." Jake knew that KC and Blackie always got along well.

"No problem. Just do what you have to do."

With that, Jake was off.

* * *

The railroad ties clattered momentarily as Jake's truck passed over the outdated crossing entering town. To Jake's recollection, this old marker of Chippewa Lake's entrance hadn't seen repair work in years, which made sense, as he couldn't remember ever having to stop for a train.

Some fifty yards after the tracks, the truck entered a narrow wooden bridge stretched over the uppermost segment of the Mississippi River within the boundaries of Minnesota's Big Bear Indian Reservation.

Nothing had changed. Not even the echo of the loose planks, he thought.

Jake looked out at the boarded-up storefronts of a town with no future. One liquor store, two bars, a small grocery store, and a laundromat provided the only signs of commercial activity. The Head Start office, a one-man post office, two churches, and a rundown town hall represented the civic presence supporting the community. The streets stood stark and unkempt. The hundred or so government-constructed houses in town hadn't been painted since they were built. Rusted and bedraggled cars that would no longer start sat in backyards like discarded beer cans. Surrounded with overgrown dried grass from summer, their final resting places provided clear evidence of their owners' poverty.

Jake eased his Yukon through town, taking in the familiar scene. Ignoring his presence, a black, long-haired, mange-ridden dog roamed across the street in front of the truck. As Jake pulled into Vern's Grocery Store parking lot, right next to the Chippewa Lake Town Hall, a group of young Ojibwe Indian men were milling around the dirty white clapboard city building. Most likely they had just stumbled out of the Night Owl Bar across the street, where the only pool tables on the reservation afforded the men daily entertainment. Several still carried longneck beers.

Jake recognized Frank "Big Lights" Johnson on the edge of the gathering. Big Lights had given himself his Indian name after spending an entire night in the forest years ago lit up with alcohol and peyote. Coincidently, the northern lights gave a spectacular three-hour performance that night, convincing Big Lights that his life and the known universe had finally come together as one.

Jake approached the group.

"Hey, Big Lights, what's up? You taking these boys' money again?" Big Lights' reputation on the table was no more than talk. Usually, he was the one with the open wallet.

Big Lights turned and offered his hand as a broad grin creased his face.

"Jake, you old son-of-a-bitch. Good to see you." Despite Big Lights' obvious acquaintance with the outsider, the others separated themselves a bit from the two. The gap between the cultures remained polarized by the simple red-and-white color difference of a man's skin.

"You heard what happened?"

"Yeah, I understand that you got your hands full."

"Did you know Two Fingers?"

"Sure. And I'll tell you right now that he never hurt a soul, Jake. None of this makes any sense."

"The murder was brutal. I can tell you that firsthand."

"Hanged, I heard?

"Yeah, from the garage rafters. Hard to understand."

"Wasn't suicide then. We've got too many other ways to snuff out the light than to hang ourselves."

"That's what the sheriff said."

"It's still good to see your big-city butt up here, but why so close to winter?"

Jake had always liked Big Lights. Despite his affinity for booze, he could always be counted on. The locals on the reservation respected him as well. They saw him as a free-spirit individualist and an informal leader within their tribal community.

"Thought I'd give winter a try. I've got a little time on my hands. What's with the crowd?" Jake asked, gesturing toward the others.

Big Lights' expression turned quickly. "You're not gonna buy this." He hesitated to see who was within earshot. "For the fifth year in a row, the casino isn't giving any of the profits to the tribe. Can you believe the only Thanksgiving payout'll be a goddamn turkey and a box of canned goods?"

"That's BS," Jake replied, recalling previous complaints and sensing the degradation in the remark. Talk of corruption and feelings of being cheated filled the minds of many on the reservation.

Big Lights shrugged as if to say, *Oh well*. Then he said, "Sooner or later, if the situation doesn't change, things'll get nasty. Some of the men are talking about a big-time shake-up of the tribal council leaders on the rez, and you know that won't go down easy."

As Big Lights spoke, Jake realized what a commanding figure the man presented. In contrast to Jake's medium-size frame and his studious and bespeckled look, with prematurely graying hair, Big Lights was well over six feet and weighed about two hundred pounds. His clear brown eyes and jet-black hair highlighted his classic Indian appearance. Big Lights stood out as unique in the confident way he carried his size. Fifteen years of construction work had kept him in reasonable shape. Although years of alcohol abuse had taken its toll on the inside of his body, at thirty-five, he remained "tall, dark, and handsome," a fact he often proclaimed at the Night Owl in mock testimony to his success with the ladies. Being considered a *rounder* by his friends for his reputation of getting around with the opposite sex only made Big Lights smile and wink.

"Things with the tribal council sound serious," Jake said. "Let's get together next week. I'd like to know more. I've also got some ideas about creating a few new jobs on the reservation someone might be interested in."

"That'll get lots of attention," Big Lights said, gesturing with both hands in animation. His own situation had been pretty good with the occasional construction work, but most were less fortunate, he thought. New jobs were always good.

"First things first, though. The sheriff has to finish his investigation and I've gotta get myself organized. I'm a greenhorn at this, and I'm not at all prepared." Jake decided not to bother Big Lights with the details about his layoff at Astro Technology that gave him the time for a winter sabbatical. With unemployment rampant on the reservation, business was always in a downturn. And in truth, Jake felt a little uncomfortable, just yet, talking about losing his job. He'd never lost a job before and despite the fact he knew his layoff had nothing to do with his performance, he was embarrassed to have been selected for a furlough.

After talking about the murder investigation some more, Jake asked, "Can you break free tomorrow morning to help out at the cabin cutting and splitting firewood?" Jake thought that with the two of them on chainsaws and Ken running the hydraulic log splitter, they could produce the eight cords that Ken recommended.

"I can do that. The boats at the Blue Star aren't going anywhere." His job winterizing boats at the Blue Star Marina was temporary, like most everything he did. "I'd feel more comfortable, though, with three chainsaws and someone to spell Ken with his bad back. I'll get Bobby Turnbull and his brother Morey."

"We're going to need everyone to bring chainsaws, wedges, mallets, and axes, too, since everything in the garage is off limits," said Jake.

"Not a problem, as long as Ken brings his log splitter and your supply of longnecks is in excellent shape."

"I'll hold up my end of the bargain. I just hope I don't have to make a habit of pestering you all winter."

"I'll bet I can drink more beer than you have projects," Big Lights said with a laugh.

Jake smiled and then said soberly, "You know, I'd like to offer condolences to Two Fingers' daughter before leaving town today, but I don't know where she lives. Do you think she'd mind if I stopped unannounced?"

"That's the Indian way. She won't mind. The house isn't far from here at all."

After their conversation Jake stopped into Vern's for some basic groceries. He quickly walked the market aisles noticing how pathetically sparse the shelves appeared. He'd have to do his complete shopping to stock the cabin at the vacationers' grocery store out by the bypass.

four

As JAKE DROVE away, Jonathan Northbird, one of Big Lights' friends from the group, returned. "Who's the white brother?"

"A friend, up here this winter for the first time. I've known Jake off and on for years, mainly just helping out at his cabin at the end of the peninsula. He's always been a stand-up guy. You know, never acting like he's better than anyone else—and fair as hell when it comes to getting paid for work. Yeah, Jonathan, there needs to be a few more like him.

"Come to think of it, he might be someone to talk to about this hosing we're taking by the casino," Big Lights said, head down as he kicked at the gravel in the parking lot. "I don't know how much he knows about casinos, but I know he's got a big job in Minneapolis. He's pretty smart and a straight shooter."

In truth, Big Lights and Jonathan, and most Indians for that matter, believed that the Mystic Lake Casino, which had pioneered Indian gaming years before, represented what should be happening on every reservation. Every Shakopee Mdewakanton Sioux tribal member received thousands of dollars monthly from casino profit distributions. Many, in fact, were millionaires. Big Lights and Jonathan didn't understand that the gaming market in the Twin Cities, where the Mystic Lake Casino was located, was worlds apart from their Norway Pine Casino on the remote Big Bear Reservation.

What they did know, however, could be summed up with the buses they saw continually pouring in from all over northern Minnesota and North Dakota. And a turkey and a box of canned goods didn't cut it for these two. What they saw was a full house of gamblers and nothing to show for it.

"Maybe he's got some connections that can help."

"Maybe," Big Lights replied. "I don't know. The only thing I do know for sure came from an article I saw in the *Bronson Times* last week. It said that the Indian Gaming Regulatory Act and the National Gaming Commission require a plan for what they called *per capita distribution*. I'd give a six-pack to each Tribal Council member to hear how they came up with a goddamn turkey and a box of canned goods."

Jonathan took a long drag from a cigarette cupped in his hand and a pull from his beer while nodding in agreement. His lips curled when he spoke, showing his yellowish-brown teeth. "It's the fucking tribal council board's fault as far as I'm concerned. They could give a shit about us. They're in it for themselves."

"This may be over Jake's head, too." Big Lights struggled to light his cigarette as a brisk wind swirled. "I'll bring it up to him anyway the next time I'm at the cabin. He also said he had some ideas for employment on the rez that I'm real interested in hearing about, too."

"He's not one of those PC Native American do-gooder types, is he?"

"No way. Like I said, he's a straight shooter."

"I hope you're right. Most of these people who say they want to help are just talk."

As if on cue, Sam Aguire and Chase Leonard, two of the Tribal Council's most powerful members, parked their car in front of the Night Owl and headed for the front door. Sam, a powerfully built Indian and German half-breed, intimidated young men half his age on the reservation. Chase, Sam's closest ally, had a calculating look about him and was known to be the brains on the council. Their presence at the Night Owl surprised no one as they regularly held private meetings at their corner table.

"That's who we need to have a meeting with, right there," Big Lights said, bristling at the men's presence.

As always, however, they did nothing.

five

JAKE FOUND LINDA'S house around two. He knocked on the front door with some hesitation. He had never met the deceased man's daughter, and he wasn't at all sure of what he would say. The house was like all the rest in town, a two-bedroom ranch in desperate need of paint and repair. True to form, several old cars were in the backyard. They probably hadn't been started in years. It always amazed Jake how messy the Indians could be with their junk, like cars, that no longer had value. As much as he tried to explain the vicious circle of what he called *downhill economics*, it never sank in to his friends.

Within moments he heard someone in the house approach. A young Indian woman first peered through the curtains, then opened the door. She was dressed in Levi's and a sweatshirt and seemed to be around twenty and about five feet three inches tall. Her features were softer, more Polynesian-like, than the rough look typical of Ojibwe. While very plain in presentation, she possessed attractiveness underneath her flat expression. She appeared to be surprised by a visitor.

Jake introduced himself. "I'm sorry to intrude, Miss, but my name is Jake Lorenz. Your father was found on my property and I wanted to stop and offer my condolences."

"Thank you for coming. I'm Linda Smith. Please come in."

Linda broke the awkward moment. "I understand that you're the one who actually found my dad?"

"True enough. It's hard to imagine how something like this can happen. From everything I've learned your dad was a good man. That's why I wanted to come by. What happened to your dad isn't right, and I'm sorry for how you must feel about everything."

"Thank you." Her distress in the loss of her father was obvious, even to this perfect stranger.

"Please sit down. Can I get you something to drink? I'm afraid I don't have much, though . . . maybe a soft drink?"

"Anything cold is fine." Jake noticed the threadbare carpet and meager decorations of the living room that spoke to a poverty-level existence so common on the reservation. A few pictures in cheap dime-store frames displayed who must be other family members. The only lamp in the room created shadows, giving the setting a black-and-white movie stage effect. The tables were absent of dust and clutter, however, which spoke to a degree of pride.

As they talked, Jake reflected on the inevitable. This young woman must have shone like an evening star in the life of Two Fingers. All parents probably feel that way, but in this case, there was so little else. In that moment, Jake realized why parents throughout the ages have placed so much hope in their children. The gap between all the possibilities Linda represented and the reality of a Native American gravedigger's life was enormous. Jake quickly saw that love and hope had moved Linda to bridge that gap for her father's sake.

"In some ways I can share the pain of what you're experiencing. I also lost the most important person in my life. Her name was Jan. We had been married a long time. When she died, it was awful. It was a traffic accident—one of those things, I guess."

"I'm sorry to hear that." Her shoulders slumped as she let out a deep breath before continuing. "My dad had so little. And it was all taken away. My mother died from cancer, and my brother, you probably have heard, was murdered."

"What happened?"

"All I remember was a lot of fighting and anger between Frank and my dad. It all happened shortly after my mother died. Frank created his own trouble with alcohol and drugs. And both of them were fighting the sadness of losing Mom. With some help, they probably could have survived together. But when Frank left for Bemidji that night, he never came back."

Not wanting her to relive the details of another death, Jake remained quiet.

After a long pause, she continued, "Reservation life can be very difficult, particularly when real solutions are so hard to see."

"And your dad? Does any of what happened make sense?"

"I always felt that something was going on. He would never say anything to me, of course, but it seemed he was involved in something that was putting a lot of pressure on him. The stress was obvious, but he never talked about it. I wish I could have given more to the sheriff's deputy who was here earlier." A feeling of helplessness fueled her despondence.

"I don't ever remember my dad wanting anything other than his family. It was taken from him. Maybe it's better that he's gone now?" Tears formed as she talked. Her hands clutched a small handkerchief she used to wipe her eyes. It was her loneliness, however, that Jake sensed. And why wouldn't she be lonely, considering she'd lost her entire family tragically and faced an uncertain future on the reservation.

Jake knew of no honest advice he could offer, nor profound words of comfort he could say about what she had to endure. "I'm truly very sorry," he said quietly as he stood in preparation for leaving.

"I hope you didn't mind my visit, Linda. I wanted to meet you and I'm glad that I have. Your father must have been very proud of you."

"Thank you for stopping and being so kind. You are welcome at any time, Mr. Lorenz. Good-bye."

He admired her courage. Yet, barely knowing her, he worried for her future—he understood the emptiness and finality of her circumstances all too well.

Jake headed directly to his cabin on the peninsula, some twenty miles from town. His mind fell into despair for about ten miles while reflecting on Linda's situation. Once he turned south on the gravel road leading onto the peninsula, his focus shifted to how he had never spent a winter at Arrowhead before. Minnesota winters held a wicked reputation for being brutal, and the cabin was extremely isolated. Regardless, Jake was committed to seize a chance to experience something new while mustering up the energy for the rest of his life.

It was the winter to-do list and the limited prep time that temporarily took center stage in his thinking while driving. I know the cabin phone needs to be upgraded to digital for the fax and computer, he thought. And there's a serious firewood task ahead; Ken and Big Lights help will be huge. Then I'll make another trip into town for supplies.

"Maybe I'll even find out what I want to do for the rest of my life," he said in a surprise whisper, confirming the real challenge to solve. What would the next year bring? Several of his friends had also been outsourced and downsized, and he knew from their experience that the job-search process was a real pain despite the company-line propaganda claiming it as an opportunity to retool and restart. "This is my mess to fix."

Still, he felt confident the coming winter would provide the time to answer many of his personal questions. He just wouldn't have Jan by his side. That all changed when a sixteen-year-old with poor judgment thought he could beat the light at the intersection of Route 14 and Main Street. Jake had never really loved anyone else. And because they were unable to have children, Jake had no family. Her death devastated him. He moved, changed jobs, and went through several therapists. He just couldn't find a way to fill the hole created by Jan's absence.

KC was his only real stability now. They trekked for many hours together in the fields of Minnesota, Iowa, and South Dakota, hunting pheasant. Jake never tired of those days together watching KC work the corn and alfalfa fields flushing birds. The bond between them was unshakable.

Yet, at forty-two, Jake felt very alone. He recalled Jan's steadfast philosophy that *life was all about learning*. He had the feeling he was about to earn his Ph.D.

six

I NEED TO check on the investigation's progress this afternoon, he thought, desperately wanting to get a go-ahead to start cleaning things up. He didn't expect much yet, however, so he decided to talk first-hand to the few neighbors who lived on the peninsula. He wanted to let them know his plans. At that thought he chuckled. Like they don't already know? Nobody has any secrets out here.

Jake chose to visit Alex Minor first. As the largest private land-owner on Arrowhead, Alex controlled the 375 acres that made up the tip of the peninsula and most of the arrowhead shape giving the peninsula its name. Jake's parcel of thirty acres abutted Alex's property to the north and essentially made up a good portion of the curved base of one side of the arrowhead's shape. Jake knew that the location of the newer Stenway Lodge, on the south shore of Eagle Feather Bay, offered an excellent vantage point of Sandy Cove. He thought that if anyone was able to observe strange activity, it would be Alex.

The bay between Jake and Alex's land presented the most beau-tiful and undisturbed wilderness setting Jake had ever seen. Called Eagle Feather Bay for the bald eagles inhabiting the peninsula and actively fishing the bay's shoreline, it served as a safe harbor to the occasional boater or fisherman caught in bad weather. Northern Minnesota weather patterns changed rapidly and could be very harsh. With over four hundred miles of shoreline on Big Bear Lake, storms could be treacherous and occasionally deadly. With its fifteen- to twenty-five-foot depth, the bay was ideal for all kinds of powerboats and sailboats. It was perfect for any summer or, for that matter, any year-round activity. Jake and Alex shared the only land access to the bay.

* * *

It was Alex's grandfather, Hans Stenway, and great-uncle, Frederick Stenway, who emigrated from Norway to northern Minnesota in 1883. They founded the Stenway Brewing Company, one of the largest brewers in North America, and were the first permanent settlers on the peninsula. With the brewery headquarters in the Twin Cities, the family maintained a firm grip on their holdings. In 1994, the family still controlled 65 percent of the company.

Grandfather Hans's skill as a businessman and great-uncle Frederick's genius as a brewmaster made for a potent team. The only serious threat to their phenomenal success had been Prohibition. As resourceful entrepreneurs, however, Hans resolved the dilemma by cultivating new channels of distribution for their product. As a result, the two became very close associates with some of the most notorious mob families in Kansas City, Chicago, and Detroit. Business couldn't have been better.

A downside, however, involved their associates' frequent conflict with the law. Both the original family lodge, built in 1886, and the newer lodge built in 1918, the year Alex was born, were virtually isolated and together served as a natural safe haven where their business associates could lay low from time to time. Reachable by seaplane only at that time, and equipped with all the comforts of the Cadillac Ranch, the newer lodge quickly evolved into the perfect refuge. Many Stenway guests found it difficult to leave, even well after the coast had cleared.

Alex was the only son of Hans's daughter, Rose, and her husband Richard Minor. Richard led the business briefly, but his tenure ended tragically when he and Rose perished in a plane crash while traveling to Arrowhead in 1934, when Alex was sixteen. As a young man, Alex showed great promise. He knew the most important clients through his frequent visits to the lodge. They all liked him. These people became his family. In time Alex took control of the Arrowhead property and Stenway Brewing.

But rather than achieving great success, Alex became an infamous case study. Every business school in America chronicled the devastating four years of his leadership as Stenway's CEO. With seemingly inborn arrogance, Alex led a management team that ignored an unparalleled rise in the market share of light beers and California wines. He declared them a fad and insisted that the drinking habits of the American public were not so easily changed. His investment strategy focused on the return of hard-liquor drinks despite mountains of public opinion and market research to the contrary. His growing megalomaniac tendencies captured the constant attention of the biggest business publications on Wall Street. The Stenway board removed Alex from office in 1979 with little fanfare, an enormous trust, and an 18-percent undiluted ownership of Stenway Brewing.

For the past fifteen or so years, Alex had been living on his vast wealth. Whatever potential his many subsequent business efforts initially showed was always overridden by his ruthless approach to people and circumstances. In the past few years, he had vanished from the business-world radar screen. He was spending more and more of his time on Arrowhead.

* * *

While Jake drove, he recalled how mean-spirited Alex had been in their few encounters in the past. As a casual visitor to Arrowhead, Jake had chosen to tolerate Alex. At times, the man was actually interesting with his stories about the old Prohibition days. Recently though, Jake had stayed clear of him. Alex had demonstrated no interest in becoming neighborly and openly discouraged visitors by restricting access to his spectacular property, even for local hikers and hunters.

The remaining five-mile drive down the dirt road to the Minor property took Jake less than ten minutes, yet the anticipation of interacting with Alex and his harsh approach made a slow acid churn in his stomach.

seven

Two large, intimidating Dobermans approached aggressively as Jake pulled up to the 1918 lodge. Not about to get out of the truck, he honked the horn a few times. The pickup near the front entrance to the lodge suggested that someone was home. In a few minutes, Alex emerged and immediately quieted the dogs. As he motioned for Jake to come in, Jake was pleased that Alex recognized him.

Jake extended his hand upon entering the cabin, as he said, "Hello, Mr. Minor, how are you?"

"Hell, nobody calls me Mr. Minor, Jake," he barked. "Call me Alex."

"I wasn't quite sure you'd recognize me. It's been a few years—except for passing out on the road every now and then."

He surveyed what used to be the main entertainment and bar area of the original mob hideaway as they walked to a sitting area. The bar itself was long gone, but Jake could easily envision the room furnished with the right motif to accommodate several dozen guests. It was quite impressive.

"It looks as if you are planning to stay the winter, Jake." Alex was always direct and it was sometimes hard to reconcile the crispness of his remarks with a body losing a battle to age. "That bad luck with the cabin, though, and the murder of that Indian gets you off to a real poor start, don't you think?"

"It sure does, but how'd you know about my plans?"

"Nobody really told me, but not too much gets by me after being on this peninsula as long as I have. In your case, it's a pretty safe bet that when someone upgrades their propane gas tank in October, their plans include using the cabin during the winter."

He was absolutely right, Jake thought. He also concluded that there wasn't much point in trying to outwit Alex either. First, he wasn't sure if he could. In his mid-seventies, this guy was still mentally on top of his game. Second, he felt that honesty would be a better basis for a neighborly relationship, regardless of what he personally thought about Alex.

"Well, answering your question about my plans is exactly why I stopped by. I do plan to stay the winter and to take advantage of the time I have since I lost my job at Astro Tech. The experience will be just what I need, I think." The hesitation in his voice was honest, as this whole cabin situation had eroded his enthusiasm.

"It's my guess that the last several years haven't been exactly what you wanted with the loss of your wife and now this job problem," Alex said after a slight pause. "It's been my experience that a clean break from the past is a better alternative than hanging on to things that are familiar to you. Have you considered a change of scenery altogether?"

"Your point has merit, but it's not easy to do. Part of my time off this winter will be to explore that very perspective. Anyway, I wanted to let you know that I would be around and not to be surprised if I show up for a cup of sugar or some friendly conversation from time to time."

"Suit yourself. But be careful of the dogs when you come over. Leo and King are trained to my command as guard dogs and boundary trained for the property. As you saw, they're aggressive. It makes me feel a little more at ease. Tony's the only other person they'll listen to." Tony Matheson had served as full-time caretaker at the property for years.

"Thanks for the warning. I think I got the picture when I drove up. Has Sheriff Betts been over to talk with you about the murder and what's happened at my cabin yet?"

"Well, he was here this morning, but I don't think he's going to have an easy time getting to the bottom of this. This kind of thing is well out of his league, and besides, the loss of one Indian isn't the kind of event that motivates the big-city police to join the hunt. It's my opinion, Jake, that this will all be forgotten in less than two months."

As Alex leaned against an antique hallway chair, Jake recognized his own antipathy over the man's dismissal of Two Fingers, or any human being for that matter.

"You're probably right, Alex. But for his daughter's sake, I hope you're wrong. All the same, you're the only one who has any kind of a view of Sandy Cove. Did you notice any kind of unusual activity in the last week? You know, boats or trucks or noises or things like that?"

"I'll tell you the same thing I told Sheriff Betts. One thing's for sure."

"What's that?"

"Whoever did it came and left by boat. That's the only way to get in and out of these places without leaving tracks from a vehicle all over the place. Of course, I knew that any hope of confirming that suspicion had vanished when I drove past your place last night. There must have been half a dozen cars up and down your access road at least two or three times. Any tire-track evidence of a previous visitor would be long gone."

Jake reflected on the validity of Alex's comment while recalling the absence of tire tracks in the soft driveway dirt the night he arrived. He decided not to say anything about it now, at least not until he could develop a stronger sense of whether Alex could be trusted.

"But to answer your question directly," he continued, "Nothing unusual came to my attention over the last several days. I've been in and out quite a bit though, with various projects. It would have been easy for me to miss something."

"I'd appreciate it if you would let me know if something does come to mind," Jake said. "In the meantime, I'm more than a little behind in getting ready for the winter."

Despite Alex's age and inability to contribute physically, Jake would have expected at least a cursory expression of neighborly support.

None came.

Jake started to move toward the kitchen as a signal of his imminent departure. As he walked through the spacious dining area with two large tables, he noticed that one of the tables was covered with a white sheet. Jake's immediate impression was that of a child's train layout, or a scale-building model of some sort. His instincts were reinforced with the architectural drawings on the seat of a chair. He made a mental note to ask Alex about the plans on his next visit when he had more time.

"You know, Jake, if you're ever interested in selling Sandy Cove, I'll give you a fair price for it with no strings attached. My guess is that the market value is about $400 to 500K."

"Thanks, I'll keep the offer in mind. See you later."

They shook hands.

The dogs remained in a stay position at Alex's command while Jake went to the truck. Beautiful animals, Jake thought to himself, even though he was not a fan of the breed.

Jake headed down the road toward Ken and Laura's place. This would be a good time to stop and it would take just a few minutes, as they lived a few miles north on the dirt road.

Replaying his encounter with Alex as he drove, it occurred to him that the man had actually been somewhat cordial during their discussion. Considering Alex's propensity to offend people, this pleased Jake.

And $500K is not a bad price either, he thought. Maybe Minor is mellowing in his old age. The possibility of a more interactive Alex Minor interested Jake, as company during the winter would be sparse. If Alex opened up, his colorful history would make for great discussions. Jake decided not to rule it out.

eight

ALEX WATCHED JAKE walk toward his truck, their encounter already replaying itself in his mind. Jake's visit had caught him by surprise. The distraction created by Sheriff Betts asking a series of inconsequential questions had misled Alex from anticipating the real speed of events. He should have realized that Jake would stop to see him first. Alex was frustrated.

And having the model of his planned real estate development for Arrowhead sitting around for others to poke their nose into just wasn't smart. Granted, the bedsheet made it impossible to tell anything. But he definitely caught Jake's look in that brief moment while he was leaving the house. He would move the model to a less conspicuous location later that day.

An all-too-familiar feeling of anxiety began to fill Alex's mood. His past was peppered with examples where he had not heeded the meaning of important events around him. There were too many times that success had been undermined by his own inability to size up events or his unwillingness to listen to the advice of business associates.

At times like this, the 1978 boardroom scene permeated his thoughts like a relentless video he couldn't turn off. That particular executive meeting at the Stenway Brewing Company blistered with Alex's one-way monologue. As Stenway's CEO, he had been unrelenting in his drive to expand acquisitions into the hard-liquor business and to continue investing in the company's stronghold in the U.S. traditional beer market to the exclusion of the rapidly growing light-beer market.

"You have to understand, gentlemen," Alex pushed. "The Stenways own the beer market in the United States. Any son-of-a-bitch who thinks he can take market share away from Stenway simply by diluting the potency of the product and losing a few calories doesn't understand our customer. No upstanding beer lover is going to identify with some faggot light beer or some fruity glass of wine as a substitute. And furthermore, I'm up to my ass in these bullshit market studies that are trying to tell us something different. If you want the truth, ask me, or better yet, I'll take you down to Pulaski's Bar & Grill tonight and wager each of you five thousand that you'll get bounced onto the street if you try to substitute some faggot alternative for real beer. Goddamn it, the real beer drinker is our customer, and there's more of them every day—people who work hard and want a break at the end of the day, not some college boy who's trying to look fashionable."

Of all the disasters in his career, it was this boardroom scene of his losing control that continually replayed itself. He swore to himself that it would not happen with Arrowhead. The groundwork for everything necessary to succeed had been laid. Farley Johnson, county commissioner for Big Bear County, had agreed to support the controversial zoning changes required for the development to take place. Farley knew the resort would not be popular with locals on the peninsula, the businessmen of Bronson, the county seat, or the Indian community, for that matter. But Alex was convincing.

Alex knew when Farley turned sixty-five last March, his chances for re-election were over. Even in this remote vacation area of Minnesota, the younger baby boomers were having an impact. Farley's age and lack of a real vision for the county would put him on the sidelines after next year's election. Alex helped him recognize this truth one night with a little persuasive effort over a few whiskeys. What sealed the deal, however, was a sweet little retirement package. The day that Alex's property on Arrowhead was approved for the 375-acre commercial real estate development, Farley would receive a clear deed to a nice little beachside bungalow at Cabo San Lucas on the Baja Peninsula in Mexico. Early family role models at Stenway had taught Alex how to influence with conviction. Combining these skills with some knowledge of small-town politics made Farley an easy mark. Alex always laughed to himself over negotiations like this. Wealth gave him the advantage. Everyone had their price.

With zoning virtually assured, Alex concentrated on how the development would take shape. Secretly, he hired Rex Meeks of the firm Meeks & Harrison, who managed the development of Port Ludlow on Puget Sound. With Rex as a houseguest for the months of May and June, they laid plans for a world-class adventure resort property. By developing Arrowhead, Alex reasoned he could establish himself as a futurist in the changing, upscale real estate development business. He had become obsessed with the Arrowhead project. He would be damned if he would let history repeat itself. Rewriting the chapters of his failed business life had become all-consuming. Nothing would, or could, get in Alex's way.

The strategy to accomplish his land development coup was clear. Route 45 from the Twin Cities ran straight north toward Arrowhead, skirting the east side of Big Bear Lake. This route provided easier access from the Twin Cities to the Arrowhead Peninsula and the lake itself than going through Bronson, on the west side of the lake. Alex was convinced that the recreation and real estate market from this small and poorly located resort town could be completely diverted to a development on Arrowhead. The remarkable geography of Arrowhead would give it an overwhelming competitive advantage as a year-round attraction. With the right developers and his vision, Alex knew winter and summer tourists could be marketed to successfully. Every version of outdoor and indoor enjoyment would be a part of the overall plan. The heart of Bronson's resort and tourism business would be stripped in no time. And if these factors weren't enough, the Norway Pine Indian Casino, not far from Chippewa Lake, was fifteen miles closer to the Arrowhead Peninsula than to Bronson. Steps were already taken to build on that advantage by linking the business interests of two establishments. The Native American monopoly on casinos wasn't about to stop him from forging a relationship with members of the local tribal council who would favor his resort.

A critical link in the overall success of his plans, however, was the development of Eagle Feather Bay. The Inn would be the crown jewel of Midwest resorts. Victorian elegance, exquisite accommodations, and breathtaking views of Eagle Feather Bay were certain to earn the inn world-class status. The bay's overwhelming beauty, unique sand beaches, and natural harbor would be the perfect backdrop for hundreds of guest rooms and corporate meeting spaces. The championship golf course would tie the resort together with a world-class spa and condominium community sharing a vast array of outdoor activities.

Alex knew his land had everything for the project, with one exception: He owned only one-half of the bay's shoreline. Jake owned the other half, the half with virtually the best sand shoreline for a beach. Finding a compelling logic to encourage Jake to sell his land had occupied Alex's thinking for months.

* * *

It was early September when Alex concluded that he needed to understand Jake's plans in order to make his own. Alex knew how things worked on the peninsula so when he ran into Helen at Eagles' Grocery Store out on the bypass, he took the opportunity to chat.

"What do you hear from Jake Lorenz these days?" he asked after a few brief introductory exchanges.

"Funny you should ask. I was just on the phone with him yesterday and he seems pretty committed to coming up here and staying the winter."

"At his cabin?"

"That's what he said."

"Is that right?"

"I was as surprised as anybody. There's never been a Lorenz visit here in the winter, let alone a plan to stay the entire time. Sometimes you can't figure people."

"How so?"

"Apparently he lost his job at Astro Tech, so now he thinks he needs to spend the winter in the woods. It sounds a lot like the ostrich sticking his head in the sand to me. It's none of my business, though. Buddy and I have always liked Jake, so we'll help out any way we can."

"Don't I remember that he lost his wife several years back? Maybe it has more to do with that?"

"I'm the first to admit that I don't have a clue when it comes to figuring out men. But if I lost Buddy and my job, the moving truck would be packed pronto. Why would a person want to burden herself with the constant reminder of sad events? 'Time to move on,' I'd say to myself."

"I agree with you," he replied, shifting the loaded grocery basket from one hand to the other. "But I don't think people see things that clearly, at least not under stress, anyway. He'll definitely have some adjustments to make in coming here."

The information changed things for Alex. Jake's presence would provide opportunities to get him to sell. He needed to know for sure, however, if this was a fact. The local phone company was his first stop.

* * *

"I'd like to check my last phone bill, Mrs. Schwartz," Alex requested at the counter of the one and only office of the Monroe Telephone Company.

"Is there a problem, Mr. Minor?"

"Well, I'm not sure, but I was close by and thought it would be easier to stop in and check with you personally. It's a billing question."

The Monroe Telephone Company had thirty-five employees and Mrs. Schwartz handled all the billing for every customer. When she was on vacation, billing changes stopped.

"You know, I ran into Helen today, and she said Jake Lorenz is planning to spend the winter here for the first time. Do you know Jake?"

"It's funny, I think I know everyone, but only the locals in person. As a matter of fact, Mr. Lorenz did call me last week telling us not to disconnect his phone for the winter and to switch it from seasonal to full-year rates. Seems like he does plan to use it."

Alex finished his business with Mrs. Schwartz, admitting that there wasn't a billing problem after all.

While fairly convinced at this juncture, Alex made one more inquiry the following week with the propane gas delivery driver who was on his normal route. He knew that no one had ever stayed the winter at Sandy Cove and reasoned that the tank probably wasn't adequate for winter use. If Jake was staying, good judgment would lead to the need for a larger tank. And, as if Alex were a prophet, the driver confirmed that he was on his way to Sandy Cove to replace the two-hundred-fifty-pound tank with a five-hundred-pound tank.

Alex concluded that if he piled a little more bad luck onto Jake's plate, he just might induce Jake to sell. And besides, Alex didn't feel he had a whole lot of time to make this land development happen. He needed to move quickly. He focused on a ploy that would cause destruction to Jake's cabin and become the straw that would break his resolve to stay at Sandy Cove.

nine

JAKE KNEW THAT a phone call from Helen would have preceded his visit to Ken and Laura's. Smiling in anticipation, he turned the corner onto their property.

Entering on the dirt and rough gravel driveway, he saw Laura attending to the pond they had built as a landscaping piece. It looked terrific when the summer flowers were in full bloom and the waterfall was active. Now, however, it was choked with dead leaves. Laura was removing them so she could drain it for the winter.

Glad for the break, she stopped her project and approached Jake's truck. He turned off the ignition and got out. She smiled warmly in response to his outstretched arms, which enveloped her in a friendly embrace.

"Jake, I can't tell you how happy we are to hear you're staying for the winter. You're still staying, aren't you?"

Jake nodded. "I'm looking forward to it quite a bit, actually."

Arm-in-arm, they walked toward the front door to look for Ken. "You look just fantastic, Laura."

She smiled, her cheeks pink with a hint of blush from Jake's attention.

True to form, they found Ken reading in the family room in an orthopedic chair.

"I've always admired a man secure enough to read a book while his wife performs manual labor in the yard," Jake said with a sarcastic smirk.

"There will be a time," Ken responded slowly without breaking a smile, "when you will be ready to learn the finer points of dilettante living, but trust me, you'll pay big time. Especially if your manners include both insulting me and hustling my wife in public." Ken always had the last word.

Since he broke his back in a snowmobile accident five years ago, Ken had struggled with rehabilitation. Plenty of rest periods combined with a steady schedule of physical exercises did, however, allow him to maintain his favorite pastime of reading. His bent for unique vocabulary flourished with an ever-growing book list. Jake took a mental note to look up "dilettante" when he got back to the Miller's.

"Fair enough, Mr. Impressive Vocabulary, but you will earn every penny of it." Jake always took a light tone with Ken. The constant pain and therapy requirements kept him from even trying to return to his regional manager position with ADT Computers. The alternative would have been a direct selling position that would put even more strain and stress on his back. As a result, Ken had remained on permanent disability since the time of his accident. It was the continual checking on his status by the insurance company, however, that truly upset Ken. Even this far north, he'd get an occasional surprise visit from their field representative.

All in all, Jake thought Ken did pretty well maintaining day-to-day civility, but the irritation generated by the chronic pain could give Ken a testy and sarcastic disposition. Today, however, was a good day.

"I can't tell you how sorry Laura and I are about the fucking crap you're dealing with at the cabin. Life's too short for this shit." In addition to a propensity for a new word-of-the-day, Ken liked to swear to make his point. It was probably a leftover habit acquired during his rehabilitation, when every other word was of the four-letter variety, but now he just seemed to enjoy the emphasis it brought to his commentary.

"It's just fucking strange how Two Fingers fits into the scenario," Ken reflected. "I mean, what could a simple soul like Two Fingers have done to merit being murdered, hanged, no goddamn less? You know, Jake, and Laura here will verify this, I'm in Chippewa Lake a lot and have had the chance to talk to most everyone at one time or another. In the two years we've lived here, I've run into Two Fingers no more than four times. And each time, he appeared to me to be a quiet, ordinary man, well suited for his job at the cemetery. It's not like he was a shithead or anything."

"Do either of you know anything about his daughter?"

"She was the pride of his life, from what I heard," Laura said. "Helen told me this morning . . ." (Bingo, Jake thought as he registered the accuracy of his prediction of Helen's call) "that she attends the University of Minnesota in Duluth on a full scholarship in marketing."

"I wonder who's going to show up at the funeral?" Laura added.

"It won't be the family," Ken replied.

"We haven't been much help, have we, Jake? What are your plans now?"

"Well, there are a number of things I'd like to do, but they all revolve around the progress being made by Sherlock Holmes at the cabin. I guess I'm not really sure, Laura."

"Don't let it get you down. Your ass will be back on track sooner than you think. Besides, Laura and I would like you to join us for supper tonight, to at least give you one thing you don't have to think about. Of course, that's only after you've given your blow-by-blow story of the day's events to Helen."

They all laughed.

*　*　*

Jake left Ken and Laura's and headed to the cabin. It was late afternoon. He hoped the sheriff would have some encouraging news.

As he drove the half-mile access road, he thought about the recent events and just how remote the cabin really would be in an emergency. Whatever the crisis, it would be long over before help could respond.

He was pleasantly surprised to see two squad cars still there. The cabin area and grounds were restricted with yellow police tape. The scene disturbed Jake deeply, as he thought of the possibilities surrounding the events. He wondered how long this feeling of uncertainty would last.

"How are you feeling this afternoon, Mr. Lorenz?" the sheriff said.

"Not quite 100 percent. What kind of progress are you making?"

The sheriff recounted the details of the investigation. As he was doing so, another officer approached. Sheriff Betts introduced Detective Jorgensen, a member of the Bronson police team on loan because of his experience with a previous murder. They shook hands and continued their discussion. Detective Jorgensen's contribution went over much of the same ground Sheriff Betts had covered the previous evening. There was no reason to suspect Jake, but they had to do their job. Jake participated in the discussion but didn't really have much to add. He could tell from their questions that they had very little to go on in the way of real physical evidence, or at least they weren't telling him. The motive, or even a theory of a motive, hadn't begun to take shape yet either.

"I don't want to seem insensitive to what's happened here, but I am hoping to begin working in the cabin soon."

"Not a problem. Winter's not going to wait, is it?" Detective Jorgensen replied in an all-business manner. "We understand your situation and our team will be done with their work by the end of the day. You can start cleaning up the cabin tomorrow if you'd like. We want to keep the garage quarantined for one more day, however."

Since there wasn't anything further that Jake could do for the men, he let them know he could be reached at Helen and Bud's if needed.

"Terrific," the detective muttered with a hint of exasperation under his breath. The sheriff rolled his eyes. Both men knew of Helen's reputation. Her firsthand knowledge of the situation would require additional damage control, particularly if the murderer wasn't found.

Jake arrived back at the Miller's around five. KC and Blackie barked and yapped while chasing his truck down the driveway but quieted when the engine stopped. Helen was another matter, however, as it was apparent that from the time he opened the door he wasn't going to get any rest until her questions were answered. She fired away as they walked toward the house.

"Jake," she gasped, "I've just got to know everything that's happened since you've left this morning! Don't leave anything out."

Before speaking, he quickly reflected on what he should and should not tell her. He decided to limit his discussion to facts he was sure she would discover on her own anyway. And maybe ask her a few questions that would stimulate her own search for new information.

"Before I begin, however," he looked her straight in the eye, "I would like your promise for some help."

"I'll try my best," she said, secretly willing to surrender her most precious possession in exchange for the details of his day.

"Would you and Michelle be willing to come down to the cabin tomorrow and help with the cleanup on the inside?"

"Oh, Jake, don't bother me with that stuff. You know we will. Now sit down and begin. You are going to tell me everything, aren't you?"

Jake assured her that he would relate every word spoken by each person he talked with throughout the day, but only after a call to Big Lights and Ken that the cleanup effort for tomorrow was on. He popped open a beer in the coziness of their family room with its openhearth fire.

ten

LOOKING OUT THE bedroom window in the morning, Jake could see it was shaping up to be a perfect late fall day, sunny with a crisp coolness that rattled your senses and made you happy for another twenty-four hours on planet Earth. Normally, the week before Thanksgiving would be cold and miserably wet, maybe including a few inches of snow, but not today. Everyone showing up to help cut firewood would enjoy the Indian summer weather.

"I'll see you both at the cabin in a while," Jake said to Helen and Bud as he prepared to leave. It was still early.

"But you haven't had any breakfast," Helen protested.

He shrugged, tilted his head slightly, and smiled as he held up his cup of coffee and an apple from the fruit bowl.

"The early bird gets the worm today," he replied in defense.

* * *

When he and KC got to the cabin, Detective Jorgensen surprised him by already being at work in the garage. Jake was beginning to take back his first impressions of small-town police work. He only hoped the detective's work ethic matched his skill in solving murders.

"You're up early, Detective."

"I didn't expect you so early either."

"How's your progress?"

"You'll be happy to know that we'll only keep the garage off limits for the remainder of today. You're free to work anywhere else."

"That is good news."

For the first time since arriving, things seemed to be falling into place. He'd lost a few days getting started, but the situation could have been much worse with considerably longer investigation delays. He decided to take a short walk while waiting for everyone to arrive. KC was all tail when he heard Jake say, "Let's go for a walk."

Walking down the access road was the perfect way to get in touch with the energy of the North Woods. Within twenty yards, KC flushed a small covey of grouse. Most of the leaves were off the trees, which made the birds easier to see as they flew deeper into the forest. A few minutes later, two woodcocks followed suit. Big gray squirrels were busy everywhere in the oak trees. All of this made Jake feel like a guest at his own cabin. After all, he thought, the woodland animals were the real residents of Sandy Cove.

The half-mile walk out to the dirt road took Jake and KC about twenty minutes. It had been a favorite after-dinner walk for Jan and Jake, and memories of the great rapport they enjoyed filled his senses. It almost seemed as if she were there. Not because of what she would have said, but because when Jan was with him words weren't necessary. Unique sensations like this happened to Jake most of his adult life when visiting the cabin. It was as if time had stopped. He had recently read an article about scientists discovering that human emotions and memory were centered in the limbic system of the brain. The concept seemed right to Jake, not because of what he remembered from his college psychology courses, but because he had lived it. Without warning, a sound, sight, or smell would trigger memories and feelings connected with the cabin. Today, it was Jan's presence on the walk. He found it very comforting.

Honkhonkhonk. The noisy interruption from Ken's truck, log splitter hitched to the back, startled Jake only a short distance into his return trip to the cabin. Jake's smile covered his annoyance at the intrusion on his private thoughts as he moved to the side of the access road. "Good morning, Ken," he said, trying to sound good-natured.

"Do you always fucking sleepwalk in the woods?" Ken replied. "I hope I didn't surprise you too badly, but it wasn't very hard. Hop in, I'll give you a lift."

By the time they had the log splitter unhooked and set up in a good location to accomplish the work, others had begun to arrive.

Helen and Michelle were next. They grimaced at the sight of the cabin. Helen was a veteran at cleaning out cabins for fisherman after their trips. She assured Michelle she had seen worse and they would not contract any lethal disease, but privately she was horrified.

Jake was feeling a little mischievous when he introduced Helen to Detective Jorgensen. Whether that would encourage him to finish early or delay the investigation, he wasn't sure.

"Nice to meet you, ma'am. I've heard so much about you, but I don't think we've ever met." Detective Jorgensen was polite, but he clearly wanted to avoid a discussion at all costs. He quickly crossed the yellow tape to the garage.

Within ten minutes, Big Lights, Bobby, and Morey had arrived as well. Big Lights made the introductions. Bobby was twenty-eight, five feet ten inches tall, and of medium build. Morey was much older, maybe in his late thirties. He was a powerful, big man. Jake estimated him at every bit of three hundred pounds and about six feet tall. Both men had the characteristic jet-black hair of Native American Indians.

Bobby and Big Lights had worked on several construction projects together and knew each other well. Their interchange reflected this relationship—light and friendly.

Jake thought Morey looked a little uncomfortable. He didn't come across as sociable like his brother. He decided that Morey's introverted demeanor would probably lead to his keeping to himself throughout the day. This was fine. He was only too happy to have the help.

Everyone agreed that eight full cords should last the winter. Sandy Cove's forested property offered an ample supply of trees felled by the storms that came through regularly. They simply needed to identify the year-old hardwoods. Anything younger wouldn't burn cleanly.

Big Lights, Morey, and Jake manned the chainsaws. Their buzz filled the air. Ken shuttled the cut tree pieces in Jake's Bobcat bucket to save his back, and Bobby ran the splitter. They estimated they would finish around mid-afternoon.

Jake knew you were supposed to let the chainsaw do the work, but eight cords is a lot of wood and he was out of practice. He pushed against the hardwood with his forearms and shoulders—within a few hours his muscles hurt and he was ready for a break. When Big Lights saw Jake sit down and wipe the sweat from his face and head, he joined him at the picnic table.

"If you don't work, I don't work," pronounced Big Lights. "Maybe you should be inside with the women, Jake. You don't look so good." The sweat continued to stream down Jake's face and dripped from the brim of his sweat-soaked baseball cap to form a small pool on the table.

"Shit, I'm fine. You just don't seem to understand the finer points of being a good host, Big Lights. If I were to make you guys look bad by doing more than my share, your feelings would be hurt."

"If that's the case," Big Lights replied, "I'm learning a lot about being a good host. It's hard to sweat like a pig on a BBQ when it's not really called for. Hell, Jake, it's my guess that you'd look downright pitiful if you really worked hard." They worked well together and Jake didn't mind the ribbing. Most of it was true anyway.

Big Lights opened a soft drink and swung his long legs in under the table. He grabbed the towel Jake had used to wipe the sweat from his face and head for the same purpose. Both men acknowledged the hard work with a tilt of their head.

"We're not getting any younger."

"You know, when I first saw you in town you mentioned that there were problems in the Tribal Council," Jake said. "Maybe you could fill me in a little, I'm interested."

"I'm not an expert on the Tribal Council political crap, Jake, but I'll give you my two cents. First, you've gotta understand that none of the Indian nations, like the Ojibwe, answer to anyone but Congress.

The president of the United States is no different from any other Joe walking down the street. Each of these Indian nations is like a sovereign country within a country. Ultimately, with all the other bullshit Congress is involved in, the tribes receive very little look-see, if you know what I mean."

"Okay."

"This opens up the door for tribal corruption, and that's pretty much been the case here. Until the casinos became the big source of power and money most of the corruption was nickel-dime stuff. There wasn't a hell of a lot to fight over. It's my understanding now from the papers that the National Indian Gaming Commission has a lot of say in the operation of the casinos, but it still seems like the fox is in charge of the henhouse.

"The Norway Pine is no exception. You probably know that the Big Bear Tribe is one of the largest and poorest in the state. I think that's where the problem starts."

"What do you mean?"

"To me, it's simple. The people on the rez have never had any idea of what a lot of money is. So it's been easy for the council to get away with making these lame revenue distributions. There's supposed to be a per capita plan to manage distributions. People are getting smarter, though, and they realize that the Norway Pine is one of the largest in the region. Did you know that Mystic Lake near the Twin Cities paid out almost seventy-five thousand per person last year?"

Even though Jake had read about the profits from Mystic Lake, he still acknowledged the comment with an emphatic "holy shit," to confirm his surprise at the huge disparity.

"Is there a distribution plan that's been made public by the Norway Pine?"

"If there is, I've never seen it. Fair's another thing."

Jake registered his concern with a shake of his head and a look of disbelief.

"Now that you understand the lay of the land, let me give you the local happenings. I think I told you the other day that the tribal distribution this year is a turkey and a box of canned goods to each family, even though the casino traffic had a record year. Hell, there are busloads of people coming from as far away as North and South Dakota to spend their Social Security checks. The numbers of employees are up, too; although that's confusing because they're hiring a lot of part-timers."

Ken and Bobby came over to the picnic table for a break also. Morey was hanging back by the tree, but within earshot, a few yards away.

"Hold the rest of the story for later," Jake said, not wanting the others to think he was getting too nosy.

The day progressed perfectly for Jake. The work was getting done, and it appeared that Detective Jorgensen was about to wrap up his investigation. It would feel great to get back to normal.

At about 2 o'clock, everyone took a break to listen to what Jorgensen had to say to Jake before leaving.

"Whoever did this was no amateur. There just doesn't seem to be anything unusual or out of place that we can use. The only prints we found were yours and those of Sheriff Betts. It's my guess, though, that at least two people were involved, but I can't even prove that. Our feeling is that Two Fingers was brought here by boat of his own free will, knocked out by a club of some sort, and taken to the garage to be hanged. If you look close, you can see what might be the dragging marks left from his boots, although there's no proof of that either. The marks on the sand beach would indicate that maybe a small boat was here. In either case, it's impossible to conclude anything. They're just imprints."

"Did you do any better in the cabin?" Jake asked.

"Not really. We dusted everything for prints and found nothing. The events may be tied together, or purely coincidental, we can't tell. The only hope we have is that the events aren't connected, in which case, our chances may increase that somebody did see something we're missing. At this point, it's a crapshoot.

"I'm going to head back to the station house to give my full report to the sheriff. All of the details will be there if you need anything for the insurance report, Jake. In the meantime, I'm not very optimistic about wiping this one off the board anytime soon."

Jake wondered privately if this was just a ploy to get the responsible parties to drop their guard. Maybe I've just watched too many B movies, he thought.

"Well, thanks for your help, Detective," Jake replied, offering a handshake of appreciation. "Everyone on the peninsula is aware of the situation here and alert to anything that looks out of the ordinary. We're still very concerned a cold-blooded killer can be this bold and nothing is found."

Shaking his head in agreement and frustration, the detective turned and left.

By then it was mid-afternoon and Helen and Michelle left as well. The inside of the cabin was back to normal. And the men only had one more cord to go. Back to work.

By 4:30, with the last of the wood stacked, Jake felt he could safely open the bar. Everyone was tired, all the equipment was turned off, and the beer tasted like honey. Helen, Bud, and Michelle would be back in about an hour. Jake had purchased some T-bones to go with Helen's famous recipe of mixed beans, hamburger, and secret sauce.

Jake truly loved being the host at events like this. After all, it would have been impossible for him to do the work himself and very difficult to hire the crew necessary to get the work done. The North Woods' business environment didn't operate like a normal economy where a project could be matched with a willing person for the right price. Here, minimum-wage projects like this one were generally accomplished because folks understood that the remoteness demanded self-sufficiency. People weren't willing to drive a long way for low pay, but they were willing to drive to help a neighbor. The balance of trade in the woods usually called for in-kind help on a similar project, like the spring and fall ritual of putting in and taking out each other's docks. In the end people would rather exchange labor and friendship than money. He enjoyed the spirit of community that was alive and well on Arrowhead.

Everyone relaxed after dinner and enjoyed one another's company. Bud did his infamous magic tricks for Laura and Ken. Bobby and Michelle talked quietly about her plans to use her geology degree. She enjoyed his good-natured attention. Morey declined the invitation to stay for dinner and left after a few beers.

Jake, Big Lights, and Helen shared stories about the old days. According to Helen, that's when people raved over the muskie fishing, and the only two telephones on the peninsula shared the same party line.

"I was impressed with your dad, Jake," Helen said. Hank Lorenz, Jake's dad, had been behind the purchase of the cabin some thirty years ago.

"It wasn't until 1985 or so that he installed indoor plumbing. Until then, that old man couldn't have been more proud of his outhouse than of a new Cadillac. He used to call the outdoor commode a 'biffy.' It stood right over there." She pointed toward the edge of the yard into the forest. "Years later, after the indoor john had been installed, he said that Arrowhead would never be the same."

Jake laughed. "Yeah, that's when he started using the old biffy to store flammables like gas and kerosene. He got a big kick out of telling people that a blast from the gas in the ground mixed with gas stored in cans would turn the peninsula into wasteland!"

The three of them laughed.

"Helen," Jake said. "Have you noticed Bobby and Michelle? They seem to be hitting it off. Did they know each other before today?"

"No, they didn't, and yes, I have noticed. No offense, Big Lights, but her mom and dad would be a little surprised to see her come home with a Native American in tow, ten years her senior, I might add. I better get over there and throw some water on the fire."

"Bobby's one of the good guys, Helen," Big Lights responded, somewhat insulted. "He's not going to scalp her, for Christ's sake."

"I know that and you know that, but it's her parents I answer to, and they're not likely to see it that way."

As Helen moved to talk with Michelle and Bobby, Jake quietly circled back to his discussion from earlier in the day. "So, are there any other problems within the tribe other than the lousy profit distribution and the shift to part-time help at the casino?"

"Well, it's tough to actually pin things down. I mean, it's not like I have the inside track. But I have heard about stuff and seen some things that don't add up, at least to me."

"Like what, for example?"

"Let's start by saying that John Fields is a good man and a good friend. Most of what I know comes from him."

"Who's John Fields?"

"He's the ex-tribal chairman brought in to clean up dirty laundry and business affairs. He was fired by the council in six months, supposedly for three things—malfeasance in the handling of tribal affairs, dereliction or neglect of duty, whatever that means, and refusal to comply with the constitution and bylaws of the tribe. It was all over the papers in Bronson. Hell, Jake, it's hard to imagine someone screwing up that badly in six months."

"You think he was set up?"

"Damn straight. I can't prove it, but when he went against the Tribal Council power structure to get things changed and improved, he lost out."

"Who took over?"

"Some dude named Don Pasquesi. But he's in the back pocket of the real power on the Tribal Council—Sam Aguire and Chase Leonard. The truth be told, I could get my ass kicked sideways with the council just for talking like this to you. Outsiders aren't welcome."

While Big Lights told his story, Jake also considered his friend's tendency to be too vocal. Jake was especially concerned he might carry the discussion to the bars in Chippewa Lake. In that venue, the outcome of his outspoken nature could easily have harsh consequences.

"I hope you're careful who you talk to."

"You're absolutely right on that one," Big Lights answered reassuringly.

Jake hoped he would remember. But he knew there was no stopping Big Lights when the beer was on the house.

"Just after Don Pasquesi became chairman, the Tribal Council hired a new outside accounting firm to check the rez's books, somebody from Eau Claire. They're called McMillan Larsen Wingfoot, I think. They're supposed to be experts in gaming and Indian casinos. But Wingfoot turned out to be Sam Aguire's nephew from one of the larger and wealthier Chippewa tribes in Wisconsin. Some surprise, huh?"

"Are they legitimate?"

"Oh, they're legitimate, all right. As it turns out, they're so legitimate that James Wingfoot is the chairman of the National Indian Gaming Commission. Who knows how much higher they go beyond that?

"Within three months, we noticed that the casino started replacing the old slots with new slots from North American Slot Machines. Some of the slots being replaced were brand-new. Soon after, a lot of people were fired from their jobs, and part-time replacements were hired. Many who lost their job are my friends. The reasons were all trumped up and related to trivial shit.

"The more I think about this affair, the more it pisses me off," Big Lights said, his tone escalating. "And another thing, what's the logic of Aguire, Leonard, and Pasquesi all being at the casino on a regular basis, and at some pretty strange hours? Don might make sense, but it's hard to justify why the other two are there."

Jake found the possibilities fascinating, although he was not quite sure what to make of them. One thing seemed clear, though. Big Lights believed that something was going on. He put his arm around Big Lights' shoulders and said, "Let me buy you another beer." He couldn't help but sense the frustration Big Lights felt on behalf of his tribe.

It wasn't really late when people started to leave, but everyone was exhausted. Jake thanked each person personally and enthusiastically for their help as they filed out to their cars. He felt a bond with these people that was hard to come by in the Cities.

Jake turned on the TV to catch the evening news. After the long day, the hour felt like midnight. His muscles ached and weariness quickly overtook him.

He and KC sat for a few minutes enjoying the silence of the empty cabin. As Jake scratched KC behind his ears, he reflected on a successful day and finished the last of his beer. He wouldn't have admitted it to the others, but he was really sore. He couldn't believe how out of shape he was. He decided to save the kitchen work for the morning.

eleven

As PLANNED, MOREY met with Sam Aguire at the Night Owl Bar & Grill in Chippewa Lake at the end of the day. He had come directly from Jake's cabin.

"Sit down and have a beer," Sam said. "Have you eaten anything yet?"

Sam liked hard facts and he was anxious to get a firsthand account of what had taken place at Jake's. Sam needed an insider to be his eyes and ears. While Morey was a long way from a perfect substitute, he did have access through Bobby. Good enough, Sam thought.

Morey knew Sam's power on the council was stronger than ever. Doing Sam a few favors would go a long way. It was a stroke of luck, his being asked to help out at Jake's. Big Lights was Bobby's friend, not his, and he had never met Jake. Even though Morey couldn't put all the pieces together, he sensed something big was happening. He wanted to be a part of it, and he would do whatever it took to stay on Sam's good side.

"No, goddamn it," Morey muttered back. "And you don't keep this machine running at full speed by holding back on the grub." He pulled his open work coat back and extended his enormous girth for emphasis.

Everyone knew that Morey loved to eat. Walking away from those T-bones that Jake was putting on the grill had only made him irritable and hungry. Despite this, the work was done there, and Morey felt out of place staying any longer.

Morey's disposition turned when Sam called to the bartender, "I want the biggest piece of meat you have for my friend here. Forget the salad and double up the fries. We'll be at the back table when it's ready."

Sam got up from his bar stool. Morey followed him to the back of the bar across from the pool table and slid his immense body into a booth. The light was dim and hid the shabbiness of the decor. What couldn't be hidden, though, was the permanent smell of cheap tap beer and cigarette smoke that permeated the brain and stuck to your clothes like a wet coat of paint.

Appearances didn't matter to Sam, however. His intense demeanor and powerful build commanded attention regardless of the setting. His pockmarked complexion and deep-set eyes highlighted a face that never smiled. People knew Sam meant business.

It was early for a Saturday night at the Night Owl. And the only two other patrons would not threaten Sam and Morey's need for privacy. They were a part of the tribe's disenfranchised army of lost and forgotten men. These two had been there for hours. Alcoholics for sure and, most likely, men who had been without a job for so long they no longer held any sense of responsibility. The Bureau of Indian Affairs documented that over 50 percent of the adult Indian men were members of this army—no job, no self-respect, and no way out. These statistics were probably low. The world outside would find it very difficult to imagine their plight. One thing was certain—they presented no threat to the prearranged meeting between Sam and Morey.

"Have a couple of beers while dinner's in the oven, Big Fella. We have plenty of time for you to eat and tell me everything that happened."

Morey knew that this is where he would earn his keep. He took his time as he began. After recounting everyone present at Jake's cabin

that day, he decided to start by telling Sam about the comment made
by Detective Jorgensen at the end of the day.

"The dick called himself Jorgensen or Swensen, or something like
that. He's from Bronson. Anyway, he said that this one's probably
going to be on the open board for a while."

"I could find more evidence in a day than this jackass could in a
week," Sam said. "Go on."

"There's not much to tell. I worked the chainsaw all day and only
got bits and pieces of information on breaks. The dick spent all day
in the garage and gave Jake the okay to start the cleanup on the rest
of the property. He said experts did the job, probably two. He wasn't
sure if Two Fingers came of his own free will or was forced. The only
thing this guy really knew outright was that Two Fingers was clubbed
and hanged. I think he was pissed when he left—he's got no clue. He
asked for people to call if anything else came up and gave out a bunch
of business cards.

"He thinks all three of them came by boat," Morey added and then
took a long pull of his beer. "There were marks in the sand, but that
don't tell shit as to who put them there."

"How about fingerprints?" asked Sam.

"None he talked about, just Sheriff Betts's and Jake's. I think he's
banking on some lucky lead that might connect the cabin mess and the
murder. He's hoping that someone else could have seen something."

Sam knew, of course, that this could not have been the case. He
thought how their approach to the cabin and garage that night had
been meticulous. The detective was right about the boat and the two
men, but these local dicks would get no further. Sam had witnessed
the low caliber of their work before.

"What else went on, you know, between the others?"

"Hell, we just cut one shitload of wood," Morey replied. "And all
I got was a free lunch and a couple of beers. Nothing else really happened."

"The tribe will make it up to you, Morey. It's important that we
find out what happened to Two Fingers ourselves. These local cops
are incompetent bastards and never do a complete job when it's just

an Indian. If this were Jake Lorenz or Alex Minor that got hanged, the whole fucking FBI would be all over the county. You know what I mean, Morey?"

Without waiting for Morey's reply, Sam went on. "Why do you think that poor fucker got hanged anyway, Morey? I'll tell you why! Remember when those three BSU college jokers burned that young Indian beyond recognition, just for the fun of it? That was Two Fingers' son. As far as I know, this is the same kind of bullshit. The same cops investigated that one, and those asshole college kids were never convicted. Hell, the only way they could possibly identify the Indian was by his dental records. To this day we don't know who did it. That's why the tribe has to stay together on matters like this. Those bastards don't know how we do things. We'll never get a fair shake if we don't."

Morey sat in silence for a few moments. Sam's comments barely registered. "One thing's for sure, though," Sam continued, his stern eye contact forcefully invading Morey's comfort zone, "old Two Fingers sure pissed somebody off, but good."

Morey didn't grasp the full meaning of Sam's last comment, but the aggressiveness of his behavior intimidated Morey. Somewhere in the depth of Sam's penetrating eyes lay the core of the devil. Morey couldn't quite describe it, but Satan was there, all right.

* * *

Over the past ten years Sam had become a powerful member of the Reservation Tribal Council, but never the RTC chairman. That was his way. Sam knew how to get what he wanted, but the kind of power he exercised didn't come with a gavel or a title on a business card. Sam was a predator when it came to accomplishing things.

Two Fingers was the perfect example. Three years ago, Two Fingers wouldn't agree to participate in a plan Sam, Chase, and Don concocted to take control of the Arrowhead Peninsula from Alex Minor. The plan was brilliant. It took advantage of the legal Native American tribal rights to take possession of land, regardless of ownership, if it turned out to be an integral part of a sacred Indian burial ground.

Numerous Indian artifacts had been discovered near Minor's property over the years and, as recently as four years ago, an isolated grave of a female Indian medicine woman was discovered less than a hundred feet from his property line. Common perception held that other sites most certainly existed in the vicinity. Alex Minor wasn't about to cooperate, and Sam, Chase, and Don did not want to press the issue without being sure of the outcome.

As the caretaker of the Indian cemeteries throughout the reservation, Two Fingers would be the perfect accomplice. A few of these cemeteries dated back several hundred years and had been long forgotten. With careful planning, including dirt composition and Indian corpses from the right time period, a sacred burial ground could be meticulously recreated on Minor's property. After all, it was ultimately the tribe's final say as to the authenticity of the sacred grounds uncovered. Once the sacred burial ground was established, Sam and Chase could take full control of the resort and casino project by locating them together on the Arrowhead Peninsula. A heritage center would be a nice addition to keep reservation members happy.

Sam and Chase developed a perfect plan to double-cross Alex and get him out of the way. But Two Fingers wouldn't agree to his critical role of exhuming the old corpses from the early known burial sites. Without his knowledge and specific expertise, the plan couldn't be accomplished. Since his cooperation was critical, Sam arranged for the savage attack, burning, and murder of Two Fingers' only son, Frank. Sam made it appear as a racially motivated attack by some BSU students, but the charges never stuck. It came on the eve of a long-awaited reconciliation between father and son and crushed Two Fingers' resolve. The final agreement was sealed with a threat of similar treatment to Linda if Two Fingers chose not to cooperate.

So for the past three years, Two Fingers did as he was told. Everything was in place for the sacred burial ground to be discovered this coming spring, after the thaw. Despite his unfailing cooperation, Two Fingers' usefulness had come to an end. He had become a liability in a high-stakes operation.

Arranging to visit Jake's cabin with Two Fingers was easy. Two Fingers had seen Alex setting up the destruction to the cabin while on one of his own trips to the peninsula. He relayed the information to Sam and Chase. They were very interested in this bizarre activity, particularly since Alex was their business partner. Two Fingers volunteered to give them a firsthand look. He thought he was going to the cabin that night as a favor to his bosses. Instead, he was taken out of the picture.

* * *

Sam's dinner with Morey was going well. He was pleased with Morey's work and felt the relationship could become even more useful. He was always looking for men willing to get things done without worrying about how. Sam was a good judge of character, especially bad character, and he intended to give Morey some additional responsibility.

Near the end of the meal, he slipped an envelope with five hundred dollars inside to Morey.

Surprised, Morey said, "You sure know how to take care of my fat Indian ass! I didn't know I was so fuckin' important. What's the big deal about the murder, anyway? Fill me in."

Sam grabbed the envelope back from Morey's hand. "Getting filled in ain't part of what you get paid for. It's questions like that that will put you back on the unemployed roster real goddamn quick. You just do as you're told. No questions, got it?"

There was a heavy silence between the men.

"But I only wanted . . ."

"What you want don't count—ever! If you're not able to live with that, then our business is over."

Morey nodded his head in understanding, realizing he could be in over his head, but still wanting Sam to take him in. Sam pushed the envelope back to Morey a second time.

"We're involved in some business that's important to the lifeblood of the tribe," Sam continued. "If you can't keep your mouth shut and do what's asked of you, you're gone."

"That's not a problem," Morey replied in quick accommodation. He finished his dinner in relative silence and started to push away from the table when Sam asked, "I want you to help me out with two more projects now that we have an understanding. This time you'll be totally on your own, though, and you can't be seen by anyone."

Sam laid out the plan. He wanted Morey to go over Two Fingers' house with "the detail of a Polish cleaning woman," as he put it. "Don't leave anything unturned and don't leave any trace you were there. Can you do that?"

"Yeah, I can. What am I looking for?"

"Anything that looks like it shouldn't belong to an Indian cemetery caretaker—unusual information, like maps, journals, or pictures. Use your head. And it needs to be done before Linda returns from college for Thanksgiving break."

"Done. What's the other job?"

"While Linda's here in Chippewa Lake on break, I want you to comb through her college apartment the same way—with one exception. Make it look like a break-in. Steal her computer, her TV, and shit like that. Get rid of the stuff so nobody will ever find it. When you're done with both projects, bring what you find to me."

With their agreements set, it was now time to go. The two and a half hours had gone by quickly. Sam paid the tab, and they began to move away from the table when Morey made a last comment about the day.

"Jake and Big Lights seem pretty chummy together. Seemed like they're big-time friends, you know?" Morey wondered more than offered.

"No, I don't. What are you trying to say?"

"Well, those two are pretty cozy is all I'm saying. Private conversations and bullshit like that most of the day."

Sam didn't like this information. Private conversations meant something to hide, maybe a problem, maybe not. He'd make a point of looking into it later.

They left the Night Owl and got into separate cars.

twelve

KC's GROWLING SHOCKED Jake out of a deep trance and onto his feet. He must have fallen asleep on the couch before shutting the cabin down for the night. A glance at the clock over the antique bookstand told Jake it was 1:45 in the morning.

KC's hair bristled on his neck, and his lips curled, baring his teeth. The growling deep in his throat became more intense. The door to the lake was closed, but some of the windows, covered only with screens, remained slightly open.

Jake could hear movement at the edge of the forest beyond the ordinary nighttime sounds. His mind struggled against a headache from the beer and the abrupt interruption out of a deep sleep to figure out what it was. His instinct felt a definite presence.

He ran to the front door. Locked it. Ran to the three-season porch door and locked it, too. He needed time to think. Was the bear coming back? Even though he had not seen evidence of the bear since his arrival, he should have figured it might return. How can I be so stupid?

"Goddamn it!" Jake exclaimed, realizing his shotgun was still back in the Yukon until the sheriff completed his investigation.

He turned out the lights in the cabin to give himself a better view of the night outside. The halogen yard light over the garage lit up most of the area on the open side of the cabin. But the side adjacent to the thick woods was pitch black.

"Damn," he muttered. "Where the hell is the flashlight?"

Jake made his way to the kitchen and groped the counters where he remembered last seeing it. He startled himself knocking over a beer bottle, surely attracting the attention of whatever prowled outside. Finally Jake's eyes adjusted to the darkness. He saw the flashlight inches away. He grabbed it and stood motionless. The typical night-time noises had now gone silent, as if time had stopped, and gave way to whatever approached. There was no escape. Jake felt his pounding heart could be heard throughout the cabin.

Minutes passed.

The noises stopped.

He decided to check things out further. Maybe whatever it was had lost interest. After all, bears around the cabin had never caused a problem in the past.

He retrieved an ax handle he always kept in the bedroom for protection from an intruder. Flashlight in one hand and ax handle in the other, he moved around in the dark cabin. His weapon wouldn't do much good against a bear, but he could be dealing with someone involved in the Two Fingers incident. With a person, the ax handle would do considerable damage.

He saw nothing in the yard. As he listened, however, he definitely could hear something prowling around. Whatever it was, it sounded heavy. Now bushes were being rustled without concern for noise. Then Jake heard guttural, snorting sounds distinctly identifying this intruder as a bear. He went to the bedroom to shine the flashlight through the window. He opened it quietly to avoid the flashlight glare from the glass.

With his nose close to the screen, he directed the beam along the edge of the woods. About twelve feet of property separated the cabin and the trees. Suddenly, in a rush toward the cabin and the light, the bear challenged and rose to his hind legs.

Jake gasped.

Cinnamon bears are normally three to four hundred pounds and five to six feet in height. The typical black bears in the area gave way to these larger cousins. But this bear appeared to be double that size, the largest Jake had ever seen.

His pounding heart and rapid shallow breathing triggered a fight-or-flight response. Every muscle in his body tensed. He was terrified.

"What should I do?" he whispered, wishing someone could hear. The bear's aggressive posture at the mere sight of the flashlight was not a good sign. The sheriff was at least an hour away. Ken was out of the question because of his back and Bud was pretty old for this kind of thing. Not exactly the SWAT team he needed.

In another instant, Jake thought of Tom Faulkner at the Cedar Lodge and Fishing Resort. Tom had hunted bears for years and had lived on the peninsula since he and his wife Cheryl purchased the resort four years ago. He would know what to do.

The phone seemed to ring forever. When Tom finally answered, it was from a deep sleep.

"Tom, this is Jake Lorenz. I'm sorry for waking you, but I've got a big problem at the cabin and need some help."

"What's going on?" Tom grunted.

While explaining the situation to Tom, Jake could hear the bear move from the side of the cabin onto the front porch. With the windows partially open, the smells of leftovers from Jake's little dinner gathering floated through the air like an aromatic welcome mat.

Jake heard breakage and a loud impact at the front of the cabin. He turned the cabin lights back on and dropped the phone to see one hell of a large bear ripping the door off its hinges. It entered the cabin roughly fifteen feet away from where he stood.

KC attacked the bear before it was through the door. Spinning toward the direction of the dog, the bear instantaneously retaliated in a huge brown blur of fury and raked its immense paw at KC, narrowly missing. Jake grabbed some dirty pots and pans from the counter and began banging them wildly, instinctively trying to distract the bear away from KC. The bear's growls, KC's barking, and Jake's banging exploded through the cabin.

The bear steered his course in the direction of the kitchen where the garbage can sat, still loaded with steak bones and table scraps. Jake noticed the shank of a hunter's arrow buried deep in its left shoulder. The discussion with Bud of an injured bear from the hunting season flashed through his mind. This bear had only one goal—complete his feeding drive for hibernation. At this late date, anything would do.

Jake had to get out of the kitchen or he would be cornered. He grabbed the butcher knife and climbed onto the pass-through counter. He would time his exit with the bear's entrance into the kitchen.

Bears rarely attacked a human. But Jake knew that this bear was different. Desperate for food and suffering from a serious and likely infected wound, this animal was dangerous. God, how he hoped Tom was on his way with help!

Suddenly the bear's annoyance with KC's barking and aggressive provocation escalated into full retaliation. Rising to his full height, he let out a terrifying roar. KC reacted instinctively and attacked, sinking his fangs deep into the bear's flank.

The bear's enraged reaction was unbelievably quick and powerful. With deadly force, this eight-hundred-pound crazed beast turned and struck KC with one paw, knocking him across the room. Jake was paralyzed. To his horror, the bear continued ripping at KC, crushing his neck in his jaws, shaking him like an old dust mop.

Jake scanned the cabin's great room for anything to help defend himself. He thought of moving toward the fireplace tools as the bear headed back toward the kitchen garbage. Out of the corner of his eye, he saw something far more useful—the antique ice-fishing spear hanging in the corner near KC's body. The galvanized steel spear was seven feet long, about seventy pounds, with six eight-inch solid-steel forked prongs at the end. These fishing spears were designed to be released through an ice hole, while already in the water, in order to deliver a certain strike on a large walleye or northern pike.

He knew he must stall the bear if at all possible. In all likelihood, Tom would be there soon with a rifle. But the cabin was small and there was no place to hide. Only the garbage stood between Jake, the bear, and a sure mauling.

When the bear entered the kitchen, Jake completed his crawl over the pass-through counter back into the great room. Stepping over KC's limp body, he quickly removed the spear from its hanging position.

Sounds of the bear rummaging in the garbage stopped in less than a minute, and Jake saw the beast turn the corner of the room toward him. No longer afraid, Jake was pissed off like never before. This bear had violated Jake's final safe haven. His anger over Jan's death, the loss of his job, the events over the last few days, and now KC's destruction detonated within him. The bear rose on his hind legs facing Jake. The emptiness of the bear's eyes displayed no human connection. He roared one final insult directly at Jake before his attack. Hot with rage and stench, the bear's breath brought bile to the back of Jake's throat. Long strings of saliva ran from the bear's open jaws. He moved in for the kill.

The predator within Jake took over. Lunging at the bear with the strength and determination of his entire being, Jake screamed at full force. All six forks of the spearhead entered the front of the bear's neck. Combined with the weight and force of the bear's charge and Jake's own power, the spear buried itself into the base of the bear's skull, completely through its neck, directly at the brain stem.

The counterforce of the bear's attack sent Jake crashing backward onto the floor, where he landed next to KC.

thirteen

FROM THE MOMENT Tom got Jake's call, he was in constant motion. Finding his pants and shoes seemed to take forever. He grabbed his 30.06 and instructed Cheryl, "Call Ben and Jim right now. Wake 'em up and tell to come a'runnin—no matter what. Tell 'em it's a bear!"

He had been hunting in the general area of Jake's cabin over the past several months and had noticed bear tracks of unusual proportion, easily twice the size of a typical Minnesota black bear. He had hoped to set a trap by baiting an area near a tree stand he'd used before for hunting. But he never even got a glimpse of the animal.

Tom knew that if this was the bear Jake now faced, he was in real danger. Something had to be terribly wrong for a bear of this size to be on an aggressive feeding pattern this late in the year in an area inhabited by people.

Tom knew these dirt roads like the plumbing in his resort and took every turn like a seasoned NASCAR driver. He didn't want to lose control of his pickup, but he sure wasn't going to be late either. Within ten minutes, Tom had covered the six miles of winding dirt road, but he feared he wasn't going to be fast enough.

Wet with night dew, the grass on the long driveway to the cabin slowed Tom down even more. He was sweating profusely. Finally, the lights of the cabin were in sight. Nothing seemed out of the ordinary from his view in the truck one hundred yards away.

He slammed on his brakes and the truck skidded across the lawn. Leaping out of the cab, Tom heard the most incredible roar from a bear he had ever heard in his life. Simultaneously, he heard Jake scream with equal strength, "You motherfucking bastard!"

Tom rushed the cabin door with his 30.06 loaded and the safety off. Entering without concern for his own safety, he felt the cabin actually shake.

Rushing past the kitchen, he entered the great room just in time to see the bear fall with its full weight on top of Jake. He raised his gun to shoot, but there was no way to immediately separate Jake from the bear. As they went down together, he could see Jake's legs buckle and only his shoulder stuck out from underneath the bear. The rest of his body was smothered. He approached and saw all six tines of the spear sticking completely through the bear's neck, just like Poseidon himself would have killed an attacking sea monster.

Tom stuck the barrel of the rifle into the bear's ear and squeezed the trigger. The shot blew a gaping exit hole in the bear's head. Brain matter and blood covered the floor and stairwell.

Jake had blacked out under the weight of the bear. The intense sound of the rifle shot, however, was an instant wake-up call. Within seconds he was frantically trying to get out from underneath the massive hulk. With his heart racing, his body covered in sweat and blood, and the sound of Tom's voice yelling for him, he realized he was all right, even though his face was buried in the bristled hair of the bear's neck and he could barely move under its weight.

"Are you okay, Jake? Are you okay?"

He wasn't sure. For several seconds he caught his breath before he answered. "I think so," he said in a muffled tone from beneath the bear. "Thank God you're here!"

After Tom struggled to pry the weight of the bear partially off him, Jake was finally able to wiggle free. In that moment, Jake saw the grim remains of KC. He picked his dog up and cradled his mutilated body in his arms.

The adrenaline receded, but Jake couldn't stop shaking. There was nothing else left for him to grasp on to. Jan, his job, and now KC—all gone. He felt completely exposed as the tears of a lifetime emptied once and for all.

part 2

fourteen

"JAKE, YOU'RE THE closest thing to a celebrity this peninsula's ever had. Look at this place. It's packed. Do you ever recall seeing this many cars at the town hall, Buddy? I mean, even the dedication didn't cause this kind of excitement." Helen was a bit worked up as the three of them walked toward the small, rustic Arrowhead Peninsula Town Hall.

"Look over there," she said, pointing to several TV trucks and media trailers.

"Calm down, Helen, you're going to make a fool of yourself if you can't act normal. Jake's excited, everyone's excited, but just let him enjoy the evening without whipping up a frenzy over everything." Bud looked at her, pleading for cooperation.

"You guys are both great to care about me so much," Jake intervened. "Everything will be okay. It's pretty natural for people to get stirred up, so let's just let them have their fun today and go home. Tomorrow will just be another day."

From the moment the news of the attack got out, Jake was a hero. Even the editor of *Outdoor Life* called and wanted an exclusive for their "This Really Happened to Me" column. Five separate newspaper reporters from as far away as Chicago and Omaha wanted interviews before he got to the town hall front door.

It wasn't just the bear attack, not that the attack wasn't worthy enough. What made the story was the fight KC put up to protect his master. Every dog owner in the Midwest, probably the country, could relate to KC's courageous defense. Jake drew the line, however, at requests for a picture showing himself, the dead bear, and KC's battered body. One person even wanted to mount the dead dog's body. Jake was offered five thousand dollars, but said "no chance," and that ended the discussion.

"This Thanksgiving party definitely is a real ballbuster—one to remember," Ken said to Jake once in the building. "I mean, can you believe this fucking place?" He had to yell to be heard, and not surprisingly, caught the offended attention of the mayor of Bronson.

Jake's guest-of-honor status stirred the admiration of locals and out-of-town visitors alike. Everyone showed up to celebrate, even Alex Minor. The event was a big deal, and besides, many here were Jake's friends.

One of the more unusual announcements came in the form of a verbal business proposal from Mike Porter, owner of Porter's Sporting Goods Store in Bronson.

"We're all proud of Jake and what's happened here. And, well, those of us here at Porter's would like to have this here bearskin mounted, proper like. We'll send it to a taxidermist and make it into the best damn bear rug you'll ever see, and we'll cover all the costs to boot. All we ask is that Jake here will let us display the rug in our store for the next two tourist seasons," he said to the audience.

"You can use it during the off-season, Jake, and then it's yours to keep after the second year. What do you say?" He motioned for Jake to respond.

"I never knew one bear hide could be so important," Jake replied, taking the microphone from Mike. "But if it makes everyone here happy, I'll go along with it, too." In the long run, the skin will make a terrific wall display in the great room of the cabin, he thought.

The crowd cheered Mike's generosity. They all knew firsthand that taxidermy could get really expensive.

The bear attack aftermath pictures had been developed for everyone to see. The amount of destruction to the cabin kitchen and great room did not surprise anyone, considering the bear's size. Seven hundred-eighty-five pounds was sure to be a near record in Boone & Crockett.

Despite KC's noble defense, the bear's size dominated discussion at this gathering. The same would be true at a ceremony held on the following Saturday by the Big Bear Lake Indian Band. The Ojibwe believed that killing a bear without the use of a gun conferred the bear's power to the man. Consequently, this unusually large bear gave Jake tremendous status among his Ojibwe neighbors. During that ceremony, Big Lights would present him with a replica of the Makwa Totem, acknowledging his bravery, in honor of Chief Makwa-oday, whose name meant bear's heart.

Alex made his way through the party taking in the comments of praise and heroism directed at Jake. And even though he couldn't help but admire Jake's courage and accomplishment, the whole notion of the peninsula being thrust into the limelight made Alex uneasy. In his estimation, too much attention put his project at risk. As far as he was concerned, winter couldn't come soon enough. The subfreezing temperatures would drive the nosy reporters away fast.

While standing alone near the temporary library section of the township hall—five shelves of donated paper- and hardback books—a disturbing side effect of Jake's notoriety occurred to Alex. Hell, he thought, it's not likely that Jake would sell his cabin after becoming the biggest hero since Paul Bunyan. The resort development plans could definitely be in jeopardy.

While partnerships often get messy, bringing Jake in might be the only way now, he reflected. The more he thought about this idea, the more it made sense. Heroes always get what they want. Maybe this turn of events would provide a backup strategy to the Farley Johnson Baja Mexico plan.

"Nobody says no to a hero," he said, half under his breath.

With new motivation, Alex observed how Jake interacted with locals throughout the day. Jake definitely had a natural way of dealing with people and seemed to have considerable influence as well. He could be a real asset to the project, Alex thought. The more he considered the idea, the more he became convinced of its wisdom. However, he also knew he wasn't dealing with the likes of Farley Johnson here. Jake demonstrated principles and intelligence. He actually cared about people in the community. His price would be higher, much higher.

* * *

As the day grew late, people started to thin out.

Michelle and Bobby had spent the entire day together celebrating Jake's notoriety, and by now, Bobby had grown restless with the crowds. He wanted to leave.

"Michelle, let's go for a drive."

"Where do you want to go?"

"The moon rising over Eagle Feather Bay is pretty awesome. Maybe we could go there."

She nodded and they exited quietly. Neither wanted to attract attention. Both knew of Helen's protective feelings as Michelle's surrogate mom. They managed to slip away in Bobby's car, unnoticed among the rest of the crowd filing out of the town hall.

Bobby found a secluded spot to park, commanding the perfect view of the bay and the full moon overhead.

"You know, Michelle, I think you're pretty special."

"I like being with you, too."

He wanted to hold her hand but the center console of the car made it awkward. Instead, they twisted in their seats a little to face each other and just talked.

"I don't think your grandmother approves of us being together, though. Big Lights told me that she's concerned about what your parents might think, you know—me being an Indian, ten years older, no less."

Bobby had been drawn to Michelle the moment he first saw her. Her relaxed way with people made him feel comfortable, but he needed to know if she would accept him. And he definitely didn't want to move too fast for fear of scaring her away.

"What do you think?"

"I want to get to know you better, too. The other stuff doesn't matter." She reached across the console, took his hand, then, smiling, squeezed it for reinforcement.

"What's your family like, Bobby?"

Bobby hesitated before answering. It caught him a little off guard. No one had ever asked about his family before.

"My mom's full-blood Ojibwe," he started slowly. "And I am very proud of her. Her life's been difficult. My father's an alcoholic and pretty rough with her. He wanders in and out of our life, mostly looking for a handout to finance his next binge. The only money she's earned came through making beadwork crafts for the trading post on the highway. It was her dedication to us during those difficult years that kept me out of trouble. She would always tell my brother Morey and me, 'You can be anything you want if you work hard enough and believe in yourself.' I always remember what she said. I hope it's true."

"She sounds like a strong woman, and there's no reason it's not true."

"Well, I try because I want to bring our family honor, but my brother Morey's another story. He's a bully. As long as I can remember, he's always been looking for a reason to fight. It makes it hard on my mom. What I mean is that he's got a police record for all kinds of crap and it hurts her. And his friends from the casino are garbage. She knows he won't change, and it makes it hard for us to be a family anymore. What's more strange is that money comes from nowhere for Morey."

"What do you mean? What kind of work does he do?"

"He doesn't, but he always has cash. I can't figure it out. You know, Michelle, the poverty and lack of education in reservation life don't always bring out the best in people. That's the hard truth. In one way or another, people get trapped." He didn't feel right hiding anything from Michelle, even if it meant she might not want to see him anymore.

"Are you trapped?" she asked, looking deep into his eyes.

"For a while. Sometimes, the reservation seems to be the only way of life. I'm trying not to limit myself, though, which is why I've enrolled at BSU for the winter semester. I hope to get a degree in forest management."

"That's great, Bobby. Why didn't you tell me before?"

"I wasn't sure I would be accepted and, well, I would have been embarrassed if I didn't get in."

Michelle squeezed his hand again and kissed him on the cheek. She trusted Bobby and sensed a kindred spirit through his honesty about his family and his situation. She didn't think he was trapped either.

They sat quietly holding hands, watching the moon over the bay, like a silver beacon to a lost locomotive among the stars. Michelle hoped Bobby would kiss her. She found his lean build, deep complexion, and jet-black hair attractive. The T-shirt under his open coat conformed to a well-developed upper body with defined forearms and biceps—she liked that as well.

She's perfect, he thought. He loved the way her blond hair contrasted with her olive-colored skin, visible even in the dimness of the car. The shadows of the moon also revealed the outline of her full breasts in perfect proportion to her athletic body.

He had never been with a white girl before. Would she want me? Will she reject me because of her grandmother? Maybe her friends have warned her about older guys wanting too much too soon. His unusual lack of confidence and the need to not make a mistake allowed the moment they both wanted so badly to pass without anything happening.

"Maybe we can commute to the campus together this winter," Bobby said, really wanting to tell her how beautiful she was.

"That's a great idea," Michelle said, trying not to show her disappointment with his shyness.

At that moment, Michelle saw three flashlight beams on the opposite shoreline of the bay. "Do you see those lights?

"I sure do." They sat up straight and strained to see the outline of a boat in the shadows. The distance was far too great for either of them to tell who the people were, but both realized instantly the suspicious nature of what they saw. At times Indians would set up for wild rice harvesting the night before, but the harvesting season had ended in September.

Bobby fixed his eyes on what appeared to be three men, one medium in size, another with a barrel frame, and one very large man holding something in his hands. The silhouette and movements of the largest man resembled his brother Morey, but he couldn't be sure. He said nothing.

Quickly the flashlights moved off into the forest.

"Whoever they are, they sure know their way around," Bobby whispered. "I know these woods, they're dark at night. And even with flashlights, the thick growth of small trees makes quick movements difficult."

The men and the lights disappeared.

On his own, Bobby might be tempted to follow. He was completely confident in the forest, with or without a flashlight. However, the unresolved circumstances of Two Fingers' murder and Michelle's presence provided sound logic to start the engine and slowly leave without distraction or notice.

"I'm sorry for bringing you out here," he said while driving. "I mean, I'm not sorry we were together. I really enjoyed that, but it could be dangerous." For his entire life, the peninsula had remained safe from any crime. It was poor judgment on his part, however, to ignore present facts, and he knew it.

He struggled to push these thoughts from his mind while walking Michelle to the Miller's front door, where he finally summoned the courage to kiss her.

Michelle responded to the touch of his lips with a kiss filled with the passion of the lost moment in the car. She wrapped her arms around him inside his coat and pulled his body close to hers. She felt his hard muscles against her breasts and wriggled to get closer.

"Thanks for a great day. Can I call you again?" He asked with renewed confidence, kissing her again.

"If you don't, you'll be riding to BSU by yourself!"

The front door closed and each smiled in their parting, sparked with the excitement of their embrace.

fifteen

Two DAYS BEFORE the Thanksgiving Day gathering honoring Jake at the Town Hall, Sam and Chase mulled over the problem at their private table at the Night Owl.

"That son-of-a-bitch is the luckiest bastard north of the Crow Wing River," Sam said to Chase in a sour tone.

"This goddamn bear attack fiasco is going to jeopardize everything we worked for. The peninsula's like downtown Bemidji with all the activity."

"We're just damn lucky the weather hasn't turned," Chase said, changing the subject to focus on what he felt was the real issue.

The two men had been conspiring on the Arrowhead Peninsula casino scheme for at least three years. As far as they were concerned, no detail had been overlooked. Their initial plan included making their way back to the six burial sites on Alex's property before winter to complete their restoration. The ground would have to look natural when the sites were discovered in the spring. Both the effects of the winter snows and new spring forest growth would complete the camouflage efforts naturally. The risk of being noticed with all the people coming and going on the peninsula, however, jeopardized their cover.

"We need to get out there quick," Chase continued.

"I'm listening," Sam said sarcastically. "Is there a solution somewhere in what you're saying?"

"The party at the town hall will give us the cover we need. Don't you see? Everyone will be there. By the time people leave, they will either be drunk or too stuffed with food to breathe. There won't be a light on anywhere on the peninsula past 9 o'clock. We can take the boat to Minor's about an hour later to be safe. We can be in and out before daybreak."

"And just how is it you know the weather will hold out? Are you a goddamn weatherman now too?"

"I'm not, but the paper is, and besides, our only other choice is tomorrow night while everyone is running around the peninsula making preparations. You know, Sam, sometimes you piss me off. I know we have a problem, and we need a solution. But if you don't like this one, give me an alternative, not some bullshit comment."

Chase was the only person who could talk to Sam like this. At five feet ten and one hundred sixty pounds, Chase made up for his unassuming physical presence with a quick, brilliant mind matching Sam's need for the unscrupulous. Besides, Sam owed Chase big-time. He was the only person who knew the real truth behind the murder of Frank Smith, Two Fingers' son.

"This job you're planning is more work than I want to take on with just the two of us. And if it does start snowing, we'll have to work even faster."

"What are you saying?"

"What I'm saying is that we need to rent a workhorse. I think Morey's our man. Tomorrow, in fact, is a big day for Morey. He's doing a shakedown of Two Fingers' house in the morning, and at night he's taking care of Linda's apartment in Duluth. I think it's time to bring him in, and if he fucks up, we'll just get a bigger rope."

"For Christ's sake, I'm not going to hang everyone who doesn't cooperate. We agree on goals, but murder isn't high on my list."

"Don't get so uptight, it was just an expression."

Privately, Chase had become disturbed over his involvement in the murder and planned to avoid similar circumstances.

"It will be easy enough to check out whether Morey does both jobs right. Then, provided that his work is good, I'll agree to bring him in. We'll limit him to only what he needs to know, which won't be much." Chase wanted to be cautious in giving a loose cannon like Morey information that he couldn't handle.

After settling a few more details, Sam left the Night Owl. Chase lingered over his drink a few minutes. Being a planner by nature, he wanted time to review the logistics without interruption.

* * *

The next day Sam left an urgent message for Morey to call first thing on Thanksgiving morning. He wanted to make sure Linda's apartment got done Wednesday night, and to let Morey know he may have another project needing his help.

Morey got the message right away.

He had tried to get in touch with Sam before leaving for Duluth to report on Two Fingers' house, where he had found absolutely nothing unusual, but he couldn't. He liked Sam's growing confidence in him. The money was good and he had no problem with the work. It would take weeks to earn this kind of money, even if I could find the work, he thought.

* * *

Morey arrived at the University of Minnesota-Duluth campus late on Wednesday night. Everyone had left for the holiday. He found Linda's off-campus apartment building easily; the listing outside gave her first-floor apartment number as 4A. Before attempting an entry, however, he parked his truck in the dark shadows of the street to observe the building for activity. For the next two hours, he saw only one person leave; no one arrived, and no lights went on or off. By midnight he felt safe to go in.

The cheap door was ridiculously simple to jimmy. A standard VISA credit card slid easily between the door and the lock. He laughed when he remembered the credit card slogan promising the card would "open up new doors in his financial future." "Promise kept," he snickered.

Inside the apartment he found the usual college apartment stuff: computer, TV, stereo, clothes. He made quick work of moving the valuable items to his car. No noise, no disruption. Everything went well. On his second trip he looked around more closely, following Sam's instructions to look for anything unusual. He kept his latex surgical gloves on the entire time. After not finding anything, he trashed each room for effect. The bedroom and dresser drawers were his last targets. In the second drawer from the top he discovered a number of silk panties and other undergarments. The thought of this young woman wearing these garments against her naked, untouched body aroused him. His three-hundred-pound sweaty body and sleazy personality kept him in the league of paid prostitutes only. His heart began to pump and within seconds he felt an erection press against his tight work pants. Using the silk panties to stroke himself, he quickly masturbated. After climaxing in her underwear, he stuffed the panties in his pocket. He left feeling a sense of gratification both in accomplishing Sam's goal and adding to his own pleasures.

*　*　*

Morey met Sam the next morning on one of the many remote dirt roads on the reservation. This particular intersection afforded them a view of anyone who might pass by without being seen themselves. Morey arrived first and waited. Within minutes he saw the dust of Sam's truck in the early-morning mist.

"I did exactly like you told me to do, but I didn't find anything at Two Fingers'. I looked everywhere. I searched the house for almost an hour."

"What about the apartment in Duluth?"

"I can show you the stuff I got," Morey said, motioning for Sam to move toward the truck bed. He pulled back a secured tarpaulin, exposing the stolen items.

"Where are you going to dump this stuff?"

"This shit don't float. I can take it to the deep part of the lake. Nobody's on the water today."

Sam handed him an envelope with another five hundred dollars.

Morey nodded nervously. "Any more questions?"

"No. You already told me you searched Two Fingers' house, and Linda's apartment was taken care of the way we agreed to. Is there something you're keeping from me?"

Shaking his head aggressively to the contrary, Morey replied, "I only meant to make sure that you had the information you wanted. I wouldn't keep anything from you, Sam."

Sam didn't want to spend a lot of time on the open dirt road with Morey. He said abruptly, "Chase and I want you to help us tonight with another project. You'll need to meet us at the Night Owl at 9 o'clock. Dress warm. We're going to be out on the lake." He hesitated while maintaining eye contact with Morey. "There will be an extra five hundred in it for you when we're done, but there's no backing out when we're finished."

"I'll be there. I'm not gonna back out. Count on it."

"Good. Bring a large flashlight and some shovels and hard rakes," Sam ordered as they parted.

*　*　*

At a boat landing on a remote site on Big Bear Lake, Morey, Sam, and Chase loaded six large bags of something indefinable into the boat. Morey knew he would find out soon enough what their contents were. It was dark, but a full moon skirting the clouds made navigation easy. The men headed across the three-mile stretch of water toward the bay. Traveling without running lights and a mild chop on the lake kept them from going full throttle.

They slowed up when they approached Eagle Feather Bay. Scanning the water for other boats, possibly night fishermen, Sam pointed to the bay's far shoreline as a heading for Morey.

Reaching the shore, they beached the boat, securing the rope to the nearest tree. Sam grabbed two of the bags. He turned his flashlight on and entered the forest. The others grabbed two bags as well, clicked their flashlights on, and followed Sam. The bags were relatively light, but their bulky contents made them awkward to carry.

"Goddamn it," Sam whispered loudly. "We're not trying to land seaplanes here. Get your asses into the woods before someone sees all these fucking lights."

They all moved quickly.

Within minutes they came to a small clearing near one of the many marsh areas in the forest. Morey could see a bare spot where the surface of the ground had been dug up recently, an area about the size of a big refrigerator on its side. Morey knew these men were capable of almost anything, yet, rather than being alarmed, his confidence actually grew. Sam must really trust me, he thought.

"I want you to do just as I do," Sam said, opening one of the bags. Morey was not surprised to see a mixture of leaves, twigs, and forest covering in the bag. That's what he'd guessed while carrying the bags, but he still didn't grasp their purpose.

"Morey, you go first. Spread this stuff carefully over the bare spot. Make it blend in with the natural forest-floor covering. Be careful not to disturb anything else."

Two Fingers had prepared this mixture of natural covering in such detail that each bag coordinated with a specific site. The only difference was who Two Fingers thought would be doing the work.

He had done his job well, too well. His life's work as caretaker for the Indian reservation's various cemeteries had prepared him for the task like no one else. And Linda's safety had sealed his commitment. Within forty-five minutes, the altered ground blended perfectly with the forest floor around it. In the spring, it would be part of the natural covering again.

Each man meticulously checked for anything unusual before leaving each site. Even though Sam, as the head of the tribal exploration committee, would be the first to find the sites in the spring, he wanted no surprises.

By the time the three men found the next location, thirty minutes had passed. The six "ceremonial sites" selected covered key segments of Alex's land and put most of the property in question.

"This is going to take all night," Sam said to the other men.

In fact, the first light of dawn glimmered when they finished their last site. The work was tedious, and both Sam and Chase were satisfied with Morey's help. If nothing else, he knew how to stay on a project until it was complete, a trait both men regarded as an asset in their kind of work.

They were on the boat around 5:30 and back to the original landing before sunrise.

With everything in place for the tribe's historic discovery of the burial sites in the spring, Sam and Chase felt secure. Thoughts of the well-executed plan, Alex Minor's defenseless surprise, and their own extravagant wealth filled both men's minds.

On the way to pick up their cars at the Night Owl, Sam handed Morey another envelope. He didn't open it and asked no questions, but instead said, "Thanks, I've always liked gardening."

sixteen

LINDA STRUGGLED WHILE the Duluth policeman took her statement. She didn't really know what had happened. When she came back to her apartment the Sunday after Thanksgiving, everything had been trashed.

"Why would someone do this?" She sat despondently, holding her head in both hands.

"My father's been murdered. My brother's been murdered. And my mother's dead from cancer. Now this," she said to a Duluth patrolman.

More than a little shocked by her situation, the officer asked the names of Linda's family members and included them in his report.

"I don't know what to do. I'm afraid. I don't even know where to go." The flow of tears streaked her mascara.

Hearing her distress and seeing the empty look on her face, the officer finally said, "You don't sound like you're going to be all right. What can I do?"

Linda burst into a new torrent of tears. "I'm trying to do my best, but it's just too hard." He listened, but didn't fully comprehend the depth of her emotional despair.

"Do you have anyone you can turn to for help?"

"Maybe my friends can help with my courses in school, but other than that, no. I'm it. No one's left."

Her demeanor resembled a small girl separated from her mom and lost in a large shopping mall. Feeling hopeless, frightened, and insecure, she didn't know what to do next. Tears continued to run down her cheeks while she finished the statement for the officer at the kitchen table.

"I'll arrange to have a patrol car drive by here several times a day. We'll make every effort to ensure your safety. My name's Colin Brady. Here, take my card. If there's anything I can do or anything else you remember, I want you to call. From my experience, it's real important to get yourself back in a normal routine. I know it's going to be hard, but it isn't likely the burglar will come back. After all, there's not much left to steal," he said with a quirky look, trying to lighten the situation.

She smiled back.

"You can be pretty sure, Miss Smith, this was just a random break-in. We always get a few over the holidays. Trust me, you'll be okay."

Officer Brady stayed until Linda regained some of her composure. He guessed she was pretty put-together under normal circumstances. All the same, he felt badly for her situation and hoped she'd get through this mess.

After he left, Linda began cleaning things up, but the weight of events kept her from feeling much better.

Her spirits improved somewhat the following day after talking to friends and knowing they would help with each of her courses. Aside from having to rewrite a partial rough draft of a paper due for marketing, the class notes necessary for final exams could be reconstructed. Her friends agreed that teaming up and consolidating their notes would benefit everyone. They would all work together. The group helped her feel included and supported. Getting her mind off the violence connected with the intrusion was not an easy task, however.

* * *

Big Lights heard the news of Linda's situation from Sheriff Betts while having a beer at the Night Owl. The sheriff mentioned he had received a call from the Duluth police department. A police sergeant who knew about Two Fingers' murder recognized the name in Officer Brady's report and decided to alert Sheriff Betts to the break-in. While no apparent connection existed, he thought it would be best for the sheriff to know.

"You know, Big Lights," Sheriff Betts commented, "that girl has a lot on her shoulders right now. I'm not sure anyone her age can handle these pressures. Is there anyone she can turn to for some moral support? She's a quiet girl and she hasn't been back to the reservation much since leaving for school. It's my impression she's been trying to make a clean break from her life here. Either she didn't have many friends or she hasn't kept up with them."

Big Lights paused briefly, his eyes downcast. "I can't say that I much blame her for that. Maybe I'll drop over to Duluth next week to see if she needs some help. I've always liked Linda, and I'd feel badly if her people didn't support her."

"Good idea," the sheriff said before taking a long pull off his beer.

"Let me know if you pick up on anything that's strange about the break-in."

On their way out, Sam and Chase walked by the table where Big Lights and Sheriff Betts sat.

"It'd be a goddamn shame if two members of the same family were murdered and neither killer was brought to justice," Sam said, speaking directly to Sheriff Betts.

The sheriff moved uncomfortably in his chair at the sarcasm-filled remark. Big Lights could see from his tense expression that the sheriff didn't like being challenged publicly. Sam Aguire obviously made him feel uneasy.

"What makes matters worse," the sheriff retorted, "is that Linda has also had some problems over in Duluth. You're right about one thing, Sam. That family has had bad luck." The sheriff was noticeably subservient in his tone.

"What are you talking about?" Sam asked.

"It seems her apartment at U of M was broken into and ransacked. Her computer and other valuables were stolen—a pretty normal campus break-in, according to the police. They say she's pretty shaken, though. Big Lights and I are going to make a visit tomorrow to see if everything is okay."

The sheriff definitely wanted to look like he was involved. After all, he may not like these men, but both were Tribal Council leaders and very influential.

"Tell me what her reservation family can do to help," Chase said. "Not many people know her, but I don't want her to think she's all alone on this. Will you do that, Sheriff?"

"Yes, and I'll pass on your comments and concern as well."

Sam and Chase walked off.

Sheriff Betts looked at Big Lights with frustration. "Sam never lets me forget about Frank's death on the BSU campus. With Two Fingers now gone, I sure don't want anything to happen to Linda. I hope you don't mind that your trip to Duluth is now official police business?"

"Not really. It's probably a good idea. Are you sure you still want me to go, though?"

"Yeah, I really do. Representation from the tribe will help. I'll pick you up after breakfast. That'll give me time to call and let her know we're on our way."

* * *

Linda was in the midst of getting things reorganized in the apartment when a sharp knock on the door broke the silence. She recognized Big Lights from the reservation and Sheriff Betts from her father's investigation.

"Come in, Sheriff . . . Big Lights. Thanks for coming"

"We won't take long, Linda. We just wanted to make sure that you're okay," the sheriff said.

"You've been through a lot," Big Lights added.

"My friends here are really helping, but it's hard to accept that my family's gone and there's no one to turn to. The police here were nice, but there's not much they can really do. I still feel vulnerable. It's difficult to put it behind me."

"The tribe wants to help. Chase Leonard himself asked." The sheriff definitely wanted to deliver on his promise to Chase and convey his personal expression of interest.

"What can we do?"

"The biggest problem is the missing computer. It contained all my course work and I never backed up my files. My friends are pitching in and helping with missing class notes and reports. They're just great. I could never do it without them. I think the TV and stereo are the only other things missing, and I can live without those."

"What do you mean, you think?" Sheriff Betts asked.

"Things were pretty messed up, so it's hard to really tell. Possibly the burglar was looking for something, I don't know. Everything in drawers ended up in a huge mess. Maybe he thought he would find jewelry or something else of value—drugs, maybe. According to the officer, this kind of burglary is normal during campus breaks. He was surprised that my apartment was the only one burglarized, though. With the whole building empty that night, he could have emptied every apartment. I'm trying not to think about that fact too much. Something must have scared him off is what Officer Brady said."

"Do you have insurance to cover the loss?"

"No, I don't."

* * *

Late that afternoon, the sheriff and Big Lights returned to Chippewa Lake. As originally thought, the Duluth PD had things under control and there seemed to be no real immediate concerns. Trying to recover Linda's stolen property would be another matter, however—a task so unlikely one would have a better chance of winning the state lotto.

"You know, I think I'll suggest to Chase Leonard that the tribe, or maybe the casino, help Linda replace the stolen items. Without insurance, there's little chance she'll ever do it on her own."

"Great idea."

"You really have to admire the courage of this young lady," Big Lights continued. "No family, nothing of any real value to her name, and still trying to move her life forward. This game face she's wearing seems pretty thin, I think. I'm no shrink, but it wouldn't surprise me at all if another emotional letdown weren't just around the corner. I'm just saying if it were me, it'd be awfully goddamn tough to handle."

Both men nodded in silent agreement.

seventeen

WHEN THE FIRST real snow came it was a doozy. It fell nonstop from November 31 to December 4. Over a foot of fresh powder accumulated before the storm petered out. The cabin and forest were like an operating room. Everything sparkled in a pure white gown. For Jake, the snow was a welcome change. It's what he came to Sandy Cove to experience. And, just for a moment, it seemed to cover over the problems since his arrival.

After the storm, Jake made it his first order of business to select a Christmas tree. He would cut it from the thousands of spruce planted years earlier by the Department of Natural Resources after the Chinese Elm disease destroyed vast portions of the forest.

It was fortunate he didn't have to walk far. He hadn't purchased a snowmobile yet—the old snowshoes hanging on the wall for years would have to do. At times like this he really missed KC. Even though KC would have struggled with the snow's depth, Jake imagined him bounding beside the old toboggan he pulled. He smiled at the image, knowing full well he would have been pulling both the tree and KC on the return trip home to the cabin.

Only in Jake's imagination had he pictured a Christmas tree in the cabin. With cabin use limited to May through October, hunting and fishing, walks in the woods, swimming, autumn leaves, fires by the beach, northern lights, sunsets, and lake vistas comprised his mental photo album. The tree symbolized a perfect beginning for this winter experience. It was a living Christmas card—one Jan would have liked a lot. Roughly about twelve feet, the tree fit perfectly in the corner on the same wall as the ledge-stone fireplace. He used the ornaments Jan had collected throughout their marriage for just this moment. Several were handmade: a sequined Bruce-the-Moose, Santa in his sleigh, a wooden man and woman riding bicycles, and a crystal starburst. It looked spectacular. The feeling of nostalgia comforted him with a renewed sense of enthusiasm to spend the winter.

He decided that tomorrow would be snowmobile day at one of the dealerships in Bronson—his Christmas present to himself. Getting the tree with the toboggan was one thing; trudging up and down the long access road all winter long was another story entirely. Besides, no one lived in these conditions without a snowmobile. It was completely impractical. He had made arrangements with Ken and Laura to park the Yukon in their utility garage for the winter with their boat. He could then use the truck after snowmobiling the half-mile out to their house. He had never owned a snowmobile before and felt exhilarated with the prospect. Some salesman would make a good commission tomorrow, he thought.

* * *

On his way to Bronson the next day, Jake stopped at the Night Owl in Chippewa Lake, where he was sure he could find Big Lights. Jake felt out of the loop, not having seen anyone since the Thanksgiving get-together. He was interested in the short-version update he would get from Big Lights, instead of the unabridged gossip dump he would get from a visit with Helen. Besides, he was hoping that Big Lights would go with him to Bronson.

Sure enough, Big Lights was holding court with a few of his cronies, a longneck in one hand and a pool cue in the other.

His broad smile greeted Jake as he walked across the barroom.

"It's beautiful, isn't it?" he said, gesturing his hands in a broad motion to include all outdoors.

"It truly is, my friend," he said, knowing he was experiencing the beauty of winter as few other outsiders had.

"I'm off to Bronson to make some snowmobile salesman happy. Can you join me?"

"If you let me finish taking these boys' money I can." Big Lights flashed his grin at his opposition across the table.

Jake ordered a beer and sat down to watch. He knew it wouldn't take long. Big Lights thought he could beat everyone at pool, especially after a few beers. The truth was that Big Lights, while good at pool, tended to buckle under the pressure of cash. Jake had tapped him for a couple of dollars himself. If these boys were any good, they would be on the road within the hour.

* * *

"Am I that bad?" Big Lights asked forty-five minutes later, as he and Jake pulled out of the Night Owl. "I mean, I choked, and they smelled the blood in the water, didn't they? I'm damn lucky I'm not rich, or I would have lost a lot of money."

"You're probably right. Maybe this is one time that not being rich is a good thing. And it really wasn't a lot of money—what, maybe fifty bucks or so? It could've been a lot worse."

"Easy for you to say. It wasn't your fifty bucks. It was money lost a whole lot faster than it took to earn. That's what really pisses me off."

Jake said nothing and locked his focus on the road.

"This is one of the things I like about you," Big Lights said, changing the direction of his venting. "You do a good job of staying out of a man's way when he's beating himself up. I guess that means you agree. I'll not hold it against you if you disagree with me, even a little."

He paused for Jake to reply.

Still nothing.

"In truth, I guess I've had about as much agreement as I can take," Big Lights finally said. Both men laughed.

The rest of the forty-five-minute drive was spent talking about snowmobiles—new versus used, engine size, passengers, clothing, and trailers. Jake got excited just listening to Big Lights. Bringing him along was a good decision, Jake thought. Not only did he know a lot about snowmobiles, but he knew one of the salesmen as well.

"Maybe I won't get taken as badly as I thought," Jake said, a renewed sense of optimism in his voice.

It didn't take long for the two of them to find a used Polaris that was perfect for his needs. The trailer was practically new. He could get all the clothes and equipment from Porter's Sporting Goods, the store that was preparing his bearskin. Jake was ready for winter.

* * *

During the drive back to Chippewa Lake, Big Lights filled Jake in on the trip to Duluth and Linda's misfortune.

"It's just one bad break after another. I don't know whether I told you or not, but I'm really impressed with her," Jake said. "I had only that one visit with her after her dad was murdered, so I really don't know her all that well. But if you look under her quiet shell, there's a pretty put-together person inside. She thinks clearly and has her feet on the ground about things."

"I hope this doesn't hurt her," Big Lights went on, "but my bet is that she's going to take the next quarter off from school. She was pretty fragile after the robbery, and I'm thinking that a break is actually a good idea. She told me it would only push her graduation back three months."

"That's just the kind of thinking I mean, down to earth. What's her major?" Jake asked.

"Marketing, whatever that's all about. Why?"

"Well, that idea I have about new jobs could use a bright person like Linda. It's been in my mind ever since I first got here. It will take some work to get it up and running, but nothing we can't handle."

"Unless you have a mouse in your pocket, I think that *we* just meant me," said Big Lights.

"Hold your breath a minute and I'll fill you in."

Over the next twenty minutes Jake outlined a plan to train a select group of local Indians to transcribe computer data collected from voice-activated telephone campaigns.

"You know that 800 number you call when you want a catalog from Bass Pro Shops?"

"Sure."

"Well, that's the kind of thing I'm talking about. Your name and address are recorded on the phone call so they can send you a catalog. Then it's transcribed and entered into a mailing-list database by a computer operator. You get your catalog right away, and they get an electronic mailing list that they use again and again for selling different products. Quite frankly, the experience would be valuable to Linda as a marketing major."

"I'm still not sure how the reservation ties in," said Big Lights.

"It's pretty straightforward, really. The reservation supplies the people for the computer operator positions. The quality and turn-around speed of these voice transcriptions are very important. The work can be done from a person's home, or anywhere for that matter, as long as the phone data can be downloaded for transcription. I know it sounds complicated, but it's not. The key to the project is to purchase some computers, get connected online, and train the interested people to do the work. We could probably get start-up funding for all three steps.

"I've got some friends in Omaha who might be interested. They're called Interactive Marketing. We could propose the idea to them; they might want to get involved. They're good people and regularly spend quite a bit of money having these transcriptions completed. My guess is that we could create jobs for fifteen to twenty people within a year, provided we demonstrate that our work is top-notch.

"If you think the idea has merit, you and I could take a road trip to Omaha over the holidays to visit with these people. You know, check their pulse."

"Are you kidding?" said Big Lights excitedly. "I think this is a great idea! The tribe will jump all over the chance to create that many jobs. Reservation life is hard enough as it is without the only opportunity to make a decent living being the casino. This sounds perfect. I don't know if I mentioned it or not, but the council is going to replace Linda's stolen computer as a community gesture. They'll like the fact that it may be used to help create more jobs."

"That's good news.

"So, what's the next step? Let's get going."

Two of Jake's favorite qualities about Big Lights were his enthusiasm and willingness to dive into something new.

"I think it's a good idea too, but we need to get our ducks in order to avoid creating a false expectation for the tribe. I don't want to get people all fired up, only to let them down. We'll need to go slowly at first, don't you think?"

Big Lights nodded to the affirmative, but only halfheartedly. It was his nature to err on the side of action.

"Why don't we talk to Linda first?" Jake said. "Check her level of interest. Her involvement would be helpful in many ways. Then we'll arrange a private meeting with the Tribal Council to gain funding and moral support. Their commitment will be important to our success with the people in Omaha. And as far as funding, I can't imagine a problem, considering the potential casino benefits and available federal job funds."

* * *

Back at the Night Owl, Big Lights and Jake threw down a few more beers while watching the pool table action from the sidelines. Their conversation continued to drift to the possibilities of the new business and the implications on computer literacy, non-casino employment, and job training.

"I know I get all fired up over things, Jake, but this is pretty cool stuff. The old Indian ways and white society have created a huge identity crisis. Young people need to see a future. And with so many people out of jobs and many of those suffering from alcoholism, this is a no-brainer. The council definitely is going to be interested." Big Lights' animated hand gestures and fast dialogue completely distracted his normal addiction to the pool game being played in front of him.

eighteen

"Sure, I'd like to be involved," Linda said the next day, "especially if we can make a difference."

She knew she had the reputation of being an *apple*, an Indian who is red on the outside and white on the inside. This might be the opportunity to overturn people's attitudes. Her acceptance of a white education and her willingness to leave the reservation justified the label. She knew that. But what others didn't know was the hurt she felt as a result of her brother and her mother. Escape was a logical reaction. Others would have realized that had they been in her shoes. But now she had a chance to mend the broken connection with her reservation upbringing. Somehow, the complete loss of her family had made her understand there were people on the reservation that needed help.

Jake and Big Lights were as pleased with Linda's acceptance as she was with the offer. She would be helpful, and the three of them would make a good team.

"My mother always used to say that things happen for a reason, Mr. Lorenz. I think I can even get course credit for the experience if I ask my counselor. This will be my first real resume material. Do you think we could call it an internship?"

"Yes, we can call it an internship, Linda, but only on two conditions. First, this is going to be a *paid* internship if the council accepts our proposal. You're too valuable to give away your talents: Marketing Lesson 101. Second, you're going to have to call me something other than Mr. Lorenz."

"Oh, I'm sorry."

"Don't be. It will just be easier. Whatever you're comfortable with is fine with me."

"Okay." She paused in thought.

"Is Mister Jake okay?"

"Sure, Linda, Mister Jake is just fine." While it made him feel a little old, he couldn't help acknowledging the respect Linda conveyed.

"I wouldn't tell anyone else this, but when my apartment was broken into after my dad's murder, it was like the final straw. I've been really down. I told people I was skipping a quarter, but in truth, I'm not sure that I wasn't closer to dropping out of school altogether. I really want to thank you for taking an interest in me."

* * *

A week later, after a complete deep dive into their presentation, Big Lights, Linda, and Jake were sitting in the waiting room at the Chippewa Lake Town Hall. The trio was about to have its first meeting with the Reservation Tribal Council. The seven-member council included Sam Aguire, Chase Leonard, and Don Pasquesi, the council chairman. It was popular opinion among outsiders that whatever these men wanted, the council approved.

"Are you sure that it's a good idea for Linda and me to do most of the presentation? I mean, if we were giving it at the Night Owl with a bottle of beer I'd be fine, but this is official business. I've never done this before."

Jake was about to reassure Big Lights when Linda interrupted, "I'm nervous too, Big Lights, but we're never going to build a business if we don't take some responsibility."

"Yeah, but . . ."

"No buts and that's final. Besides, you'll do just fine. This is my first time too. These are our people; we need to take the lead."

Linda had taken to this project like a duck to water. Early on, she had shown her leadership on several issues. Jake marveled at the perfect fit.

The three of them had developed the presentation to show the benefits of the *Omaha Project*, as they called it. Special focus would be given to the hot buttons in the proposal that were sure to get the council's interest—employment, job skills, and technology. Jake's experience and participation in many such meetings at Astro Technology served their preparation needs perfectly.

"But we don't have thirty-five thousand to fund a project that has a 50/50 chance of failing." Chase objected to Big Lights' request for seed money two-thirds of the way into the presentation. His objection came at a critical juncture in gaining the council's agreement.

"Look at it this way," Jake said, jumping in for the first time. "The business can be set up as a Minnesota corporation with federal support money. This council can serve as its board of directors. Big Lights and I will serve as unpaid advisors to the corporation during the initial set-up stage. Your only ongoing commitment to expenses will be Linda's intern salary and a small office to operate from. You have to admit that this represents a very low risk considering the upside. Besides, down the road those new job skills will transfer very nicely to existing businesses like the casino."

Jake's words hit the mark. The council voted unanimously to support the program with an initial pilot involving five to seven participants, but only if the interest with Interactive Marketing proved to be real. Linda would start working immediately for the Reservation Tribal Council under the direction of Jake and Big Lights. The council agreed that once the Omaha Project was established, the final organization of "who does what" would be decided. One council member noted the "enthusiasm value" of the project as winter was a particularly depressing time on the reservation.

Afterward, Jake, Linda, and Big Lights celebrated at the Lodge Pole Supper Club.

"Jake, you're a genius," Big Lights exclaimed for about the tenth time during dinner. "Isn't he just unbelievable, Linda?"

Linda nodded and smiled.

"It was a team effort and we all have reason to take pride in what we did today," Jake said.

"Mister Jake . . . "

Jake had tried several times over the week to get her to change from Mister Jake, but he'd made no progress. No looking back now, he thought.

"I've got a million questions to ask, and I don't know where to begin. A week ago, I had no idea what I was going to do, and now I have a full-time paid internship. I really want to do a good job. Do you think that Interactive Marketing will be in favor of this project? We have to impress upon them how much this means to our people and that we can't let them down."

In the last week, Jake had learned a lot about Linda. She was very bright, but she lacked the confidence Jake expected in a young person of her caliber. Still, he knew the Native American world was different. Their culture and infrequent interaction with white people outside the reservation made success hard to find. And even more than most Indian people, Linda hadn't had much to smile about lately. But when she did—when her brown eyes sparkled with interest—she was quite stunning.

"What should we do next, Mister Jake?"

Recognition of Linda's potential added to Jake's developing protective attitude. Her reactions as they discussed the Omaha Project and the way she called him "Mister Jake" didn't hurt matters.

"We're going to take this project one step at a time. None of us want this to fail. So it's my suggestion that we meet early tomorrow morning to map out the work. I'll call my friends at Interactive Marketing to set up a meeting. The holidays are generally slow for them and will probably work. In the meantime, we need to develop a profile of our potential Big Bear Tribe workforce. That's going to be your job, Linda. Why don't you think about how you will approach gathering the information tonight, and tomorrow we'll talk about it.

"Big Lights, I think that your services can best be used to decide on a location where we can run this business. In time, people will be able to do this job from their homes. In the beginning, however, it will be important to have a central location that gives us a place to train people and deliver top-notch work."

* * *

Half a mile away from the Lodge Pole Supper Club, Sam and Chase were having a highly agitated dinner at the Night Owl.

"Doesn't it just piss you off the way we're being manipulated by this Jake asshole? If we're not careful, we'll be building a fucking totem pole telling his life story. I don't like outside intrusions, and I goddamn don't like the interference they bring in making our decisions."

"No disagreement from me. We're definitely better off keeping things just the way they've always been. Now we've got an Omaha Project to contend with, just what we don't need. This guy's got us wasting thirty-five thousand on some do-gooder project. And in the process, we're giving Linda a job and spending fifteen hundred to replace a computer we paid five hundred to destroy. I don't like this shit at all," Chase said in an uncharacteristically emotional tone.

The project presentation had been so well done that neither Sam nor Chase wanted to raise suspicion by voting against it. With the RTC acting as its board of directors, however, they could at least monitor activities—a small victory, in their opinion.

With Christmas and New Year's Eve coming, however, Sam and Chase would have to set aside concerns about the Omaha Project and give their full attention to the casino. New Year's Eve weekend represented the best payday of the year. Since the new slot machines had been installed, the two men had accumulated millions in a simple skimming process. And with the funds safely tucked away in a Bahamian bank account, they were itchy to move to the next phase of their Arrowhead plan. The more money they could get, the better. By spring, they estimated that their holdings would be over twenty million, enough to fund their Arrowhead project privately and take Alex Minor out of the picture completely.

nineteen

PREPARATIONS WERE WELL underway for the New Year's Eve gala at the Norway Pine Casino. Competition for an extravagant party in north-central Minnesota was nonexistent. If the weather held, people would come from all over. Sam and Chase expected about eighteen to twenty-two thousand guests from all walks of life. It wasn't just the gambling that attracted people. The casino's New Year's Eve party held the reputation of being a first-class shindig. Gambling was simply an added attraction to the food, music, floor shows, and door prizes. And the addition of a new Jeep Grand Cherokee as the grand prize for the annual blackjack tournament guaranteed excitement. There was something for everyone, including Sam and Chase. If the casino revenue was anything like last year, it would break the three-hundred-dollar-per-person barrier for a two-day total of about six million dollars. Not a bad take for a sleepy little Indian casino.

For Sam and Chase, this meant another generous deposit to their Bahamian investment fund. However, everything had to go just right. Walking through the skimming process one more time had become a ritual for the men. There had never been a problem in the past; their discipline in examining procedures served them well.

In most casinos everyone was on the take; this was a given. Sam and Chase made sure that wasn't going to happen at the Norway Pine. They needed to run a *clean operation* to maximize the bottom line. And the last thing they wanted was any suspicion on the part of the Indian Gaming Commission. James Wingfoot was their buffer as the gaming commissioner, but they had to do their part and stay out of the limelight. The trick was to make their 10-percent skim without the reservation becoming suspicious. Sam's harsh methods of dealing with people and the casino's reputation for airtight control made this possible. It was well known that no one would live to enjoy anything illegally taken from this casino. The illusion of propriety was complete with a clean bill of health validated annually by the accounting audit conducted by James Wingfoot in his role as audit partner for McMillan Larsen Wingfoot & Co. In order for all these elaborate efforts to make a difference, though, the skim had to go right.

The casino was set up like all others; the foreman watched the dealers and the boxman who counted the chips. The pit bosses and shift bosses, who were watched by the casino manager, watched the foremen. The eagle in the sky, the twenty-four-hour surveillance system, watched everyone. Even Chase, as casino manager, was vulnerable to this sophisticated camera and security system, good enough to back up their *No One on the Take* policy.

The computer design of their slot machines accounted for the beauty of their system. Through a quiet little deal modifying the technology on their new slots, and a kickback arrangement with the president of Universal Slot Machines, the 10 percent that Chase and Sam needed never hit their books. Before being delivered to the casino, a chip in the motherboard of every slot's computer was replaced with a chip designed to perform a new form of math. For every one hundred dollars taken in, only ninety dollars was recorded. With the hourly totals from every slot machine electronically captured and recorded into the casino's accounting system, 10 percent of the real slot-machine take was unaccounted for.

The transfer of the money out of the casino was trickier, however. Coins are heavy and bulky. The skim had to be converted to bills during the daily routine without raising suspicion.

At this point, Chase and Sam had to take active control of the cash transfers. The count room was the perfect location. The vault and adjoining count room were secure offices where the money was counted and packaged for Wells Fargo pickup. Occasionally, James Wingfoot would help make the transfer if Sam and Chase were absent. Only the three of them knew the procedure.

Money and fill slips from each of the gambling games were routinely brought to the vault, the staging area for the count room. Twice a day, either Chase or Sam would control the money's exchange to the count room. It was relatively easy. Since the computer already held a figure that was 10 percent lower than the actual cash amounts from the slots, calculating the amount of folding cash that had to be skimmed from the gaming tables was simple. This amount would be removed and new fill slips supplied for the accountants in the count room to balance against.

Once the money was transferred to the official count room, the accountants would balance their physical count to the original totals, following strict procedures. Frequently, the manager would demand recounts to guarantee accuracy. Naturally, no difference existed.

At all times, armed security officers guarded both the inside and outside of the vault and count room. The paper money switch to the audit bag Sam or Chase carried in the casino took place out of the view of the inside security guard, who was on the opposite side of a partition and was focused on the outside door. When Chase or Sam left the vault with their standard accounting audit bag filled with bills, everything seemed normal. Because of the live security involved in this staging area, the eagle-in-the-sky capabilities were never installed. The added expense had seemed unnecessary.

Exiting the casino was easy as the audit bag, Chase and Sam's ongoing expected presence, and the mind-numbing routine were accepted procedure.

The money was held in an outside location known only to Chase and Sam. On a very irregular schedule, it would be packaged in a locked, metal container for transfer to the Bahamas. The container would be booked on one of the regular air cargo services out of the Bemidji airport. The men's only requirement was that the air cargo service have electronic tracking and tracing to ensure recovery if lost. Airborne, FedEx, UPS, DHL, and Northwest Airlines all provided this level of service from Bemidji. The container contents were marked business documents and routinely shifted from service to service.

The customs agent in the Bahamas was well paid and very motivated to arrange for a courier to ensure the final leg of the container's journey to the Sawgrass Investment Fund on the island. Occasionally, Sam would visit the island to reinforce the custom agent's motivation. Sam's resourcefulness in learning where the custom agent lived and what schools his children attended paid off. Two Fingers had known this method all too well.

The New Year's Eve holiday came and went without a hitch. Their predictions of a successful event were right on the mark and a four-hundred-fifty-thousand-dollar contribution to Sam and Chase's investment fund would soon be on its way to the Bahamas.

twenty

"MERRY CHRISTMAS, MR. Minor. Thanks for the presents."

Tony's children had never really liked Alex because he basically ignored them the rest of the year. But on Christmas they made an exception. In truth, children were an annoyance to Alex. He made an effort, however, and the gifts were well received.

"I'll see you tomorrow, boss. Thanks for coming over. I'm sure the kids will love their gifts."

Alex left Tony's family and headed back to the lodge. Despite the loyalty Tony had displayed as caretaker for both lodges for ten years, Alex wasn't comfortable socializing with his family. He felt better if he simply dropped the presents off the day before Christmas. His stay was brief—a beer, some cheese and crackers, and a little polite conversation—no more than a quick visit.

Alex found himself pondering his reclusive nature and his estrangement from people as he drove back to the lodge. There was a time when people liked me, he thought. As a young boy, even as a young adult, I interacted with others easily. People would always draw me into their conversations and activities at the lodge. How did I become so different?

Images of boardroom battles, leadership demands, and lost market share flashed through his mind's eye—people's faces were nondescript. In truth, individuals never mattered much at Stenway. People were replaceable. It was the bottom line that counted, always the bottom line. Power and wealth are master craftsmen when it comes to shaping who we become, he thought.

The barking of Leo and King at a FedEx truck in his driveway quickly brought him back to reality. The driver pulled up behind Alex's truck near the lodge. With more people living on the peninsula, express deliveries had become a little more familiar over the last few years. Just five years ago, it would have been a rare occurrence.

"I've got a delivery for you, Mr. Minor," the driver said. "I hope you're enjoying your Christmas."

"Yeah, thanks," Alex grunted under his breath. He reached for the package, scribbled his signature, and turned toward the lodge, not looking back.

The driver stood motionless and stared, expecting a polite holiday exchange or some acknowledgement of his role in the delivery of an important document. The social side of this encounter, however, had never occurred to Alex. It was nothing personal and probably never would be, not to Alex anyway.

"Merry Christmas," the driver uttered dutifully, and left.

Alex's interest focused on the package. The day after the discovery of Two Fingers, he had contacted Sam for some inside work. He wanted his land to be thoroughly canvassed for anything suspicious that could link him to the murder. As his partner, he was confident that Sam knew how to get things done quietly. The search didn't turn up much, only some work gloves, a flannel shirt, and unaccounted-for tools. Tony was adamant about not missing anything from their supply rooms. Alex sent the items to Chicago, where old family contacts could conduct an analysis without raising suspicion. This must be the reply he had been waiting for from the criminologist.

* * *

Once inside, he reflected that the report on the glove and tools was most likely a waste of time and expense, since the murder of Two Fingers had quickly become old news. In just over a month, it hardly merited any mention in Chippewa Lake gossip, beyond an occasional "Will the murderer ever be found?"

Alex removed the contents from the envelope and noticed an invoice in the amount of four thousand five hundred dollars *for services rendered.* In the old days he would have taken this request for payment as an insult, but he knew his political connections were fading. Any influence he possessed came as a courtesy to the family name. The money wasn't the issue anyway, he thought. The report is what mattered.

The document's contents were organized and direct. The torn shirt offered no information, although several analysis procedures had been performed. This was not unusual, as cloth rarely provided useful identification. The rake and shovel, however, both had clear fingerprints identified as those of Two Fingers Smith and Sam Aguire.

His thoughts went directly to his discussion with Sam the day he ordered the search of the property. Tony, not Sam, had found the tools, shirt, and gloves. This evidence logically placed Sam in proximity to the tools. What had he been doing?

The work gloves were made of leather and coarse fabric, the type you might find at any construction site. This analysis was revealing because dirt had accumulated in the material and in the crevices where the material was sewn to the leather. Apparently the soil had caked, leaving enough dirt for analysis.

Two items immediately caught Alex's attention.

The first was a reference to traces of garnet and iron found in the soil. Earlier in the year, Alex had the people from Meeks & Harrison Development do several soil studies as part of the planning for the Arrowhead Resort project. He didn't recall any reference to garnet and iron. They were minerals generally found in areas of higher terrain. A quick check of their report in his files confirmed his recollection.

The second finding was even more peculiar. The same soil also contained traces of a black spruce pitch and a dandelion oil concoction that the first criminologist reported as unusual and outside his office's experience.

Alex quickly concluded that this substance was what had delayed the analysis and report for more than a month. He could see from the invoice that several expensive tests had been performed by some pretty distinguished government agencies. All came back with inconclusive results, except one. An outside testing agency working with the Department of the Interior and Bureau of Indian Affairs identified the mixture as one used by Indian medicine men in belowground burial ceremonies.

An attached document explained the Indian belief that the dandelion oil mixture protected the body from the evil spirits during the deceased's spiritual journey. The black spruce pitch was used in the construction of a birch bark canoe necessary for the safe journey of the deceased.

Indian tradition had favored cremation or aboveground burial houses for centuries. Not until the late 1700s did belowground burials became accepted, probably a result of the European and Christian influence from traders and missionaries. The analysis also provided a little history on the origin of the practice and concluded that this method of anointing the ground around the corpse with the spruce pitch and dandelion oil stopped in the mid-nineteenth century for unknown reasons.

A footnote alerted the reader that the discovery of this substance might be connected with the presence of a sacred Indian burial ground or property. Any such findings were to be reported to the Bureau of Indian Affairs Office or directly to the tribe or reservation on which the findings were discovered.

Alex spent hours going over the report, searching for hidden implications. What could these findings mean? After much contemplation, the only tangible connection he could make regarding the foreign mixture was that Two Fingers had been the caretaker of the reservation cemeteries.

But what would be the logic in that connection? And why, or better yet, *how* did it get onto his property? Alex tried to draw a picture that somehow led to Two Fingers' murder. He turned the possibilities over and over in his mind, realizing he was getting nowhere. The image of Sam and Two Fingers together did not fade, however.

"What am I supposed to do with any of this crap, even if I do figure it out," he muttered as frustration sat in. "I'm almost seventy-seven years old, for Christ's sake. This isn't the battle I want to fight."

After more consideration, however, it occurred to Alex that this was exactly what he needed to open a discussion with Jake about working together. If they were digging on his land, there was a good chance they had been digging on Jake's as well. Even though he didn't have the slightest clue where this would go, he put on his wool coat, scarf, gloves, and hat and headed out the side door of the lodge. He decided to take his truck since Jake's access road was still passable with 4-wheel drive. He was on his way to Jake's with a sense of urgency and deep conviction that a partnership had to be struck.

Bored with the lack of activity in their insulated doghouses, Leo and King sprang into action at Alex's whistled command and jumped into the bed of the truck.

During the short drive, he reviewed his plan with Jake. I should go slow and stay away from anything that arouses his suspicion or smacks of foul play. He decided to stay centered on the possible implications from the criminologist's report and Jake's land.

"Who knows what we'll ultimately find?"

With Alex, the extroverted self frequently responded to the mental challenges of the introverted self.

"Not much if I don't get some help soon."

Must be all the time alone in these goddamn woods, he thought.

twenty-one

JAKE WAS ENJOYING an uncharacteristically lazy day reading a book by the fire when he heard a vehicle approach. He went to the back door and recognized Alex's truck.

"To what do I owe this unexpected surprise?" He extended his hand, motioning for Alex to come into the cabin. "Merry Christmas, Alex."

"You too, Jake. You know it's going to take a while to get used to the idea that you're here."

They exchanged the normal holiday chitchat for a few minutes.

"You want coffee?" asked Jake.

"Sure." Alex hesitated until Jake returned to the kitchen table and his cup was full. "I came over, Jake, because of some information that has been made available to me. It might have some bearing on Two Fingers' murder, as well as have potential implications for both of our properties."

"You know, I just knew that this wasn't going to go away." Jake had always thought that what happened was bizarre—a murder, a hanging, no less, and the property destruction—these things were way beyond normal. "I'm all ears. Tell me what you've got."

"I think that you knew from the beginning my confidence in local police abilities was very shaky," Alex said. "So I decided to take it upon myself to uncover anything that might implicate my property. It was obvious to me that whoever committed the murder hadn't come to the cabin by car or truck. I wanted to find out if these scum had involved me or my property in any way."

"Makes sense."

"This is going to take a minute, but I need to fill you in."

Over the next hour Alex explained everything in detail. "The night after you arrived and discovered the body, I began a close surveillance process of my own property. Covering 375 acres isn't easy, so I hired some locals who know the woods pretty well. Sam Aguire's a local Indian I know with a reputation of getting things done. He served as my go-between in Chippewa Lake to find the right people for the job. I thought I could trust him.

"I instructed the men to stay out of sight and to maintain a twenty-four-hour-a-day surveillance on the two resorts, the lakeshore perimeter, and the narrow access to my property from the rest of the peninsula. Leo and King were kept in close check during their presence.

"In less than a week after the discovery of Two Fingers, it was my carekaker Tony, however, who found things that seemed out of place—a shovel, torn work shirts, gloves, a rake—stuff like that. I told Sam to search the property again for more items. Take an extra few days if you need, I told him. Nothing else was found.

"Then I called Rex Meeks, a contractor who worked on the property earlier in the summer, to see if the tools belonged to his crew. The answer was no, everything was accounted for. Hell, I even had Tony check the supply of tools we kept at the two resort buildings again to be sure they weren't ours. Tony was positive, however; nothing was missing."

"I can see why you were concerned. This is puzzling."

"For a moment I considered turning everything over to Sheriff Betts. I rejected that idea in favor of a more discreet analysis by some old connections in Chicago. You know, Jake, City Hall family ties and such."

Jake knew better than to question the identity of these sources. Instead, he just nodded his approval.

"It would take several weeks, but I would be sure to get a complete investigative analysis by trained criminologists." Jake was listening intently, but staring off in order to process what Alex was saying. This guy doesn't miss much, he thought.

"You may think I'm a pretty suspicious guy, but my instincts for foul play are generally pretty accurate, even if I don't have much to go on. If something had happened on my property that could be connected to the murder, I wanted to know about it. I even checked in Bronson, where I have some contacts that would be motivated to help. Nothing.

"Basically, what I'm trying to explain is that a lot had happened in a short time, and I just don't like the feeling of 'pieces not coming together'—you know what I mean? Patience seems to be a skill my temperament sorely lacks."

Jake brimmed with questions but had held off until Alex finished. Alex's confidence grew as he talked, knowing he had made the right decision to involve Jake.

"Your instincts are pretty unbelievable. I am impressed with the level of your research," Jake said, drawing a deep breath. He privately wondered just how deep Alex's family connections went into the Chicago police family. "Have you formed any opinions as to how all of this fits together?"

Alex answered, "It's difficult to form a conclusion other than the obvious one that there was more to the relationship between Two Fingers and Sam than originally believed. It also seems strange that the rake and shovel had both sets of fingerprints, almost like they were doing some work together. And if there is a connection to the spruce pitch and dandelion oil concoctions, it most certainly would be with Two Fingers. But *why* is hard to imagine. According to the analysis, this method of burial hasn't been used for more than two hundred years."

"You must know Sam well enough to trust him, or at least do business with him. What do you think Sam wants most?" Jake asked.

"What do you mean?"

"Well, what would he kill for?"

Alex thought for a minute about the partnership he'd made with the tribe and the casino in order to build his new resort.

"It would have to be power and money," he said.

Both men reflected quietly on that statement and the obvious conclusion that people are likely driven to commit crimes by basic needs. And what keeps most people from committing crimes is a value system of right and wrong.

"Are you saying that Sam's need for power and money could lead to murder?"

"That's a big step," said Alex. "One thing is for sure, though; Sam's connection with the tools certainly places him in a position to be investigated as a possible suspect. It's hard to speculate on a motive, but if he was involved, I'll bet my inheritance that the connection is in this report somehow."

"You're probably not too happy you hired him to do the surveillance either."

"No shit."

"If what you say is all connected, I'll also bet that the destruction to my cabin is somehow connected."

Outwardly, Alex appeared indifferent to the comment. Inside, the connection made him very uncomfortable. At some point in the future, he thought, it would be wise to take responsibility for the cabin, at least with Jake, before it incriminated him unwittingly as an accomplice in the murder of Two Fingers. Now, however, was not the time.

"You may damn well be right, Jake," Alex replied without making eye contact.

"You know, even though I don't generally warm up to the idea of a partner, in this case it may be worth talking about. I just can't get the idea out of my mind that everyone is missing a huge piece of the puzzle. Somehow, our properties are part of the mix. We should work together to get to the bottom of this, Jake, however we can. If this arrangement between us is okay with you, I'll cover the expenses involved. Whatever we learn will be just between the two of us until we can make a move with confidence."

"I'm normally a rule-follower by nature, Alex. My first instinct is to involve the police, but considering the circumstances, I believe your idea makes sense. You obviously have access the sheriff doesn't. It also doesn't seem fair to Linda not to have the truth about her dad's death. Yep, I think you're right," Jake repeated thoughtfully after removing his glasses and pushing the heels of both hands on his forehead as if to seal the bargain. "But there will be a time when the authorities need to be involved. When that time comes, we'll need to act fast. From what you've said, and if you're right, Sam is not a man to fool with. And I doubt he's acting by himself."

"Agreed."

For the next two hours, Alex and Jake discussed their plans, formulating several strategies that needed to be accomplished right away. Alex knew the close-knit nature of the community made this project a little dicey, at best.

First, they agreed that it would be more natural for Jake to be the one to make some discreet inquiries. It would be totally out of character for Alex to initiate conversations with locals. A few of the inquiries made sense to do right away. Linda was first. Jake would explore her dad's work relationship with Sam in more depth. The men hoped she would also agree to a more thorough search of the house for clues the sheriff may have overlooked. Specifically, Jake wanted to find another pair of gloves that could be tested. He was quite sure that Linda would cooperate.

The other person who might have information would be Ken. Everyone knew he was addicted to night fishing and could be found on the bay at least three or four nights a week. He may have seen something and not realized it. Jake and Ken had been peninsula neighbors and summer friends for a long time. It was a long shot, but Jake felt he could make the inquiry without attracting attention.

Alex, on the other hand, would have Tony show them exactly where the gloves, tools, and shirt were found. While they weren't quite sure what the location would reveal, both felt it was a necessary piece of the puzzle. Alex mentioned that he also had a big map of the peninsula, on which they could plot the location of anything else they discovered.

Last, Alex would use his Chicago connections to conduct a background check on Sam and perform tests if anything was found in Two Fingers' house.

"It's going to be real important for us to go slow and not to attract any attention." Jake nodded his agreement. "I think I'll begin with Linda. We have a meeting tonight on the Omaha Project, and I'll have a chance to approach her then. She trusts me. Near as I can tell, her friendships seem to be limited to Big Lights and me, so I don't think there's much chance of her spreading information. Big Lights is another matter, however. He's never been tight-lipped about anything. I'll make sure Linda understands to keep the information to herself."

"Good," said Alex. "And on second thought, I'll have Tony show me the location of the items without involving you. It will raise less suspicion and I can show you on the map later."

"Why don't we plan to meet by the end of next week to compare notes?" Jake proposed.

Alex nodded, adding, "By the way, in case it doesn't show, I'm pleased that you're willing to work with me on this. I think we're the right duo to make something happen."

As the two men stood, Alex preparing to leave, Jake smiled and shook hands with him. Their eye contact was honest, but something seemed odd to Jake. In all his experiences with Alex, he'd never heard a compliment come from the man's lips, not about anything or anyone.

* * *

Later that evening Jake arrived early to the Lodge Pole Supper Club, where he, Linda, and Big Lights had agreed to meet to discuss the Omaha Project. He had hopes of talking to Linda before Big Lights arrived.

"Hello, Linda," Jake said as she approached the table.

"Hi, Mister Jake. Where's Big Lights?"

"Do you really need to ask? If you haven't noticed," he said smiling, "Big Lights does not respond well to structure, which makes him tough to nail down. What I'm saying is that last-minute diversions are part of who he is, and this probably won't be the last time he's late. I don't mean this negatively, however. His spontaneity will definitely make him a very good team member. Anyway, this will give us a chance to talk privately for a few minutes before he shows up."

Jake got down to business quickly. For all he knew, this could be Big Lights' inaugural opportunity to be on time.

"I can't give you a lot of details, Linda, but I have some information regarding your dad's murder. It's possible that it may be more complicated than a random act of violence."

"What have you found out?"

"Don't get your hopes up, because I can't prove anything yet. Nor can I reveal my source of information. But what I do have leads me to believe that your dad was involved in something beyond his control. And for some reason, this cost him his life."

Her smile transformed into a fixed gaze. "Do you think that my dad was doing something against the law, Mister Jake?" Even the thought of her dad's potential connection to criminal activity brought a sense of hurtfulness to her emotions.

"No, I don't, Linda, but he may have been mixed up in activities he didn't really want to be involved in. Tell me what you know about your dad's work at the cemetery. Was there anything unusual about his hours or his business relationships? Did you ever see him with Sam Aguire?"

"I don't like that man." She involuntarily tightened her lips and bristled in disdain.

"What do you mean?"

"Well, every once in a while I would see Mr. Aguire with my dad after work during my summer vacations. Sometimes he would be with my dad until late at night, like midnight or even later. My dad always seemed upset when Mr. Aguire was around."

Jake took clear note of this connection, but he needed to move on to the topic of the house inspection before Big Lights showed up.

"That's very interesting. By the way, how long did it take the sheriff to conduct his search of your dad's home after his murder?"

"Oh, probably about an hour or so. Why?"

"It's really a question of thoroughness, Linda, and I'm wondering whether they were looking for the right things. With your permission, I'd like to do my own search. And I need to keep it just between us. Not even Big Lights can know. It just wouldn't be good for certain people to know we're poking into your dad's murder. If I'm right, finding out why your dad was murdered could become dangerous. I don't want to risk any harm to you, or anyone, that's for sure."

"You can come over this Saturday afternoon, Mister Jake. I trust you a lot, and I want to do what's right for my dad. He was a good person."

"So, what are you two planning behind my back?" Big Lights boomed. Neither Linda nor Jake had seen him approach the table and his voice startled them both. Jake handled the surprise without missing a beat.

"Just because you're late doesn't mean we can't begin to get things done without you, does it? Linda was just beginning to tell me about the workforce profile she's been working on. Do you want her to continue or start over?"

twenty-two

ACTIVITIES OVER THE past month or so had put Two Fingers' death out of Jake's mind. Now his eagerness to examine Linda's house from top to bottom dominated his attention. How could someone's life be so easily forgotten? Alex's prediction had been right on the money.

Jake's feeling of remorse only got heavier. Perhaps it was because the murder took place on his property or, more likely, because he was beginning to feel a bond with Linda. Jake realized he probably hadn't done enough for her. The only real contact with Linda came through their interaction on the Omaha Project. Important, sure, but it certainly didn't fill the waking hours of her day. What was she doing with herself? Was she making new friends? How was she coping with the inevitable loneliness?

He made a mental note to talk with her more and to learn more of her day-to-day circumstances before rushing into the house search. Maybe there was more he could do.

On Thursday he stopped at Ken's to see what he could uncover by gently probing into Ken's recollection of events in the weeks prior to the murder.

Laura answered the door.

"Come on in, Jake. Get yourself out of the cold," she said, smiling.

"Thought I'd pay you two a neighborly call, if the timing is okay."

"That's what I like about you. Giving us the credit that we might have something else better to do. I know this is new to you, but believe me, we get pretty hungry for intelligent contact in January. It's not like I'm living with Ian Fleming or something."

"Ken," she called out. "Jake wants to know if you can break away from your classified job with the CIA to keep our friendship alive."

"What the hell does he think this place is—a fucking support group? Tell him I'm too busy measuring the size of the January snowflakes." Ken wore a big grin as he came around the corner of the entryway from the kitchen.

"Well, if I run out of sarcasm over at my place I sure know where I can find an extra supply."

"Take a load off, neighbor," Ken said as he settled in one of the kitchen chairs.

"Want some coffee?" Laura offered.

They hadn't really talked much one-on-one since Jake's celebration. He knew he had no excuse, so he offered none. Jake was always surprised how good-natured the two of them seemed to be despite Ken's chronic back pain. Their transition from an active life in the Twin Cities to the remote and sedentary life of backwoods Big Bear Lake seemed natural for them.

Their cabin decor looked like a scene from *Northern Exposure* and reflected their comfort with the wilderness lifestyle. The fish and game mounts were evidence that Ken was still a pretty good outdoorsman despite his condition. And the natural decorations of dried flowers and pussy willows combined nicely with the local craft items to create a warm feeling. They mirrored Laura's easy way about herself and gave evidence to her complete adaptation from city life.

They talked inconsequentially of how Jake was getting along in the cabin and what to do to stay active. Ken related in detail the possibilities of a new spinal fusion procedure he had read about for his back, something involving the insertion of a wire through the back tissue and muscle, with heating controls to every exact point on the wire. The significance for Ken, and others in his condition, lay in the possibilities of using the procedure to perform various spinal surgeries without the traditional invasive methods. Ken's hopes were up, although he had learned over the years not to get too excited. Jake was patient in their conversation, enjoying the interaction with his friends. The topic would shift soon enough toward the purpose of his visit.

After a while, Laura brought up Two Fingers. Once again Jake was amazed where the murder ranked as a topic of social conversation. Nonetheless, this was the opening he'd hoped for. He skillfully played the conversation until they were talking about the weeks prior to the murder and the possibility that intruders had made a series of visits onto the peninsula by boat.

"You know, I talked with Alex about that very point when this shit first happened," Ken said. "I think Alex is right. I mean—it only makes sense—easy access, undercover, no tracks."

"That's interesting," Jake replied. "You spend a lot of time on the lake. When you think back, do you remember seeing anything that seemed unusual?"

"It's hard to pinpoint any one thing. During daytime fishing you basically think about fishing. At night, though, it's a whole other trip. Time is weird. If the fishing is good, the action is your clock and time passes like a bat out of hell. If it's bad, though, it's like you're smoking weed. You become a part of the natural lake thing—a moment in time—a small, barely visible appendage to the fucking universal order."

"Why am I not surprised," Laura interrupted, "only you could make fishing sound like an LSD trip."

"I do recall a period when it seemed like there were more people fishing than usual—trolling for walleyes is my guess. That may be unusual in itself, however, since Eagle Feather Bay has never been known for its walleye fishing. I suppose I could have been more observant," he lamented.

"Not to worry."

"I do remember one boat, though, that left each night, going onto the main lake and around the tip of the peninsula. At least I think it was the same boat. It struck me as unusual, since the direction they took led only to uninhabited Indian reservation land. And, now that I think of it, goddamm it, it was late for someone to be moving on to a new fishing location."

"Did you notice anything else?"

"Only that they were active for about two weeks, around mid-October, and then it stopped."

"Do you think it means anything? I mean—could you have seen something that might be a clue?"

"That's a tough one. Maybe. It's more likely it was a late vacationer from one of the resorts trying to get his money's worth out of a fall vacation. My better judgment tells me that if this damn murder is really dependent on us for a solution, it'll never get fuckin' solved. And besides, I'll bet the resorts would dearly love for this puke to just go away."

"You're right. Murder can't be very good for the family vacation business." Jake walked over to the picture window facing the lake and watched the many birds at the feeder as they talked. Their color stood out against the white snow like a box of crayons on a white piece of paper.

"You know," Laura interjected, "Helen and Bud Miller are coming over for dinner tonight, and we're going to play some dominos afterwards. Why don't you stay? Dominos are one of the required winter survival skills on the peninsula."

"All the more reason to stay—thanks." He wondered if Helen would still be talking about the murder. It would be a true test of the community's thinking. If she wasn't, the issue was in the scrap pile for sure.

* * *

The discussion that evening contained only two references to the incident, oblique remarks regarding the sheriff's competency or lack of it.

While Laura served dessert, Helen said, "You know, Jake, just yesterday Michelle and Bobby said they saw some flashlights on Minor's shoreline the night of your party. Three of them, I think they said."

"Really! I'm surprised they made no mention of them until now."

"It's probably my fault. They wanted to say something, but were afraid to tell me they were out there—alone together, I mean. I think I've been pretty hard on Michelle about not getting too involved with Bobby, him being an Indian and all. It's important for Buddy and me to look out for her, because of how her mother thinks. Personally, I think Bobby's quite a nice young man."

"Actually it was Bobby who came to us," Bud said, "something about three men with flashlights who disappeared into the forest. It bothered him for weeks because he couldn't come up with a good reason why they would be there. To his credit, he did volunteer the information. Apparently Big Lights had passed on a comment to Bobby that Helen made about the two of them being together."

"I remember saying it the day everyone was cutting wood over at your place. It was pretty negative," Helen said apologetically.

"With the snow we've had and the storm coming tomorrow, it's too late for the sheriff to do any follow-up, that's for sure," Ken said. "It's supposed to be a ballbuster, according to the weather channel."

twenty-three

AFTER RUNNING A few errands, Linda headed back to the house to be there for Mister Jake's arrival. She was looking forward to his visit. While not quite sure what to expect, the thought that he might shed some new light on her father's murder was encouraging.

On the drive from Vern's Grocery Store to the house, she thought about her return to the reservation. She didn't want to drop out of school, but the break-in proved just how real the danger was in her life. The isolation she now experienced didn't help either. Her only regular contact was with Big Lights and Mister Jake.

As a quiet, introverted person growing up, she never expressed her constant feeling of wanting to leave reservation life. This preoccupation with moving away left her isolated; she was a wallflower during high school. Lack of popularity meant no real reservation friends to come back to.

In truth, Linda had changed a lot. Her late development into a very attractive young woman with a stunning face and a beautiful body was not lost on the young men who took notice now. Linda recognized some of them, but she didn't think they really recognized her. Their focus was on booze and drugs, and what she wasn't willing to give. She had overheard their disgusting comments. And the way they looked at her made her feel dirty. She knew they would have nothing in common. She thought about what a real boyfriend would be like, but had no reference point.

Consequently, she placed great importance on her time with Mister Jake and Big Lights. The two of them and her work on the project kept her from going into a self-destructive cycle of depression. She recognized her growing dependency on them. It was difficult not to overemphasize the importance of their meetings.

She walked into the house with her sack of groceries. The day was heavy with snow clouds, and the gray sky filled the rooms with an overwhelming dreariness. In truth, the house was pretty depressing all on its own. Two bedrooms, one bathroom, a kitchen, and a living room were all there was to this small forty-year-old house. The drapes were tattered and dirty, and the vintage rug was stained and faded.

On the reservation, you grew up pretty much accepting what you had. No one remodeled or redecorated. There weren't even any stores where you could buy nice things without driving all the way to Bemi-dji or Bronson. But the real barrier wasn't the distance to the stores. The Ojibwe made use of things until they no longer had value and then dropped them, literally. It was as simple as that. Decorating or remodeling were activities for white men, and besides, where would the extra money come from anyway?

Just as tears welled in her eyes, a prelude to an all-too-familiar pattern of despair, a knock on the door brought her back to reality. Linda took a moment to answer while she composed herself.

"Hi, Mister Jake. Come in."

"Hello, Linda. Are you OK?" Jake couldn't help feeling Linda's sense of isolation and abandonment. Her life at U of M had plenty of activity and lots of people; here there was emptiness.

"It's nothing, really. I think I'm just feeling a little sorry for myself, that's all." Giving Jake one of her game-face smiles, she said, "Why don't I get you something to drink before you get started?"

It was easy for Jake to see that Linda had anticipated his visit. They chatted while he sipped his soft drink, and Linda opened a little to her feelings. Jake felt good that she trusted him.

"It's the loneliness more than anything else that makes it hard. At school my friends were always there. Other than a few phone calls, they're gone now, too. Maybe I made a mistake dropping out."

"Some questions only time can answer, but I can tell you one thing for sure, Linda. This Omaha Project wouldn't exist if it weren't for you. Whether you realize it or not, the council needed to see someone of your age and determination involved in order to be confident. You're already making a difference. I know it's hard, but when you start working with others, you'll feel better. When Jan died, it was my job and friends at Astro Tech that kept me going. You'll see."

"Thanks for the pep talk and letting me talk, Mister Jake. I don't know what I'd do without you."

"You'd be just fine, that's what you'd do."

They talked continuously while Jake explored the house. He tried to think like someone who was trying to hide something. It helped to have Linda at hand to show him each room. They were sparsely furnished and easy to survey. It was obvious to Jake why the original search had gone so quickly. If something were out of place, it would be a no-brainer to spot. He looked for places where things could be hidden.

It wasn't until he had inspected every room and crept through the attic and the crawl space of the house that he said, "Maybe I'm wrong, Linda. I was hoping to find something, and all I've accomplished is to get your hopes up."

"I'll check the storage shed out back before leaving. If I find something, I'll tell you. If not, I'll just leave. This storm is building up fast. And if anyone asks about my visit here, let's just agree that it was Omaha Project–related."

Linda nodded in agreement.

"Oh, that reminds me. You're holding an introduction meeting tonight at the school for the project. Are you sure you don't need any help?"

"No, I don't think so, Mister Jake. These are my people. I'll do fine."

"Remember, be straightforward about the goals of the project in order to set realistic expectations."

"Will do."

*   *   *

The small shed at the back of the lot was a waste of time also. It was virtually empty. Other than a few gardening tools and some miscellaneous garage-type items hung on the walls, there was nothing, not even a shovel or a rake. Jake stood hunched over by the low ceiling of the aluminum shed and thought *something isn't right*. Sparse is one thing, but missing essential tools is another.

Suddenly it occurred to Jake: he was looking in the wrong place. Two Fingers wouldn't jeopardize his daughter by hiding incriminating evidence in his home. Jake would be more likely to find the items he was looking for by searching the storage and tool sheds at the cemetery. How could I miss such an obvious connection? he thought.

It was about three o'clock in the afternoon as Jake walked toward his car. The sky had become very dark, and the storm was beginning to build for its attack. After starting his Yukon, Jake sat for a few moments and contemplated just how long it might take to wander around the cemetery on his own. Would he be noticed and, if so, how would he explain his presence?

He decided that the time was right. The snowstorm would likely eliminate any visitors at the cemetery, and the thought of seeing his aunt and uncle's grave gave him the excuse he needed to explain his presence. Technically the cemetery was available to the public, but for practical purposes burials were mostly Indian because of its location adjacent to the reservation. His aunt and uncle were locals with no money to speak of, which made this their logical resting spot. It would take ten minutes to get there, and no more than another half-hour to nose around. He had a flashlight in the car that would help in the sheds, given the typical limited visibility of a winter afternoon.

Arriving at the cemetery, he parked his truck in full view, as if to demonstrate his perfect right to be there. The snow came down hard as he crossed the small field of scattered tombstones and Indian burial houses. Murmuring a short prayer of gratitude at his uncle's grave for all the fishing trips as a kid, he moved on toward the two outbuildings.

There was one wooden, garage-size building and another small one. Before entering the larger one he called out, "Is anyone here?" He waited a few moments, heard no reply, then opened the side door and called again. Nothing. It was dark inside. He experienced a flashing déjà vu feeling simulating the initial discovery of Two Fingers in his own garage. To his relief, the flashlight erased all connection to that encounter.

Inside were all kinds of tools. Obviously Two Fingers wouldn't have had to purchase his own.

The garage hadn't seen any activity recently. Layers of undisturbed dust covered the disorganized workbench. It's likely that Two Fingers was the only person to ever come into this building, he thought.

Rummaging around, Jake noticed some five-gallon gas cans lined up away from the workbench. He lifted them and gauged the contents to be fuel. He opened one can, and the fumes confirmed his guess.

Away from the cluster of these cans stood a single one. Why had it been separated? He immediately judged the contents to be different, not so much by the weight, although it did feel heavier, but by the way the fluid moved in the can—thicker and more sluggish. He opened the can and sniffed. He'd never smelled this combination before, but he recognized the aroma right away, a mixture of dandelion and pine tar of some sort.

He filled a small jar to take for analysis by Alex's people and continued to look around. He knew he was on to something and didn't want to miss anything. He took his time.

Outside, the snow was blanketing everything. He estimated that staying too long could present a problem for the trip back to the cabin. He couldn't believe he'd been there an hour already. What else could there be? He tucked an ordinary pair of work gloves hanging on a nail into his pocket. If an analysis showed the same results as the other gloves, a solid connection would be made between Two Fingers, the odd mixture of substances, and the activities on Alex Minor's property and, most likely, a clear link to Sam Aguire.

Scanning the room one last time, he noticed a small framed picture of Linda and her dad. She looked to be about eight or nine and was holding a large walleye while standing on a rickety old dock. Her smile was happy, more than likely from the praise being bestowed upon her by Two Fingers. It was sitting on the workbench and Jake guessed she would like to have it. He slid it into his larger coat pocket. He found nothing else of importance in the garage or the smaller shed.

Satisfied with his visit, Jake wanted to head for home right away. This was a snowstorm like none he had ever seen.

He pulled onto the street not looking both ways and almost hit another truck virtually camouflaged by the blizzard. Miraculously, they missed each other, and in seconds both trucks disappeared— headed in opposite directions. Jake knew he owed someone an apology, but it happened too fast to determine who. There was no damage done, and the snow buildup on the road was easily seven to eight inches by now. Time to get going.

Jake drove deliberately, slowly making his way back to the cabin. The normal thirty-minute drive took well over an hour. The snow came at the windshield in horizontal sheets. With his wipers all but frozen, visibility was drastically reduced. He needed to really focus to stay on the road. Still, he couldn't help but turn the day's discoveries over and over in his mind.

When he reached his access road, a quick assessment led him to backtrack and leave his truck at Ken's. The snow was already deep and drifting badly. "This is the last time I'll leave the snowshoes in the cabin," he said, berating himself under his breath. The normally comfortable walk was a memorable hike from hell.

twenty-four

MOREY LEANED FORWARD in the driver's seat and wiped the windshield just in time to see the other truck pulling out of the cemetery parking lot. The driver didn't see him at all. Morey's instincts helped him swerve away from the Yukon when it pulled into his path in the oncoming lane.

"Fuckin' idiot."

He recognized Jake's truck. He thought of chasing Jake down and beating the shit out of him, but he knew better. Swallowing his intense flash of anger did not come easy. Had it been one of his less-fortunate Indian brothers, the story would have been much different.

"Who the fuck does he think he is? Our little local bigshot should take some goddamn driving lessons."

What he had just seen dawned on him after his rage began to subside about a half-mile down the road. What the hell was Jake doing at the cemetery? Knowing that Sam didn't like Jake gave Morey cause for second thought. If there was information that would put Morey in good with Sam, it would be information about Jake. It might even be worth another five hundred.

He wheeled his truck around in the snow and headed back to the cemetery. Within a few minutes he was parked in the small lot.

The snow was falling so hard that Jake's tracks were disappearing quickly. This was beginning to look like one of the worst storms in years. Morey made it to the large garage by backtracking Jake's footprints. Once there, he realized he could barely make out Jake's arrival tracks; only the tracks leading away from the garage were recognizable. This could only mean one thing. Jake hadn't just walked by the garage casually. He had actually been inside it for some period of time.

"Our little hero's been snooping around," Morey muttered. But when he looked around inside the garage and the shed, he didn't see anything unusual.

This was Morey's first visit to these buildings. It would have been a good idea to check this place out, he thought, when I did the once-over at Two Fingers' house. He was sure, however, that it hadn't been part of Sam's instructions. The possibility of not following through for Sam produced a quick jolt of anxiety.

Morey tried to check Jake's arrival tracks again on his way back to the truck. But now they were gone all together. He knew Sam would want to know about this situation right away. Instead of going home, he headed straight for the Night Owl on the bet that Sam and Chase would be there.

twenty-five

JAKE FELT LUCKY to reach the cabin. He had truly never seen a blizzard of such magnitude. For five days, the storm pounded the cabin. Ultimately, it dropped over five feet of snow with drifts easily double that. He could never remember snow accumulating at the rate of a foot a day.

The old cabin windows were not thermopane, which caused a substantial buildup of frost and ice on the inside. When the storm finally broke, Jake was eager to see something—anything other than the cabin's walls. It took considerable scraping to get his first look outside. At first, he saw nothing but an unimaginable volume of white snow. All recognizable items on the ground, like the large boulder by the driveway, the propane tank at the side of the cabin, and the telephone connection box by the garage, were completely buried. Looking toward the garage where the snowmobile was parked, he could see nothing but a massive snowdrift sloping toward the top of the garage starting from a point about twenty feet from where the side door to the garage would normally be found. Not that it made any difference; the snowmobile would be totally useless in this depth. It would sink like an iron boat. It's not like people hadn't warned him ahead of time about the likelihood of getting snowed in, he thought. He realized that he would be here for a while.

He also knew that snowshoes would be dangerous. A person could easily get marooned in one of those large drifts, only to find the struggle to get out could take hours—a heart attack waiting to happen.

Looking out the window on the other side of the cabin, Jake saw a large oak tree on its side, half buried in snow. The raw power of the blizzard winds had ripped the tree from its roots, twisting the trunk with its force. Jake counted his blessings that the tree had not fallen on the cabin.

The power and telephone had been out for days. He instinctively knew that trees were assuredly down everywhere, taking service lines with them. The emergency channel on the portable radio gave a general description of the state of affairs in the county and, among other things, provided instructions on how to survive without electricity. That was helpful, particularly the comments on taking inventory of supplies and conserving essentials. After five days, the food supplies were dwindling fast.

A brief moment of optimism flashed in his mind when he thought of his cell phone, only for the feeling to leave just as quickly, as he remembered he had left it on the front seat of his truck.

"Damn. That would have been nice," he said loudly.

He groaned with the thought of getting more wood. But his last fire went out yesterday and the remainder of the wood was under a drift similar to that covering the snowmobile. The break in the storm made access to firewood his first priority. As the snow between the cabin door and the woodpile was exceptionally deep, his only option was to burrow a half-exposed, WW II–like foxhole trench. This could happen only after removing the storm door that swung out. He started on the trench right after breakfast, using the snow shovel left on the porch. By mid-morning he had covered half the fifty-foot distance. Completely drenched in sweat, he went inside to take a break and avoid a chill. By early afternoon he was done.

Surveying the outside of the cabin the best he could from the woodpile, Jake realized how fortunate he was the cabin held up as well as it did. The sharp pitch to the roof, complementing the Bavarian motif, prevented too much snow buildup. He knew that excessive accumulation could easily cave in the roof, causing the same damage as a fallen tree. Hank had definitely done his homework when he designed the cabin, he thought. It was solid.

With the power off, he needed to organize the remaining refrigerated food in a makeshift icebox carved into the wall in his trench. Foraging animals were an issue he hoped he would not confront. One thing at a time, he thought. There was no running water as the well ran off a submersible electric pump. And since he hadn't purchased a generator, he had to melt snow with the heat of the fireplace for water to drink, cook, wash, and flush the toilet.

All in all, there was little he could do other than accept his need to hunker down for a while. Stoking the fire around the clock kept him busy, but there wasn't much else to do. His restlessness increased.

Around the seventh day, Jake became distressed, and loneliness began to take center stage in his emotions. Another storm added two more feet, requiring another half-day to reopen the trench. Despite his efforts to maintain the fire, the temperature in most of the cabin had dropped to below freezing, at least solving his problem of having to keep the refrigerated foods outside and vulnerable to critters. He was living in a thirteen-hundred-square-foot refrigerator!

Adding to his desperate situation was the dwindling supply of battery power in his two flashlights. What was left he would preserve for an emergency. The thought of spending more time in this cold and dark isolation was claustrophobic. It had already been too long, and it could easily be five more days. The thermometer hanging on the post near the porch ceiling confirmed outside temperatures holding at ten below zero—no chance of getting out.

He started to lose the focus required by his daily routine that had kept him occupied for this past week and found his thoughts wandering for long periods of time. He had read everything in the cabin, his computer was useless without power, and the lack of interaction with others was taking its toll. He tried keeping a log of events, but became muddled in his thoughts, confused over time and priorities, and gave up. His food supply was reduced to canned goods. He was becoming weak, which caused a huge loss of energy and additional anxiety. Long onsets of depression became routine.

With darkness coming as early as three in the afternoon, the supply of candles had long since been consumed. During these prolonged stretches of emptiness Jake fell into severe stages of melancholy. Insecurities about his ability to rebuild his career dominated his thinking for days. His thoughts perseverated over the things he could no longer control. Why didn't I put in the work to complete my resume? I can't believe I'm so stupid to allow this much time to go by without a serious job-search effort. I should've done a lot more networking, but I let myself get distracted. People who know me will think I'm ridiculous to hide in the North Woods, away from reality, away from my responsibilities.

This downward spiral of negative self-talk continued. The lack of any job progress, coupled with the recognition that an Internet employment strategy from the cabin was more than a little naïve, fueled his mounting frustration. Major doubts with his decision to stay through the winter escalated.

"What good is this damn cabin anymore, anyway—all I'm doing is hiding in the past. The truth is," Jake said, more and more relying on talking out loud to stay on track, "I haven't received one inquiry about my status since leaving Astro Tech. Shouldn't my reputation count for something? Shouldn't it!" his voice stabbed at the air in a verbal Don Quixote–like lunge.

"Why do you think you're so friggen special," he countered in continued self-flagellation. Dwelling on the fact that he knew very competent engineers who went unemployed for eight to twelve months didn't help. Being cut off from the electronic world and the people world was a double whammy to Jake. The fact still remained, though; he hadn't received any calls, and it polluted his mind.

At 4:44 A.M. on the tenth day, Jake awoke in terror, reliving the bear attack in his dreams. This was the third consecutive day that he'd awakened at 4:44, each time from a different, very vivid dream. His sweat stuck to the sheets, preventing him from comfortably returning to sleep. His thoughts of KC brought back feelings of acute melancholy. His vision of staying the winter in the cabin had definitely included KC's companionship. The void created tortured him, especially now.

In the discomfort of these early morning imaginings, half asleep and half awake, unresolved thoughts continued to haunt him. His subconscious ground away during the sleeping hours of night, only to wake him with one last piece of unprocessed data.

"What's with 4:44, anyway? Is this some kind of message that's supposed to mean something?"

The real truth for Jake lay not in KC's absence, however, nor in the loss of control over his job search, nor in the storm, but in the enormous void created when Jan died. Thoughts of them together would consume his mind as he struggled in these early morning recurrences. He could feel her lying next to him and hear the soft inhale and exhale of her sleep. He imagined the smell of her favorite Herbal Essence shampoo in her streaked blond hair on the pillow, her eyes still closed in rest.

The years since Jan's tragic accident had not erased anything. He could still see and feel her presence—their walks down the driveway, simple bicycle rides, skipping stones on the quiet water, fires on the beach, and excitement shared in sex—everything they had shared together. He always knew he was lucky when he heard his friends talk about not communicating with their wives. Even in their worst times, which were rare, their mutual respect and love went unchallenged. Their sharing of every thought and enjoyment together created a bond that even the physical separation of death could not eliminate. There were times he wished he'd been in the car with her.

At other times he thought they might have been *too* close, and maybe that had kept him from moving on. And in truth, he really hadn't progressed past the point of her death. The therapy sessions had been helpful, but they never resolved the longing that had become a part of his daily makeup. His friends had stayed close and even introduced him to new prospective female companions. The jokes of being a good-looking bachelor having his way in a sea of willing female partners were a staple in conversations with his buddies. He never made it past first base, however, with anyone. It wasn't as if there weren't opportunities. In fact, he was astounded with the open offers for sex. What Jake had experienced with Jan in their relationship was so meaningful, however, that these rushes to intimacy paled in comparison to memories that were once real for him.

Lying there, half asleep in the cold darkness of the bedroom in a bed piled high with blankets, he felt a longing for Jan that brought tears to his eyes. Some were in recognition of the beauty they shared and some lay in the accelerating despair created by the isolation. Jake knew he was trapped—nearing a breakdown.

Intellectualizing the solution was easy, he thought. Doing it would be hard. Letting go of the most beautiful and exciting part of his life would not be achieved without a price. The tears continued. He fell back into a semi-sleep.

He held on to whatever peace and serenity his thoughts about Jan could bring over the next few days. He tried to focus on his routine of stoking the fire, clearing snow, eating, and basic hygiene needs in order to keep himself together. After all, she had walked every square inch of this cabin many times herself. It gave Jake a sense of visceral connection. He knew she would be disappointed in his wallowing like this, as it was her convictions that enabled him to believe in himself and move forward. Her unfailing commitment to him had been a true source of his strength.

On the morning of what he thought to be the eleventh day, Jake woke and tended to the lifeless coals of yesterday's fire. He had come to dread the bitter cold of those first few morning hours. Once the fire was revived, he began his routine of checking the cabin on the inside for structural damage from snow weight on the roof, melting more water, and preparing breakfast.

Suddenly, he heard a banging on the door. At first, the sound was like an abstract irritation. His routine had become so internalized that this seemingly common occurrence startled him. When he got to the door, there stood Tom. With his full winter beard and his snowmobile suit, he looked like someone from an Antarctic expedition.

Jake stood motionless in disbelief. To his judgment the depth of the snow was still impassable and it looked like more was on the way. Yet there stood Tom, as if he'd come over to go ice fishing.

"Open up, Jake. It's colder than a well-digger's ass in the Klondike out here."

Snapping out of his stupor, Jake opened the door.

"You are a glorious sight, my friend. How did you make it back here?"

"It was a bitch—no less than three hours from the road to your place. Luckily, I've done this once or twice."

"God, am I happy to see you. I'll get you some coffee while you warm up."

As they drank, Tom gave him the details. Jake could see that Tom was in a solid state of sweat from the effort.

"Why don't you take some of your clothes off and let them dry before we head out of here?"

"Not unless you want a roommate. There's more storm coming before noon. We're getting out of here as soon as I finish this coffee and get some food. You do have something left to eat, don't you, Jake?"

"How about my last can of baked beans?"

"Perfect. You know, we were beginning to worry a bit for your well-being, Jake. This was a big snow by any measure, and with you being a greenhorn and all, well, we thought you may have had enough."

"How long has it been?" Jake wasn't actually sure. Some of the days were a blur, especially the ones full of thoughts involving Jan.

"Thirteen," Tom responded matter-of-factly.

"I can't believe it. I would have bet money that it was eleven."

"Why don't you get ready to leave while I finish eating? We can talk more in the truck."

The hike out took the men less time since they were able to follow Tom's tracks.

They went directly back to Tom's place. As it turned out, Tom's visit was part of a peninsula-wide rescue effort being coordinated from the Cedar Lodge and Fishing Resort. Six other people who had been rescued so far were at the lodge. All had been in straits similar to Jake's. The volunteer team knew that it was the people who were off the road by some distance, like Jake, who would be in trouble. The rule of thumb was to give them about twelve days, however, before hiking in. Any earlier and some were likely to consider it an intrusion. According to Tom, isolation was a positive part of the winter experience for some folks.

From Jake's point of view, they could have come twelve days earlier. Another shot of Jack Daniels quickly put some spirit back into his step as he realized that his world had stopped spinning for almost two weeks. His head, however, still had difficulty reconciling this monumental episode of isolation, loneliness, and frustration.

The storm had given him a chance to relearn something about himself, though. Jan was most certainly the high point of his life. But he owed himself the benefit of moving on. Maybe the storm would serve as a metaphor for his struggle. No matter how devastating, all storms come to an end.

twenty-six

SAM AND CHASE were just about to leave the Night Owl to get a head start home on the storm when Morey walked in.

"I thought you'd want to know what I just saw."

"What are you talking about?" They stopped, somewhat puzzled by the confrontation.

"Jake—snooping around the cemetery storage buildings. Didn't make sense to me, thought you'd want to know," Morey said, looking squarely at Sam.

The veins in Sam's neck instantly turned blue. Morey could never recall seeing Sam this pissed off.

Knowing nothing of what Jake might or might not have discovered, Chase immediately decided the buildings had to go, and now. Too many opportunities for things to go wrong, he reasoned, if they remained.

"Morey," Chase said. "Go saddle up to the bar for a few beers while Sam and I talk a minute." This was an easy order to follow. Beers on the house and the prospects of another payoff represented the high point of Morey's week.

"These buildings are where Two Fingers spent a good portion of his waking hours," Chase said to Sam.

"Any screwups on his part involving our plans were likely to happen in those buildings. How could we be so stupid as to overlook them?" His voice quivered with frustration.

"We're goddamn lucky that ol' Sheriff Betts isn't any smarter than we are," Sam finally said, shaking his head in disgust.

"Well, we can't let him investigate them now, that's for goddamn sure. Who knows what Jake may have found? And for Christ's sake, why was he even there in the first place?"

Jake Lorenz was becoming an all-too-common topic for these men. What to do about him, however, was unclear. On the other hand, the decision about the cemetery buildings was easy. The impending blizzard was the perfect cover to burn and destroy the buildings. The local volunteer fire department wouldn't even know about the fire until it was over. After a quick review of the plan and their options, they summoned Morey back to the table.

Morey had not wasted his opportunity. The bar bill showed two beers and three shots.

After receiving his instructions from the two men, Morey headed toward the door. On his way to the cemetery he stopped at the State Liquor store and picked up a twelve-pack before they closed up. A good late-afternoon buzz shouldn't be wasted, he thought. I can nurse this one right into a full-blown drunk with a little help.

Everything he would need to torch the buildings was already in the garage. The one-mile drive took about ten minutes in the snow. As expected, nobody was in sight on the streets or at the cemetery. He sat in the parking lot for a few minutes planning his strategy, which mostly involved drinking another beer before starting the fire.

Finally he left his truck and started trudging through the snowy cemetery toward the buildings. He had decided to burn down both at the same time and get out quickly. He located the line of gas cans in the shed.

He poured the gas around the inside base of the building walls on the windward side of the buildings. The wind would fan the flame perfectly throughout each structure. Everything went as planned. He ignited each building from the inside doorway and got out fast, narrowly escaping the small explosion of the gas cans that quickly followed.

He hustled back to the truck as quickly as his big body would allow, but the snow was deep and his three-hundred-pound frame made the short distance an effort. He sat for a few minutes in the truck, his chest heaving as he caught his breath.

Quickly the flames reached over forty feet. He could feel the intense heat even in his truck. The scene excited him, so he allowed for a few extra moments to take everything in. He finished the open beer and popped a fourth to celebrate. In a few minutes he pulled away.

Maybe he would get lucky tonight, he thought. He knew a couple of local ladies who were always eager to earn a few extra dollars. And he surely would have a few extra dollars.

twenty-seven

DURING HER DRIVE to the high school the storm's obvious intensity concerned Linda, but she had made a promise. And the people coming to the school really wanted a job with the Omaha Project. They were all high school graduates and eager to get involved, particularly with the promise of learning some basic computer skills. She knew they would show up despite the storm, and she didn't want to disappoint them. Besides, many of them didn't have phones and couldn't be notified.

The meeting started right on time and their enthusiasm for the project kept the discussion going for well over an hour. Using her own computer, Linda showed the candidates what would be involved. Even though each person's keyboard skills varied, she didn't want them to be intimidated by the job requirements involving the computer. Linda answered all the questions before closing the meeting. She was very pleased with the results. People were optimistic. She was quite sure at least four of these candidates would create a solid nucleus to launch the project.

Everyone hurried to leave, as the storm was becoming dangerous.

Linda stayed a few more minutes to pack up the computer, turn off the lights, and lock up. When she got to the front door of the school she was amazed by the snow's accumulation. She could barely make out her dad's van in the lot. Concerned about driving, but more apprehensive about staying overnight at the school, Linda hurried across the parking lot. She bent her head against the harsh wind, slipping with each step through the drifts.

Cleaning the windshield with the snowbrush hardly made any difference. The snow-blinding visibility would be perilous. She guessed she could make it home in less than a half-hour if she took her time on the main road between Bemidji and Chippewa Lake. Easy enough, she thought, until the van spun out through a sharp curve. She felt the tires lose their grip, putting the van in a slow-motion 360. She was out of control before she could slow down and skidded off the shoulder and into a swale, completely bottoming out.

Frustrated and a little panicky, she tried to calm herself down. "This is nothing serious," she said aloud for reassurance.

She spun the wheels a few times in a futile attempt to get out. I'm not going anywhere, she thought as her shoulders slumped in resignation.

Surely someone would be along soon, she thought. Hiking the remaining few miles in the dark blizzard seemed impossible. Her concerns escalated as time passed.

"Come on," she pleaded quietly in the hopes that someone would be on the road.

At last she saw the headlights of an approaching vehicle.

"Finally," she said with hopeful expectation.

She got out of her car to make sure the driver would see her. The lights of the coming vehicle moved slowly through the unplowed road and, to her relief, finally stopped.

The passenger window to the pickup truck rolled down and she recognized Morey.

He smiled with a crooked grin and slurred his offer for help. "You lookin' for some help, pretty lady?"

"All I need is a ride, Morey. I can get the van later," she insisted urgently. She only knew him casually from his reputation—not someone she would associate with on normal terms. Instead, he got out of his truck to check out her situation.

"You're in bad straits here, honey," Morey observed, motioning her toward the van. "Get in and out of this fucking storm, and I'll tell you what I can do."

Linda had always been afraid of Morey. He never looked at her as a person. His eyes were always fixed on her breasts. Her college friends would have called him a sleazebag.

"I don't want to get in, Morey! Can't you just give me a ride home? Please!" She resisted getting into the van, but Morey opened the back door and forced her inside.

"Now you look here, you little bitch. You have a problem that I can fix and I got a problem that you can fix. Comprende?"

She could smell the alcohol on his breath. "I don't know what you mean. I only want some help. Please, just a ride into town!"

"A ride is what you want and a ride is what you'll get." He laughed. "It's about time we see what's inside those panties of yours."

"I don't want to cause trouble. I just want some help," she pleaded. "Please," she begged. Tears came quickly. She feared the worst.

The back of his meaty hand came crashing across the side of her face and knocked her across the cargo area. He snorted like an animal.

"What you want don't count, honey. I've had my eye on you for some time, and I expect to treat myself to a taste."

She saw that his pants were undone and his penis was bulging in his stained underwear. He ripped at her blouse and began grabbing at her breasts.

"Stop, you're hurting me. God, please don't!"

Another blow from a closed fist knocked her senseless against the steel paneling. From that point on, she went in and out of consciousness.

Morey's appetite for Linda was uncontrolled. He repeatedly forced himself on her. The only clothes left on her body were her torn blouse and her socks. Her panties had been ripped off early in the assault when he buried his head in her vagina. In her few moments of consciousness, she experienced sheer horror as he raped and sodimized her. Luckily, those moments were brief. Linda would be spared most of the memory of this sacrilege—participating only unconsciously in his vicious orgy.

Morey's overwhelming desire for Linda's body, combined with his obsession with his own physical pleasures, obscured any notion of keeping track of time. For Morey, the hour passed as many of his dreams, fuzzy in time and truth, lacking any sense of real connection. The reality check of his truck possibly running out of fuel while idling for such a long time, however, finally snapped him back into the moment. He realized he needed to get out of there.

Zipping his pants, he said, "Is there anything else I can do for you, you piece of trash?" Her incoherent murmurs infuriated him and were the catalyst for him to lash out once more. This time, his huge right hand delivered a blow directly to the center of her face, smashing her nose and cheekbones. Blood spurted in every direction, covering the cargo area, including Morey.

He exploded, screaming, "You dirty little bitch," over and over as he hammered her head against the steel paneling until deep lacerations in her forehead and skull gushed more blood. A clump of her scalp hung semi-attached to the metal edge of the sidewall. Her body went limp well before the attack ended.

* * *

Morey drove back to his rented hovel, spinning out several times on the way. He threw his clothes in a pile to rinse out later. He could remove the bloodstains entirely with a washing at the laundromat in town. He added the panties to a growing pile of similar garments in his closet. It was a gruesome trophy case—a graphic representation of his perverse mental state and sick connection with the women in his life.

Time passed while Morey watched TV and sobered up. Vague regrets for killing Linda started to surface. It was not what he had intended. He rationalized his feelings, though. After all, his needs were no different than any other man's. He just wanted to have sex, and things got out of control. Why shouldn't he be able to have sex with women? Any regrets had little to do with remorse or guilt. Concerns of what Sam and Chase would do when they found out did begin to enter his mind. He had to make sure that didn't happen. A sense of urgency found its way into his mutated reasoning.

The more he sobered up and the more the facts became clear, the more Morey knew that he had to go back to Linda's car and eliminate any evidence connecting him to her. "Maybe a fire is the solution for this problem as well," he murmured.

Despite the blizzard's relentless attack, he put on clean clothes and headed out again. Luckily the thirty-minute trip back to Linda's car didn't require a fill-up; he didn't want to stop for fear of being associated with the scene later.

twenty-eight

BOBBY AND MICHELLE had been seeing quite a bit of each other since Thanksgiving. Commuting back and forth to BSU accounted for about two hours round-trip. They managed to get classes on the same days, which simplified their schedule.

The awkwardness of that first night in the car was long gone, and it was easy for anyone to see that they were definitely an item. They could always be found together studying, laughing, fooling around, and genuinely enjoying each other.

Helen was so completely taken with Bobby that she even paved the way with Michelle's mother and father, describing him as the most handsome and intelligent young man in Chippewa Lake, regardless of heritage. She wasn't doing this just for Michelle's sake. Both Helen and Bud had observed Bobby closely before giving their approval. He got nothing but A's at BSU and demonstrated a respectful maturity that was good for Michelle.

That Saturday Bobby and Michelle had been working together on a community project sponsored by BSU for the benefit of local elderly people. It was mid-afternoon by the time the school heeded the storm warnings and canceled all activities. While having a late lunch, the two of them debated what to do about the drive home.

"Aunt Helen will understand," she said, hoping to convince Bobby. "This is the logical decision to make." Michelle wanted to stay the night.

She knew Bobby's incredible sense of duty would compel him to try to get her home safely. He desperately wanted to earn Helen and Bud's respect. It was admirable, she thought, but becoming a stumbling block in moving forward. She was secretly hoping the chance of being snowed in would create the opportunity for them to be together for the night. Both of them wanted it very badly.

"I don't think we'll have any real problems if we leave soon and take the drive slowly," Bobby replied. "The truck has four-wheel drive, and besides, there are lots of people who will need help if this storm is as bad as predicted."

"Bobby," she pleaded, head against his shoulder.

"You've never seen what happens when the peninsula becomes snowed in. People will need to be rescued. It happens every five years or so."

"Don't you ever think of us?" she petitioned. "I mean, sometimes you treat me like your sister. Don't you ever want to be really alone together? This could be the perfect opportunity."

"There's nothing I'd like better, but I don't want to think just of myself when I know others are going to suffer and could use my help." In his mind, he could see how perfect it would be, just him and Michelle together the whole night. His sense of duty prevailed, however, as they got up from the table looking at each other.

"It's just going to have to be at another time. I love you and the idea of being together, but I know I can help, and I don't know how to say 'no' under the circumstances."

She knew Bobby was right, but that's not what she wanted. They headed to the truck.

She pouted for the first half-hour of the trip while the snow pelted the windshield.

Bobby was glad he had thought to gas up before leaving. Gas could become a premium if they got stuck and had to stay the night in the truck. He kept his focus on driving while entertaining visions of how they might be together.

Darkness came and they were barely halfway to Chippewa Lake. Bobby was beginning to think that Michelle's suggestion was, in fact, the better course of action.

"Are we going to make it, Bobby?" Michelle asked without one hint of an "I told you so."

"We'll be okay as long as we don't get stuck. I haven't seen anyone in a while. We don't have any choice but to keep moving," he said while keeping his undivided attention on the road.

By the time they reached the outskirts of Chippewa Lake, hours had passed.

"I can't wait to get home—Helen and Bud will be worried."

"No argument from me," he replied empathically.

At that moment, Bobby saw a vehicle on the side of the road, well off the shoulder. "There's no way it's going anywhere without a tow truck."

"I'm glad it's not me."

"I can't see any signs of people, can you, Michelle?"

"Nope. Maybe someone has already helped. If they were still there, someone would be waving us down."

As he drove past, he also thought the driver might have fallen asleep or possibly be hurt. He slowly came to a stop and backed up, making sure to remain in the middle of the road.

"You stay in the car, Michelle. I better check this out. There's no reason for both of us getting wet and cold."

Bobby approached. The van looked as if it had been there a while. The windows were covered with snow, preventing him from seeing inside. When he walked around to the other side, however, he opened the rear door to get a look.

His adrenaline spiked after cautiously opening the door. The half-naked, lifeless body covered in blood was barely recognizable. A woman for sure, but hard to tell much else as the face had been beaten into a pulp. Indian, maybe. The scene led Bobby to draw the obvious repulsive conclusions. Disgust and despair took over as his mind searched for what to do next.

Before going back to tell Michelle, he decided to check for a pulse in the unlikely event that this person was still alive. To his shock, his fingers detected a very faint throbbing on the left wrist.

He quickly returned to his truck.

"This is serious! There's a woman in the car, barely alive. She's been badly beaten, probably raped. We're going to have to get her covered up and into the truck so we can move her to the hospital. Let's move fast—I don't think she has much life left."

"Oh my God! Who is it?"

"Can't tell, and we don't have time to spend on that now."

Within moments of viewing the body, Michelle was choking back bile.

"I don't think I can do this."

"You can. You have to!"

She took a deep breath of the cold air and began working with Bobby to get things done. They rolled the body onto a blanket Bobby had in his car, then covered her with a second blanket. Using the first as a stretcher, they managed to get her into Bobby's truck. Within minutes, they had the woman positioned between them in the truck, collapsed, with her head on Michelle's lap. There was no movement, and her breathing was nothing more than a whisper. Neither could recognize the woman, even with the truck dome light on.

As quickly and safely as possible, Bobby drove to the Indian hospital in Chippewa Lake. Services there would be minimal, but no other choice existed. During the short trip, Michelle managed to keep her own emotions over the viciousness and baseness of such an act in check. On their way they saw only one other truck going in the other direction. Bobby debated if the driver could help, but reasoned that time was their real enemy now. He continued.

Luckily, a doctor and two nurses were still on duty. The doctor had decided not to risk the trip home to Bemidji. The nurses were there to provide twenty-four-hour first-aid support. After lifting her onto a gurney, they wheeled Linda into a small emergency room for treatment.

Michelle called Helen from the hospital to let her know about the awful situation. "We're okay, but we're not going to be able to make it home. We can stay at the hospital. It's crazy to try anything else. Don't worry, Aunt Helen, we'll be fine." This time Michelle didn't consult Bobby, and she wasn't leaving him an option. After the phone call, they waited to hear from the doctor on the woman's condition.

Shortly before 11 P.M., the doctor came out.

"This woman is lucky to be alive. She's very fortunate you two came along when you did. My guess is that she would have died within the hour."

They nodded in understanding, grateful for their ability to have helped.

"Do you have any idea what happened?" the doctor asked.

Bobby explained the few details they had.

"Can you tell who she is, Doctor?" Michelle asked.

"Yes, one of the nurses recognized her. Her name is Linda Smith. Do you know her?" Bobby and Michelle looked at each other in astonishment before responding.

"Oh my God. Yes," she said, hesitating to take a deep breath. "We do." Michelle clasped Bobby's arm while she spoke. "She works with Big Lights and Mister Jake, Jake Lorenz, on the Omaha Project."

"I just can't believe this, Bobby." Her look for support from Bobby drew a blank stare.

"Did she say anything about who did this to her?" Bobby asked.

"No, and she won't. She's in a coma and appears to have sustained serious brain damage. We'll need to get her to the Bemidji Hospital if she stands a chance of surviving."

Making a vague gesture to the outside weather, the doctor continued with a doubtful expression, "I don't think the storm is going to permit that. Normally, a helicopter can be flown in within a half-hour, but that's unlikely tonight."

"Can we see her?" Michelle asked.

"Yes, but only for a minute."

They stood there quietly with the emergency curtains pulled back as the nurse adjusted the IV and continued monitoring the life-support systems. Linda's bruises and extensive stitch work were awful to look at. "You probably know there's nobody to notify," Bobby said.

"The nurse here is aware of her situation," the doctor replied. "We'll make her as comfortable as possible and hope for the best until we can get her to Bemidji."

"Not very reassuring considering her condition." The doctor's despondent look was his only reply to Bobby's comment.

"At least she's safe and warm with people who will care for her," Michelle said, holding Bobby's arm for support.

Bobby and Michelle were given some blankets and pillows; they curled up together on one of the waiting room couches, happy to be together and out of the storm. With her head on Bobby's chest, Michelle began to cry. The images of their ordeal made her feel deeply vulnerable. Bobby held her close, trying to erase the horror of what he knew they both were thinking.

"I couldn't have helped her in time without you," he said, brushing away the tears on her cheek.

"You were right for us to come home tonight, Bobby. She'd still be out there if we had stayed in Bemidji. I love you."

twenty-nine

MOREY WAS SOBERING up quickly, and the seriousness of his situation was now very clear. He passed the oncoming truck headed toward Chippewa Lake, hoping they had missed seeing Linda's van in the ditch. He didn't recognize the truck or the drivers, and he certainly didn't want to be recognized by stopping. It occurred to him that any connection to this part of the road, under these circumstances, would mean a prison sentence.

He soon came to Linda's van. His plan was to stuff a kerosene-soaked rag into the throat of the gas tank. After lighting it, he would move off quickly before the explosion.

Everything seemed as he had left it. Then he saw tracks in the snow leading to the van. He quickly opened the rear door. It was empty.

"Fuckin' son-of-a-bitch!"

He paced for a few minutes trying to clear his mind. He had definitely sobered up now.

Realizing the van was full of evidence, he continued with his original plan. Finding her body was one thing, but finding evidence leading to him was another thing entirely.

After pulling his truck down the road a hundred feet he went back, stuffed the rag into the gas tank, and lit it. He struggled in the deep snow, getting barely fifty feet away before the gas exploded, engulfing the car in flames. The shock wave knocked him to the ground. Unhurt, he got up and continued plowing through the deep snow toward the truck.

He wasn't waiting around to watch this fire, even for a minute. Time to vamoose. He drank his last beer while driving away as quickly as the snow would permit. Linda's van exploded once more as the fire ignited the gas in the carburetor. Crushing the empty beer can in his hand, Morey pitched it onto the passenger side floor.

thirty

WORD SPREAD QUICKLY about Linda's attack. People found it unbelievable that one family could have been the focus of so much brutality. It was beyond bad luck. The locals were afraid. The reservation and peninsula communities were living in near panic knowing that a vicious killer existed among them. Something dreadful could happen again, they thought, with good reason. A few men and women on the reservation even started carrying guns despite the tribal prohibition against concealed weapons.

The pressure on Sheriff Betts mounted astronomically. He brought arson specialists in from the Twin Cities to investigate both the car and the cemetery building remains. Nobody in their right mind believed they weren't connected. Yet all traces of evidence had been eliminated. If the fire didn't destroy the evidence, the blizzard did—footprints, tire tracks, everything.

A 24-hour guard was placed around Linda. Everyone prayed for her recovery, and for the coma to release its grip. She was lucky to have had constant emergency attention from the doctor and nurses during her initial confinement in the Indian hospital. Nevertheless, she was transported via helicopter to the Bemidji Hospital during the first brief break in the record-setting storm. There she was placed on the critical list, as her vital signs continued to remain weak.

Nobody was more affected by Linda's attack than Big Lights. His fondness for her surfaced during the crisis. It was apparent that his commitment to Linda had grown substantially—well beyond the simple working relationship offered by the Omaha Project. He never left the hospital and held on to his firm belief that her spirit would receive strength from his presence.

After a week of investigations though, no one had been arrested. The cycle of inconclusive police work was becoming all too familiar. Even the DNA evidence didn't reveal anything. People were outraged.

* * *

For Chase and Sam, however, the story was different. What could have looked like an accident or a simple case of vandalism at the cemetery had now become another full-scale investigation. The situation was once again out of control. This time, however, they could do something about it. Morey needed to learn a lesson. And that lesson was about to be administered in a maintenance building behind the casino, out of sight and sound of anyone.

"But I did everything you asked me to do, didn't I?" Morey pleaded.

"Shut up," Sam said as he jammed the barrel of a loaded .45 pistol into Morey's mouth. Chase strapped the revolver in place with duct tape as a bizarre appendage to Morey's head, while he held the handle of the gun steady with his hand. It took every bit of Morey's concentration to control his gag reflex.

"It's simple," Sam said with such destructiveness in his voice that even Chase said nothing. "We placed you in a special position of trust to help us with our work. We've paid you well beyond your worth and asked that you use your eyes, ears, hands, and brain, nothing more. And you've misused that trust."

Morey's right hand was secured in a table vise at the wrist. The cold look in Sam's eyes added to Morey's increasing terror of what would come next. With quickness and precision, the cold steel of a razor-sharp fish-cleaning knife was buried completely through the palm of Morey's right hand, pinning it to the workbench. Blood gushed from the wound, ran down the blade, and pooled on the wooden surface. During the muffled, choking sounds of pain that followed, Chase opened Morey's left hand, which had been secured with rope to the workbench. The crushing blow from a claw hammer was delivered with brutal force.

Morey gagged in pain with the .45 still taped to his mouth, gasping for consciousness. He would have passed out if it weren't for the smelling salts Chase jammed into his nostrils. They wanted him conscious.

"Of course, you'll have to find an explanation for all of this if medical attention is needed," Sam warned. "You need to know what happens if we have to deal with this kind of bullshit again. We would consider another error in judgment to be a fatal misuse of your talents." He paused purposefully. His eyes bore a hole in Morey's wavering awareness of what was happening.

"We still want you involved, but your future is totally up to you now."

In his life Sam had learned that absolute control really was a derivative of fear. Adolescent beatings from his father had secured that belief long ago. As a practical matter now, Sam always found brutal harshness his best tool for getting results, especially when failure could not be tolerated. Efficient and effective, he reasoned.

Chase removed the .45 from Morey's mouth and fired it into an exposed joice beam, which shattered on impact. The object lesson was not lost on Morey. With his face two inches from Morey's, Sam said, "Don't fuck up again."

thirty-one

ACROSS THE LAKE on the peninsula, the township meeting was in full swing with Sheriff Betts trying to explain to people what the police were doing to find Linda's attacker.

Finally, after much discussion, and with little accomplished, Bud stood up to address his neighbors.

"I've lived here, like most of you, for a long time. Helen and I came to the peninsula because of its beauty and quiet way of life. Hell, we've never even locked our doors.

"I'll be damned if I'm going to let some lowlife take that away from us. Now don't get me wrong, we are locking our doors now, and we are afraid for our safety, like every one of you. But letting this situation get out of control is the wrong approach.

"We've always accomplished everything as neighbors. Hell, we built this Township Hall together with our own sweat and our own tools. Arrowhead Peninsula belongs to us, but in order for us to keep it, we're going to have to take matters into our own hands."

"Now don't go tryin' to take over, Bud," the sheriff said nervously, concerned with the direction of Bud's speech. "Taking the law into your own hands won't work."

"That's not what I'm proposing, Sheriff."

"Well, then, what is it that you are proposing? We ain't got all night," someone yelled from the audience. Everyone laughed and the tension broke.

"To me, it's simple," Bud continued. "Sheriff Betts here is only one person. He's having a hell of a time just trying to keep this situation from blowin' sky high. The way I see it, he needs more help, at least for the short term. I think it would be wise for the sheriff here to deputize a few of us so we can patrol our own peninsula legally. People have been doin' it for a hundred years. Why, I'll bet it would take no more than six of us, taking turns patrolling these roads, to ensure that no more shenanigans take place. Give us a radio and some instructions, and you'll be in control the whole time, Sheriff."

The people in the audience clapped enthusiastically in support of Bud's proposal.

"So, what do you think, Sheriff?" Laura piped up, filling the void created while the sheriff formulated his response. "We can't wait for more men to be killed and women to be raped."

Sheriff Betts asserted himself by walking to the center of the room. With his hand to his chin he responded slowly. "I think your proposal has merit, Bud, but only if I pick the volunteers and am placed in complete charge of the operation."

"Then let's get to work," someone said.

Over the next ten minutes, they discussed who would make the best volunteers. Jake was left off the list because of his part-time experience with the peninsula. Alex was too old and, quite frankly, not trusted all that much. Tom, Ken, Bud, Tony, and the two Schafer brothers from one of the other resorts were chosen based on their knowledge of the peninsula, their ability with guns, and their willingness to volunteer. Tom would be the lead deputy. The sheriff swore each man in before the meeting was over.

The six of them stayed behind with Sheriff Betts after the meeting broke up to work out a schedule for patrolling. They agreed that twenty-four-hour coverage was needed, with each taking a four-hour watch. The watch time slots would rotate each week so no one person got permanently stuck with the midnight shift. Everyone hoped the criminal would be caught soon, within the next few weeks anyway.

* * *

As everyone headed toward the parking lot after the meeting, Jake motioned Alex to come near. "I've got some information that may be very important. Let's meet at your place for a few minutes on the way home, and I'll fill you in. By the way, were you able to have Tony show you where he found the tools and gloves before the snow came?"

"No, I haven't had much luck on that or the other item as well," he said, referring to the background check on Sam. The storm had delayed their promised meeting, as well as Alex's progress, much longer than either of them had expected.

They exchanged nods. "I'll see you in a few minutes," Jake said. It was getting late, but neither man wanted to delay the discussion.

Jake held back in his short drive to Alex's lodge in order not to appear to be following. He wasn't exactly sure why, but the prospect of raising curiosity wasn't a good idea.

"Do you want a beer while we talk?" Alex offered once inside the lodge.

"Thanks, that sounds good."

Jake summarized his conversation with Ken as well as he could, without leaving anything important out. He focused on Ken's recollection of seeing one boat in mid-September going around the tip of the peninsula onto the main lake each night for about two weeks. Alex listened closely, raising his eyebrows and nodding his head at various times.

"There's not much to go on here, but that's all he could recall."

"Well, if there is a connection, it's most likely an Indian one."

"Why's that?"

"The direction Ken saw the boat take leads to uninhabited wilderness shoreline, odd for that time of night," said Alex. "Other than a few remote Indian hunting shacks on reservation land, the nearest non-Indian cabins are thirty miles by water. Not a trip anyone with any sense would take at night just to catch a few walleye. Oddly enough, the only boat landing for miles is near those shacks. It's used only by the local Indians during the wild rice harvest."

"Do you know how to get there?"

"Sure I do, but it wouldn't do us any good in this deep snow. In a week or so, if this snow melts a little, we can take our snowmobiles there by ice. Even then, it might be a waste of time. To find anything, we may need to wait till spring."

One of the real learning points for Jake during his winter stay was the propensity for people to travel on ice. Over at Bronson, actual streets had been plowed on the ice and were maintained by the city for ice-fishing traffic and general transportation. Without a lot of snow, it was not unusual to see cars and trucks on the ice, even on this remote side of the lake. With reasonable snow depth, however, the snowmobile was the vehicle of choice. Before coming up to the cabin, Jake thought that winter made the cabin more remote, when in fact it was just the opposite with the opportunity of easy access on ice.

"At this stage, any information will be useful," Jake said. "Anyway, I'd like to know where the boat landing is for my own information."

Alex pointed at a spot on his large map of the peninsula. "It's right about here."

He then said, "I also heard from Helen about the people who were seen on my property over Thanksgiving. Something about Bobby and Michelle out necking by Eagle Feather Bay when they saw men with flashlights. Do you know anything more about this? She didn't give me much to go on."

"No, nothing at all. I wanted to follow up, but the storm came right after they told me. With all the phones down, I couldn't call you, or even Sheriff Betts, for that matter. I'm afraid that lead is buried, like so many other things."

"This damn storm was real convenient for people who were up to no good, wasn't it?"

"Sure was," Jake nodded.

They went on to discuss Jake's findings at the cemetery storage building. They chewed over the possible implications for a while before deciding Alex would arrange to deliver new samples of the spruce pitch and dandelion oil and the second pair of gloves to his contacts in Chicago for more analysis. Their various speculations about the meaning of events—if the sample turned out to be the same as that discovered on Two Fingers' gloves—all led to a conspiracy of one sort or another. About what, however, they had no idea.

When Alex went to the bathroom, Jake considered the circumstances surrounding the cemetery further. It was obvious the torched buildings were the work of an arsonist, but was there a connection to the fact that he himself had been at the cemetery just a few hours before? And did any of this create a link to Linda's attack? He would never forgive himself if it turned out that his actions had somehow endangered her.

The pure coincidence of the near sideswiping of that truck at the cemetery remained unanswered as well. Was the driver connected to the sequence of events and, if so, how? One other thought nagged at his consciousness. If the driver was involved and also recognized him, was he now in danger? His inability to provide either a description of the truck or the driver plagued his memory of the event. Despite mental rehashing, he simply couldn't recall anything tangible. His report to Sheriff Betts involving a description of a dark truck was all he had. The lead was cold before ever becoming warm—a dead-end.

* * *

Other than the obvious one, Alex's reason for going to the bathroom was to give himself a few minutes to consider disclosing what he'd done to Jake's cabin. It seemed like the time might be right. His lack of forthrightness had been gnawing at him ever since he and Jake had entered into this partnership. Alex's nature was not one of teamwork. So this decision was hard. In the beginning, he believed he could use Jake to achieve his goal without ever having to disclose the transgression. Now things were getting messy and dangerous. He certainly didn't want to risk being implicated in these crimes. And how could he and Jake be successful in their efforts with a serious gap in knowledge and trust?

This wasn't like Alex, but he was going to have to be straight with Jake and it was going to have to start now, regardless of the consequences.

As Alex walked back into the room, Jake spoke first. "You know, Alex, I've had some other thoughts you need to know about before we finish."

The idea flashed through Alex's mind that Jake may already know about the cabin. "Hold on to them for a second. I need to fill you in on something you should've known some time ago."

"What are you talking about?"

Alex's concept of a destination resort didn't surprise Jake, particularly after recalling the bedsheet he'd noticed covering the table on his first visit. What he heard next, however, was unbelievable.

"Your property was in the way and I wanted you out. And I made some bad decisions thinking you would sell if you got discouraged." Alex shifted uncomfortably while leaning against the stairwell.

Jake's silence forced Alex to continue.

"I knew the peninsula had an excellent population of bears. As near as I could tell, I had only a few weeks, so I started baiting your cabin. None of this makes sense as I look at it now, but I felt the destruction would discourage you from staying. It was my plan to buy your property for a fair price, if that makes a difference. What I didn't count on was the large wounded cinnamon bear that showed up."

"The one I met up with?"

"One and the same. It was weak with infection and hadn't eaten enough for hibernation.

"So, every three days or so, I put a couple large sections from a deer kill and some generic dog food in the boat and took a trip to your place at dusk. It was easy to stay out of sight along the shoreline.

I kept the dog food purchases down so as not to be noticed in Chippewa Lake.

"I was convinced that this whole escapade would get you to sell. And everything was in control until you arrived and discovered Two Fingers." Alex stood erect to make a confident final point.

"You gotta believe me, though, when I say I'm just as much in the dark as you are over the murder. It's important that you believe me."

Jake said nothing during Alex's little speech. How could someone be so desperate for achievement and recognition?

"This is absurd," Jake finally said in total astonishment.

"You're right."

Jake stared at Alex's slumped shoulders and contrite expression. He guessed that this was probably the first time in the man's life that he was genuinely taking responsibility for the destructive consequence of his actions.

"People are supposed to get smarter in their old age, not dumber. You mean you were actually plotting to get me to sell out so you could build a resort?" Jake paced for a minute trying to collect himself.

"Goddammit, that was stupid! Now I'm just supposed to forget about all of this and pretend we're working together as a team? Forget about KC? Forget about the fact I almost got killed?" Jake knew that his going off on Alex wouldn't solve anything, so he just stopped talking, but in his unwavering stare at Alex, he maintained a look of complete contempt.

"I'm embarrassed, Jake, and I'll make it up to you. I have no excuse for my actions and wouldn't hold it against you if you chose to press charges."

The room was very quiet. Alex paused before continuing.

"This situation is real serious, and I don't want this bullshit of mine to confuse the real facts when they ultimately do come up. I'm sorry, Jake."

While Jake wasn't thrilled with the idea of a major resort on Arrowhead, he suspended any further comment to focus on the fact that Alex had just taken a major risk in exposing his true character, and for some reason had chosen to do it with him. Alex's demeanor assured

Jake this wasn't just some ploy to maneuver him away from taking responsibility for his actions. This clever, devious, mean old son-of-a-bitch had just apologized.

The men held eye contact for some time before Jake responded.

"Well, Alex, life does have its ups and downs, doesn't it? Aside from some bills of mine you need to clear up, there's not much else you can do that this apology hasn't covered. I'll try not to hold it against you, Alex, but it will take me some time."

"Thank you. I understand."

"It's clear to me that your goal wasn't to hurt me as much as it was to achieve a need inside yourself that probably doesn't hold the value that you think it does."

"True words, Jake. True words."

*　*　*

Jake changed the subject. "I'm not sure what to think about the person in the truck I barely missed. If the driver is involved, it's likely he isn't in it alone."

"I think we should proceed very cautiously on this issue," Alex responded slowly with deliberate emphasis. "If a conspiracy does exist, we'd be well advised to figure out who the players are before sticking our nose in without a strategy."

"You're right. Let's just wait for the results from Chicago before making any major moves. In the meantime, we'll just hold tight."

"That's probably all we can do. I'll let you know when I get the report."

Jake left the lodge seriously questioning his own sanity in partnering with Alex. He sensed an authenticity in Al's confession, which was the only element in his mind holding them together. He decided to suspend judgment in order to weigh his impressions against Alex's future actions. Jake knew from experience that when people changed, it often came from a deep-seated need to fulfill something that had been missing for a long time. He chose to take Alex's forthright act of honesty and integrity at face value.

thirty-two

ALEX HAD GROWN impatient waiting for the response from his Chicago connection. Despite assurances, the analysis work seemed to take an unusual amount of time. Typical government inefficiency, he thought, while mulling over their lack of progress two weeks after sending the gloves and mixtures by overnight express.

So, when the FedEx truck pulled down his driveway the following Thursday afternoon, he was more than a little excited. He immediately went outside and headed toward the truck, waving at the driver before he could come to a stop.

"Looks like you're expecting something pretty important, Mr. Minor," the driver said. "And by the looks of this envelope, you've gotten it. You're the first person on Arrowhead I ever knew who received a FedEx from the U.S. Government—Department of the Interior in Washington, D.C., I believe."

Alex resented the personal inspection of the return address but as usual said nothing. His standard grumble was the extent of his communication. Already, his mind was trying to connect the Department of the Interior with the expected criminology report.

Inside the lodge, he ripped open the envelope and began reviewing the contents. At the top of the two-page letter was the normal government case number and reference to the letter's purpose.

*   *   *

United States Government Department of the Interior
Bureau of Indian Affairs
Notification
Native American Sacred Burial Grounds Act
Official Investigation.

We are notifying you that your property on government tracts 34 through 42 is currently under investigation as a protected Native American sacred burial ground. Pursuant to the Native American Sacred Burial Grounds Act, a team of Department of the Interior agents will be contacting you within the next thirty days to conduct a full site survey, which will include all necessary tests to determine the validity of the Big Bear Lake Ojibwe Reservation Tribal Council claim related to your property located within the general boundaries of the Big Bear Lake Indian Reservation.

Contact Agent Donna Lynch at the Washington, D.C., office with any questions prior to the investigation team's arrival on March 29, 1995.

*   *   *

The letter continued with the standard legal references, compliance obligations of the recipient, and various telephone numbers. It was signed by Jordan Barnhart, Secretary of the Interior.

Alex stood motionless in the kitchen. He reread the letter two more times trying to rationalize the logic of its demand, knowing full well that altering any course of action by the Department of the Interior on a matter such as this was tantamount to stopping an out-of-control freight train. Beyond being convinced the letter was some sort of mistake, Alex's thoughts were paralyzed. Having anticipated that the FedEx truck held his criminology report, this particular delivery came as a huge shock.

It was the first of March, and he knew that most of the winter snow would be gone in three weeks or so, making such an investigation possible. Scheduling the investigation at the first possible opportunity after winter's conclusion had given it a very high priority.

The implications of a burial grounds accusation were significant. If proven correct, the land involved could be transferred back to the local tribe for jurisdiction and management. He would not only lose control, but could ultimately lose ownership and rights. While sacred burial grounds legislation varied from state to state, it ultimately represented one of the strongest land control powers of Native American tribes throughout the United States. He knew the tribes functioned as sovereign nations with separate and often conflicting treaties and rights with both state and federal government jurisdiction.

Letting the issue sit for a few days didn't really clear anything up. And when he called Agent Lynch on Monday morning, Alex was ready to go to war over what really caused the action.

"Good morning, Agent Lynch. My name is Alex Minor, and I'm calling to find out about this ridiculous notification I received last Thursday." Alex's adrenaline injected high octane into his tone. Several pumps of his heart passed before Agent Lynch replied.

"We try not to send out ridiculous notifications, Mr. Minor. Can you tell me what you're referring to?"

"You know damn well what I'm talking about. How many sacred burial grounds notifications do you send out?"

"I can assure you, Mr. Minor, that our notification is in full compliance with the Native American Sacred Burial Grounds Act, and it is not being done with a facetious or trivial intent."

"How could that be?" Alex said. "This property has undergone the most stringent tests for title contamination and has proven to be clean from any reference to Indian origin. The title documentation has been approved and placed into record at the county courthouse. In fact, the title has been ensured to be free of any Indian *cloud* relating to ownership. You'll find, Agent Lynch, that this can all be verified through your National Archives in Aberdeen."

Agent Lynch knew that all properties that change hands in Indian reservation areas are routinely reviewed for Indian *clouds,* that is, something in the history of the property that would put into question the legitimate title of the current owner. The truth is that many past underhanded activities took place to legally move the deeds of properties away from Indian ownership. Generally, the local Indian agent was the one having direct or indirect involvement. Knowledge of the government system, coupled with the ability to read and write, provided an agent with the unusual authority and power to get away with anything. For years nobody in the government system really cared enough about the corruption, and there were plenty of people of means willing to buy these lands.

Agent Lynch listened, but she was quickly irritated by Alex's pushy manner. "If you think you're going to accomplish anything by calling this office and insulting the people who work here, you're wrong, Mr. Minor." She had heard it all before, so she wasn't unsympathetic to his plea. But she wasn't going to put up with his rude behavior, either.

"Listen, Mr. Minor, this request for investigation has the full approval of the Secretary of the Interior. I'm not going to dispense with our responsibilities just because you're upset. All of your questions will be addressed during our investigation later this month. So, if you'll just be patient . . ."

"Patient! You may have all the time in the world, but I don't. I've got plans for this property and they have to go forward."

"Your plans are going to have to include our department now, Mr. Minor. There's nothing more I can do today. We will confirm our exact arrival date with you in a few weeks."

Alex's rudeness had eliminated any opportunity for Agent Lynch to reconsider. His phone call had done nothing other than to increase his blood pressure. Their discussion never made any real progress. He didn't know the origin of the investigation, the purpose of the investigation, or how long the investigation would last.

* * *

Alex pounded the steering wheel of his truck repeatedly during the five-minute drive to Jake's. He had reached his limit; complete frustration consumed him.

"Now take it easy," Jake said, "and start from the beginning." It was obvious that Alex was furious about something.

After patiently listening to his monologue about government inefficiencies and "bullshit bureaucrats," Jake finally understood what was happening. He also realized that Alex was not the person to be dealing directly with these people.

"Alex, you gotta listen to me. You're just going to piss these people off, big-time, if you keep blasting them in every conversation. From what you said, I don't think you're going to stop this investigation. But tell me, don't you have a law firm somewhere in the brewery business that can let these people know that you're serious as well?"

Alex confirmed the existence of such a law firm in Chicago and agreed that its direct communication with the Department of the Interior would be useful. Stenway Brewing had had several past encounters with government officials on their landholdings. Privately, however, he hated to involve them because he knew it would mean others in the family would become aware of his dilemma. He wanted a success, not another blotch on his record.

"Do you have any idea who this is that the notification was copied to?" Jake asked offhandedly.

"What do you mean?"

"Well, look here," he said as he directed Alex's attention to the bottom of the letter. Sure enough, there was a "McMillan, Larsen & Wingfoot," with no other identification.

"I guess I was so fired up I never noticed. What do you think it means?"

"I'm not sure, but it seems someone else is interested in this investigation, too. Sounds like a law firm, or maybe an accounting firm. Yes, come to think of it, that's exactly what it is. I do remember Big Lights' making a comment when I arrived, referencing a new accounting firm the tribe engaged. I'm sure this is the firm's name."

"This is complete lunacy."

"It might be a good idea if I call this Donna person to try to patch things over. I can present myself as a concerned neighbor and maybe find out a few more details. You know, like, what the origin of this investigation is, and what McMillan, Larsen & Wingfoot's interests are in this matter . . . stuff like that."

"Give it a shot, but I'm not sure they'll even take your phone call after the damage I caused."

thirty-three

FOR ALL PRACTICAL purposes, Big Lights had lived at the Bemidji Hospital since Linda's attack. Even though he was in the way most of the time, the staff couldn't help developing a liking for him.

All of his life, Big Lights had rolled spontaneously with the motion of general events. His need for freedom never allowed for a permanent friendship, female-wise that is. Just when a relationship would start to turn serious, Big Lights was off to another "emergency." These emergencies included construction jobs all over the state of Minnesota, opening-day fishing trips in the spring, Indian powwows throughout the Midwest during the summer, all sorts of hunting trips in the fall, and the occasional drinking binge to fill the time in between.

All in all, Big Lights was one fun-loving guy, a party waiting to happen and tough to nail down if that was your intention. Most of the local ladies had given up, despite his good looks and his genuinely likable personality.

Big Lights had surprised himself with his attachment to Linda Smith. Originally he attributed his enthusiasm to the Omaha Project and the opportunity to contribute to the community. Granted, opportunities like this were rare, but he began to respond for a different reason. He really liked Linda. Everything about her attracted him. He'd even backed off on his drinking over the last few months, not so much on purpose—it just happened.

He kept his feelings to himself, however. One of the reasons was her continual state of vulnerability ever since he had met her in Duluth. The fact that she was about fifteen years younger than him only further convinced Big Lights that he would be taking advantage of her situation. He remembered Helen's comment about Bobby and Michelle, and their age gap wasn't nearly that of his and Linda's. Last, he respected Jake a lot, and he wasn't sure Jake would approve either, which is why he'd been planning to talk first with him about Linda the week the attack took place. None of this mattered now.

Since Linda's attack, Big Lights had been unable to control his need to be by her side at the hospital. Initially the hospital staff objected. He wasn't a relative, and as far as they could see, his presence was unauthorized. Consequently he sat for days in the intensive care waiting room.

Over time, however, Big Lights convinced the nursing staff of his importance to Linda and hers to him. After all, she had no relatives and very few visitors. He told the nurses he and Linda were close working associates and very close friends, not engaged or anything, but close enough to imply commitment between them.

They had never even been on a date, or in fact, had never even talked about a date. But this wasn't important now. Big Lights knew Linda needed his help. He mentally pictured her coma as a disaster within her control. If she felt an instinct to stay alive, she would. If she didn't, she would let go.

"I know you can hear me, Linda. Stay with it and you'll be okay. I've fallen in love with you and I've got to tell you. Please, please hang in there!" He needed to express his feelings out loud to her, whether she could actually hear him or not.

He talked to her virtually nonstop over the weeks in the hospital, never showing any hint of giving up. The staff developed a deep admiration for his determination and devotion. In time, they treated him differently and provided him the information and privileges of a relative. As a result, he knew her condition hourly. It was fragile. While there was no permanent structural damage, the broken cheek and jawbone would take months to heal. More critically, though, her vital signs were not good and the coma continued its hold over her. She remained on life support—an insurance policy against the likely risk of heart failure.

Big Lights held her hand, rubbed her arms, and talked to her for three weeks.

During the coma, Linda's brain was a firestorm of missed electrical connections, like a Fourth of July celebration out of control. At times the explosions were so strong her system could hardly stand the strain. Muscles would lock up and twitch irregularly as her body reacted uncontrollably to the nightmare.

Barely responding to the essential nutrient supplements keeping her alive, Linda's body grew weaker. The brutal destruction in her brain continued its course. She remained unaware of the events and the battle taking place.

It was during one of these seizures when Linda's mind went calm. Her consciousness was drawn toward the peacefulness of a white light. For the first time, her subconscious made its presence felt, and the firestorm disappeared. There was no more twitching or muscle spasms, and to Big Lights, her face held the peaceful appearance of a celestial spirit.

"Linda, Linda, Linda," Big Lights called loudly. "C'mon, sweetheart. Don't give up on me now!" Over and over and over he called, pleading with her to wake up.

The nurses who had witnessed his commitment for weeks privately hoped for a miracle. Technically it could happen, too. Her vital signs had improved a bit and a breakthrough was possible. Their fear, which Big Lights could never accept regardless of their advice, was the likelihood of severe and permanent brain damage. To what extent was impossible to predict. Time continued to be the relentless enemy, though, as full recovery became less and less likely.

That morning his miracle came—with no more fanfare than the passing of a moment, Linda opened her eyes.

She had no recollection of where she was or how she got there. Her eyes scanned the surroundings. She looked at this man who had been yelling her name and wondered who he was. Why was he there? Did she know him? The tears in his eyes and the look of joy on his face would certainly indicate that he knew her. She looked at him but said nothing.

"Linda, Linda," this person said. "Talk to me. Are you okay?"

She was sure she could talk but wasn't at all sure what to say. Trying very hard to collect her thoughts, she realized that she had no idea as to why she wouldn't be okay. But she knew she was definitely in a hospital.

"What am I doing here?" she said quietly.

"Thank God you're okay," he responded joyfully.

"Everyone has been so worried and now you're okay. This is just fantastic!" Her voice was a wonderful sound to Big Lights. The celebration of her recovery was captured in his broad grin.

Without taking a breath, he took her hand, looked into her eyes, and said, "Linda, I waited too long, and I'm not waiting anymore. I love you, and I want to be with you forever. I know you may be surprised by this, and maybe I'm not the perfect man, but whatever my shortcomings, I promise you today that I will work very hard to fix them in order to be with you."

"Linda," he said, his voice trembling, "Will you marry me?"

Stunned, she said hesitantly, "But, but, I don't know who you are."

The expression on his face collapsed. Inexplicably, this scruffy man, long overdue for a shower, had just proposed. And she didn't know who he was.

Not knowing what to do, Big Lights just sat there, holding her hand quietly and lightly stroking her forehead with the other hand.

"Well now, it looks as if our sleeping beauty is back," the doctor said, walking into the room.

"Doc, she doesn't seem to remember much of anything. In fact, she doesn't remember anything at all."

As one of Linda's permanently assigned nurses walked into the room, the doctor responded to Big Lights, "Why don't you give us some time with Linda, and we'll check everything out. It's not uncommon for some amnesia to be present, and under the circumstances, I'm not surprised. We'll give you a call when we're done." He motioned for the nurse to assist Big Lights to the waiting room.

To Big Lights, the waiting was pure torture. It twisted his insides. His incessant pacing of the tiled floor manifested his deep anxiety. Time continued to be his master, and he was not a loyal servant.

Consumed and preoccupied, Big Lights didn't notice Bobby and Michelle walking down the hospital corridor toward him. Frequently they stopped by to visit Linda on their way back to Chippewa Lake from their classes at BSU. Other than Jake, they were the only other consistent visitors.

Big Lights' agitated behavior was a clear signal that something was up. Their hopefulness shifted to real concern when he explained what had happened.

Frustration continued to build in Big Lights during this exchange, but as it did, a new emotion began to take over. "You can count on one thing for goddamn sure, when this whole mess is over. Whoever did this to Linda is going to pay, and I mean pay with their ass. It's not fair that this scumbag goes unpunished. Betts isn't going to let this one get away, goddamn it. I'll drag the son-of-a-bitch in myself." Big Lights' anger erupted with a punch at the wall with his fist.

"You're right. This jerk needs to pay," Bobby said as his emotions merged with Big Lights'.

"I can't wait until her memory is back and she can ID this freak," Michelle added, hugging Big Lights in support. Tears of anger and hurt filled her eyes.

The trio soon learned that the complete story would not be forthcoming, at least not in the near future. The doctor emerged from Linda's room to deliver a firsthand report. He respected their loyalty to Linda. When this ordeal had run its full course, the doctor said it would be friends like them who would get Linda back on the road to recovery. Their knowledge of her condition would be an asset in providing the care needed.

"The news I have to give on her condition is distressing. While her physical recovery will be acceptable, and I expect her to be back to normal within six weeks, her recovery from the amnesia is not so positive. At this stage we'll have to do a series of tests, but you need to know that a reversal to full memory sometimes never happens.

"It will take a while to determine whether we're dealing with the physical damage to her brain or the emotional scars from her ordeal, or both." His voice softened as he looked directly at Big Lights and said, "I'm sorry, but we'll just have to take this one day at a time."

Big Lights felt the emotions stemming from Linda's coma recovery, his spontaneous proposal of marriage, the bile of contempt he felt for the scum who did this, and the disappointing news of her future recovery pull him into darkness. His shoulders fell and his tired face drooped with obvious despair.

Bobby put his hand on his friend's arm. "Let's go grab a beer and some decent food, buddy. We're in this with you all the way, but it's going to take some time."

thirty-four

JAKE GAVE HIMSELF a few days after his discussion with Alex to consider his approach in calling the Department of the Interior about the notification. Since he wasn't the owner, his call could easily be dismissed before he was even connected with Agent Lynch.

He decided to take the helpful approach, knowing that most government workers responded positively to available information that would simplify the task at hand. He would present himself as a friend and neighbor of Alex Minor's, someone knowledgeable about the peninsula. He wanted to establish himself as a resource, one that would be easier to deal with in keeping discussions on a businesslike basis.

Donna's administrative assistant answered Jake's phone call and listened to his request to speak with the agent. She put Jake on hold and relayed his interest to Donna.

"If that's Alex Minor on the phone, take a message," Donna responded with a *don't even think about it* tone in her voice.

The assistant indicated it wasn't Mr. Minor, but a Mr. Lorenz. "He seems very nice and willing to help with information relating to the survey."

Donna was skeptical. However, she knew that cooperative contacts in the local community could make these investigations go much easier. She decided to take the call.

"This is Agent Lynch, Mr. Lorenz. How may I help you?"

Jake immediately communicated his knowledge of her previous discussion with Alex and said, "I don't know how to put this any other way, other than to say that Alex can be a real pain in the butt to work with sometimes. I apologize on his behalf. My purpose in calling is to see how we can start over and cooperate with your efforts.

"Besides," he said lightheartedly, "We tend to take a more neighborly approach than Alex probably let on. I don't want you to think we're part of some radical militia."

"That's refreshing to hear," she said, reflecting on her personal experience where fair resolutions to disputes had been facilitated by a cooperative third party.

They spent over forty-five minutes on the phone, talking about the background of the investigation and the ambiguous nature of the decision process regarding Native American rights. While it was unclear as to how the claim evolved, it was clear that the Big Bear Lake Ojibwe Reservation Tribal Council had instigated the investigation and was convinced there were several burial sites on the land parcels.

"These investigations are never what they appear, Mr. Lorenz. My team is responsible for validating the claim and uncovering the surrounding circumstances of the claim and counterclaims. It's never easy. And I can tell you one thing, the truth is sometimes hard to find."

She went on to explain that the burden of proof was on the local tribe, yet the validity of the evidence uncovered would be primarily judged by their available tribal experts.

"I'll admit that this can be a real catch-22 for the landowner if the tribal motivations are not of the highest integrity. The vast majority of times, however, the dispute is resolved quickly with no damage to either party."

While her comments were informative and helpful to Jake, they didn't really put his mind at ease. Donna seemed a very likable person committed to doing her job responsibly. On the other hand, the process of the investigation was very nebulous. How had the request escalated to a full investigation? Why had this investigation received such an urgent priority? These were just a few of the questions needing more answers. Donna was being very cooperative, but clearly the decision process went well beyond her control.

During their discussion, Jake explained that his property bordered a considerable portion of Alex's and that property lines get very confusing without a survey and the right equipment or a firsthand understanding of the land.

"You know, Donna, it might be useful for me to help out as a local property guide of sorts when you get here. It would probably save you a bunch of time. And if you'd like, I could also be an outlet for communications with Alex Minor, if necessary."

"That would be helpful, Mr. Lorenz, although we will come fully prepared equipment-wise. We have done a few of these investigations before. I will take you up on your offer, however, as long as Mr. Minor consents. It's his property we're investigating."

"It's my guess he'll agree completely. He realizes he's off to a bad start. And if you don't mind, please call me Jake."

"Alright, I will. I'll give you a call when I arrive, Jake. My plans put me in Chippewa Lake a day or two before the investigation team arrives and the real work begins."

"I'll wait for your call."

He also suggested staying at the Cedar Lodge and Fishing Resort owned by Tom and Cheryl, explaining that there wasn't much in Chippewa Lake other than a rundown motel on the highway. Tom's cabins were clean and much closer to the property and besides, they weren't rented on an hourly basis as those out on the highway.

"Thanks. One of the perks of being an agent doing site investigations on various reservations is the choice of lovely accommodations." They both laughed.

"I must tell you, Jake, that I was reluctant to take this call when my assistant told me it was about Arrowhead Peninsula. It's not our intent to make things difficult for taxpayers, so when Mr. Minor reacted as he did, my guard went up." She thanked him for his cooperation and promised to call immediately on her arrival.

"One last thing, Donna, if you don't mind."

"Not at all."

"I noticed that a copy of the notification was sent to McMillan, Larsen & Wingfoot. I am aware of their accounting firm relationship with the local tribe, but curious as to their role in the investigation. Would you mind . . . ?"

"Not at all. As you accurately stated, they are the accounting firm of record for the Big Bear Lake Tribe. You may not know, however, that they represent the entire Ojibwe Nation as well. I believe the firm is located in Wisconsin. I can't give you all the details because I'm not sure I have them all myself. But what I can say is that they have taken only a passive fiduciary interest in this investigation at this point. It may be of interest to you to know also that James Wingfoot, one of the firm's partners, is Sam Aguire's nephew. James is also a commissioner on the National Indian Gaming Commission—very influential, to say the least."

"Wow."

"Do you know Mr. Aquire? He's one of the board members of the Big Bear Lake Reservation Tribal Council."

"Yes, I've met Sam Aguire, and Chase Leonard as well. Their reputation among the local Indians is one of being very heavy-handed."

"Well, regardless of their local reputations, they seem to have considerable clout through James Wingfoot, leading right up to Mr. Barnhart's office. He's the Secretary of the Interior and my ultimate boss."

"That's a lot of visibility for one investigation. We'll try to help you keep your job," Jake replied with a smile in his voice.

She laughed. "You really are helpful."

Once off the phone, Jake's expression indicated welcome surprise. Donna Lynch was not only bright, but competent and cooperative as well. She sounded like someone he would ordinarily like to meet.

Within minutes, Jake was on the phone with Alex relating the details of their conversation. After summarizing the facts, Jake concluded, "Alex, your temper is going to be a problem if you can't curb it. These people are just doing their job. It won't do any good making enemies of them. Treat 'em like human beings, and they may act reasonably in return."

He and Alex agreed to look for an opportunity for Alex to turn on some charm in an attempt to mend fences with Donna.

"You're right, I'll give it a rest. But I still don't like the way this is shaping up. This connection of Sam's to the Department of the Interior is too convenient. Plus, I just got the results of my background check on Sam, and the bastard's as clean as a whistle. Coming from his circumstances to where he is today, I don't buy it for one minute. I may have been born at night, but not last night."

"Just remember one thing, her group may become the allies we need," Jake said, reinforcing one more time Alex's need for civility with the Department of the Interior people.

He also knew that Alex was uptight about the lack of response from the promised Chicago analysis of the spruce pitch, dandelion oil, and work gloves. So he decided to change topics, for Alex's sake. Alex's need to control events made him a poor partner when waiting was a required ingredient.

Jake gave Alex the update on Linda's condition since he knew Alex would never think to ask himself. He also shared his continued concern that there may be a connection between the cemetery, the unidentified driver, and her attack. He conjectured that when the attacker was discovered, the connection would become clear. In any event, the violence might also be related to Two Fingers' murder, Linda's break-in, and Linda's attack. If, in fact, this was the case, the prognosis for more violence was very high. Extreme caution was necessary.

They reconfirmed their agreement to hold off on any actions until the report from Chicago arrived.

part 3

thirty-five

Time flew between Jake's first call to Donna Lynch and the arrival of the investigation team. They had arranged a first meeting, as Donna promised, and agreed to have dinner together at the Lodge Pole Supper Club at 5:30 p.m. Jake felt that the choice of the club would help, in a small way, to make a good first impression, as it was the only decent restaurant in the area.

The one important matter to be accomplished by Alex and him over the past few weeks, however, was the final receipt of the Chicago analysis, and important results they were. The two concoctions Jake found in the cemetery shed matched exactly the black spruce pitch and dandelion oil mixtures discovered in the fabric of the gloves found on Alex's property earlier. Also, since there was a small bloodstain in the second pair of gloves found in the shed, a DNA test was ordered. The blood belonged to Two Fingers. While this wasn't a surprise to Jake and Alex, it was important. The combination of the oil and pitch match with the two sets of gloves gave Alex and Jake positive evidence linking Two Fingers and Sam to the cemetery and the activities on Arrowhead. Elusive thoughts linking these men to a conspiracy of some sort entered both men's minds.

While waiting for Agent Lynch, Jake turned this information in his mind, as he had many times already. He had arrived a little early at the Lodge Pole, since he didn't want his guest to be kept waiting. A table reservation really wasn't necessary, but he did want to have a private setting that would allow them to talk. The booth in the corner with a view of the frozen lake met his needs perfectly.

*   *   *

At precisely 5:30, what looked to be a Ford Taurus rental car pulled into the parking lot. From the lobby, Jake could see a casually dressed woman walking toward the restaurant. Jake admired punctuality and her timeliness impressed him.

He remained at the hostess check-in station to greet Donna. Her attractive and confident demeanor immediately struck Jake when she entered. She was in her mid-to-late thirties, about five feet six inches tall with dark, wedge-styled hair. Even with her ski jacket on, he could see that she was well proportioned and in excellent physical shape.

"You must be Jake Lorenz," she said, anticipating his introduction. Her pleasant smile and forward approach caught him a little off-guard. His thought pattern actually went blank for an instant. Maybe it was because he hadn't been around an attractive woman in a while. But he held his smile for a moment longer and gathered himself before answering.

"Yes," he answered with a slight catch in his voice. "I am. I'm glad to meet you, Agent Lynch." He surprised himself with his sudden nervousness. He hoped she hadn't noticed.

As they walked toward the corner of the restaurant, Jake couldn't help being aware of her striking figure. He fought to get his mind back on track while sliding onto the bench seat.

"Well, Agent Lynch, where should we begin?"

"Probably by calling me Donna; that is, if you don't mind."

"Donna it is."

They filled each other in with a sketch of their personal backgrounds, finding some similarities. He grew up in a suburb of Minneapolis and she in a suburb of Cleveland. Both had been raised in college-educated families and had earned college degrees themselves. His was in computer sciences from the University of Minnesota. Her undergraduate degree in forestry was from Michigan State University. She also had a doctorate in history, specializing in Native American cultures, from the University of Wisconsin. Neither had immediate families. Jake had lost Jan in the automobile accident, and Donna's husband, Ed Lynch, had died two years earlier of an early stroke at age thirty-eight.

Since she and Ed had gone to college together, Jake estimated that she was about thirty-eight to forty, privately noting that her age would be hard to guess without the facts. Her skin was unusually smooth, despite a job requiring considerable time outdoors. Jake quickly concluded that her green eyes were the immediate focal point of her personality and attractiveness. They were almost shamrock and offset her natural tan like emeralds. He wasn't sure where the business discussion would take them, but he knew he would enjoy being around her.

"You know, Donna, Alex wanted to join us for dinner tonight in the worst kind of way. He feels bad about being aggressive and rude on the phone and is anxious to make it up to you. I suggested that he go slow and let me do the honors tonight. I hope that's okay."

"Good choice. He does have some repair work to do, but I'm not ready for it tonight after traveling all day."

While they ate their salads, Jake filled Donna in about the Stenway family history and Alex's plans for his property. He asked that she keep this information to herself as it had been only recently communicated to him in trust. At the same time, he also displayed his personal disapproval of the commercialization plans for the land.

"The Arrowhead Peninsula is as beautiful as any natural setting I've ever seen," he said. "It doesn't seem right for it to go the way of the bulldozer and resort. I think you'll agree when you see it tomorrow."

"I am anxious to see it. I was on Big Bear some years ago and remember it as being pretty special. I don't recall seeing the part of the lake where the peninsula is located, though."

"My guess is that you already noticed the peninsula's isolation on your maps. The intermingling of national-forest land, the Indian reservation, and segments of privately held property keeps our little part of the world pretty much to ourselves, the way the locals like it."

"I'll bet."

"Alex is pretty bent on changing all that with his development. I don't think it will go over well. It's a private matter at this stage, though, so I haven't made my feelings public. I think he's going to get more local resistance than he's bargaining for."

"It must be hard to work with him, having such different points of view."

Jake shrugged, "Somehow I got elected."

"Mr. Minor already pressed his case with me over the phone on this exact matter. It seems like he's in a real rush."

"Well, in his defense, he is getting on in years and doesn't have much runway left, as they say. I think he sees this project as a personal statement. You know, a feather of achievement of some sort. I do know he considers it very important."

Despite Jake's disapproval of the project he did his best to represent Alex 's thinking fairly. Donna nodded and raised her eyebrows, passively accepting his explanation.

"What do you think we're in for here? I mean, with all the investigations you've done over the years, wouldn't it be fair to say that you must have some general feel for the outcome?"

"That's an interesting observation, Jake. Normally I could make an assessment, but this one is different. It's not unusual to uncover an occasional burial site for a variety of reasons, but to uncover various sites within close proximity is unique. Most Native American history has been reasonably documented, and to miss a sacred burial ground would be unusual, to say the least. But there are some compelling circumstances that make this area of Big Bear Lake a good bet for a possible surprise," she said.

As she shifted gears in her conversation, Donna no longer seemed like the visitor who had just arrived. She took control of the conversation, describing the investigation process and indicating the need and appreciation for cooperative relationships during the process. It was easy to see that she meant business. Jake admired her assertive character and, almost subconsciously, noted a similarity to Jan.

It was still early evening when they finished their meal and ordered coffee.

"You know, Donna, if you're not in a hurry, I'd love to hear more about the background to this project." Jake saw it as an opportunity to learn something interesting about the peninsula—besides, he was enjoying her company.

"That's fine with me, but I'll warn you that I can go overboard on this stuff."

"Don't worry."

"Well, to start with, you're probably aware that the Arrowhead Peninsula has considerable history for the Ojibwe tribes. I'll try to make my point quickly, but I do need to lay an important foundation first.

"As you may know, this part of Minnesota played a significant role in fur-trading in the 1700s and 1800s. Even before that, however, Indian activity was widespread, back to what was called the *Muk-ud-a-shib* or Black Duck culture. It was the earliest record of the Ojibwe totemic system. Since that time, there have been fifteen to twenty recorded Indian families or tribes, each claiming a separate badge representing the different family totems. The badge is important as each family is represented differently in the afterlife. Consequently, the artifacts buried with the body will tell a story of what family that person represented. Consistency with the badge is critical."

She sipped her coffee, creating an opportunity for questions. Jake wasn't ready yet, so she continued.

"During the early 1700s, however, the tribal families of the Ojibwe were driven from their homelands by the Dakota Sioux because of the fertile hunting grounds. The growing demand for beaver hats in England and the plentiful supply of beaver in this wilderness area made life for the Indian tribes very dangerous. The Dakota Sioux were powerful and had strong relations with the early traders, so the Ojibwe were temporarily pushed out. My point here is that there has been constant tribal activity and wars for hundreds of years here. From the standpoint of our investigation, this means one thing—plenty of opportunity for burial sites."

Jake's elbows were on the table, with his body leaning forward and his eyes closely following every one of Donna's facial expressions.

"Most significant about this history is the period from the early 1700s to the early 1800s in what was referred to as the 100 Years War. The battles between the Dakota Sioux and Ojibwe were brutal and nonstop, with the Ojibwe ultimately winning. Their success came down to two elements: good leadership in the person of *Esh-ke-bog-e-coshe*, or Flat Mouth, as he was known by the whiteface, and good strategy by aligning with the United States. With the Northwest Angle established as the northern border between Canada and the United States at Lake of the Woods, the American Fur Trading Company ultimately took fur-trading control from the Northwest Trading Company. The trading company's mutual bond with Flat Mouth and the Ojibwe was strong, and the business relationship prospered. As the leader of the Ojibwe Pillager Band with central headquarters on Sandy Lake and Big Bear Lake, Flat Mouth was looked upon as the chief among chiefs. During his thirty-year leadership, he drove the Dakota Sioux from the Ojibwe ancestral hunting grounds forever. You might find it interesting, Jake, to know that he is one of only three Indian chiefs in the United States to have his likeness, in the form of a bust, displayed in Congress in Washington, D.C."

"I had no idea."

"Are you sure I'm not putting you to sleep?"

"I gotta tell you, I love this stuff. Please, go on. This is absolutely fascinating." Jake reacted much as a schoolboy fawning over a favorite teacher's lesson. He was also hoping, for Alex's sake, to see if she would soon make a specific connection to their situation.

As if on cue, Donna said, "All of this does have a point. It is believed that the headquarters' post of the American Fur Trading Company was located on Arrowhead Peninsula, most likely on Mr. Minor's property. The trading company's underground foundation may even be the very same as the Stenway Lodge foundation—the one built in the late 1800s.

"You might want to brace yourself for the final chapter, though," she said in an empathetic tone.

Jake could already see how her brief and exquisite history related to the investigation. It was coming very close to home. Yet in his wildest dreams he could not have predicted the final link to the story.

"For thirty years," she continued, "the main village of Flat Mouth was located within one mile of that American Fur Trading Company post."

Jake's mouth dropped. "You mean . . ."

"Yes, the original village location may be on either Mr. Minor's land or yours."

"This doesn't make any sense," Jake said, thinking that the pieces didn't seem to fit all of a sudden. "A village of that size would certainly be commemorated in Indian history and never have been turned over to outsiders."

"True enough, except for one fact. Once the true flowage of the Mississippi River was determined not to go through Big Bear Lake and the beaver trade disappeared, alternatives for managing the lake waters opened up. One of those was the dam on the Sugar River built in 1884 to facilitate the vast amount of timber cuts that needed to get downriver to Stillwater. The logging demand was insatiable and the supply in this area was immense. When the dam was turned on, the level of Big Bear Lake rose seven to ten feet. The Indian village, which was most certainly located on the shoreline to avoid the mosquitoes and black flies, would have been buried underwater."

Jake looked at Donna with disbelief, unable to say anything, realizing the possible consequence to his property. He had never really questioned the existence of the small dam on the other side of the lake, believing it had "always been there." Now he knew differently.

Shifting in his chair and taking a drink of his coffee gave him a moment to think.

"What can we possibly hope for?"

"Well, for one thing, that the burial grounds are located somewhere else. And for another, that the placement of the village is in error."

"How could that be?"

"Well, even though the two prominent explorers at that time, Zebulon Pike and Henry Schoolcraft, both identified the village near the American Fur Trading Company post location, the post itself has never been found. Without the trading post location, the village has been hard to pinpoint. The good news for American history is that this investigation may solve that riddle. If it does, Jake, I'm sorry that I'll have to be the one to break the bad news. You obviously care about this land very much, but if the premise of the investigation is proven, the land will surely fall within the rightful claim of the Big Bear Lake Reservation."

"Unbelievable."

For a few moments they both just sat there. It was now 9 o'clock, and the Supper Club was closing. As they got up to leave, Jake thanked Donna for devoting so much time and for buying him dinner.

"It's the least your government can do."

"I'll see you back to Cedar Lodge if you'd like," he said as they walked across the parking lot.

"No, that'll be okay. I can find my way."

"We are going to start work at 9 in the morning the day after tomorrow with a meeting with Mr. Minor if you'd like to join us. In fact, we would appreciate it if you would."

"You can count on it," he replied with obvious anticipation.

thirty-six

JAKE ARRIVED AT Alex's about half an hour before the investigation team. This gave him time to brief Alex on his dinner with Agent Lynch the evening before last, and what to expect from her today.

"She's smart, competent, and nobody's fool. You may not want to hear this, but I think our best course of action is to cooperate completely. There's so much historical evidence against us that our only hope will be to make sure the facts of the investigation are valid, and that they truly do match up with the theory presented. We have to count on her professionalism and sense of fairness to ensure both arguments are heard."

"What do you mean, historical evidence? Hell, our family's owned this property for over a hundred years, and that's a proven fact."

"I'm afraid that this tribal claim will take us back a lot further than that," Jake said as he gave Alex the abridged version of Donna's history lesson. "The net result is that they're going to be real interested in the old lodge. It seems to be at the heart of their theory."

"What do you mean?"

"Has anyone ever suggested that the old lodge sits on top of the American Fur Trading Company foundation?"

"I remember something like that when I was a kid. It was just talk, though."

"Well, I think you're going to actually find out whether it was talk or not. She seems to think the theory has merit."

As Alex and Jake talked over coffee in the large kitchen, Leo and King started to make a racket outside barking. They could hear the dogs coming down the entire distance of the winding driveway, about three hundred yards, as they followed two cars onto the property.

Alex promised to be at his best and, in doing so, he was quick to heel the dogs and chain them to a wire-running line out of the way.

Jake was surprised to see five people pile out of the cars. It hadn't occurred to him to ask the size of the team, but their number immediately established a sense of purpose.

After pleasantries were exchanged, Jake formally introduced Alex and Donna. Then Donna made the introductions of her team. Despite Alex's age, he generated a strong first impression. His physical appearance and self-confidence were striking. All those years in the boardroom were not lost when it came to creating a stage and being in charge. This was easily accomplished with a handshake, steady eye contact, and a warm greeting.

"Good morning, Agent Lynch. It seems as if your team has chosen an exceptional day on our peninsula to begin our work together."

"We have at that," said Donna. "I must say that in all of my travels in Minnesota I've never seen beauty as unique as your peninsula. If it weren't for the elevation differences, Eagle Feather Bay would strongly resemble Emerald Bay on Lake Tahoe. Your position on the peninsula, however, adds a dimension that Emerald Bay could never achieve."

Jake enjoyed observing the skill each person used in jockeying for position. Always focusing on control, Alex had chosen a brief comment directly establishing his ownership to "our" peninsula, yet deferred to Donna's authority by using the phrase "working together."

Donna, on the other hand, chose an approach that leveraged her charm and knowledge. Within her comments on the peninsula was the subtle implication that her expertise was not accidental or limited.

She had guessed right in assuming that Jake had briefed Alex on their dinner conversation.

If nothing else, Jake thought, this investigation was absolutely going to be worth the price of admission.

"Why don't we go inside the lodge where we can talk about what you're going to need," said Alex. "Afterward I'll give you and your team a complete introduction to the property."

"Fair enough," Donna said, keeping pace with Alex step for step.

* * *

Inside, after everyone's coffee mug was filled, Alex began a tour of the lodge.

"This building was essentially the party house back when business relations were maintained on a simpler basis. When I was here as a young boy, Stenway customers would be invited for extended stays. They must have worked very hard while they were here since they always brought their secretarial staff along," he said with mock seriousness, which raised a smile from the male members of the team.

"No disrespect intended, of course. I was too young to know what was really going on," he said, directing the comment to Donna.

"None taken."

As they toured the lodge, it was easy for the guests to visualize what Alex had meant by a "party house." The large entertainment area and the many bedrooms upstairs could accommodate various guests. But more important, it was evident that this building was a piece of American history and their tour a special opportunity. Alex finished the tour at the opposite end of the lodge, where a large conference-style table dominated a comfortable meeting area.

After everyone was seated, Alex continued, "Jake and I respect the importance of this investigation, and we recognize that it may involve both of our properties, although sheer magnitude makes mine the focus now. I know you will respect our need for an expeditious process. And," directing his comment to the team members, "I am hopeful that Agent Lynch has informed you that we do have business plans for the property later this spring. In the meantime, we will support and cooperate with your efforts in any way possible to move the investigation along."

During Alex's prologue, Donna reflected on the value of Jake's involvement. With Alex's immense wealth and power, this investigation could literally take years if he chose to make it difficult. She hoped she hadn't overestimated Jake's forthright nature as a facilitator of coming events. He had made a good first impression and she didn't want to see him get hurt.

Donna took Alex's concluding remarks as her cue to begin a review of the process her team would undertake during the investigation. She outlined the approach on a flip chart.

"We've discussed this project between us, prior to arriving, and decided on the following steps. I'll review them in order of priority. Please ask questions at any time." She wasted no time taking control of the discussion.

"First, we'd like to take you up on your offer for a general overview of the property. We plan to survey and mark the boundaries, as well, for clarity. While this is being completed, we will begin our examination of the exterior foundation of the old lodge—weather permitting, we'll start tomorrow. I'm sure Jake has informed you of its importance."

Alex nodded.

"The day after tomorrow we will conduct a joint review of the Reservation Tribal Council evidence. Our focus will be solely on the point of view presented by Mr. Chase and Mr. Aguire. You're welcome to participate, Mr. Minor, but I'll understand if you don't.

"Based on the tribe's preliminary report, we believe that several sites will be identified for sono-probe focus. This is an archaeologist's device using echo-sounding waves to discover objects in sedimentary layers. Whether or not we find what we're looking for will determine if we proceed to the next step, which would involve selective excavation."

"What you're looking for is corpses, I presume?" Alex asked.

"That's right."

"Will it be limited to just human remains, or is this sono-probe just an excuse for a fishing expedition?"

"As you suggested, Mr. Minor, time is of the essence. If you don't mind, we will limit our discovery work to human remains only, as you say. Without them, there is no evidence to support the sacred burial grounds claim. Are there any other questions?"

"No."

"The investigation will come to a conclusion with a formal public report reviewing our findings. Any actions or recommendations will be clearly stated and based on hard evidence uncovered during the investigation. It's important for you to know, Mr. Minor, that theory alone will not create an obligation on your part."

"I'm happy to hear that."

Donna was not someone who was going to complicate matters. Even Alex admired her for her direct, no-nonsense manner. He recommended that a title search be conducted for both properties, not just his, and she concurred. Privately he and Jake knew it would validate their position and remove any doubt of an Indian cloud over ownership. It also might help minimize a dispute if the evidence discovered was not substantial enough.

"If there are no further questions, I'd like to recommend we begin the general property overview today. Since the snow will make for a difficult walk, we've arranged for our own snowmobiles." Donna pointed outside the meeting room windows as almost on perfect cue, a truck pulled up hauling a trailer loaded with snowmobiles.

"We assume that you have your own. If not, we can double up," Donna said.

Alex wasn't about to put himself in a lesser position and ride in back, even if he hadn't owned his own snowmobile. Jake, however, decided that it would be too much of a delay to go back to the cabin for his and would ride as Alex's passenger.

*　*　*

Once outside, they proceeded to unload the five snowmobiles. The day wasn't cold enough to warrant full jumpsuits, so they were underway, heading down the road in no time at all to begin their inspection of Alex's 375 acres.

By this time the team's thorough preparation was evident, and neither Alex nor Jake was surprised when everyone on the team produced detailed maps of his property. With a lot of ground to cover, Alex was about to suggest a course to follow when Donna interrupted with several questions regarding wetlands, existing ice ridges, and proximity to Jake's land—the result of which changed his recommendation.

In the end, it didn't make much difference to Alex or Jake which route they followed. They exchanged glances, however, acknowledging the full-scale preparation and planning the team had gone through prior to arriving.

"I see what you mean," Alex said quietly to Jake regarding any connection to the bureaucratic incompetence and bungling he may have expected.

March was actually a pretty good time of year to be traveling through the forest. The snow cover was compacted and the lack of foliage allowed for good visibility. Within minutes of starting, they all pointed eagerly in the direction of a twelve-point whitetail buck as it bounded off into more dense cover.

Around noon, Donna stopped the snowmobile caravan and suggested that they take a break for lunch. As the snowmobiles powered down, one of the men opened a large duffel bag filled with sandwiches, energy bars, and drinks.

"It looks like you kept Cheryl and Tom pretty busy this morning," Jake said in a grateful tone.

"I grew up with four brothers and learned a long time ago that if you want their help, you'd better be ready to feed them. Besides, I think Cheryl welcomed my help with the lunches. Tom was happy too. It looked to me like he would be better at filleting a walleye or skinning out a bear than making sandwiches in the kitchen."

Jake laughed. He had personally eaten a few meals prepared by Tom at the resort and she was right; food preparation wasn't his strength. Donna's ability to grasp the essence of a situation was apparent. He privately admired her skill and her easy manner in getting things done.

With about an hour of light remaining, the team pulled up in front of the old lodge built in 1886, the one believed to be located on the original building foundation of the American Fur Trading Company Post. It was situated at the very southern tip of the peninsula, about one thousand yards from the newer lodge Alex lived in. Lake access to this location two hundred years ago, whether via water or ice, would have made it an ideal site for a trading post. Alex offered to take them inside. There wasn't much time left for doing anything meaningful outside.

The old lodge was a three-story structure of virgin timber that had weathered to a dark brown over the years. The two aboveground stories had been living quarters and the five-foot crawl space below ground had served as a fruit, vegetable, and wine cellar.

"This is a superb specimen of white pine functionality. Can you imagine what a home built using today's materials would look like after a hundred years?" Donna speculated.

"That's not a pretty picture," one team member said.

Alex led the group into the lodge through a service door to the kitchen. Except for a microwave and externally mounted electricity fixtures on the walls, nothing had been changed. The two large wood-burning cooking stoves were magnificent. Oil lamps sat on open wooden shelves everywhere, and a large butcher's block was in the center of the room for meal preparation. Around the corner a modern refrigerator had replaced the original icebox.

From the kitchen the team proceeded into an eating area with pine tables and chairs able to accommodate about twenty people. The windows were all beveled glass, with wood-framed screens to match, and styled to swing inward toward the ceiling, where they could be secured by a hook-and-eye latch. The porch dining area was so rustic and appealing with its hand laid hardwood floors, open-beam ceiling construction, and authentic period furniture that they could almost smell the bacon and eggs and see flapjack stacks steaming on tin plates.

They walked slowly through an entryway to the left of the dining area. Jake whispered to Donna, "The next room is truly one of a kind; it's my favorite."

As they entered what one might feebly refer to as a "great room," Jake watched as Donna and the team automatically looked up. The ceiling was about twenty feet high. An elevated, lodge-pole pine catwalk stretched about halfway up on two walls and led to the bedrooms. The central focus of the room was a fieldstone fireplace about twelve feet across at the hearth and tapering the entire twenty feet up though the hand-hewn open-beam ceiling. Two very old trophy mounts, a Boone and Crockett caliber moosehead and an impressive whitetail buck, flanked each side of the fireplace. One could easily picture the musty presence of a Teddy Roosevelt–type figure, smoking a cigar and sipping his brandy, sitting in one of the large, overstuffed, leather armchairs in front of the fireplace. Additional tables, chairs, and couches made for an intimate and comfortable setting for about a dozen people.

Everyone was quiet, just drinking in the atmosphere, when Alex said, "I've been fortunate all my life to be surrounded by nice things. I want you to understand that what you're looking at now and what you've seen today represent for me the happiest and most important part of a pretty crazy life. I'll work with you, but I don't want to lose it."

Donna was smart enough to know that there was no good response to his comment. She also began to understand the potential for a very difficult struggle between Alex and the Ojibwe tribal council. Both sides had major historical ties to this land that would not be given up easily.

The day had been very productive for both groups—each established its boundaries and laid a foundation for future work together. However, there would no doubt be some dicey times ahead.

It was after dark, and everyone was tired and cold by the time they returned to the main lodge. Donna declined Jake's invitation to dinner, saying she needed to prepare for tomorrow, when her team would determine the nature of the old lodge's foundation before meeting with the Regional Tribal Council. If the evidence pointed to a trading post, that would provide the basis for a specific discussion with the tribal council. Without that discovery, however, the burden of proof would become more difficult for the Ojibwe.

Easy, Jake, he scolded himself. There will be plenty of other times for dinner.

Donna's team left tired and slightly unsure of what the next day would bring. Alex's offer to store their snowmobiles in his barn was acknowledged appreciatively. The time and effort saved at the beginning and end of each day loading and unloading would be useful. Jake stayed behind to chat with Alex for a few minutes about the day.

Both agreed that the team was very well prepared and in charge of what they were doing. All in all, there were no real surprises.

"I'd rather work with competent people," Alex said, acknowledging the team's skills.

"I'm glad you see it that way. I was impressed with Donna at dinner. And it looks like her whole team is good."

"That doesn't mean I'm going to let them win on this damn investigation," Alex said.

"I would be disappointed if you did." Jake slipped his jacket on, saying, "I think I'm going to stop over at Helen and Bud's on the way home. She'll have a fit if she doesn't hear things directly from me. Besides, it will help us if she has the real story and doesn't feel the need to make one up."

Alex shook his head in disgust; he considered Helen's gossip tedious.

*   *   *

"So what's for dinner?" Jake piped up when Helen answered the door. His timing was excellent. And Helen always had extras.

"Jake, you old rascal, where have you been? You're the one person who can make my day. Come on in and wash up. We're just about ready to eat."

To his surprise the whole family, plus Bobby, was there. Michelle and Bobby were quite the item now, having dated regularly since the Thanksgiving Day celebration. Michelle's mom and dad had even visited over the Christmas holidays. They met Bobby and, to everyone's relief, liked him very much.

Jake said his hellos to everyone, paying particular attention to Bobby. He'd only met him a few times and wanted to form his own opinion of the young man. After the small talk died down, Bud said, "Well, Jake, you're not getting out of here without giving us a full report on the investigation activities down at Alex's. Do you want to start now or wait until after dinner?"

"Now's fine. Just give me a few breaks for food along the way. There's nothing more important than Helen's meatloaf," he said, giving her a big smile. This was as close to a real family as Jake had, and it felt good to be here.

By 10 P.M., the recounting of the investigation, as well as Jake's first dinner with Donna, was complete.

"If you're sure there aren't any more questions, I'm going to turn in. I'm exhausted and tomorrow will be another busy day. Thanks again, Helen, for the superb meal. I promise to keep you in the loop.

"Good night, everyone," he called out as he opened the door to leave.

thirty-seven

EVERY MEMBER OF the tribal council showed up at the tribal center in Chippewa Lake the following morning, anxious to meet the Department of the Interior investigation team, especially the pretty lady agent. Most members of the council participated minimally while Sam and Chase dominated the discussions. They reconvened at Alex's property in the early afternoon. Sam conducted the snowmobile tour, clearly demonstrating his familiarity with the Stenway estate property. He masterfully orchestrated the route to coincide perfectly with speculation about the presence of burial sites.

Throughout the day, Sam and Chase ignored any opportunity to interact directly with Jake. And at one point, clearly irritated, they raised his presence as an issue with Donna, saying they felt it was not warranted.

"Gentlemen," Donna said. "First, you should know that Mr. Lorenz's involvement today is at the request of Mr. Minor. Mr. Minor's age limits his activities, and Mr. Lorenz is willing to help out. Also, if Mr. Lorenz's land ultimately does become involved, I want to avoid the need to backtrack in our efforts, which will only waste time. Keeping him informed now will save time in the end and serve both our purposes."

Sam and Chase knew any further protests on their part would certainly appear to be biased. They dropped their objections.

"Bullshit," Sam said under his breath, privately fuming while getting back onto his snowmobile. His hard glance toward Chase made his already apparent views crystal clear.

Overall, Jake felt the tour provided little hard evidence. What Sam and Chase did offer was a convincing presentation using a very old map to identify the presumed location of the trading company and the estimated location of Flat Mouth's village. Sam pinpointed the alleged burial grounds based on the triangulation of those two fixed points and a third point—the location of an Indian medicine woman's body discovered four years prior. While he acknowledged that that initial investigation had concluded the body and burial site represented a person estranged from her village, as was historically the case with individuals who were out of favor and banished from the tribe, he also concluded that a burial ground location on Alex's property was likely because of the very assumption of a village in the first place.

"The truth of what we've presented today can only be uncovered through selected excavations after the ground thaws," Chase said to emphasize a required need for action.

Regardless of what else happened that day, Sam and Chase did lay a convincing foundation for the investigation team to conduct several excavation efforts at Sam's direction. It was agreed that if the sono-probe confirmed human remains, digging would begin in about six weeks—after the thaw.

As everyone was leaving Alex's property at the end of the day, Donna pulled her car next to Jake's truck.

He rolled down his window.

"Jake," she said in a businesslike tone. "I have a few more questions I'd like to ask. Can you drop by the resort later this evening?"

Jake didn't care what the topic was, or could be, for that matter. He was delighted to be helpful and, in the process, recover from yesterday's turndown for dinner.

He kept his cool this time and replied in a level tone, "No problem. I'll be there about 7:15." The exactness of time came out of his mouth in a feigned attempt to establish his need to attend to other priorities. Don't want to appear too eager, he thought.

"That'll be fine," she replied. With one gentle look, Donna completely penetrated his little ruse at playing hard to get.

"Should I bring anything?" he asked, thinking that he was never good at social games. Or maybe I'm the only one playing, he reflected.

"Just yourself," she said.

* * *

"I don't know what the fuck that little bastard thinks he's up to now, putting his nose into our business," Sam said. "I'll guarantee you one goddamn thing for sure. If he gets in our way, there's going to be hell to pay." Sam was furious as they drove away. Chase was quiet in his agreement.

"Look at that little son-of-a-bitch now, kissing ass with Donna-what's-her-fucking name. It won't be long until he's banging the bitch. And what's with that bullshit age excuse of Alex's? The son-of-a-bitch could walk us all into the ground if there was a sawbuck in it for the winner. Old my ass!"

* * *

Back at his cabin, Jake agonized. The minutes seemed like hours. He wasn't at all sure what Donna wanted to see him about. He probably should have asked more questions, but the car-to-truck conversation didn't lend itself to getting details. Anyway, it was now ten after seven, so he left for the resort. The ten-minute trip would make him about five minutes late, belying his eagerness to see her again.

* * *

Jake had walked into Tom and Cheryl's resort hundreds of times, but never with this level of anticipation. He immediately saw Donna at one of the tables with a few members of her team. He decided that his best course of action was to talk with Tom for a few minutes first at the bar, in order to settle himself down before approaching her table.

It was one of those busy nights, though, and before he could say anything to Tom other than ordering a beer, Donna approached him.

"Thanks for coming over."

"Happy to oblige."

"Today was interesting, and I really want your candid opinion of what went on, if that's okay."

"What do you mean?"

"Well, for example, did you notice anything peculiar in the way Sam and Chase reacted to you?" She wasted no time getting to her point.

"No," he paused. "Well, I'm not really sure. What do you mean?" He was a little surprised by the directness of her question, and also a little let down by the lack of a more social interaction before business.

"Clearly, I'm new to the mix of people in this investigation, Jake, but it seems to me that they are very uncomfortable with your involvement. Why do you think that is?"

Jake's mind raced through the calamitous events since his arrival for the winter. He believed Sam was involved, but there was nothing that he could prove. The thought that Donna had detected something in their first meeting alarmed him with the possibility that Sam and Chase were on to his suspicions as well.

"Donna," he began slowly. "I'm not sure what you're picking up on between us, but regardless of what it is, you get full credit as a first-class investigator."

His immediate instincts were to be completely honest with Donna. As always, it was Jake's style to err on the side of openness in forming conclusions, even if they couldn't be fully supported by the facts. Intuition, big picture, inductive thinking—call it whatever you like—Jake always gravitated to the overall theory of things first.

As he was formulating a way to proceed, Donna responded, "Investigations are never what they appear to be, Jake. Motives are very hard to read. Our purpose, on the other hand, is almost always clear. Is there enough hard evidence that would warrant a decision to declare the land a sacred burial ground?"

It was as if her matter-of-fact statement was designed to reinforce the team's purpose with him first. But I know the purpose, he thought, where's she going?

"I repeat," Donna continued, "motives are another thing entirely. For example, the historical theory supporting this investigation has been known for some time, but the assertion is only taking place now. Why is that? Are there reasons beyond the burial ground premise that would promote significant financial gain? Who will really benefit by the outcome? What will the real impact be on the community at large? These are just a few of the questions I need to get answered. So you see, Jake, what you know may be far more useful than you imagine. I hope you'll trust me that the information will be used properly."

Jake decided on his course of action right then and there. If Donna was going to be a useful ally, he reasoned, she would need all of the facts surrounding the events of the last several months. "I'm not sure that I can give you exactly the information you need, but there definitely is more to the story. If it's fine with you, I can do that better by showing you things while I'm telling you about them at the same time. We can do that now if you'd like."

"I'm ready if you are."

"Let's take a ride then. We'll be gone a few hours."

"Don't wait up for me," Donna said to her co-workers before leaving.

Donna considered the possible outcome of this discussion while walking to Jake's truck. She had noted Jake's honesty right from their first phone conversation. His willingness to disclose what he knew seemed to reflect well on the trust developed in their short relationship. Her instincts told her that this investigation was going to be unique. For Donna, the element of complexity added to the project's excitement. Somehow, she also knew Jake's involvement was essential. To what extent he actually knew it himself, she wasn't sure.

The hospital in Bemidji, by way of Chippewa Lake, was their first stop. While driving, Jake gave a detailed account of all that he knew—in chronological sequence since his arrival in November. He identified where Linda lived and the charred remains of the sheds at the cemetery. He also pinpointed the precise location of Linda's attack on the highway. He purposely made an effort to elaborate the details, recognizing that Donna's mind gravitated toward logical, bottom-line information. She will sort out what information she needs and what she doesn't need on her own, he figured.

"I'm certainly not an expert in these matters, but to me, Two Fingers' death is too suspicious, particularly considering the incriminating information we now have against Sam from the lab tests. As for Alex's involvement, I don't believe that was anything other than a mean-spirited maneuver to get my land. The mindless attack on Linda makes no sense, however.

"I guess what I'm saying is that I can see some of the pieces to the complete picture, but most are still like one of those giant jigsaw puzzles with lots of sky and water."

She absorbed the information with great interest, asking only a few questions for clarification as Jake related the story. Her ability to formulate a plausible connection to the investigation might be the only link to these events and the destruction of two people's lives. In her mind, unique was no longer the word she would use in characterizing this investigation. Risky seemed more fitting. And, while she would not compromise Jake's position, she knew she'd have to prepare her team for the possibility of violence. Over their years together, they had developed a respect for her instincts.

Their visit with Linda at the hospital was brief but enjoyable, as her spirits were clearly on the mend. Her short-term memory of the attack had not improved, but for the first time since before the attack she addressed Jake as "Mister Jake," which made him grin. His personal respect and interest in her were obvious to everyone in the room. And Donna was touched by his fatherly attention to Linda's concerns.

And, of course, visiting hours weren't complete without Big Lights.

"Jake," he announced. "You're a breath of the pine forest air after a spring rain. This girl needs every bit of help she can get, and it's good to know she can count on the likes of you." Big Lights' upbeat attitude added to the enjoyment of their visit. He and Jake had not seen much of each other lately.

As they shook hands, Jake smiled and said, "Big Lights, I'd like you to meet Agent Donna Lynch. She's here to conduct the investigation about Alex's land."

"So you're the pretty government investigator everyone's told me about," Big Lights said with a broad grin.

Donna actually blushed. "I'm happy to meet you as well. Jake's told me all about you. Your flattering description, though, probably has more to do with the fact that I'm the only female on the team."

She was amazed how fast the knowledge of investigations traveled in remote communities. Here she was talking to someone she had never met, who probably knew more about her and her activities than she would ever guess, and she and her team had been in the community for only a few days.

After leaving the hospital, Donna said, "You treated Linda like she was your own daughter."

"Linda's a remarkable young woman, isn't she—one any father for sure would take great pride in. I guess I have taken a special interest in her."

"Maybe this is a way to be the father that you never were," she said softly.

"Thanks, that was nice of you to say. I've been very impressed working with Linda on the Omaha Project. I like her ability to take responsibility, and her willingness to give back to a community that has given her precious little. It's remarkable."

"And what about Big Lights? He's obviously attached to her."

"This may be the one blessing coming out of the whole sad story," Jake said, explaining that Big Lights' declaration of love and support was a surprise to everyone, including Linda.

"It does seem like she's responding to his attention, doesn't it? It must have been quite a surprise to come out of a coma only to have a person you don't recognize at all propose marriage and an undying lifelong commitment to you."

They both laughed. And in doing so, a bond of friendship began.

They were quiet for most of the short ride back through Chippewa Lake and on to Tom's resort.

Donna's mind was bouncing back and forth between the investigation and this wonderful person she was getting to know. Not since her husband's death two years ago had she felt this way toward another man. In fact, there had been no other men at all. She would have to stay focused on the purpose for the trip, she thought, although she knew it would be difficult.

Jake, on the other hand, was no longer focusing on the investigation. He felt a tremendous relief having passed his entire knowledge of the events and suspicions on to Donna. First, her competence and position gave him the confidence that he had done the right thing. Second, at least one other person now knew the whole story—besides him and Alex—an important insurance policy should something happen. And third, most of all, the last two hours had allowed him to break through the formality of their relationship. It was now Donna and Jake as new friends. Her manner of talking with him during the entire evening suggested that she shared his feelings.

They arrived at the resort well after closing time. Only a few of the cabin lights were still on. Jake felt like he was on a first date, returning under the watchful eye of protective parents. He kept a casual manner so as not to attract undo attention in case someone was watching.

"You know, Donna, it might be a good idea to see my cabin, where this all started last November. I can give you a pretty good summary of the police report and a firsthand look at the crime scene. Maybe there's something that you can uncover from the cabin and the garage where Two Fingers' body was found. And besides, I make a mean lasagna."

"That's a great idea. Just tell me what day's best and I'll be there."

"How about tomorrow?"

"Sounds fine to me," she answered. "I want to thank you for being so open tonight. I hope you know that your information is safe with me. It really does help to know the whole situation. As I mentioned earlier, nothing in these cases ever seems to be what's presented.

"I'll see you tomorrow then." She turned and walked to her cabin.

"Good night," Jake said, keeping a watchful eye until her cabin door opened.

thirty-eight

SEVERAL WEEKS HAD passed since Donna's team had arrived on the peninsula. Other than their initial meetings, some survey work, and the removal of a few core samples around the foundation of the old lodge, little had been accomplished. Sam, Chase, and even Alex wanted faster results.

"It's the government," Chase said as he and Sam sat at their usual table at the Twin Pines. "I don't think we stand a chance of telling them how to pick up the pace. If we press them for faster results, they'll just go slower. Hell, as far as I'm concerned we're doing okay just to be on track with the current plan." Chase was trying to calm the storm he knew was brewing in Sam.

"That's just fucking beautiful. Now I've got a partner who's a goddamn bureaucrat, too."

Too late, Chase thought. "Relax, Sam, everything's under control. Have another beer before you do something stupid."

"Stupid! You'd best rethink who you're talking to before this conversation turns ugly."

Sam had returned from the Bemidji Airport an hour earlier in a foul mood. Their weekly cash drop was on its way to the Bahamas, via Minneapolis/St. Paul, Akron/Canton, Pittsburgh, and New York.

There was always risk with these shipments. Intentionally using different airlines, airports, and routing helped make tracing difficult, but the airlines weren't always reliable and shipments were occasionally lost. Two months ago it actually happened. A shipment was misplaced for three weeks—400K lost in space. Sam was always on edge after a drop; Chase knew the pattern all too well. He was venting and the slow progress of the investigation team was a convenient excuse for his temper.

"You know, Morey's going to be here in a few minutes. There's no way we can be linked to this jackass," Chase said, changing the direction of the conversation.

"Rumor has it that Linda's amnesia isn't any better, but we both know her recovery is just a matter of time. And when her memory does return, no one's going to say a word that would put her at risk. No, what's going to happen is that Morey's going to get a surprise knock on the door by Sheriff Betts, and that'll be the ballgame. There's no chance for him not to implicate us. He's not smart enough."

"What are you saying?" Sam wanted to know.

* * *

This meeting with Morey would be important. Just yesterday Sam and Chase had heard that Linda had been moved from the hospital and placed under the temporary care of Helen and Bud for further recovery. Michelle had volunteered their home because Linda had nowhere else to go. She certainly wasn't ready to live alone. Helen and Bud were happy to help. Bobby, Michelle, and Linda had become very close and with Bobby being Morey's brother, the mess could only become worse. Chase and Sam knew they had to distance themselves from Morey.

As they agreed on a plan, Morey walked into the bar.

"Get another round," Chase said, motioning Morey toward the bar.

Morey delivered the drinks and slipped into a chair opposite the two men.

"How are your hands?" Chase asked. Morey's left hand was still in a cast, making it awkward for him to carry three beers.

"I owe you guys. Believe me, I'll never do anything stupid again," Morey muttered in his usual slow-witted tone while settling his girth into the chair. His baseless promise was witness to his stupidity.

"We believe you, Morey," Chase said.

Sam remained quiet and sullen, incapable of playing the role of the good guy.

"I'm sure you understand, though, that your actions are still causing some serious problems."

"You're not going to hurt me again?" Morey said in alarm, pushing his chair back from the table. The sight of this large man acting in childlike fear demonstrated the complete control they had gained over him.

"No, we're not," Chase continued. "But there is some unfinished business that needs fixing right away."

Chase recounted his and Sam's thinking about Linda, and how close her recovery was to a long prison sentence for Morey.

"Worse yet, it'll connect you with us. We can't have that kind of visibility. You're going to have to finish what you started, and soon."

Morey never really knew what led to his destructive actions. It was always some overwhelming impulse that ruled his thoughts, some kind of temporary insanity. He had beaten other women in the past, but none had been foolish enough to go to the police. This was different, however. Morey knew what Chase meant by "finish what he had started." This would require planning, but he didn't have much time. He thought he had finished the job that night, but his own do-gooder brother had fouled things up.

"How soon do I need to take care of things?"

"Don't waste time. Word is that Linda's recovering fast. And I don't need to tell you that a screwup here wouldn't be good."

While Chase and Morey talked, Sam stayed silent. His dark, lowered eyes produced a menacing stare that foretold the consequences of any failure.

"I'll fix it right this time. I'll fix it right away," Morey repeated nervously. "Don't worry."

thirty-nine

ANXIOUS TO PROVE his loyalty to Sam and Chase by acting quickly, Morey planned to act that very night. They would be proud of him; he just knew they would.

Within hours of their meeting and with only a trace of sunlight remaining, Morey maneuvered his snowmobile through the forest on one of several intersecting snowmobile trails on the peninsula. He turned south on the trail that went near the Miller house. He was careful not to be seen while finding a well-protected spot that gave him a clear look into the living room. Loading a stolen 30.30 deer rifle, he surveyed the scene through its high-power scope.

The scope brought Helen and Bud as close as if they were all sharing a cup of coffee. If they walked by the big picture window he could tell the shape of the buttons on their clothes. There was no sign of Linda.

Morey worked hard to quiet himself. His heart pounded, and he perspired heavily despite the cold evening air. But the only thing he could do was wait until it was completely dark.

Within the hour, Bobby and Michelle showed up with Jake Lorenz. Morey wasn't comfortable with the number of people, but it did seem to guarantee that Linda must be there. Hell, even Morey could figure that out. Plus, he would have the element of surprise and the darkness of the trails to give him the cover needed for his getaway.

Linda finally walked in front of one of the smaller kitchen windows. Not nearly enough time to sight in a clear shot, however, and the angle was bad. Be patient, he thought. He could feel the sweat running down his large body. His right-hand trigger-finger was ready. The knife wound had mended well and wouldn't restrict his ability to shoot. His entire left hand, however, the one that took the hammer blow, felt frozen. The stiffness of the cast, coupled with the restriction of movement inside it, made his hand vulnerable to the frigid air.

For the next hour and a half, he waited.

"Goddamn," he muttered over and over again in growing frustration. He would have to get closer to the house, where he could get a better look.

Morey edged his way next to the house where the kitchen window was located. He could see in, but the bay window was still too high for a shot. If he could only find something to stand on he could easily finish things—100-percent-accuracy range, he thought. Sam and Chase would be happy and he'd be off the hook.

After looking around in the dark, he finally discovered some cut firewood logs he could stack. It would elevate him the necessary two feet. Stacking ten or so pieces in a herringbone fashion, Morey was confident that the makeshift platform would do the job. He could make his shot and be out of there in minutes.

The late-winter snow was wet and heavy, making trips to the woodpile exhausting. He plodded back and forth three times, breathing heavily. The heat buildup in his snowmobile suit made his sweat sticky. Nothing was ever easy, he thought. The voice of Chase's last instructions, "stay with it and finish the job," echoed repeatedly in his mind. He would be done soon, he promised himself.

Once on the temporary platform, Morey could see everyone in the room through a break in the curtains. These same curtains protected him from their view nicely. With his 30.30 loaded and the safety off, Morey raised the stock to his shoulder. He was so close. Linda was sitting at the kitchen counter in clear view. The scope was completely unnecessary. Like ducks on a pond, he reflected. This would be easy.

As he took final aim, Blackie came charging around the corner of the house. Barking aggressively in an obnoxious off-key pitch, he caught Morey completely by surprise. Blackie continued the ruckus at the base of the woodpile.

Looking down at the dog, Morey lost his balance slightly. Instinctively shifting his large mass on the firewood platform, he grabbed for the window ledge to steady himself. He realized too late that with the rifle in his right hand his casted left hand was not up to the task.

Instantly, his large body crashed to the ground.

The rifle discharged. The shot went wild.

Blackie accompanied the chaos by barking loudly within inches of Morey's face. Morey panicked as he tried to scramble to his feet. Failure, failure, failure—his mental alarm sounded along with the vision of Sam's face! He needed to get out of there without being recognized.

Inside the house, everyone dropped to the floor behind anything affording an element of safety. No one moved until they heard someone running across the yard. Thinking it was safe, Jake edged his way to the window. He saw the shadow of a man behind some trees by the outline of a snowmobile.

Within seconds the snowmobile started and the intruder was maneuvering toward the trail. It was impossible for Jake to make out anything definite in the darkness.

* * *

After filling his gas tank, Tom mounted his snowmobile to begin the late shift on community patrol. The patrol had not seen or heard anything suspicious yet—in fact, there had been discussion just two days prior that entertained the idea of dropping their rotations completely.

When he heard the nearby shot, Tom immediately headed in the direction of Bud and Helen's. He deduced that the man on the snowmobile heading toward the lake trail was the source of the problem.

He estimated that his capacity for miles was greater than that of the fugitive and he kept his distance with his headlights off, as the nearly full moon gave the light he needed. He would follow as long as he could without being noticed.

After less than a mile, however, the other snowmobile left the lake trail for the open ice in an obvious attempt to put distance between himself and the scene. Tom followed, knowing that his cover would be blown once on the open lake.

* * *

Morey's only goal was to get out of there as fast as he could. The course he chose would take him across a large stretch of Big Bear Lake's open ice—distance from the scene was critical. His Artic Cat was fast and once across the lake, he could blend his tracks with many others on the heavily used trails near Bronson. He could hide the snowmobile any number of places for a pickup later. Everything would be fine.

Morey's own engine sound and the dampening effect of the woodland cover drowned out the noise of Tom's pursuit. The thick trees and the winding turns of the trail also obscured Tom from Morey's view. That changed quickly as both snowmobiles entered the open ice.

Alarmed, Morey continued his navigation by moonlight—a dangerous strategy as there were soft spots in the spring ice. He knew the ice-fishing houses had been removed at least two weeks ago. For locals, this occurrence marked the end of winter. At fifty miles an hour, however, any direct weight on the ice from the moving snowmobile would be minimal. Morey kept the throttle wide open.

There was enough moonlight for Tom to keep the fugitive in view. His snowmobile was equally high powered, and he found himself closing the gap. In a short while, he was within about two football fields of Morey.

Morey's plan wasn't working. He couldn't outrun his pursuer. The menacing look of Sam's face blazed across his mind's eye. Chase's instructions of "Don't screw this one up, Morey," bore a hole in his subconscious. He concluded that his only hope was to level one good shot at the pursuer when he got within range. He pulled his snowmobile to a stop and positioned it broadside for protection. He used the engine hood as a rifle rest to sight in his target and steady his shot. He wouldn't have a second chance.

At about 100 yards' distance, Tom realized that the fugitive had stopped. Out of gas, he thought. Maybe, but he wasn't going to take any chances. He quickly slowed down, which was dangerous on the fragile ice, so he kept moving slowly in circles while keeping his distance from the other man.

With the aid of the moonlight, a shot at this distance would not be that difficult. Morey had killed deer at this distance. He steadied his rifle and sighted Tom in, recognizing him on his slowly moving snowmobile. A set-up shot, Morey thought. Just relax—squeeze the trigger.

The slug ripped through Tom's left shoulder, shattering his collarbone and knocking him completely off the snowmobile. How could I be so stupid? Tom thought in his shock as the pain rushed through his shoulder.

Lying bleeding on the ice, Tom looked toward the other snowmobile to determine his attacker's next move. The shooter was waiting, a luxury that wouldn't last. Tom started to belly crawl back to the snowmobile where it had stopped ten feet away. Thank God for the emergency shut-off feature on the sled.

He needed to get out of the shooter's sight immediately despite the excruciating pain. He had reached within a few feet of the unit when another shot shattered the ice with the impact of a land mine two inches from his head. Ice shards pierced the exposed skin on his face. Tom scrambled the last few feet to safety behind the snowmobile.

After removing the ice from his face and catching his breath, Tom reached for his 30.06 case. All the while, volleys of shots kept coming.

Morey had plenty of ammunition, but no time. He could feel the soft ice moving under the snowmobile. Was his pursuer armed or not? Given the boldness of the chase, Morey figured that he was. He would try a few more shots before leaving. His engine was still running so his getaway would be quick.

Tom knew that his opportunities were limited. A return shot would have to be his best ever. The searing pain in his shoulder challenged every movement needed to get his rifle into position. The magnitude of his task dawned on him when he realized that the shattered collarbone would allow him minimal support to sight in the target. All he could do was to lay the rifle on his lifeless arm while peeking out from behind the snowmobile. He saw some movement, but not enough for a clean shot.

In a moment of inspiration, Tom's next move became crystal clear. He, too, had sensed the instability in the ice and knew from experience that it was very dangerous. With his decision made, he took careful aim.

Within an instant of squeezing the trigger, Tom's decision was rewarded. The slug penetrated the snowmobile's gas tank, causing an almost instantaneous explosion. The fireball ignited the sky in a display of victory and as quickly as the explosion had taken place, the snowmobile and driver were plunged into a twenty-foot-wide hole of icy water.

Tom's feeling of relief disintegrated when he saw a six-inch undulation in the soft ice coming directly toward him. He hadn't anticipated the cause and effect of his actions. In fact, he had never seen this before. He rolled and rolled to distance himself from the weight of his own snowmobile. Ignoring his pain, he continued rolling in the seconds he had left. He waited for what he surely thought would be his demise, as well. The wave went under him like a small tsunami. He was a toy boat in a bathtub. When it was over he turned and looked, only to see a huge hole in the ice. His snowmobile had disappeared—like an illusion into the depth of the lake. In a desperate attempt to save himself, he fought the pain and exhaustion to roll even farther while keeping his weight distributed on the ice. Finally feeling some stability in the ice again, he was relieved to be alive.

In the distance, he could hear the fugitive's anguished attempts to escape from the icy water. Who was this man anyway?

* * *

The thrashing and flailing only broke more ice in Morey's path. His snowmobile suit had filled with water, making escape virtually impossible. He was a three-hundred-pound hog weighted down with cement blocks. His face charred beyond recognition from flames and searing heat and his suit ballooning with freezing water sealed his death as he lost his grip on the ice and slipped beneath the surface.

forty

Jake poured another glass of chardonnay for Donna as they sat in front of the fireplace at his cabin. Admiring its natural ledgestone design, he remembered the argument that he and Jan had had about the expense of the fireplace, he being much more practical and she insisting on the added atmosphere it created. He was pleased that he'd given in to Jan's aesthetic influence.

"You seem to have a knack for being in the right place at the right time," Donna said.

"I think you're giving me more credit than I deserve. It wasn't an act of genius to follow the two snowmobiles onto the lake. From there, anyone within twenty miles could see the explosion. If there were survivors, it was obvious that they would need help fast. I just happened to be there first. Anyway, maybe it's karma, since Tom saved me the night of the bear attack."

"Regardless, I think you acted bravely."

Over dinner and a few glasses of wine, Jake rehashed the scene of Two Fingers' murder for Donna. His perspective shifted somewhat as he related Alex Minor's role in the cabin mayhem. Donna didn't say much during his tale—a few questions from time to time, but nothing more.

What was absolutely incredible to both of them was the life Morey had led and the web he had woven involving Linda. In the two weeks of intense investigation following the chase on the ice, Morey's life had been exposed. Everything became known. The pawnshop receipt for Linda's stolen computer was found in one of his bedroom dresser drawers. More disgusting was the pair of panties in another drawer, identifying him by a semen DNA analysis as the rapist. It seemed as if Morey had been stalking her for some time. And while no hard evidence linked Morey to the murder of Two Fingers, people were confident that they had their man for that crime, too. The coincidences were too strong, and it was very easy to imagine Two Fingers catching Morey red-handed in an attempt at some other sleazy perpetration. People reasoned that Morey would not be one to deliberate long when confronted with an incrimination. Sheriff Betts, as well as most others, concluded that a hanging murder would have matched his brutal style.

"I imagine everyone in town feels a whole lot better about not locking their doors now," Donna said. She shifted on the couch to a more comfortable position closer to Jake.

"Well, yes and no. I really feel badly for Bobby in this whole mess. Here's a young man trying his best to break away from a lousy system only to be put needlessly under the microscope just because he has the same last name as Morey. He didn't choose him for a brother and had no involvement other than blood. It's not fair.

"On the other hand, with the knowledge surrounding Morey's death and, in particular, the evidence of his stalking Linda, both the Indian and white communities have literally breathed a huge sigh of relief. All their questions are answered, and their feelings of danger are gone. The disbanding of the patrol itself seems to have lifted any remaining pressure. All of this I like.

"But I guess I'm still concerned," Jake said with a lack of resolution in his voice. "I can't reconcile the other facts pointing to Sam's involvement. Plus, where did those large cash deposits in Morey's bank account come from?"

"I don't think there's any question; you're right to be suspicious. But even though I'm an investigator, I don't know where to tell you to look for the answer," Donna said. "More information is definitely going to be necessary."

Not wanting Morey's demise to occupy their whole time together, Donna changed the subject back to the investigation team's findings. She indicated that selected excavations after the ground thawed would be the only way to uncover the truth about a sacred burial ground. The team had made their plan and marked the locations for digging with the help of the sono-probe research covering a significant portion of Alex's land. They had pinpointed six proposed dig sites.

"It's possible that the investigation will ultimately include your land also. We won't know, however, until we're done at Minor's."

"It will be good to have this behind us," Jake said, offering no objection. He had expected as much. At this point he held no ill will toward the process being conducted. And how could he possibly hold any negative feelings toward Donna, or her team? They were only doing their job.

"I'd like you to go to Washington, D.C., with me next week when I give my interim report," Donna said, catching Jake by surprise.

"What?" he said, twisting his face in bewilderment.

"I think there's foul play here too, but I'm not sure that my story will be convincing enough on its own to warrant an additional investigation. You would be an asset to the meeting I have planned with Jordan Barnhart, our U.S. Secretary of the Interior. For some reason his interest level is very high on this investigation and he wants a complete firsthand progress report.

"What do you think? Can you make the trip? Your government will foot the expenses," she persuaded with a friendly smile. The shift in her position to him and her hand on his knee suggested more.

The firelight, the wine, the trust developing between them, their closeness on the couch, and the openness she offered with her smile caused Jake to react rather than respond. He slowly put his hand behind her neck and confidently pulled her close and kissed her.

The room went quiet as the kiss lingered—a gentle touch, a silent promise, an open invitation for more. For the next few minutes, they shared a closeness that neither had enjoyed in some time.

For Jake, however, pleasure mingled with guilt. Traces of Jan's memory were always present. For Donna, the moment was exactly what she had hoped for—men like Jake were not plentiful, and rarely single.

"I take it that was a yes," Donna whispered as she brushed the gray hair across his temples.

"Trust me, it's only my civic duty that calls me to make such a perilous journey," he said lightly.

The moment was over, and each knew that pressing their emotions forward was beyond what the evening called for. Besides, everything was just perfect as it was.

It was getting late. Donna gently pushed away and stood up in a move to leave.

"You sure know how to show a girl a good time," she said as she gave him another light kiss on the lips.

* * *

The access road to Jake's cabin was still blocked with dirty piles of late-winter snow, so they took his snowmobile to her car. Jake positioned himself in the driver's seat, and Donna snuggled in behind him with her arms wrapped around his waist, a gesture noticeably different from the trip in. Even through his ski jacket, the pressure of her soft breasts against his back was a pleasant distraction. Maintaining his concentration while driving was difficult as thoughts of their D.C. trip filled his mind.

Donna gave him an extra squeeze before getting off the snowmobile, as if to say, "there's more to come." They kissed once more in the crisp winter air under the shadows of the moonlit forest before she got into her car and drove away.

Jake watched her car's taillights until they were out of sight. He stood there quietly for several minutes. For the first time since he could remember, a woman other than Jan occupied his thoughts and senses. It felt right.

forty-one

BARELY AFTER SUNUP the next morning, Jake heard frenzied pounding on the rear cabin door. He couldn't believe it. Who in the hell could it be? He slipped on a pair of Levi's and stumbled onto the porch balancing his cup of coffee.

"Jake, man, I've got to talk to you right away," Big Lights blurted out as he gasped for breath from his hike down the access road.

Jake hadn't seen much of Big Lights other than during the visits to the hospital, where Big Lights was totally focused on Linda. That was fine as far as Jake was concerned.

It was obvious to Jake that Big Lights hadn't slept or been home in days. His long hair was greasy, his breath was sour, and his clothes smelled from some pretty heavy body odor.

"I'll get you a cup of coffee. You know you look like shit, don't you?" Jake said as one friend to another.

"Thanks, buddy." Big Lights fell into the large leather chair by the fireplace.

"You'll know why in a minute. There's some funky crap goin' on and I need you to listen, Jake, and help me figure out just what the bejesus I've been seein'."

With his hands cupped around the steaming mug, Big Lights began his story. It came out jumbled and mixed-up. At times, Jake would have to slow him down to make sure he understood the order of events.

"Since Linda moved in with Bud and Helen, I've inherited a sudden supply of time. I just don't seem to fit in with that whole family scene. It's awkward for me. On top of that, work's real slow right now. I'll be honest with you, Jake. I've got too much time on my hands and the casino was calling my name. But that's not why I'm here."

"Take your time." The expression on Big Lights' face definitely commanded Jake's attention, and his normally lighthearted tone gave way to a seriousness Jake had rarely seen in his friend.

"What I need to tell you about is a whole series of strange events. It all started when I noticed Sam and Chase at the casino. At first, everything seemed normal-like. I mean, it's not like they're not supposed to be there. Something kept bugging me, though, but I couldn't put my finger on it. Well, it hit me one night watching Chase go to the count room, like both of them do all the time—way too predictable for me. All of a sudden their routine seemed staged, like their purpose wasn't the real purpose at all. And why did they need that big briefcase? Every day one of them brought the same big briefcase."

For someone who lived totally in the moment and had difficulty planning a trip to Bronson, it wasn't a surprise to Jake that Big Lights found the ritual of this procedure unusual. Logical or not, though, he knew that this wasn't the real point behind his story.

"Keep going."

"It's been my policy to stay clear of these two guys. They're bad news as far as I'm concerned. Always have been. And the few comments I've overheard from you tell me that things don't add up from your viewpoint either. You know, foul play and shit like that."

For the first time, Jake wondered privately just how much Big Lights had figured out on his own.

"Anyway, all this stuff just made me think. Finding out what was in that briefcase they carried every night became kind of a mission for me. Now it gets good, Jake, because this shit gets pretty amazing from here on out."

"Let me have it."

"Every night the guy carrying the briefcase would place it in the trunk of his car, only for the other guy to retrieve it in broad daylight the next day while having drinks at the Twin Pines. From there, the contents of the briefcase, now wrapped in brown-paper packages, were delivered once a week to two separate bus-station lockboxes in Bemidji."

"How did you figure that out?"

"Like I said, I had time on my hands, and it was easy to follow them. So I decided to hang out at the bus station. It took three days to unravel things. Last Tuesday, around four in the morning, turned out to be my lucky day. I'm still not absolutely sure about anything yet, but I'd bet my paycheck that the contents of the briefcase and the wrapped bundles are one and the same."

"I'm getting confused. Tell me every step."

"Late that night, a man I'd never seen before came and opened both lockboxes, retrieved the packages, and left. He was the only one in the bus station—no attendant, no one at all. I was in my car across the street, out of sight. When he went in, I followed and saw the collection through one of the windows. They were filthy, but I was able to wipe away the soot and see inside.

"It was a little difficult to follow this guy since we were the only two cars on the street. I can say this, though, he was very confident of his routine. He turned on his headlights, like he was running an errand to the hardware store, and drove away. I followed as close as I could with my lights off. Five minutes later he turned into the airport and went inside the cargo building.

"There was no question in my mind that this little routine was no coincidence and would repeat itself next week. But what had I really seen? Money was my answer, but there was no way I could be sure with just what I had."

Big Lights sipped his coffee thoughtfully, his large hands wrapped comfortably around the cup. "The following week was different, because I was ready. You'd be proud of me, Jake. Here I am, sitting on the bus station sidewalk smelling and acting the part of a total stiff. I did that well," he commented as an aside.

"And sure enough, here my man comes, like exactly at 4 A.M. This is too weird, I thought. He walks past me as if I didn't exist and goes straight to the lockboxes."

As a drunken Indian on a binge, Big Lights had no peer. His intoxicated presence at the bus station would have been as normal to the stranger as the station's dirty linoleum floors.

"On his way out, though, I managed to stagger into him in the doorway. The packages flew everywhere.

"He was pissed and called me some rude Indian name. I stumbled and faked some dry heaves in his direction. It gave me time to pick up one of the packages as he scrambled for the other. Well, surprise, surprise, my good buddy—it had a shipping label on it. And guess where it was going?"

Jake always loved the way Big Lights lived his stories, so he played along. "I have no idea, but if I did, I still don't think it would be the end of the story."

"You are 100-percent right," he continued. "Does the name McMillan, Larsen & Wingfoot from Eau Claire, Wisconsin, ring a bell?"

This was the third time Jake had been confronted with the accounting firm's name in the past several months. He acknowledged Big Lights' question with a nod and a raised eyebrow. He encouraged him to continue with a circling motion of his forefinger and hand.

"It was an Airborne shipping label and I remembered I had a drinking buddy working there, but I didn't want to lose the trail by getting sidetracked. So after this guy left, I went directly to the airport and asked when the next flight to Eau Claire left. There was one leaving at 7:35.

"You probably already guessed my next move, as I had no choice. I got a ticket. I just knew those packages were on that flight, I just knew it."

This was classic Big Lights, Jake thought. Acting on pure instinct without any real proof of how *A* was going to connect with *B*.

"And the money, where did you get the money for the flight?" Jake asked, doubting its existence.

"Not to worry, my good friend. Even a blind squirrel finds an acorn every now and then. I had a pretty good run while checking these guys out at the casino. It's just money anyway, and I knew I'd spend it before the week was out.

"Hang on to your shorts, though," Big Lights instructed, "because now the story gets really interesting."

Like it wasn't interesting already, Jake thought.

"I made a beeline for the Airborne counter when I got to Eau Claire and waited some more, but not for long. Some Indian in a business suit claimed the packages and took them directly to the UPS counter in the next building. I'm figuring that someone didn't want these packages tracked.

"Well, I waited for a few more minutes and went back to work as a drunk. You'd love their expression when I spilled my entire cup of coffee on one of the packages and the manifest paperwork the UPS guy had just completed. For a minute, I thought the guy in the suit was going to lose it. He got over it when the clerk said not to worry about it; he'd fill out new paperwork, which is exactly what he did. My man in the suit just paced and stared at me.

"To make a long story short, I waited outside until the coast was clear and went back to the vacant UPS counter. I'll be goddamned if that dirty paperwork wasn't in the wastebasket just like I thought it would be."

Big Lights smiled, almost smugly, and took another sip of his coffee. "Sometimes I think I have a gift."

"That was two days ago," he continued with a "here comes the best part" look on his face.

"As it turned out, this package was about to make a milk-run route from Eau Claire to Dulles Airport in D.C. From there it went to Miami and on to the Bahamas. Here's the manifest."

"The Bahamas!" Jake said disbelievingly as he looked at the coffee-stained document.

When he looked up he recognized Big Lights' familiar "I'm not done with my story yet" expression. "Don't tell me!"

"You guessed it—I've always wanted to go to the Bahamas."

Jake's mouth hung wide open.

"My luck ran out, though, when I got to Miami. Hell, I didn't know the Bahamas were a foreign country. I thought it was part of Florida, you know, down by Key West or someplace like that. Anyway, they wanted to see a passport or a visa. I showed them my credit card, but that's not what they meant."

"You are truly a piece of work." Jake shook his head in admiration.

"Well, I didn't have a passport either. I showed them my reservation ID, which did no good at all. They started getting a little edgy with me. This escapade had involved several days by now, and I was getting pretty ripe. People were giving me lots of room. It was either that or they thought I might scalp them if they got too close," Big Lights said with a grin.

"They probably thought you were a terrorist."

"My question for you now, Jake, is this. Do you recognize the name on the manifest—Sawgrass Investment Funds?"

"No, not really."

"Cause I sure didn't have a clue. That's when I knew I needed to talk to you, and quick, so I returned on the next flight. I missed the connecting flight to Bemidji, though, because of mechanical delays and crap weather. I rented a car in the Twin Cities and drove directly here. I couldn't wait out on the road any longer without falling asleep."

Jake was transfixed. If this could be proven, Sam and Chase would be implicated in grand theft and money-laundering, just for starters. It was hard to imagine how long this had been going on and to what extent it involved others in the tribe.

"You are unbelievable. Talk about being in the zone!" Jake was so impressed he hardly knew where to start.

"First, I believe that your suspicion on what was in the briefcase was right from the beginning. From what you've described, there's no question that it's money," Jake said as he explained to Big Lights the Bahamian position on banking and tax-free investments.

"But you've got to keep this information to yourself. No one can hear this, particularly from you. Are you sure you understand how important this is?"

Big Lights made a promise of silence, no matter what.

"Too many people have already been hurt. I have reason to believe that it's all connected. If it is, and I believe that it is, this evidence will be crucial." Jake's steady tone expressed his genuine concern for Big Lights' welfare.

It was about 10 o'clock when Big Lights finished breakfast and several more cups of coffee. As he left, Jake asked if he had plenty of soap and laundry detergent at home.

Big Lights answered with a one-finger wave.

Jake wanted to call Donna but felt he needed to bring Alex up to speed first. Feeling cooped up in the cabin, he opted for a snowmobile ride over a phone call. Within minutes he was headed down the peninsula toward Alex's lodge.

Tony, the caretaker, met Jake with a cordial wave as he continued his work in the garage. Leo and King were their aggressive and noisy selves, but Jake was no longer intimidated. He talked to the dogs reassuringly as he made his way to the door.

Alex was surprised with the visit, but he had developed a liking for Jake and welcomed him inside.

He stayed an hour, giving Alex all the Bahamian fund information. This was also his first opportunity to let him in on Donna's invitation to go to D.C.

"Jake, I'm real concerned that Big Lights' little escapade will lead back to us. Are you sure that he wasn't recognized at all?"

"My guess is that he could be recognized, at least by the Indian in Eau Claire if he saw him again. Big Lights swears, though, that they've never met."

"We've got to keep it that way. " A look of distress was on Alex's face as he pressed for additional details that Jake didn't have. Alex wasn't very good with only half the information to anything and he quickly became frustrated and irritable. He wanted conclusions, and there weren't any.

"On another point, I'm not too thrilled that you confided in Donna before we had a chance to discuss it. You're too trusting, Jake. You think that all these people are going to do the right thing. Well, I'm here to tell you that they won't. Sooner or later they'll look out for ol' number one. They always do."

"For Christ's sake, Alex, that's why we're a team. If we don't involve her we'll be over our heads real soon. Besides, it won't be long until everything's out in the open. And there's no question that we're going to need real law enforcement. It can't be just the two of us trying to figure this out. She's got access to the FBI, Alex. They're the ones with legitimate authority in reservation matters of this magnitude, anyway."

Alex threw up his hands in mock surrender to Jake despite his inner turmoil for immediate answers. He wanted nothing more than to break ground this summer on the resort, but he knew that this entire scenario put matters beyond his management.

"I'm not good with all of this," he said, knowing that even Jake was probably going to object to the resort development before events were over. The loss of control and the overwhelming feeling of swimming upstream against circumstances generated way too much tension. The recurring sense of alarm played hell with his blood pressure.

"You've got to calm down and trust me on this. I know we're going about it the right way. I can keep Big Lights and Donna on our side and under wraps." Jake tried his best to reassure Alex that they were on the right track before he left. Usually very logical, when Alex lost it, his track record for rash behavior was legendary.

"Isn't this why you involved me in the first place?" Jake reminded him.

forty-two

MOST OF THE investigation team accompanied Donna and Jake on the Northwest Airlines flight out of Bemidji to D.C. Consequently the two of them had little time to talk privately. Even with a two-hour layover in the Twin Cities, there was always someone around. It did give Jake some time to read a book, a luxury he had all but forgotten about.

He made little progress with the novel, however, as unresolved issues nagged at his concentration. When they arrived at Reagan International Airport he had covered only fifty pages and forgotten most of the story. But he had come to the conclusion that this whole winter retreat idea had been a big mistake. Truth number one, he had made absolutely no progress in moving on with his career. And to his amazement, he hadn't even turned his laptop on to check for e-mail messages in over a month—completely unlike him. As a professional technocrat he lived by electronic communications. This whole involvement with the peninsula—the murder, the Omaha Project, Linda, Morey, Donna, and now Big Lights' story—had consumed his thoughts and diverted attention from his reason for deciding to spend the winter on Arrowhead in the first place.

Truth number two, it was beyond comprehension how he had allowed himself to become so wrapped up in these criminal affairs. Certainly somebody doing investigation work could pursue the bad guys well enough to make an arrest. Was he just kidding himself with the importance he placed on his and Alex's involvement?

In contrast, he realized, part of his life was taking a real turn for the positive. His daydreams about the next few days with Donna definitely kept his attention as he reflected on the intensity of her kiss at his cabin and the logical conclusion of more time together in D.C.

After landing, he and Donna walked down the jet bridge together.

"You know, I'm not even sure I should be here. I've been thinking quite a bit, and frankly, I'm becoming a little concerned about my involvement in this whole affair."

"Now don't go and get cold feet on me, Jake. Your purpose here has real value, and you don't strike me as a person to run from a little controversy, particularly when it's the right thing to do."

Jake knew she was absolutely correct about him. It wasn't his style to turn his head and ignore an injustice of any sort. "You're probably right, but I'm still uneasy."

How did she always know the right thing to say when it came to encouraging him to get involved? Was he that easy to read? He didn't really mind it. He just found her insight rather amazing.

Donna waited for Jake as he picked up his luggage from the carousel.

"Let's share a cab and get you to your hotel," she said in a cozy manner. "It's right on the way to where I live in Georgetown."

* * *

They were quiet as the cab passed the Washington, Jefferson, and Lincoln monuments. He hadn't seen these beautiful sites since a family vacation when he was a child.

"It's wonderful how these places never change. It's as if the whole purpose of the city and the monuments is to keep the importance of our freedom alive. Come to think of it, it works," Jake said, realizing his offhand observation was pretty obvious.

He slid his hand into Donna's as they made the rest of the trip to the hotel, a large Marriott overlooking the Potomac.

When they rounded the driveway to the hotel's entrance, Jake turned and looked directly into Donna's eyes. "I'd like to see you tonight, Donna. What I mean is I'd like tonight to be just for us."

"Your wish is my command. You are my guest, remember, and I would be negligent in my hostess duties to ignore you. How about if I go home for a short while to take care of a few things and come back here around 5:30 for dinner? I know a nice place on the river that you might like."

"Perfect."

* * *

When the call to his room came precisely at 5:30, Jake was more than ready for an evening without the ever-present investigation team.

The restaurant exceeded the personal review she gave Jake during their taxi ride. Definitely five-star by northern Minnesota standards, he thought, and in a great location that allowed them to sip wine while watching the April sunset and the boats on the river. The glass doors to the river view were open, allowing the spring breezes to ply their spirits. Sitting next to each other at their table with their backs to the rest of the restaurant, Jake and Donna felt the gentle warm air intoxicate their winterized brains.

Since their meeting with Jordan Barnhart was not scheduled until the following afternoon, they felt free to simply talk and enjoy each other's company. They discovered that it wasn't just circumstances fueling their blossoming connection. Their chemistry and the wine made fine partners.

Jake loved the way Donna listened. It was as if he held some special license to whatever topic he chose, regardless of how insignificant. Her eye contact and smile not only encouraged his discussion; they made him feel smarter about whatever he was saying. Even when she disagreed with him, she did it in a way that complemented his thought process.

Donna found Jake's confidence sexy. And his priorities were intact. Here's a guy out of work for close to six months, she thought, yet he's able to lead an effort involving many others without once complaining or posturing for his own benefit. Plus, he looks great in jeans and a flannel shirt, even if it's not the normal evening attire for men in D.C. To the contrary, his casual attire emphasized his unique attributes, especially the way the small tuft of chest hair curled from the open collar of his shirt.

They ordered a second bottle of wine before the main course, instructing the waiter to keep a slow pace. The she-crab soup Donna recommended as an appetizer tasted like nothing Jake had ever had. He methodically enjoyed every spoonful of the East Coast delicacy.

"Do you think this counts as our first date, or is this just the ongoing hospitality of our government to its out-of-town guests?"

Donna smiled. "Well, that depends, Mr. Lorenz, on two things. If you're examining my expense report for the investigation, this dinner is clearly all business. But, if you behave yourself like a gentleman, it's not only a date, but a very important date."

As she spoke, she slipped her hand into his and gave him a small kiss below the earlobe.

Jake melted with both the softness of her touch and the implication of her comment. A very important date, he thought, feeling a touch of nervousness mixed with excitement. She had definitely taken the initiative. Like in so many matters, she seemed to do the right thing. Did she know that his personal struggle to move on hadn't been resolved? How could she be so confident? His thoughts were rescued from this eddy of self-doubt as he smelled her hair and gently kissed the temple of her forehead.

They both reflected quietly on the impact of the moment. How had two such different people from different parts of the country become so attached so quickly? In their thoughts, each acknowledged that this might be the right person and the right time.

The moon's reflection on the river and the relaxing privacy of their dinner gave a slow-motion effect to the evening. As they finished the last of their wine, Donna was surprised that only three hours had passed—like a private time warp.

"I'm not sure I want this evening to end right now," Donna said softly.

"I don't either. A nightcap back at the hotel would be perfect," he offered. "After all, the room provided by our government has a beautiful river view and it would be wasteful not to be efficient with its use."

She laughed at his comment, feeling good about his comfortable approach.

* * *

The cab wait was an eternity. Jake marveled at how inviting Donna looked. Her low-cut dress was far removed from her regular government-style field attire and revealed a sophisticated side Jake hadn't seen. The combination of her striking physical appearance, incredible sex appeal, and natural outdoor beauty was breathtaking. While the valet hailed their cab, they shared a brief face-to-face embrace, and each began to interpret the desire and willingness of the other.

The ride to the Marriott was a blur. The lights of the city glistened against the sky as they crossed the Potomac River. Springtime had definitely arrived in D.C. They kissed and embraced during the short trip, both of them feeling a little out of place, almost adolescent in their attraction for the other. When the cab stopped, Jake handed the driver a twenty, not waiting for the change.

"Thank you, sir! Have a good evening," was the grateful reply.

The ride to the hotel's twelfth floor seemed awkward. Jake felt a bit on display surrounded by the bright lights and mirrors of the elevator. Another couple shared the elevator with them. Donna and Jake stayed silent and smiled playfully at each other, trying not to attract attention.

* * *

The floor-to-ceiling windows of Jake's corner room displayed an impressive view of the Potomac and the city. Enough light came from outside to eliminate any need for interior lights.

Neither Jake nor Donna held any misgivings about their intentions or their willingness as they embraced barely inside the room. Relaxed, they let their emotions act as a guide.

"Would you like to see the rest of the room?" Jake murmured in a soft voice, expecting to move to the couch.

"Yes I would, Jake," Donna said, taking his hand and leading him directly to the bed.

Jake could barely cope with the splendor of Donna's naked body. And wrapped in Jake's arms, buoyed by the sight of his strong muscles and his lean torso, Donna felt lightheaded. They fit together like two lost pieces of a jigsaw puzzle.

Later Jake asked hopefully, "Can you stay the night?"

"I can't think of anything else I'd rather do."

After midnight their lovemaking reached a high-water mark. The first time had marked the initial explosion of their physical emotions, the second time ventured out into unmarked terrain, and this, the third time, established a level of trust and openness that allowed and encouraged each other to reach a new level of satisfaction and giving. By 1:30 they were both asleep in each other's arms with a sheet partially covering their exhausted bodies.

Each awoke occasionally during the night and marveled at the comfort and natural completion that the presence of the other provided. Occasional exchanges of light touches reassured each that the evening wasn't a dream.

At eight o'clock the aroma of brewed coffee edged its way into Jake's awareness. He reached for Donna but her side of the bed was empty. The coffee should have been his first clue, but it was the sound of the shower that gave him the answer he needed. In minutes, she came out wrapped in one of those white terry-cloth robes with the Marriott monogram. To Jake, her natural beauty was unparalleled, wet hair and all. The contrast of her outdoor complexion and the white robe was too much for Jake to take as he motioned her toward him. He stood up, comfortable with his own nudity, and removed the robe, slowly kissing her lips and neck.

"Good morning to you too," she said in a tone of total surrender.

During the next hour, their lovemaking was so complete that it sealed any doubt of their mutual intentions. "This," said Jake, "is the real magilla."

"Now that we've totally taken advantage of my government expense account, it might be appropriate that we do some work in return," Donna said in a reluctant tone.

Jake smiled as he held her for one more moment. "You and I are important for each other. Let's work together and see where it takes us."

With an unexpected tear of happiness in her eyes, she nodded affirmatively and brushed her hand over Jake's lips.

* * *

The rest of the day unfolded inconsequentially as far as the two of them were concerned. The meeting with Jordan Barnhart proceeded as planned—complete with a thank you to Jake, an offer of support to Donna, and an admonishment to both to be careful.

"Jake, I'd like you to think about curtailing your involvement somewhat, particularly with the potential for danger." Secretary Barnhart seemed genuinely shocked with the accounts of and future implications for violence.

"I'm sure you'll recognize, sir, that the peninsula is a relatively small community and my land is involved. Removing myself completely just isn't practical."

"I understand; just be careful."

"I'd like to have more specific information about your traveler friend, the one who tracked these packages to the Bahamas. Our people take this stuff seriously and it would give us more to go on."

"As I said, Mr. Barnhart, he's my friend. I can't reveal his identity until I have his agreement. I gave him my word." Jake and Donna could see his response irritated the secretary.

"I'll accept that answer for now, but if this goes further, the information will be imperative, regardless of your commitments and friendship."

"Fair enough."

* * *

They left his office after two hours of discussion covering all aspects of the investigation. The springtime weather continued and flowers were starting to bud. Walking across the National Park grounds on the way to the hotel gave them time to talk.

"Jake, I've given what I'm about to say a lot of thought," Donna said slowly, causing Jake an immediate feeling of hollowness.

"What do you mean?"

"These weeks together have really helped us to get to know each other. We both respect and trust each other."

"Couldn't agree more."

"Yesterday and last night were a perfect beginning to something beautiful and important. I want you to know that you have become very important to me, and I think I'm falling in love. What I'm about to say isn't going to make sense exactly, but it is why our relationship needs to go on hold while this investigation is carried out."

"I have no intention of giving you up."

"Nor I you, Jake," she responded emphatically. "I just want to do it right, and I'm afraid that the pressures to do both, at this time, will be a risky proposition. And I can't risk losing you or compromising the investigation."

The logic held, but Jake felt like he'd been punched in the stomach. "I know," he responded slowly. "It's the right thing to do, isn't it?"

She smiled and gave him a big hug. "Thanks for understanding. Most men probably wouldn't."

* * *

His late-afternoon flight to the Twin Cities allowed Jake to connect with the 10:30 flight to Bemidji. The trip gave him time to think, not about Two Fingers' murder or his career, or about the cabin and his winter experience, but about a new life. The uncertainty of future possibilities ranged from a sense of anticipation to a notion of improbability. They created an uneasy pleasantness during his trip back to Sandy Cove.

forty-three

SECRETARY BARNHART LEFT his office early that day. While the parking lot attendant brought his car around, he contemplated what he should do next.

No one in the U.S. government outside the Department of the Interior really paid attention to the licensing of Indian casinos. So when James Wingfoot approached him on behalf of a select group of men from various reservation tribal councils, he was interested. He never once thought that his agreements with these men would jeopardize his long-standing record in public office. He'd protected his thirty years on the hill like a pit bull.

The meeting with Donna Lynch and Jake Lorenz made it clear, however, that things had gotten out of control. Is it really possible that this murder and rape are somehow connected to my agreement to authorize a new casino license on the Big Bear Indian Reservation, he thought to himself. What started as an opportunity to offset some uncomfortable gambling debts with little risk had now reached a stage where Agent Lynch suspected that his reservation business partners were involved in serious criminal behavior. He paced nervously, wondering how he ever allowed himself to get into this gambling mess and Indian casino thing in the first place.

"Mr. Barnhart, Mr. Barnhart, sir," the parking attendant called as the secretary stared into space, lost in thought.

"Are you all right, sir?" the attendant asked, not wanting to embarrass the Secretary of the Interior.

"Yes, I'm just fine, Nick," he replied. "It's just been one of those days. You must have them in the parking lot business too, don't you?"

The young man nodded as he held the car door while the secretary got in.

* * *

Jordan drove around the city for an hour contemplating his next step. My involvement in these casino licenses in the past has always been simple, almost transparent; certainly no one ever got hurt, he thought. While easy money always had strings attached, this situation promised to be different. All that was required on his part was a favorable ruling on a sacred burial grounds investigation and approval of the new Norway Pine Casino license. Basically, his department responsibilities encouraged cooperating with local tribal councils on matters such as these.

"It's my job," he rationalized, as if speaking it out loud legitimized the claim.

The $100,000 payoff that had been promised was gravy. He could still back out completely if he hadn't already accepted a $20,000 advance. But maybe it wasn't too late. A call to James Wingfoot made sense under the circumstances. Jordan knew that by letting him know of his discovery, James would respond with good judgment. As a partner in the accounting firm McMillan, Larsen & Wingfoot, James would certainly understand the risks involved in proceeding with a faulty plan.

An airport pay phone provided the best place to make the call without creating attention. It was late in the afternoon. If he hurried, he could still reach James in his office, thanks to the one-hour time difference.

* * *

By 5:50 P.M. he was at Reagan International dialing the call.

"Just a moment, sir, and I'll connect you with Mr. Wingfoot," the receptionist replied.

"James, this is Jordan Barnhart."

"Hello, Mr. Secretary."

"I've got some very disturbing news that we need to discuss."

"This is a bad time. Can it wait?"

"No."

"I'm in a meeting right now. Give me a minute."

Jordan waited less than thirty seconds.

"Okay, I can talk now. What's the emergency, Mr. Secretary?"

Over the next twenty minutes, Jordan retold most of the story reported to him by Donna and Jake, including their suspicions of Sam Aguire, possible connections to the murder and rape, and the money-laundering allegation. "I don't want to be involved in this Norway Pine deal anymore." The alarm in Jordan's voice was noticeable.

"You know, Mr. Secretary, people's imaginations sometime get the best of their good judgment, particularly during long winters in the North Woods. It's certainly unfortunate that this one family has suffered so much, but I do believe that you'll find that these events are completely disassociated from each other. I can assure you that our efforts are not connected in any way."

James's success as an accounting firm partner evolved from his ability to comfort businessmen and build trust in difficult situations. Few Native Americans had penetrated this industry so deeply or achieved such prominence.

"These alleged connections to our efforts are totally without merit, Mr. Secretary. It's best to let me check into things before we do something rash."

"Well, this may be easy for you to swallow," Jordan said, "but it's not your butt hanging in the public press when things go wrong. I want you and your group to know that my support is withdrawn at the first sign of foul play. When we first discussed this, it was a simple matter—casino licensing and burial grounds investigation—that's it. Breaking laws, and even the hint of being linked to murder, are not part of the bargain."

"Please, Mr. Secretary, relax. Everything is under control. Just let me handle the details. And if it helps put your mind at ease, let's just forget that $20,000 advance and call it a bonus. You'll see the full $50,000 when the investigation is complete and another $50,000 when the casino is licensed."

"I appreciate your generosity, but there's no amount of money that's going to make up for a screwup here, James. I want you to pass on my concerns, do you understand?"

"I do, Mr. Secretary, but you'll need to have more confidence in us as well. And to keep you more informed, I'll call you with anything that doesn't match up with our agreement. Fair enough?"

At that point, neither person wanted to add more. Concerns were registered and assurances were given. Both left the conversation, however, with significant misgivings.

* * *

What James had just heard left him very disturbed. His uncle Sam had a predisposition for violence, but James was also confident that Sam was too smart to get caught in this kind of low-life crime. The money-laundering allegation was another matter altogether, as James was up to his ass in several similar schemes on different reservations through a network of accounting firms in which he had control. They all shared the similarity of having Indian gaming expertise. He wished the secretary had more complete information.

He struggled to identify a possible breach in the money transfer process. There was the paperwork mess thanks to that Indian drunk in Eau Claire, but he couldn't connect the face at all. He wasn't totally sure that he could recognize the man again—thirtyish maybe, taller than normal, but not a lot more to go on.

As he left Reagan International, Jordan's mind raced. He didn't want the end of a successful political career tarnished, or more likely ruined, with connections to crime and foul play. Sure, he had acquired large amounts of money from the management of the casino licenses, but thanks to his gambling habit, most of it had been returned to the casinos as quickly as it was received. In the end, however, the debts at the Indian casinos could be managed with political clout and position. The private gambling escapades in Atlantic City and the associated losses wouldn't succumb as easily, he worried.

He needed to have another meeting with Donna—tomorrow. He must register his concerns once more and instruct her to keep the investigation out of local activities where it didn't belong.

"God, I can't wait to get off this treadmill," he said. Retirement couldn't come fast enough. He would be out of this dirty business, able to live his life without any of the backroom deals.

"Donna, this is Secretary Barnhart. I didn't expect to catch you in as it's after eight, but I did want to leave a voice message to arrange another meeting tomorrow before you leave. Be at my office at 10:30."

forty-four

"Our friend the secretary is putting himself on a limb he doesn't want to be on," Sam responded after hearing James's assertion that Jordan was skittish and may want out.

"Half this stuff is none of his damn business anyway, and I'm not going to waste my time talking about it, particularly over the phone. In the meantime, we need to know if we have a problem with our shipments out of Bemidji. I'm shutting down everything until we've talked more when you're up here in two weeks."

As a partner in the tribe's accounting firm, James's annual visit to conduct normal audit procedures was imminent. It was his job to insure that the accounting records would attest to the validity and accuracy of the casino financial statements. James's complicity in the entire land scheme involved more than just accounting paperwork, however. The audit, the rigged slot machines, and the movement of the skimmed money to the Bahamas could all be linked to him as easily as connecting the words of a crossword puzzle. His motivation to know of any compromising irregularities well surpassed Sam's.

* * *

Two weeks later, with everyone as nervous as a cat, James arrived in Chippewa Lake. Avoiding the inevitable attention associated with a meeting at the bar, Sam, Chase, and James decided that taking a drive would ensure a completely uninterrupted discussion. It was just as well. Sam's need to keep his hands on the wheel would lesson his likelihood for violent expression.

"It's easy to figure this fiasco out, James. I haven't been sitting on my butt since your call. Somebody is sticking his nose into our business, and when I find out who the son-of-a-bitch is there'll be hell to pay. We've checked our movements at this end and nothing unusual has come up," Chase said. "In fact, the only thing that occurred worth mentioning was on a pickup several weeks ago. Some fuckin' drunk Indian stumbled into our pickup man at the Bemidji Bus Station late one night. Drunk Indians are pretty common around here, so I don't think it meant anything."

"What night was it, do you remember exactly?" James asked with a look that said he was just then connecting the pieces of a puzzle.

"What do you know?" Sam responded tersely. Emotions ran hot in the car as each man privately considered the possibility of getting their ticket punched with some serious jail time if this project unraveled.

It took only minutes to coordinate the dates of the so-called accidental bus station run-in and the encounter later the same day at the UPS desk in Eau Claire. Two drunken Indians answered to the same general description in two towns hundreds of miles apart.

"This is no accident." Sam pounded both hands on the steering wheel.

"I grew up my whole life around these Indians. Drunks like this one. He pushed all my old buttons. I didn't want anything to do with him," James said. His vehemence had little impact on the other two men. It was clear to them that their routine had been breached. That's all they cared about.

Chase finally spoke. "Do you think you could recognize this guy?"

"Maybe. It's going to be difficult, though. It's not like it was yesterday. And if he was undercover, the filthy drunken Indian look was probably a disguise."

Sam turned his head on a swivel from the driver's seat and glared at James in the backseat. "This is where you earn your keep. Difficult isn't a word we want to hear." Nephew or not, Sam meant business.

"This may not be as hard as we think," Chase offered, "even with James's blurred memory. It's not likely that James will be able to look at a photo of every Indian male adult on the reservation, but we do take pictures of all potential new-hire casino employees. That's the majority of the halfway ambitious ones. Most of the others have police records of some sort. I'm sure our friend Sheriff Betts would help us out with those if we made it worth his while."

"It's a start," James responded. "I'll spend as much time as necessary on whatever pictures you can scare up."

In the meantime, everyone agreed that the routine of cash movement from Bemidji to Eau Claire to the Bahamas had to be changed. They agreed to initiate all new shipments through Fargo, 110 miles away, with either Sam or Chase present at every pickup. Two pairs of eyes ensured tighter security. Last, each promised to be on the lookout for an Indian with the general description of "tall, about thirty, with an assertive nature." Not much to go on, except for the assertive quality. Assertiveness generally didn't fit the attribute list of Indian males on the reservation.

The next topic for discussion concerned Alex Minor.

"He's spending way too much time with Jake, as far as I'm concerned," Sam began, "and that makes me nervous. In the beginning he acted on his own. Now, I'm not sure. I think it's time to remind our silent investor of his promise to remain silent. A visit to our partner Mr. Minor is definitely in order."

* * *

Sam swung a U-turn and headed toward the peninsula. By dusk they were pulling into the parking area at Alex's lodge. Leo and King charged the car, and Chase and James shied at the idea of opening their doors. Sam, however, bristled at allowing the animals' intimidating behavior to deter him from the purpose of the visit.

If it weren't for the clamor created by the dogs, Alex wouldn't have heard the vehicle arrive. Looking out the window, he recognized the car and immediately became upset. Very little happened on the peninsula without someone noticing, and while a visit from Sam wasn't noteworthy, his and Jake's growing suspicion that this man was somehow involved with the murder caused him great discomfort. His blood pressure rose as he headed toward the door.

While crossing the living room, Alex heard one of the dogs growl viciously and take a stand with one of the men. Within seconds, he heard a hateful retaliation from the intended victim, undoubtedly Sam, he thought. Aggressive shouting and cursing mixed with loud cries of inflicted pain came from Leo.

Alex rushed to the door, opened it, and saw Leo lifeless in a pool of blood with Sam hovering like a wild animal. King was positioning to attack.

"King, stay!" Alex commanded the dog.

Alex held excellent control over both animals and King immediately stopped. After leashing him, Alex turned and said, "What the hell did you do that for?" The veins in his neck were throbbing.

"Your dogs are overrated, old man, and so are you," Sam said with ice in his voice. As he wiped the blade of his forged-steel hunting knife on his pants, he maintained a cold stare at Al. "I'll buy you another fucking dog and maybe this one will learn some manners." Chase and James recoiled in shock with Sam's loss of control, fearing that their intervention in the situation would only add to the chaos.

Alex was not to be put off by the bully, however. "Who do you think you are?"

Sam replied quickly before Alex could finish, "I'll tell you exactly who I am, old man. I'm your partner in the development of a resort that has ties to our casino. That's who I think I am. And I'm beginning to think that your new buddy-buddy friendships are getting in the way." Sam pushed, badgered, and bullied Alex for ten minutes, privately hoping that he would fight back.

"So I suggest you terminate your friendship with Jake Lorenz and start paying more attention to our business agreements. If you don't decide to play ball, you may be spending more time than you want explaining what you were doing on Jake's property last November. Who knows what people at the zoning commission, or the police for that matter, will think?"

This was the first time Alex had been confronted with his possible involvement at Jake's cabin. It caught him off-guard. He stared at Sam in contempt.

"You remind me of that dead fucking dog over there, all bark and no bite. I'm not about to put up with your bullshit any more than his," Sam announced as he finished cleaning his knife.

Alex stood there not knowing what to do as the men turned and got in their car.

"I think he got the point," Chase said to Sam while leaving.

"That's an understatement," said James. He could taste the bile at the back of his throat.

* * *

For the first time in his life, Alex recognized that he was in over his head. Just what these men knew for sure, he couldn't tell. The original business plan had been simple. He had agreed to quietly invest money in a business partnership between the Norway Pine Indian Casino in Chippewa Lake and his resort. Everyone would win. He couldn't imagine how his current interactions with Jake could cause this much malice. And these men were not privy to his conversations with Jake. To his way of thinking, the agreement with Sam and Chase still held, unless something had happened. He knew one thing for sure. Their knowledge of his involvement at Jake's created an unrelenting feeling of inner tension.

Alex had desperately wanted to distance any connection between his visit to Sandy Cove and the murder of Two Fingers. He knew that Jake's reasoning about the murder was on the right track, which is why he helped him with the Chicago lab analysis information. He came very close to telling Jake the whole truth about his business arrangements with Sam and Chase that night with Jake over at the cabin. But Jake was so honorable in dealing with Alex's confession, he couldn't bring himself to let Jake down with the whole truth of his corrupted partnership. He also knew that the traffic and congestion created between the new resort on the peninsula and the large buses to the Norway Pine Casino would upset everyone.

For a moment that night, however, Jake's integrity and character lifted Alex's personal dignity. And, as Alex remembered it, the feeling was like an aphrodisiac—one he had never experienced before. To be treated with such respect, and forgiven without judgment. Sadly, Alex had let the opportunity for the complete truth to slip by. The guilt of not being completely forthcoming in that moment stuck like a burr.

The pressure to find a solution consumed Alex well into the evening. In reality, the answer drifted further away as the circumstances became more complex. He wanted out of his bargain with these men, and they obviously weren't going to let that happen.

King's lonely whimpers reminded him to call Tony to come and help him with Leo. They planned to wrap the dog in a salt-soaked sheet as a form of preservative and place the animal's carcass in the tool shed to freeze. A proper burial would have to come after the ground thawed.

This had all the makings for a long night.

*   *   *

Sam, Chase, and James went straight to town for a few beers and something to eat at the Twin Pines.

"What are you staring at me for?" Sam said to James. "His money, his arrogance; I can't stand the guy. And that stupid dog got what he deserved."

Sobered by the day's events, their discussions wandered, adding nothing new to their conclusions. They ate quickly and headed for the casino. It was early and Chase wanted to complete the weekly collection. James wanted to get a start on reviewing the employment photographs. Both men wanted to distance themselves from Sam's vile anger.

*   *   *

The casino parking lot brimmed with cars, which was always a good sign for business and the men's spirits. They proceeded directly through the gaming area toward their respective duties.

One player was about to have a "luck of the draw" experience that had nothing to do with the game being played. While quietly celebrating a blackjack on a fifty-dollar bet, Big Lights captured an image out of the periphery of his vision. He instantly recognized a critical piece of the puzzle in the form of James Wingfoot, the well-dressed Indian from Eau Claire, walking stride for stride with Sam and Chase. The image spoke volumes.

Without attracting attention, he cashed in his chips and left the casino.

forty-five

DONNA AND THE investigation team returned to Arrowhead within the week. They dedicated Saturday morning to the final review of their plans before beginning the excavation that afternoon. With the spring thaw almost complete, the ground had softened to the point where work could begin. Everyone chomped at the bit to get started.

The Cedar Lodge game room became their conference and planning area to organize the excavation efforts. Large-scale government section maps hung on one wall, identifying virtually every piece of Alex and Jake's land. The goal that afternoon was to create a grid by visually marking all the survey stakes. Coordinate-scale mapping would pinpoint the exact discovery locations throughout the excavation process.

Just prior to the meeting's conclusion around lunch, Jake walked in. Not having seen Donna since his departure in D.C. forced Jake to exercise considerable self-discipline not to embrace her, even in a friendly manner.

"Good morning, Jake," she said cordially. The team members also greeted Jake and shook hands; his cooperative efforts had created good relations across the board. He helped himself to a cup of coffee and a donut and sat down at the large table, trying not to engage Donna's beautiful eyes.

God, she's gorgeous, he thought.

"Even though we'll be a while before finishing the investigation on Mr. Minor's property, I want the team to show you their plans for your land, should additional excavation be necessary and we start tramping all over it. The maps are marked with the likely spots for digging."

"What do you think the chances are for discovering burial sites on my property?" Jake's tone was businesslike.

One of the investigation team members motioned for Jake to come closer to the map, indicating that the answer was going to be more than just a quick response.

"We want to be very open with you, Jake. We know that it's only through your permission that this informal part of the investigation can proceed."

"Why hasn't the local tribe filed an additional request on their own to include my property in the investigation?"

"That's a very good question. Their lack of initiation is part of what has us confused. Let me explain what I mean," Donna said, moving confidently toward the map. "I know we talked about the history of the peninsula before, but it bears repeating in order to be clear in making my point."

She went on to summarize some interesting facts about the peninsula. Some Jake remembered from their first visit and others he didn't. Regardless, her explanation connected the history to their investigation in a way that demonstrated that these people had truly done their homework.

For everyone's benefit, she briefly recapped the historical facts regarding the peninsula from the perspective of the documented explorations of Lieutenant Zebulon Pike and Henry Schoolcraft. Jake knew that both men had been commissioned by the U.S. government in the early 1800s to discover the headwaters of the Mississippi River. He had forgotten that people then believed that Big Bear Lake was the logical choice. Therefore, both explorers spent considerable time on the lake.

"Even though Lake Itasca ended up as the definitive source of the big river, their efforts on Big Bear were obviously not an accident," Donna said. "And it appears that the facts recorded in their official journals are very relevant to what we're doing in our investigation.

"You'll remember that both explorers pinpointed the existence of a Hudson Bay Trading Company post on Arrowhead Peninsula. This trading post was taken by Pike from the British and converted to an American Trading Company post early in 1807.

"What makes this important is that the exact location of the trading company has never been found. I know I'm being repetitious, but our core samples absolutely support the theory that its original foundation is under the old Minor lodge.

"History lesson number two," she went on while pointing to a different location on the map, "is that the location of Chief Flat Mouth's village for over thirty years was about a mile east of this same post. The chief had tremendous power among the Ojibwe. As a result, this village is believed to have been one of the largest intact villages for at least several decades. And, as a longtime friend of the U.S. government during the Hundred Years War, Flat Mouth's village had enormous historical significance."

"Come on. And we're supposed to believe that we're the first ones to find it. How can that be?" Jake's facial expression mirrored the skepticism in his voice. "I remember the part where the lake was dammed at the Sugar River to float the white pine to Stillwater, but I'm still not connecting this history lesson to why my land wasn't included in the official investigation. Sure, it's easy to see that the village was probably wiped out when they created the dam. I'll grant you that, but they're claiming only six burial sites—not a lot for a substantial village."

"That is why these sites are so important. They may be the only remaining connection to this important village," Donna replied.

"Added to the conclusive results that the old Minor lodge is the original site of the trading company, we believe the chances are very high that these burial sites on Mr. Minor's property are, in fact, real. But as you say, if all the historical facts are in evidence, then six sites don't make sense to us either. The RTC tribal leaders know this, but they've chosen to investigate only Mr. Minor's property. We need to find out why. The answer may be literally buried on your property."

"As always, you people have done your homework. I can't say that I wish you the best, but I will promise my complete cooperation." There was nothing else Jake could say or do.

He motioned to Donna for a private moment before leaving the lodge.

"I know the historical facts make sense, and I agree with your need to answer the question about Sandy Cove, but something is still very wrong." He quickly gave her the new information from Big Lights about the identification of James Wingfoot as a part of the suspected money courier process.

"Unbelievable! But Jake, you've got to trust me on this. I agree with your instincts and there clearly appears to be criminal intent. But for some reason, I'm on very thin ice with the secretary. Hopefully, this new information will be the connection we need, since money-laundering is a federal offense."

"How could the secretary be anything but 100-percent convinced? And what do you mean, 'thin ice'?"

"After you left D.C., he called me for one more meeting. He told me in no uncertain terms that I needed to prevent this investigation from straying into local politics, as he termed it. He went so far as to tell me that 'if I was not able to control the direction of the investigation,' I would be replaced.

"When I asked him about the reference to McMillan Larsen Wingfoot on the original notification, he shrugged it off as natural involvement by an accounting firm with its client. It certainly seems that it may now be more than that. But in the end, I'm not sure how much latitude I'm going to get to expand this investigation."

"Do your team members suspect anything?"

"Only that this investigation is very important and has the potential for conflict. I think they suspect you and I are a little more than friends, as well."

"I'll be happy when this is over and we can remove all doubt of that fact," Jake said with a smile.

Her smile in return gave him the reassurance he needed.

"Secretary Barnhart instructed me not to get involved, but he didn't instruct me not to involve others. So, I've made a decision to call a friend from the FBI. As you probably know, the reservation made a declaration about twelve years ago as to the kind of law enforcement support they would want for serious criminal activity. Their options included either the local county marshal or the FBI. The Big Bear Lake Indian Reservation, like most large ones, chose the FBI."

"I'm aware of that."

"This will definitely work to our advantage, particularly considering this new information. I just hope you've warned Big Lights of his vulnerability."

"I have, but I think we need to bring him in on our efforts, if for no other reason than to protect him."

"Agreed."

"What I want you to do is to call Agent Warren Thompson in the Twin Cities office tomorrow. Tell him everything. He'll know what to do. I'll let him know to expect your call."

"Will this put your job in jeopardy, considering the secretary's stance?"

"Maybe, but I can't worry about that. What's most important is that we get to the bottom of this snake pit."

"Be careful."

They parted, and Jake walked out of the lodge. Alex was just pulling into the parking lot.

"It looks like it's your turn, Alex."

"Yeah, something like that," he mumbled.

Jake dismissed Alex's bad temper to the fact that he was about to be grilled by the investigation team. He also noticed that Alex didn't look so good. His skin was clammy and covered with a light sweat. Maybe a spring cold or the onset of the flu, he thought.

forty-six

THE RESPONSE THAT Jake received to his phone call to the FBI was very cordial. Either it was Donna's influence or the compelling circumstances of the story, or both, that stimulated immediate involvement. Regardless, not two days went by before he and Big Lights linked up with agents Warren Thompson and Joseph Brightstar in a face-to-face meeting. Donna's generous introduction paved the way for them, Jake thought, as he noticed an immediate demeanor of trust and friendship.

Agent Thompson was older and gray around the temples, about six feet two inches and well built. He had worked out of the Twin Cities office for twenty years and was the FBI lead involved in this inquiry. What surprised Jake was the fact that Donna had originally started her career with the bureau; Agent Thompson had been her first boss. He and Donna had worked together for almost ten years. Over that time, however, her husband, Ed, became very uneasy with the risks associated with her investigations. To save the marriage, Donna got reassigned to the Department of the Interior. Her not wearing a weapon was a big deal for Ed.

Agent Brightstar was an Ojibwe Native American who grew up on the La Du Flambeau Indian Reservation in Wisconsin. As such, he had an insider's viewpoint of Native American problems, which facilitated his effectiveness in going undercover. His passion was for the battle against fraud and corruption being fought on reservations across the country. Since he was young and single, Brightstar's five-year tenure with the bureau had been laced with high-risk assignments. This was his first, however, on the Big Bear Lake Reservation.

Jake had originally approached Alex to be a part of this first meeting with the FBI as well, but Alex declined for reasons he couldn't quite pinpoint—intuitive gut feel. Big Lights, on the other hand, couldn't be contained when Jake suggested his involvement.

Linda continued to make good progress in her recovery, which gave Big Lights the self-delegated latitude to pursue anyone he thought had any involvement with her attack. He had known that Morey was a bully. But he also didn't believe that Morey was smart enough to act alone on anything. There was always someone behind his actions. Now he had been given the chance to find the connection.

From the very beginning, the team of men jelled as if they had worked together for years. Maybe it was the sense of common purpose, maybe it was the motivation of Donna and Linda, or maybe it was the anticipation that something very important was about to happen. Regardless, the four teamed up under Warren's direction to build a plan to expose the truth. Jake and Big Lights promised to participate only as directed, though. Based on Warren and Joseph's suspicions, the likelihood of violence hung heavy in the air.

The first part of the plan was easy.

"You mean you want Jake and me to go to the casino every day to bet the government's money, and we get to keep what we win," Big Lights said. Sheer delight caused his feet to twitch while he sat.

"Hell, Jake, we're gonna be rich."

"Let's not get out of control before we start," Warren said, sensing that perhaps one member of their team wasn't as disciplined as the others.

"First off, all of us are going to be there in some capacity or another. I'll be the fisherman from Iowa staying at one of the local lodges. Joseph will be the typical itinerant Indian recently released from the Hennepin County jail for a drunk and disorderly conduct conviction, and you two will be local, ordinary faces that are familiar to the dealers."

"Now listen up." Warren rapped the flip chart for emphasis. "Contrary to your idea of throwing all kinds of money around, which would only attract attention, we are going to lose money gradually, or launder our own, so to speak. Not so we'd look foolish, but in such a way that we can get five thousand dollars of our marked bills into the casino tills. All we need is for just one of those bills to show up in a package sent to the Bahamas and we'll be in business."

"Do you think you can do that without drawing attention to your actions?" Warren's comment was meant for the group, but his eyes were fixed on Big Lights.

"It seems like he's just asking you to play your normal game of blackjack," Jake responded lightheartedly, glancing at Big Lights.

The group laughed as Big Lights mumbled some indignation about Jake's manhood.

"Listen up . . . a couple more items, guys. First, even though this is Joe's first assignment at Big Bear Lake, he is known by many people in the Indian community. His disguise will protect him as long as we don't make any foolish acknowledgments to his identity. Second, we've had our eye on McMillan, Larsen & Wingfoot for some time. We've always known that an Indian Mafia exists, and it's our belief that this firm is a major player in their casino corruption operations. And for sure," motioning toward Jake and Big Lights, "play it safe and conservative. There's no reason for either of you two to be taking risks. We appreciate your involvement, but we don't want to see you get hurt. If something happens, get out immediately. Understand?"

"We got it," said Jake, as Big Lights nodded.

* * *

Over the next week, agents Thompson and Brightstar established a surveillance watch over the casino to validate the movement of money. Just as Big Lights had predicted, the accounting briefcase found its way into the casino via Chase and Sam every day. The packages, however, never made it to the bus station lockboxes in Bemidji. Something had changed.

They didn't want to start their infiltration of marked bills into the casino until they knew the exact procedure. So the following week, Joseph set up surveillance to retrace the physical movement again. His careful scrutiny led to the discovery that the new shipping location was out of Fargo. The routing had also been changed to avoid Eau Claire. The fact that James Wingfoot had taken himself out of the handling process could only mean that they were nervous, maybe suspicious. How this happened, nobody could pinpoint. Nonetheless, it was obvious the team would need to redouble their efforts and be very careful.

*　*　*

With their plans now complete, each man began his effort to lose a few thousand dollars or so over the next several days. They wanted the money to be in the next weekly drop in Fargo. For the most part everything went well. One run of great cards, however, put Big Lights up a thousand dollars on the second day. It broke his heart to piddle it away with naïve bets and high-risk hits on the blackjack table. The men spread their time out over multiple shifts, but always in pairs, in order not to attract attention. The money slowly slipped out of their hands and into the casino tills.

At about 11:30 on the fifth night, James Wingfoot walked across the casino floor after completing the audit. On the way out he chose an exit path coincidently intersecting with Big Lights' blackjack table. Big Lights saw him coming and kept his head down to avoid eye contact. It would be game over if he was recognized. James kept walking and continued scanning the players as he approached within fifteen feet of Big Lights' table. Big Lights hunkered down as if he'd dropped something, hoping that James would walk by without seeing him.

Warren doubled down on a blackjack bet not far from Big Lights when he saw the direction James headed while leaving the casino. It took Warren two seconds to realize what was about to happen. That son-of-a-bitch was going to recognize Big Lights.

Without another moment the action started.

"Goddamn it, learn how to play the game or don't play at all! This is the last time this jackass is going to screw up one of my hands," Warren yelled as he took a swing at the player next to him.

This attack took the other player totally by surprise. The player retaliated with a flurry of punches in order to defend himself and counter Warren's attack. Within seconds the pit was in an uproar, and the attention of the entire casino shifted to Warren's table. In a few more seconds, three security guards subdued Warren as the instigator of the altercation. James's natural instinct to get involved overtook his casual departure from the casino. He motioned for more security guards to the scene to resolve the problem quickly.

Big Lights saw the commotion caused by Warren's outburst and at the same time saw James turn away from his table. He knew the distraction was his signal to get out, and get out quick. Gathering his chips, he left the casino before the security guards had Warren under control.

It took about ten minutes to settle the issue. Warren became very humble and apologized for losing control.

"That's my paycheck I just lost," he said, desperately.

The other player decided not to press charges as he had seen Warren lose money all night. Besides, he had gotten the best of the punches.

Security escorted Warren to the door and gave him a clear directive not to come back. "You're damn lucky the management isn't pressing any charges," one of the officers said.

James turned to leave, when the security chief distracted him again, asking if he was okay.

"Yeah, I'm fine. Does this happen often?"

"First time ever for me," replied the security guard. "Must be a full moon. Is there anything I can get you before you leave, Mr. Wing-foot?"

"No, I don't think so."

James left the gaming area of the casino and walked down the hallway toward the connected hotel rooms, happy with the thought of heading back to Eau Claire in the morning. After working sixteen hours a day for five days straight to complete the casino audit, he was exhausted.

*　*　*

At breakfast the next day, the four men assessed damages and concluded that Warren's actions warranted an Oscar, and that Big Lights really had paid attention to their pre-game instructions.

"I know the look, guys," Warren was saying. "This James Wingfoot character was definitely sizing you up. It's hard to say where his mind is now, but we'll watch him closely for a few days to see if he acts normally or not. In the meantime, you and I are eighty-sixed from the casino until this inquiry is over. Jake and Joe will have to finish things up."

"That shouldn't be too hard to do, boss," Joseph replied. "We've got only seven hundred left among the four of us. From the looks of things, we'd better keep our day jobs. I don't know about you guys, but I didn't have to try very hard to go through my money."

forty-seven

LINDA'S CONDITION IMPROVED immensely over the weeks she had been staying at Michelle's grandparents. Mothering from Helen and sisterly care from Michelle provided her with a well-received drip therapy for the soul. The psychological impact noticeably accelerated her physical recovery.

Jake's visits also provided an important recuperative element that only he seemed able to supply. They connected like a father and his adult child—concerned and caring on Jake's part, respectful and reliant on her part. Throughout her recovery, he had become the main source of strength necessary to cope with her emotional battle. His sensitivity and understanding helped her break through the emerging and terrifying images that surfaced as she relived the true horror of her attack. Recovering her memory was a blessing and a curse. Long hours of crying were interrupted with delicate discussions of self-worth. Jake's ability to guide her at these times facilitated Linda's mental reconstruction.

The fact that Morey had died held no importance for Linda. Jake reveled in this, as he knew that her future had no connection to Morey's existence, regardless of its destructive nature. The good news for everyone lay in her renewed confidence and involvement in the Omaha Project. Jake thanked God when he finally realized she was out of the woods.

Most special, however, was Big Lights. She had fallen head over heels for him. He brought out the fun and excitement of being alive and loving another person. His passion and spontaneity for life were the perfect ingredients she needed. He'd even dramatically cut back his beer intake, realizing that those days were over if he expected to live up to his promises to Linda. She had been searching, but she didn't really know what a good partner looked like until she met Big Lights. In her mind, he filled her needs completely, which is why she accepted his proposal of marriage, but only after making him do it over again.

And Big Lights did rise to the occasion.

"This time I want witnesses," he declared right after a Sunday dinner with Helen, Bud, Michelle, Bobby, and Jake present.

Very dramatically, he got down on one knee in front of Linda while she sat on the living room sofa.

"Linda," he said after taking her hand, "I want you to know that my love for you will last as long as the stars in the sky. My commitment to our life together will not be shaken by all eternity. You make me happy and I want to share everything I have with you. Will you make these promises come true by marrying me?"

Even though his proposal didn't surprise Linda, tears welled in her eyes and she smiled beautifully.

"Yes, yes, I will." Her nervousness and tears cut her response short, but the magic between them was obvious to all.

In the bargain that day, Linda also received the gift of love and support from her new family.

* * *

Helen struggled to find an appropriate engagement gift for Linda. She wanted it to be special. She hoped the gift would capture the need for family connection they all had observed in Linda. The following day it struck Helen to reframe the picture of Linda and her father that had stood as his reminder of her in his work shed—the one that Jake had found. The picture recaptured one of the few happy connections to Linda's real family and she knew that the young woman treasured it dearly.

While removing the five-and-dime frame, Helen noticed an interesting drawing, more like a sketch or map, under the backing of the picture.

"Oh, my goodness!"

In a primitive way, Helen saw the Arrowhead Peninsula outlined with several easy-to-recognize landmarks, like Jake's cabin and both Minor lodges. Six additional X's were also on the map, each with a date from last year in parentheses.

"Linda, would you come in here for a minute," Helen called out from the study.

"I really wanted this to be a surprise, but I found something that can't wait," she said excitedly, holding up the picture removed from its frame. "Look at these markings on the back of this picture. Do they have any significance to you? Are they something that you and your dad talked about when you were a girl?"

"Let me see."

For what seemed like several minutes, Linda studied the drawing, trying to connect it to her dad.

"It looks like an outline of the peninsula, but I don't remember my dad showing me this. It's his handwriting, all right, but I'm also pretty sure that I've never seen it. What I do remember is this picture sitting in the cemetery shed for years. It always made me feel good that he kept it."

"Well, I'm about ready to wet my pants if it's what I think it is," Helen replied. Helen was always about ready to wet her pants when something exciting was about to happen. In fact, according to Bud's testimony, at times she did. But she would always deny it emphatically, saying, "it's just an expression."

Important or not, Helen wasn't about to let this discovery go by without full attention from Donna and Jake. Her compelling phone call to both of them generated the appropriate response. They convened in Helen's living room within the hour. Even though Linda owned the picture, Helen clutched it like it was a hundred-dollar bill in a windstorm. She kept her discovery a secret until both were there. This was Helen's fifteen minutes of fame. She milked it for everything it was worth.

* * *

"Do you think this is important?" She asked them several times.

"You did the right thing by calling and you're absolutely right, Helen, it is very critical to our investigation. But you've got to listen to me now," Jake said, making clear eye contact with one of the world's most prolific gossips. Jake was totally confident in Linda's ability to hold information close to her vest, but Helen was another matter.

"I'm going to ask you to do something very important and very difficult. You've got to promise me not to tell anyone about this, not Bud, not Big Lights, not Michelle. Nobody! Can you do that?" His emphasis was not understated.

Before she could respond, Donna echoed the urgency of Jake's direct request. "This may be the most important discovery of the entire investigation, but it will become worthless if we lose control of it by others finding out now. We need both of you to be on our team 100 percent." Once again, Donna's innate knowledge of human nature played perfectly in generating the needed response from both women.

Linda was first. "I know how hard both of you have worked to get to the bottom of what's going on. There's nothing I would do to jeopardize that, I promise."

When Linda finished, Helen said, "I would feel better if you swore me in or something like that. I've never been on a government investigation team. Taking an oath would make it official. I would never break an oath."

"I'm glad you said that, Helen," Donna replied in stride. "I'll swear you both in right now with Jake as a witness. Both of you must understand, though, that breaking this oath would be a federal crime." Donna's look of seriousness matched the importance Helen felt in her discovery.

With the promise of both women, Donna proceeded with the most official-sounding swearing-in ceremony one could ever hope for, considering she had to invent the oath while she talked. Using a Bible in a not-so-subtle stroke of genius reinforced the importance of their vow of silence.

"Should we plan on being part of your official investigation meetings over at the lodge?" Helen asked with a great sense of solemnity.

"Let me think about that," Donna replied slowly, knowing privately that that was the last thing she wanted.

"At this time, it may be too much of a safety risk. If people saw you coming to our meetings it would raise questions and possibly compromise your position on the team. Plus, it might be difficult for you to explain to Bud what you were doing. No, for now, I think we're better off maintaining a clandestine involvement on your part."

The look of grave disappointment on Helen's face was priceless, but her acknowledgment of Donna's logic sealed her lips forever.

* * *

When Donna and Jake had left Helen's house and were out of sight beyond the garage, Jake looked at Donna and said with a mocking look on his face, "Are you going to swear me in as well? Because if you are, I think maybe I should have my lawyer present."

She slugged him playfully on his right shoulder.

"You, mister. We have special plans for you if you break the rules. And I'll be the one to administer the punishment."

"I can't wait."

He paused. "Seriously, though, isn't it amazing how something so important can just sit under our noses for months? Now all we have to do is to figure out just how and why Two Fingers was involved."

"Very important. No doubt, it's also what got him killed."

Once they reached their cars, Donna said, "It might be a good time to come over to the lodge to look at the results of the latest sonoprobes from your property. I think they should be finished by now. We'll need to coordinate our activities by making sure you're up to speed on our next steps."

"Fine with me."

* * *

Inside the lodge, one of the team's specialists explained what they believed they had discovered in the printouts. "Our consensus conclusion from the sono-probe activities on your property is amazing, to say the least." His excitement reminded Jake of an expectant father showing off his pregnant wife's ultrasound.

"It's hard to say how many burial sites actually exist on your property, Mr. Lorenz, but it's safe to say that fifty to sixty is conservative."

"What!" Jake stated in true amazement.

"I gotta tell you, Mr. Lorenz, that our confidence in validating this discovery is very high. But it sure does add to the puzzlement of the six sites located on Mr. Minor's property. I mean, if your property is the true sacred burial grounds for the Flat Mouth village, what are these six isolated sites all about?"

"He's right, Jake," Donna added. "I don't know of any previous fieldwork where a large concentration of burial sites was peppered with multiple random outlying locations like this. It's a very unusual pattern."

"Absolutely amazing! Just tell me what you need from me."

"I'm anxious to begin excavating your property also, but I think we should start with the six separate sites first. When we're done with them, it will be important to excavate on your land. It's also a good idea to have your authorization in writing as an official part of our records. We'll draw something up for you to sign, if that's okay?"

"No problem. What I will want in return, though," said Jake, "is an agreement to keep the results quiet once the analysis is complete. I want to see how Sam and Chase react as a result of the original six discoveries. These six sites are critical to their plan. I believe that we may ruin our chance to uncover that plan if the information from my land is allowed to become public knowledge too soon. Since the research on my property isn't an official part of the investigation, at least not yet anyway, I want to have final say on any announcement of the findings."

"You've earned the right to have the final say. There isn't one of us who disagrees with your logic." Each team member willingly nodded his approval, confirming their respect for Jake's insight into the complex circumstances of this investigation.

forty-eight

WITH ONLY ONE road onto the Arrowhead Peninsula, it was like living in a fishbowl. Any activity or disturbance was noticed or heard by someone, regardless. And that night was no different as the ambulance raced along the dirt-road artery.

The year-round residences definitely heard the ominous sound. It could only mean that one of their neighbors was in trouble. Bud and Ken were both at home and took up the call by jumping in their trucks, following in the direction of the siren on its way toward Eagle Feather Bay.

The minimal growth of the spring foliage provided no filter at all for the flashing red light. Without ambient light and amidst the subtle nighttime forest sounds, the intrusion ripped away at the forest's serenity with the progesssive movement of the ambulance. Bud and Ken arrived at the Minor lodge almost simultaneously to see Alex, strapped to a gurney, being lifted by paramedics into the vehicle.

Tony just stood there lost. He had found Alex on his back, gasping for breath, semi-conscious, obviously in great pain.

"Make way, guys," one of the paramedics announced. "We've got to get this guy to the hospital fast."

As they hurried past, Alex made a feeble grabbing motion toward Bud, trying to get his attention. His hand swiped once and missed, but on the second try he managed to seize Bud's winter jacket by the pocket.

"Tell Jake to come," he said in a slurred voice. "I need . . . talk . . . important . . ." His face was gray and flushed. A look of desperation and fear was punctuated with reddened eyes. Within seconds, he threw his head back in the grip of a new seizure that rendered him unconscious. The paramedics lifted the gurney into the ambulance and slammed the back doors.

Ken backed away in shock and put his hand on Tony's shoulder in a comforting gesture. Despite what people thought of Alex, Tony had worked for him for many years and Ken knew Tony respected him. Full-time caretaker jobs in the area were scarce. Tony knew that Alex was generous to him.

"What the fuck happened?" Ken asked in disbelief.

"I don't really know. I just found him in the pole-barn on the dirt floor, barely conscious. King was barking out of control, which is what attracted my attention. When I got there, King was pacing, but wouldn't leave Alex's reach. It was like he was on an invisible leash. Other than that, I didn't hear a sound, nothing. It's hard to say how long he had been like that. My guess is that he had a stroke."

"Did he say anything else, like why he wanted Jake?"

"He was hard to understand and not making a lot of sense. He just kept saying he needed to talk with Jake, but never gave any reason or said what it was about."

As he backed out, the ambulance driver said they were going to the hospital in Bemidji, and that they would do their best to get him there in time.

After talking with Tony for a few more minutes, Bud and Ken realized that they could do nothing to help at the lodge now. They decided to go to Ken's to make some phone calls to locate Jake.

Alex faded in and out of consciousness during the trip to the hospital. At times he thought he was actually talking to Jake, telling him how much he wished he could take things back, and that Jake was a friend, maybe the only one he had. In truth, though, he wasn't absolutely sure what he thought or said. Nothing really registered.

"Jake, it'll be okay," the drivers heard him say more than once during the trip.

At other times, he argued with Sam and Chase, knowing he was being double-crossed, and that it was a bad bargain from the beginning. "Can't trust . . . sons-of-bitches. Bastards. Why . . . involved?" More mangled thoughts whirled in his brain.

In one brief moment of clarity, Alex wanted Jake to know the truth about Two Fingers, the land, the burial sites, the bargain with Sam—the whole truth, and that everything would be okay. "Be okay," he slurred. "Taken care . . . everything." And then silence.

The incessant alarm of the heart monitor signaled the story of the flatlining graph. Time no longer mattered.

* * *

Ken and Bud tried everywhere but couldn't find Jake. Finally they thought to call the rented office headquarters for the Omaha Project. Jake, Linda, and Big Lights were there reviewing new candidate resumes for computer-specialist positions.

In seconds, Ken relayed the situation to Jake, and within minutes Jake and Big Lights were in Jake's truck racing toward Bemidji.

"Man, I don't get it," Big Lights said somewhat incredulously. "This guy all but fucks you and you're still driving like an idiot to do what he wants."

"I'm not entirely sure what's going on either," Jake replied, keeping his attention on the road. "It's as if I know Alex from another time. I can't quite explain it. I don't want to make excuses for him, but it seems like there's another Alex who wants to do what's right and every so often he shows up. I've just got a feeling that this is one of those times."

"It may be his last if what Ken said about his condition is true."

They flew across the highway, shaving fifteen minutes off the normal trip to the hospital. Once in the emergency room, Big Lights began asking the questions. Everyone in the hospital knew him now as Linda's fiancé.

"There was a man brought here just a short time ago, an older man . . . name's Alex Minor. We need to see him right away, if that's possible."

One of the nurses approached soberly and spoke directly to Big Lights. "I'm afraid that the news isn't good. Mr. Minor died during his trip to the hospital. The paramedics did everything humanly possible, but apparently there were two more strokes. The time comes when it's just over."

"Thanks for the information. Would it be okay with you if we talked to the drivers? Are they still around?"

She motioned to the two men at the end of the nurses' stand and said, "I don't know why not."

Jake was clearly shaken. He grabbed the nursing station counter with both hands and leaned forward as if out of breath.

After asking a few questions it was clear that Alex had not divulged any other useful information. The comments the drivers relayed about "everything's okay" provided little comfort to Jake; he couldn't help feeling that the comment was very far from the real truth.

* * *

The ride back to Jake's cabin was strangely silent. For one time in his life Big Lights could think of nothing to say. Jake's mind tumbled back and forth between the human loss and his concern about the loss of critical information possessed by Alex. Regardless of whether or not the information would have been admissible in a court of law, Alex did have a firsthand understanding of the deal that was going down. He also had the result of the analysis done on the gloves. He may have actually known who really murdered Two Fingers.

"Two Fingers was murdered, Linda's been raped, Morey drowned, and now Alex is gone," Jake said, punctuating the silence. "A lot of people hurt. And we may be further from the answers now than ever before."

"Are you okay, Jake?" Big Lights asked.

"Where is this thing going, Big Lights? How many more people are going to be impacted?" The despondency in his voice actually scared Big Lights.

"I don't know, man, but you don't sound all right at all. This isn't like you."

"I'm okay, I'll be fine," he mumbled disbelievingly.

During the remaining ride home, Jake continued turning the facts around and around in his mind, looking for new insights. He couldn't find any.

forty-nine

OVER THE NEXT two days, the burial sites on Alex's land were excavated in painstaking detail. The sono-probes proved to be absolutely accurate in their determination. Six bodies were found, one each in the general vicinity of the sites originally identified by Sam and Chase.

At the last excavation site, Sam and Chase surveyed the work crew's activities, as they had all the others, and talked quietly off to the side, away from Donna and the other men.

"I think our goddamn luck is finally starting to change," Sam said. "With that son-of-a-bitch dead, any thoughts I had of a double-cross are gone."

"You're absolutely right. He was beginning to worry me more than a little. I think the old bastard was actually starting to go soft on us. I also think that this Donna bitch is going to play right into our hands as well."

"How so?"

"The way I see it, Agent Donna Lynch is about to confirm the authenticity of the burial sites and our work. It can't get any better. Any conflict-of-interest questions that might have come up will be moot points. She's the expert, and all we have to do is to agree with her findings. The decision will be easy and the land will rightfully revert to our control. And with Alex gone, legal interferences should be nonexistent."

As usual, Chase had analyzed the situation thoroughly. The only real possibility for a screwup now would come from a discrepancy in the authenticity report given by Agent Lynch. He wasn't worried. She was one competent broad, particularly in the area of Indian history and culture. The careful attention to detail they had taken with Two Fingers in replicating the Ojibwe burial customs was about to pay off. As a longtime caretaker of the cemetery, no one could have been better suited for the task. Chase was positive that Agent Lynch's report would validate his conviction.

"You seem mighty confident, my friend. For our sake, you better be right."

Donna walked up to the two men just as they finished their conversation.

"Have you put that Ph.D. of yours to work so we can move forward with what we already know?" Chase's implication and tone showed indignation.

Donna didn't like either man but remained businesslike in her reply.

"The results of the excavations over the past two days are very significant and could well support your position that the land may be part of a sacred burial ground. I'm not prepared to make any decisions on my finding today, though, not without considering all the facts. With the fieldwork finished, I'll be ready to give you my written report by the end of the week." Donna knew better than to discuss the findings informally with these men any further.

Sam disliked the ease with which this white woman addressed his heritage. Her tribal knowledge intruded on his Native American turf and his need to be right. That pissed him off. As the appointed member of the Reservation Tribal Council, he would be the one to declare the site a sacred burial ground, not this bitch. The angry expression on his face overrode any attempt to conceal his feelings.

Donna walked away without waiting for any formalities that would indicate that the discussion had ended. Her practice of not negotiating her conclusions would not be violated, particularly with this scum.

* * *

The spring thaw had melted the dirt road into a combination of mud and ice. Driving on this partially frozen slime was treacherous, and Donna maneuvered carefully back to the lodge, reflecting on her pending conclusions.

There wasn't one piece of evidence that would dispute Sam and Chase's claim. In fact, on the contrary, every piece completely supported their claim. Her report would have to deal with that reality, which would certainly justify invoking the Sacred Burial Grounds Act to transfer the land's guardianship, and ultimate control, from the Alex Minor estate to the Big Bear Lake Reservation Tribal Council.

On the other hand, her team's unsanctioned research into Jake's property would equally justify an investigation as to how six burial sites could logically have been located so far from the main burial location. But so far, she had been unsuccessful in gaining approval from Secretary Barnhart to proceed with the necessary excavation work on Jake's land—still an unproven allegation. Donna knew whatever such an investigation uncovered would ultimately link Jake's land to the tribal claim. And as the final decision-making body, the RTC would likely receive another gift of thirty acres. Not a big piece of land in the grand scheme of things, but a very important piece of real estate to Jake Lorenz. Jake could lose everything he'd worked so hard to keep.

But the truth remained that the RTC hadn't expressed any interest in his property. Since only a recognized Indian tribal authority could initiate a government investigation, any fieldwork on Jake's property without the secretary's approval would have to be done outside the investigation team's official jurisdiction. This would certainly and most positively taint the results with an air of impropriety. In the end, Jake could be further exposed to these ruthless people.

Then again, she thought, if everything she and Jake believed was completely true, some bad people could be sent to jail for a long time. The risks, regardless of the path chosen, were very high.

By the time she reached the lodge, she realized that her first course of action was clear. Her team must complete the investigation she had been sent there to do. To do anything else would compromise the validity of any other argument or proposal eventually presented.

With dispatch, she began compiling the evidence and preparing her report.

Her education and years of field research had taught her that the Ojibwe believed that their home after death lies westward. The road to this home was referred to as Ke-wa-kun-ah, or homeward road. Logically, the body of the deceased was positioned facing west, in a sitting position, to enable the soul to stand immediately after death and begin the journey. The articles needed in life for such a journey were buried with the deceased. For a man, these articles included his gun or bow and arrows, blanket, kettle, fire steel, flint, moccasins, black spruce pitch, and dandelion oil. For a woman, these articles included her moccasins, axe, portage collar, blanket, kettle, black spruce pitch, and dandelion oil. Some of these items would carry images of the deceased's family totem.

In the excavation sites, the team discovered four women and two men. Their totems accurately represented the Pillager Ojibwe claim to the Me-she-num-aig-way, or immense fish. Each of the bodies possessed a physical uniqueness particular to the Pillager people, who enjoyed long life and a fineness of hair, especially in old age. Every artifact uncovered was accurate and authentic. And the presence of spruce pitch and dandelion oil for the spirit's journey were found in all six sites. The fact that there were more women than men was explained by the harsh reality of the times. When men died in battle, their bodies were rarely recovered. As a form of disrespect, the bodies were mutilated and dumped in mass graves by their enemy. The two men discovered, along with the women, all died of natural causes in their later years. In addition, all of the dating tests confirmed these corpses to be from the early 1800s, the time during which the village of Chief Flat Mouth thrived on the peninsula.

In her report, the only conclusion to cast even the slightest doubt on the sacred burial ground theory was the minimal numbers of corpses, which inaccurately reflected the size of the thirty-year-old village. Donna devoted several paragraphs to this important point. She wanted to establish a possible link to the real burial grounds that she believed existed less than half a mile to the north. Without this discovery on Jake's land, she knew it could also be argued that the main burial grounds had been covered with water when the dam was constructed. Two hundred years of water and fish life would eliminate any trace of their existence. She had to find a way to complete the investigation on Jake's land without jeopardizing everyone involved.

* * *

True to her word, two days later Donna assembled all parties involved for a formal summary of her report. She briefed Jake with the bad news beforehand and, after completely understanding the facts, he supported her strategy 100 percent.

At the end of her verbal report, Sam was quick to add a lengthy proclamation that this discovery represented the most significant in the history of the Ojibwe, as it linked the local tribe to the home long believed to be that of Chief Esh-ke-bug-e-coshe.

Both he and Chase broke into a spontaneous, albeit phony, victory dance with chants and invocations in the center of the Cedar Lodge game room. Sam then declared the Alex Minor estate a sacred Indian burial ground under the act of the same name. Preparations would begin immediately to celebrate the discovery with all Native American brothers and communities at the four-day powwow planned for the Memorial Day weekend.

Within forty-eight hours, the RTC received official notification from Secretary Barnhart's office. The judgment rendered placed the Minor estate under tribal council supervision pending final disposition.

Donna's attempt to prevail with the "wrong location and sinister plot" logic was completely ignored. She was removed as the investigation team leader for ignoring direct orders and overstepping her supervisory role.

* * *

"Once and for all, Agent Lynch, I want you to know that we can't act on our own and use government funds to probe into local possibilities that don't impact our direct duties. We don't need agents shooting from the hip and conducting their personal investigations. And we won't use government funds, power, and technology to penalize these people once again. Enough is enough."

"That's not fair. I mean . . ."

"No, what's fair is that I'm giving you another chance by not charging you with the insubordination so clearly evident during this investigation," Barnhart interrupted. "Your refusal to follow direct orders by taking your team in an unauthorized direction is unacceptable. Fortunately for you, agents with your experience are rare. Consider your immediate reassignment to the Jicarilla Apache Indian Reservation project in New Mexico as my way of saying that the department will give you another chance. But it's your last chance if you plan to remain an agent of the Interior."

Considering all that Donna knew, Secretary Barnhart's admonishment in the private phone call was unreasonably stern. How could he be so stupid?

Orders were also sent that day for one of Donna's assistants on the team, Mark Arnold, to take over for her immediately and to wrap things up within the week.

Jake was heartbroken. "This is so unfair to your efforts," Jake said. "Talk about the consummate bureaucrat—this guy won't take any risks with this tribe at all. This makes absolutely no sense!"

fifty

THE NEXT DAY, Donna assembled her investigation team for a complete debriefing prior to her departure for New Mexico. Agents Thompson and Brightstar, as well as Jake and Big Lights, were present. She presented the entire story for the team, sparing none of the details and allegations, right down to Morey's DNA deposit on Linda's panties and Secretary Barnhart's unusual resistance.

"I'm concerned that you haven't nailed down the motive," said one of the men. "Some big pieces of evidence are missing."

"Or dead," said one of the others.

"That's our concern, also," Agent Thompson volunteered. "Without a clear motive, all we have is a random series of events, not connected or convincing enough for a serious prosecution.

"It's important for you guys to know that despite the Department of the Interior's hands-off policy, the FBI is taking an official position on behalf of the U.S. government. I'm sure that each of you has been around long enough to know that the bureau has jurisdiction on the reservation in matters like these. Quite frankly, we wouldn't have any authority here had the local tribe not made that choice themselves years ago." Agent Thompson purposefully went slowly. He knew the men would be uneasy in taking a conflicting position against their own chain of command.

"It's the evidence of money-laundering and tribal council fraud that we're most concerned about right now, which is why the Interior's authority is being overridden.

"During the upcoming week I don't want you to discuss this case with anyone other than me, Agent Brightstar, or the men in this room. It bears repeating that Jake and Big Lights have been sworn in as deputy agents." His gesture of inclusion toward Jake and Big Lights was followed by several nods of approval.

"Your responsibility to the normal chain of command does not exist anymore," Donna interjected to ensure clarity. "Mark is positioned as the team leader to appease Secretary Barnhart, but Agent Thompson is your command leader until further notice."

"Each of you has the option to see me separately on this issue, and if need be, resign from the team," Agent Thompson emphasized. "It won't be a problem if you choose to do so. When this is over, I don't want any of you exposed because someone thought you acted on your own or out of a mistaken loyalty to Agent Lynch."

The men did not overreact, but they were obviously concerned. The discussion and the present renegade direction of the project clearly altered their normal expectations. After all, these men had been paid to follow the chain of command most of their careers. It was like a surreal script from a Harrison Ford movie. None of them had ever been an official part of a covert FBI activity. How could the Secretary of the Interior be linked to possible Indian Mafia activities? How could large sums of money be transferred on a regular basis from a casino in northern Minnesota to a tax-avoidance venue out of the country? These questions and allegations of murder, fraud, and conspiracy were alarming realities. It was their commitment to Donna, ultimately, and her conviction that this was the right approach to take that settled any remaining concerns. It also helped that, to a man, they were steamed that she was taking a hit for this.

Privately, they also knew that Donna and Jake had developed a genuine interest in each other. They had worked for Donna for a long time, back to the days after her husband had died. They saw her struggle to build a new life but never quite reach a point where she enjoyed real happiness. They all witnessed the change in her when Jake was around. As a matter of fact, they all changed when Jake was around. Seeing the two of them forced to split up just wasn't right.

As always, though, Donna kept the discussion on the business topic at hand.

"First of all, I can say with the highest degree of confidence that this project is being run by the best the bureau has to offer. Listen to them. Their plan's a good one, but it will require some extra work and patience on everyone's part. I know that you've never once questioned doing the right thing, nor resented making the extra effort for the benefit of the project. I've always been proud of this team and I know I can count on you to give the same commitment to these men. But there are risks."

Donna proceeded to lay out the plan.

"The bottom-line goal is to completely excavate Jake's land before the end of the week, which is just three days away. It took us two days to uncover six burial sites, so uncovering the large numbers believed to exist here will mean long hours. Let me repeat: We're off the books on this one. Washington has no clue what we're up to, which is why the deadline is so critical. I want you to know that I am in complete agreement with our new course of action." She finished by covering the details and reiterating the risk that Jake was taking—possible loss of his land by the very act that brought them into this project.

There was a quiet sense of determination in the room. To a man, each person was committed to make the sacrifice necessary.

Mark spoke first. "You can count on me to get the secretary whatever he needs. We don't want to raise any suspicions. I'll give you every hour I have after that to help the team meet this deadline. If there's a chance to buy time, I'll review it with Agent Thompson, although that doesn't look likely right now." Mark came forward from his position in the back row of chairs when he finished speaking.

"Before Donna leaves, I'd like to say thanks from all of us for the great leadership she's given. There's no question she's been the best boss I've had by a long shot, and I know every one of you feels the same. It's been a great run, Donna."

"Thanks, Mark. I appreciate your comments. Each of you is special to me, and I can't begin to tell you how important our work together has been. Not just for the people we serve, but for me personally."

Their spontaneous clap of appreciation caused Donna to blush. They stood, continuing to clap, expressing their heartfelt admiration.

"It's not in my nature to say good-bye, so I won't. Good luck to each of you. Be careful in wrapping this one up."

In her remaining time, she spent a few moments with each person expressing her gratitude for their excellent work and loyalty during their time together.

Before long, Jake and Donna left for the airport, a drive he didn't want to make.

"It was probably good timing that Alex died last week," Jake said to Donna while holding both her hands at the gate. "I'm not so sure he would have handled this very well. He respected your work."

"There's no question that he could be a bastard at times, but I really think he was in over his head on this one, Jake. There's a connection we're missing that affected him. We have to find it."

"I want you to be very careful, do you hear me?" Donna said, expressing her only real concern.

"Do exactly what Warren and Joseph tell you to do, but only if you're sure it's safe. I admire your commitment to bring these thugs to justice, but I love you more than any one project or piece of property can ever be worth. I don't want us to miss our chance together."

Their embrace was intense. They both knew that the separation was going to be difficult.

"I love you, too. And don't worry, I'll take care of myself."

* * *

The men worked nonstop for the next three days. Little mention was given to their schedule as the people on the peninsula had become used to their comings and goings. The wet, cold spring weather, combined with the lack of convenient access to Jake's property, kept the curious at home. As far as the locals were concerned, the investigation team was just anxious to finish the project and go home.

Sam and Chase were nowhere to be seen. In their minds, the issue of control was already settled.

By Friday noon the team had uncovered eighty-four burial sites! Pictures of each corpse were taken, and extensive details recorded about its condition and accompanying artifacts. Samples verifying authenticity, dates, and tribal heritage were kept. They respectfully returned each body to its exact resting position.

Agent Brightstar made arrangements through FBI connections for two American Indian history experts from the Smithsonian Institute to complete a preliminary, confidential study and analysis of this remarkable archaeological find within ten working days. Each of these men marveled at the magnitude of the discovery and pleaded for more time. They would get more time, Joseph promised, but only after they completed this high-priority initial report to the FBI's satisfaction.

Throughout this effort, Big Lights took it upon himself to sanctify each corpse with a mixture of birch bark ashes and dried ferns before the skeleton was returned to its resting place. He called upon the collective spirits of these ancestors to invoke their powers over this sacred ground and to guide this team in their work. He himself became transfixed—a self-delegated protectorate during this disruption in the body's journey. At the end of the team's eighteen-hour workday, and after all the men had left for the lodge, Big Lights remained with his departed brothers and sisters to guard against the entry of evil spirits into their disrupted resting places.

During these nightly stays, he had visions of totems and battles, hunting parties and lost relatives, and even a visitation by the great Chief Esh-ke-bug-e-coshe himself. These experiences confirmed for Big Lights that this place was truly the most sacred of Ojibwe burial grounds.

* * *

Jake got what little sleep he could each night before the next day's work began. Close enough for Jake to hear the chanting, Big Lights' vigil continued. On the second night Jake became concerned because of the miserable weather, knowing that Big Lights had only his blanket. While not wanting to interfere, Jake felt compelled to check on his friend to see if there was anything he could do to make the night more tolerable. The cold wind and rain were incessant, without any forecast of a break.

Jake approached Big Lights quietly. He saw his friend sitting cross-legged on his blanket, alternately chanting and talking as if other people were there. At times Big Lights got up and spoke as if he were addressing a large party of guests. He spoke in an ancient Anishinabe Indian tongue that Jake did not recognize.

Jake watched quietly for at least thirty minutes without disturbing his friend. During this time Big Lights kept up his constant dialogue and interaction with his spiritual guests.

"Can I help with your work in any way?" Jake asked upon approaching his friend. "Can I get you something from the cabin—food, another blanket, hot coffee?"

Big Lights turned and faced Jake. He did not appear wet or cold, nor were there any signs of tiredness from the day's work. On the contrary, Big Lights bore the appearance of a strong leader fresh from an exhilarating oratory.

"Are you all right?" Jake persisted.

"How could I not be all right, my white friend? These are my people who have gathered strength from many lives and by valiantly fighting in many battles. We are their children's children. They are here to protect us from the evil spirits that live in their world, and I to protect them from the evil spirits living in ours. I know you cannot see them, but believe me in knowing that they will protect me and bring me no harm. Whatever I need, they will provide."

Jake felt his body receive new life as the pains of the day melted away. He responded, "May I stay a while and learn from your ancestors?" Big Lights smiled and offered a spot next to him on his blanket.

Jake remained the rest of the night, experiencing what he could through varying states of consciousness. At one time he dreamed that he also was talking in ancient tongues but awoke and lost clear memory of what was said.

Soon it was daylight. As they stood, dry and comfortable, they clasped their arms and embraced, acknowledging their brotherhood. Their eye contact was the only communication necessary.

In time, there would be an opportunity for Big Lights to tell these stories, and many more, to others on the reservation. But for now, he was the protector of these ancestors and he did not sleep once in the three days the investigation team worked.

fifty-one

SAM TOOK A long pull from another cold Budweiser as he and Chase discussed their victory at the Twin Pines.

"I think our goddamn luck has finally changed, Chase. We've put up with a lotta outside bullshit, but we're over the hump now. In fact, I don't think there's anyone around, or alive, who has any hard facts that will give us trouble."

After two hours of celebrating they were feeling pretty good about things.

"Two Fingers, Morey, and Alex all could've caused real problems had the three of them ever gotten together, but that's not fuckin' likely anymore." Chase laughed. He tipped his beer in a mock toast.

"I believe you're right." Sam's look of self-congratulatory smugness ranked right up there with the definition of arrogance itself.

Even though Chase privately harbored thoughts that something had been left undone, he knew it would only upset Sam if he told him. Sam would want facts, and he really didn't have any—just the anxiety of nearing the final step of their plan, he rationalized. Just a feeling.

"In any case, I do like the idea of getting things moving on the land," Chase segued, referring to the agreement with their architect to complete a rendering of the new resort and casino within a few weeks. The unveiling would take place at the tribal assembly during the Memorial Day powwow just a month away. The architect had also committed to finishing a survey and assessment of the property next week. The combination of a casino, a first-class resort, and an Ojibwe heritage center to honor the Flat Mouth Village promised to be a home run, especially for Sam and Chase. By their estimates, they stood to collect a cool two million apiece each year, even after all expenses.

Last, they had concocted a brilliant scheme to squelch any potential tribal disagreements to their plan. The new casino on Arrowhead would make a one-time commitment of $10,000 for each reservation family. The money would be put in escrow and paid out at the casino's first-anniversary celebration. A lot of money, the men thought, but the casino would finance the payout—not one dime would come out of their pockets. More important, it would create enough persuasive leverage with the tribe's members to pass the vote to approve the project. $10,000 goes a long way on the reservation. Every angle had been covered. The new jobs created would be an overwhelming incentive alone. Jobs, a payout, a new heritage center—neither man could conjure a reason for anything but a landslide response.

The official RTC Board approval would come within twenty-four hours of the tribal assembly vote. Construction could begin right away. The board would arrange for an official groundbreaking the last day of the powwow with thousands of Indian visitors from tribes throughout the Midwest present. Plans were to open the casino within a year. The grand opening for the resort would take place the following summer and capitalize on the running start created by casino publicity.

Part of Sam and Chase's scheme to solicit support included various leaks of information about the $10,000 and the heritage center prior to the assembly. Rumors on the rez always spread quickly.

They decided to name the complex The Pillager, honoring the old Indian name for the Ojibwe tribe that Flat Mouth led. The center would be called the Esh-ke-bug-e-coshe Heritage Center. Their marketing vision foresaw that the resort and casino would draw people from all over the country, and from foreign countries as well, to learn about the Flat Mouth Village and the Ojibwe Nation. Reservation pride would swell.

By the time the assembly took place in four weeks, they knew that any possible objection would be buried under the weight of community pressure.

*   *   *

Agent Thompson's daily progress meeting the following day suffered from the ill effects of these rumors.

"This is getting depressing," Big Lights commented, referring to the obvious advances being made by Sam and Chase. "Have you seen people's reactions?"

"We've got to do something fast," Jake added. "In the end, our people are going to look like idiots," Big Lights continued, "and not just to other Indian communities, but to anyone who comes to this resort. Our heritage will be distorted by lies, just as the white man has done in the past. But this time we're doing it to ourselves, and for what, to make these two bastards rich."

"And with the investigation team leaving this afternoon, we're out of time." You could hear the frustration in Big Lights' voice and see it in his pacing across the meeting room.

"Well, you do have to admit one thing, though," Joseph chimed in. "We don't have to look very far for a motive anymore. All we have to do is to connect the dots with some evidence to nail these two pricks with a prison sentence for a long time. Although I will admit, they've given this plan a lot of thought."

"It still doesn't make sense," Jake said. "I don't believe for a minute that Alex would turn over his property to the tribal council, all for the sake of an on-site casino. Alex had everything he wanted with the casino right where it was." He paused for a moment.

"With all we know now, it's easy to see that this sacred burial grounds scam was perfect only for the tribe, not for Alex. I'll bet a million dollars that he was set up. His stroke was the lucky break that sealed everything. We'll probably never know what really went on between them, but you can absolutely bet that Alex wasn't voluntarily giving up control of his property. It meant too much to him."

Agent Thompson decided to take control of the meeting and walked toward the flip chart in the front of the room.

"Welcome to the real world, gentlemen," he said, getting the group's attention. "If all the crooks were stupid, our jobs would be easy. But then, we wouldn't be making the big bucks now, would we?

"The key here is that we've made big progress, as Agent Brightstar has pointed out. It's the motive that we've been missing. And I agree with Joseph; this looks like it."

He focused the group by printing the motive in bold letters on one sheet of flip-chart paper and taped it to the wall. *Gain control of Minor land on Arrowhead to build a combined casino and resort.* He then led the group through a brainstorming exercise.

"On this sheet, I want your ideas on possible circumstances," he said, pointing to a new sheet with the heading *Circumstances*. "And on this one, I want your ideas on real evidence." He labeled the second sheet *Real Evidence*.

"We're going to start from the beginning, again. I want to chronologically organize everything we know about this case under these two headings. I want to create a new image about what we know."

After just thirty minutes of discussion and brainstorming, Jake stopped the meeting's progress. "I can't believe it. It's too obvious. It's the dandelion oil and black spruce pine tar or pitch, or whatever it's called!"

The group didn't connect his comment.

"Don't you see," he continued. "They could recreate everything about the burial but the oil and pitch."

"Explain it for us, Jake," Agent Thompson said.

"The six bodies discovered on Alex's land were moved from old burial sites on the reservation, which is why Two Fingers was so important. It's also why the map on the back of Linda's picture matches so well with the six locations. The corpses and artifacts were easy to move and re-intern. But the original oil and pitch, having been sprinkled on the soil around the corpse hundreds of years ago, would not be easy to move. Am I right, Joseph?"

Agent Brightstar nodded. "You're absolutely right. And it would be very difficult, and noticeable, to attempt to move large amounts of dirt from around the corpse at the cemetery to the peninsula. It's not something you could easily take across the lake in a boat. Plus, there's a good chance that the composition of the dirt on the peninsula is different from that at the cemetery. Even if they could transport it, the soils wouldn't match. But they still needed the presence of oil and pitch to authenticate the burial grounds."

Jake jumped back into the now-freewheeling conversation. "It's the only real evidence that we have. I'll bet my cabin and all my land that the chemical makeup of the oil and pitch found at the six sites is very different from that found in the soil on my land after two hundred years of deterioration. And I'll double that bet on the chance that the oil and pitch found at the six sites matches exactly with what I found in the can at the cemetery storage building. That's probably how Morey fits into this whole scheme. He was an errand boy for Sam and Chase. And come to think of it, Morey's burglary of Linda's apartment was most likely a scare tactic, just in case she knew anything."

"This is good, very good," Agent Thompson said. "Let's get on it."

With limited time left, the team worked feverishly to check out their new theory. It took them less than two hours to get the answer they wanted. One of the team members who had expertise in chemical analysis volunteered to conveniently miss his flight back to Washington, D.C., in order to document the dandelion oil and pine tar analysis as corroborating FBI evidence.

fifty-two

EARLY THE NEXT morning the news for the FBI team got even better. Agent Thompson had been successful in getting some help from the State Department involving the investigation surrounding the Sawgrass Investment Fund. The FBI generated assistance from a special Bahamian police team that had been handling criminal banking and organized crime activities. It was a cooperative government-to-government covert operation.

"Listen up," Warren said. "I just received an e-mail that a substantial sum of money was electronically transferred to McMillan, Larsen & Wingfoot from the Sawgrass Investment Fund."

"Yes!" Simultaneous overtures.

The four men exchanged high-fives, punctuated with whoops that declared impending victory.

A month after their marked money had entered the cash flow of the Norway Pine Casino, Warren had involved two undercover agents from the Twin City office to track the money's movement from the various airfreight offices in the Fargo Airport. The agents had been placed to work the airport as shipping clerks for UPS and Airborne. Warren wanted no chance of them being discovered.

"From what they told me," Warren said, paraphrasing his e-mail, "it took only two attempts to locate some of the marked bills from one of the packages delivered to the UPS counter. Everything was captured on surveillance tape. Apparently, all the packages were temporarily 'misplaced' in the UPS system to enable our guys to validate the existence of the marked bills. This is good news. Fourteen bills in all were identified and logged as evidence against the case file.

"And that's not the end of it. The audit trail is completely documented all the way to the Bahamas. Apparently our package still made the flight out of Fargo. They were able to identify and track it at each airport stop throughout the trip. The Bahamian police team validated the arrival of the same fourteen bills, like clockwork."

"Check," Agent Thompson said, noting they had reached the penultimate position—one step away from closing the case.

Confidence soared.

"Money-laundering is a federal offense," Joseph emphasized. "We can nail James, Sam, and Chase right now if we want."

"What's holding us up?" Big Lights was excited.

"Relax. We want to arrest all the players. In the end, James, Sam, and Chase will be easy marks with what we have. Answering the question of who else benefited from the money, however, may be more important to the case."

"Absolutely right," Warren said, emphatically reinforcing Joseph's remark. "The documented movement of the $200,000 that took place yesterday will allow the bureau to track disbursements from McMillan, Larsen & Wingfoot. We want anyone and everyone who's connected with this money flowing into the Indian Mafia organization.

"It's important we don't overreact to this information and scare off any of our suspects, though. Besides, we've cast a pretty wide net. Let's see what else swims in."

fifty-three

WITH THE GROUNDWORK laid, Thompson, Brightstar, Jake, and Big Lights began their work. Their strategy entailed a counteractive effort to the all-out campaign by Sam and Chase to presell the resort, casino, and heritage center concept to the reservation. The team believed they could flush out all the players involved in this scheme by blocking Sam and Chase's goals. Patience had lost its virtue, however. Time was short and they had to be aggressive enough to make things happen immediately.

Each man gravitated naturally to his role. Agent Thompson would remain as the team leader and FBI liaison. Big Lights and Jake would begin to visit with small groups of Indians all over the reservation. They would tell the story of the real Flat Mouth Village, generating support to swing the vote at the upcoming assembly. Their reputations on the reservation were as good as gold, but they still had to overcome the $10,000 distribution. People were poor; the money might be too much to resist. Everyone needed to know that Sam and Chase were the source of the paltry casino distributions in the past and weren't to be trusted. Agent Brightstar would uncover whatever information he could from the two lodges on the Minor property, while also acting as a shadow safety net for any violence that Jake and Big Lights might encounter. It would be easy for Joseph to blend in while the other two traveled the reservation.

The men agreed to meet every day. It was imperative that they stay on top of each other's progress.

Big Lights wanted to start his reservation-wide road show that afternoon and, as usual, Jake had to slow him down by suggesting that they put together a plan first.

"But I know what I'm going to say already," Big Lights protested.

"I'm sure you do, but don't you think it might be more effective if we have a specific itinerary to follow? We don't have enough time as it is. A lot of people don't even have phones and we could end up just driving around."

"Okay, okay, but I'm not good with itineraries." He knew better than to dispute Jake's logic. "I suppose now's the time you're going to give me the tortoise-and-hare speech."

"You're absolutely right. And even though I know that you can talk a bear out of its dinner, a little rehearsal would be a good idea, too."

Once back at the cabin, Jake said, "You know these people better than anybody, Big Lights. It would be real easy to overwhelm them with too much information, and besides, they're going to be afraid of repercussions from Sam. We have to keep the talks nonthreatening to give people a chance to really understand the truth."

Jake took his glasses off and sat down at the kitchen table where they were going to work. He was determined. After four hours of planning and practicing Big Lights' talk, both men were very confident they had a story that would work.

"You've got this story down pat. You're good to go," Jake said, praising Big Lights' skills as a master storyteller. "It's not because you're a bullshit artist, although it does help. It's because you lived the story, all the way from the apartment break-in in Duluth to the visitation of Chief Flat Mouth last week."

* * *

The next day the two men began presenting the real facts about Flat Mouth's village to members of the tribe. Both Big Lights and Jake earned the respect of their listeners. The inherent risk they incurred in speaking out marked them as brave men and it was obvious that they spoke the truth. Regardless, Big Lights and Jake took great care not to arouse suspicion.

The photo album they had assembled documenting the burial site and eighty-four ancestral corpses was compelling proof of their story. And while it would have normally been unusual for a white man to participate in such intimate reservation matters, those who knew Jake welcomed his involvement. He had earned his status as a friend to the reservation from the Omaha Project, and he was considered a man of power after killing the bear. Those who didn't know Jake found his involvement equally convincing because of his decision to gift his land on Sandy Cove to the tribe, no strings attached. A real heritage center could be built on its rightful site. Jake's pride in their history was a beacon for their own community spirit.

Most people they talked with committed to support a "No" vote at the coming assembly and praised it as the right thing to do. The rumors of the $10,000 distribution, however, remained very strong medicine among others. Big Lights hoped that his talk of building a reservation with a reputation of "shining for all generations" would convince even the most skeptical.

"I know you want to believe that these good people can look past the $10,000, but I'm not convinced," Jake said halfway through the day.

"How can you doubt the integrity of my brothers' words?" Big Lights was offended by Jake's skepticism.

"Put yourself in their shoes."

* * *

On their way back to the cabin in his truck after talking to many people that first day, Jake struck on an observation that could potentially seal the "No" vote for sure.

"At our meeting tomorrow morning, remind me to get some help from Agent Thompson about the Sawgrass Fund."

"I've seen this look before. What do you have up your sleeve?"

"I just don't think that we're getting through to everyone."

"Sure we are," Big Lights defended.

"What I mean to say is that the story you're telling is powerful and there's nothing that can be added that I can see. But, Big Lights, the look in their eyes tells me that the money is important, too. After all, we're asking poor and desperate people to turn down $10,000. In the end, we may be expecting too much."

Big Lights just stared, not knowing what to say.

"I've been doing some basic math in my head regarding the Sawgrass Fund. I'll have to admit up front, though, that I don't have any real knowledge about what happens with the money in the fund when it's recovered."

"What do you mean?"

"Well, assuming that the money will be returned, it has to belong to the reservation, I would think. That means every man, woman, and child. It's hard to figure just how much there might be, but my guess is that Sam and Chase have been at this for some time, which means there's a lot of money. I'd like for Warren to contact one of his FBI companions in D.C. Maybe they can get an estimate of the amount. If I'm right, there's enough to make offsetting cash distributions now and to build the heritage center later this summer. I'm thinking that fighting cash with cash will help our story a bit. Don't you?"

"You're a genius, Jake," Big Lights said with a broad grin of confidence.

* * *

"I completely agree with your logic, Jake. Let me see what I can find out from the bureau." Warren's optimism was encouraging. "As for who gets the money, I'm optimistic that it will be returned to the reservation. I'm sure, though, there's going to be the standard red-tape government delays."

Instead of shadowing Jake and Big Lights that first day, Agent Brightstar had spent hours rummaging through both of the Minor lodges. "I will say one thing," Joseph said, starting his report. "Mr. Alex Minor lived one very colorful life: mob connections, corporate executive, and millionaire recluse. Someday someone's going to write a book about this guy, and I want to be first on the list to read it."

"Regarding our project," Joseph said, getting back to the point of the meeting, "I have two important and possibly useful discoveries to cover. First, I did locate the scale model of the resort that you talked about before, Jake, and you were right, it did not include a casino. The developer's business card was there, however, a Rex Meeks of Meeks & Harrison."

"That's the name Alex talked about," Jake confirmed.

"Well, I gave him a call. At first he stalled, but after the formal FBI introduction he opened up right away. Said he had been expecting a call from Alex for some time and seemed genuinely surprised to learn of his death. Rex acknowledged that he had the casino model in his office and was waiting for Alex to call to set up a meeting with two people from the local tribe, Sam Aguire and Chase Leonard. There is one small hitch, though. The model he designed is a replacement structure for the existing casino in its current location."

Warren's eyes went up and Big Lights whistled.

"This is proof that Sam and Chase wanted Alex's land," Jake stated emphatically. "Alex's deal was to link up with the casino in its current location—not on the peninsula."

Joseph continued, "He asked if I knew of Sam Aguire and Chase Leonard."

"I said yes. He was anxious to set up a meeting with them. He said something about not getting paid for his fees until they approved the model. Anyway, his office is in Bemidji, and I have a meeting with him tomorrow. He doesn't sound like he's connected in any way other than as a contracted architect. If he continues cooperating, he could become a major asset in linking our two friends on the reservation with Alex Minor. And if you're right, Jake, maybe even to a new location for the casino."

"Do you think he would wear a wire?" Warren asked.

"I don't know, but the thought definitely entered my mind. I'll check it out if his story holds."

"Another interesting discovery came from reviewing Mr. Minor's checkbook still lying in his office. Before I forget, though, is this guy's family ever going to begin the settlement process? I mean, it's as if nothing's changed in either lodge since he died."

Jake interrupted with an apology, "I'm sorry, but it totally slipped my mind. I ran into Tony three days ago and he said that the family law firm is sending somebody up next week to begin the process. I should've remembered. Sorry."

"That's okay. It's no big deal," Joseph continued. "I was just curious. Anyway, the name Farley Johnson keeps coming up for checks: $5,000 here, $2,000 there, and one for $10,000. Does this name ring a bell for anybody?"

"Yeah, sure it does," Big Lights responded. "Old Farley is the county commissioner for Big Bear County."

"Sounds right to me," Jake jumped in. "If Alex was planning a resort, it would make perfect sense to have a politician in his hip pocket to influence zoning."

"Interesting," Warren replied. "Why don't you check him out as well, Joseph. Great progress for one day; nice work, both of you."

* * *

Each daily status meeting over the next two weeks confirmed that their case was falling into place perfectly.

Farley came across as the ultimate marshmallow now that Alex was dead. While he tried very hard not to incriminate himself, he agreed to testify confirming Alex's ongoing pressure for favorable zoning decisions. However, he maintained that the various donations to his campaign fund were "unrelated acts of generosity."

Within days Rex Meeks had his meeting with Sam and Chase, and he agreed to wear a wire. He taped the men admitting that Alex's replacement casino held the tribe's interest early on, but it never got off the ground. They explained that it was Alex's brainchild. All in all, the tapes directly supported the team's conspiracy suspicions, yet were hearsay without Alex's corroboration.

In the meantime, the effort to track cash disbursements by the State Department team hadn't revealed any conclusive evidence either; at least none that Warren could talk about. The Meeks & Harrison architect fees of $25,000 represented one large exception. The check issued for the casino model was paid directly from the McMillan, Larsen & Wingfoot account. Since they were the tribal accounting firm, however, the transaction didn't raise any eyebrows. However, another check made out to cash for $50,000 was being tracked closely.

Jake and Big Lights also made progress. They literally worked day and night to visit everyone on the reservation they could. Other than a handful of itinerant drunks, who most likely wouldn't show up for the assembly anyway, they talked face to face with almost every adult on the reservation over a two-week period. In total, about two thousand people heard Big Lights tell his story firsthand.

They knew Jake and Big Lights were incurring risk of retaliation and, to a man, each guaranteed their silence on the "No" vote topic. But both men knew their luck wouldn't hold out forever.

* * *

The inevitable confrontation with Sam took place three days before the assembly meeting As Jake and Big Lights left a small cafe in Chippewa Lake, Agent Brightstar shadowed them from across the street, smoking a cigarette. Sam walked directly into Big Lights' path and stuck his face two inches from Big Lights' nose. Keeping their cool, Jake and Big Lights waited for Sam to commit himself, which took about two seconds.

"Big Lights! You asshole." Sam had a way of lowering his body, much like a pit bull readying to attack. It looked like Sam was going to get into it with Big Lights right then and there. "I understand you're the newly appointed storyteller for our Ojibwe brothers. People tell me you're filling their heads with a bunch of crap-stories about sacred burial grounds, visions, and crimes committed by members of the Tribal Council."

"So what's your point?" Big Lights responded in an aggressive posture matching Sam's. Joseph immediately walked across the street toward the group.

"Well, my point, smart ass, is to tell you what you've really found. All you've found is more evidence that the sacred burial grounds exist. Another thing to keep in mind, asshole, is to remember who the fuck you're accusing of committing crimes. I happen to be one of those Tribal Council members."

Sam's use of the word *asshole* pissed Big Lights off. If this was the time and place to get into it with Sam, so be it. He probably wouldn't win a fight against Sam, but he'd give it hell for Linda's sake.

"You can take your self-righteous bullshit and . . ." Big Lights started to respond.

"Hold on, you two," Joseph interrupted, stepping between the men.

He looked directly at Sam. "Did you say Big Lights?"

"Yeah, so what? Who the fuck do you think you are?" Sam replied. "You got no business in this matter. Get your ass out of the way unless you want part of what this Indian's gonna get."

"Oh, I think I do have business here. I'm Agent Joseph Brightstar with the FBI," he replied forcefully, displaying his FBI badge. "We've been looking for this guy for a while. I'm putting this man under arrest for interstate car theft. We've been trying to nail this joker for six months. Now, if you don't mind, back off." He turned away from Sam and muscled Big Lights against the building, kicking his feet apart, frisking him, and then reading him his rights.

"Tell me this isn't true, Big Lights," Jake said with urgency. "This can't be true." Jake's spontaneity and expression of futility was perfect in supporting the incredulous turn of events.

Big Lights hung his head in shame.

What an actor, Jake thought, admiring his "I'm trapped" demeanor.

"I've got the man I came here to get, and I'll be leaving with no further interference from either of you." Agent Brightstar cuffed Big Lights.

Sam bought the charade completely. "Your actions are nothing short of treason to the tribe," he asserted, upset that he couldn't kick Big Lights' ass on the spot.

"If you've got other charges that affect our jurisdiction, I'll add them to the list. Here's my card," Agent Brightstar said. "Otherwise, I'd advise you to move on. I don't want a scene."

Sam looked at Big Lights, and then at Jake, and then turned to face Agent Brightstar again. "This man is not to come back on this reservation without the council's permission. I want that understood in your report."

"Stupid fuckin' Indian," Sam mumbled as he turned and left.

* * *

That afternoon the investigation team hit pay dirt again while wrapping up their day at the Cedar Lodge. Warren confirmed that two more direct deposits from McMillan, Larsen & Wingfoot had been made. One went into the account of Sam Aguire, and the other into that of Chase Leonard, each in the amount of $50,000.

fifty-four

Warm, spring-fresh air arrived in time for the Memorial Day weekend. People were happy that winter had passed. The delicate green forest growth exploded. These early pale shades of new-growth leaves would soon give way to a much darker and richer green for the remainder of the summer. With its puffs of clouds, the blue sky added to the perfect outdoor setting for the powwow.

Memorial Legion Park on the Big Bear Reservation proper was always the location of choice, as no other facilities existed large enough to hold a crowd of this size. The weatherman forecasted temperatures in the seventies all day. People arrived in good spirits. It was the first all-reservation assembly held in many years that asked for a vote. Each person anticipated that something good was about to happen.

James Wingfoot felt differently, however. Reservation assemblies like this all thrived on a common theme of renewing the old ways and building for a better future. Even though James hadn't grown up on Big Bear Reservation, his familiarity with these events resonated with monotony, as they varied little from reservation to reservation. He found the repetition of tradition quaint, but obsolete and without merit. He always felt that his Indian brothers spent too much effort hanging on to a past that had no future. People should take more time to make themselves useful in the outside world—off the reservation— in the real world, he thought. In his viewpoint, casinos represented the only financially stable byproduct created out of reservation life for the past hundred years. He felt no guilt profiting from their existence. He knew it was his skills, and the skills of a few men like him, that made the casinos successful. If casinos were left to the average Indian, he reflected, nothing more than rundown, smoke-filled buildings where the drunks and unemployed could hang out would exist. Despite this perception, however, today did symbolize a day of promise for him. The rewards of a multiyear plan that would make him financially set for life were about to unfold.

While James wasn't expecting anyone at his motel room door at 6 A.M., he wasn't particularly surprised with the knock. It was probably Sam, he thought, with another question about how the money would be distributed once the resort and casino were in full operation. He had been up for an hour and already had the coffee brewing.

"Hold on, hold on. I'll be right there," he said.

As he opened the door, three armed officers grabbed him and spread-eagled him against the wall. His face was pushed against the frame of the door as they yanked his arms behind his back into a hammerlock. It hurt.

"What the hell's going on here? Why are you doing this?" was the only thing he could say before someone told him to shut up. The pressure on his face barely allowed him to speak at all.

"Read 'em his rights."

"Mr. James Wingfoot, you are being arrested for grand theft larceny, the laundering of U.S. currency, and criminal conspiracies against the U.S. government. You are also being charged as an accomplice in the murder of Two Fingers Smith. Anything you say or do can and will be held and used against you . . . ."

By 6:15, Agents Thompson and Brightstar were interrogating James in a secure Winnebago motor bus just a few miles away. The FBI used

the Winnebago in remote field cases such as this one for confinement
and questioning. It allowed them to keep their business on a low profile and exempt from local police interruption.

Because of James's role in the accounting firm, they believed he was
a central figure in a growing Indian Mafia, one who could link them
to many others involved in similar criminal activities. As much as he
disliked it, Agent Thompson felt that making a deal with this character would successfully set the Mafia back for years.

"I want you to keep your mouth shut while I lay out your options,"
Agent Thompson directed while pacing menacingly in front of
James.

After constructing a detailed framework of their investigation,
emphasizing the connection to the murder of Two Fingers, Agent
Thompson made a simple proposition. "What you tell us now, before
the assembly begins, will determine the future of your adult life. Give
us the names and details regarding your connections over the past five
years at McMillan Larsen & Wingfoot and we'll recommend that your
next stop will be a witness-protection-program office in Minneapolis.
Don't cooperate and you'll be somebody's girlfriend in a maximum-
security prison for a long time. It's time for you to make a decision."

The room remained silent for several minutes. Then, after just a
few questions about the security of the protection program, it was
over. James had always been the smartest of his friends in high school
and college. This time he chose to exercise his intelligence in a productive manner. Warren and Joseph exchanged glances. Their strategy to
arrest James first had paid off.

Thirty minutes later, Agent Thompson conducted a conference call
with agents in other field offices covering the Midwest and West that
would quickly lead to the simultaneous arrests of twelve tribal leaders on seven Indian reservations. As the call wrapped up, he said,
"No, we won't need any more help here. We can handle our two local
heroes ourselves." Agent Thompson liked using the term *hero* sarcastically for criminals who invariably thought they were such big deals.
Sam and Chase were no different. Just two bullies masquerading as
big shots.

"Well, gentlemen, we've got what we need. Let's go to work." Agent Thompson shifted into high gear now, focused on bringing this case to a swift close.

"With the assembly starting in less than an hour, we don't have time to arrest Sam and Chase beforehand. We'll set up our command post in the parking lot. We can nail them when they get out of their car. And, for your information, men, a lot of people have already arrived. I don't want anyone else hurt. These arrogant pricks still think they're coming to a celebration in their honor. Let's not disappoint them."

* * *

Sam and Chase enjoyed a leisurely drive over to the Legion Park. Their conversation reflected a last-minute preview by Chase of the next several hours—a perfect culmination to years of planning and work.

"Don's going to make the opening comments and announce the official beginning of the powwow," Chase said. "As tribal chairman, he will invite all ceremonial dancers to participate in the grand entry. After the dance, Sam, you will make your presentation and unveil the proposed renderings of The Pillager building and the Esh-ke-bug-e-coshe Heritage Center. Give the people some time to walk around and see the models up close. I'll bring the crowd back to order and propose that a vote be taken. After collecting the votes, we'll let the various tribes lead the assembly in chants and dances while we tally the outcome. To make things official, Don can then make the announcement that the proposition has passed."

"A walk in the park," Sam said smugly. "A walk in the park."

Their maroon Lincoln Town Car turned from the highway onto the dirt road leading to the Legion Park and baseball fields. The sun was bright, practically beckoning their pending triumph. Lots of people had already arrived. One little boy with a baseball glove and bat waved to them as they drove by.

Big Lights, Jake, and Linda watched from a distance, following strict orders from Warren to stay out of the way. From their vantage point, they could easily observe both men getting out of the Lincoln.

Instantly, six FBI agents descended, pulling them from their car and aggressively breaking them down to a prone position in the dirt. The nightsticks were applied expertly and with brute force as the agents buried Sam and Chase's faces into the parking lot gravel. The men were quickly subdued, eliminating risk to others. The scuffle attracted a lot of attention and a crowd quickly gathered. Sam tried to make a break for it after they brought him to his feet. Agent Brightstar caught the big man from behind within seconds. He brought his nightstick across the back of Sam's right knee with such force that the knee joint shattered, sending Sam to the ground again, sweaty and writhing in pain. Another officer buried his nightstick in the base of Sam's skull, forcing him to breathe dirt. He choked on the dust. Familiar with the stories of this man's brutality and corruption, the agents weren't about to ease up in their arrest.

Three men dragged Sam to his feet as Agent Brightstar positioned himself directly in Sam's face.

"Stupid fuckin' Indian," Joseph said in mockery, expressing the hatred he held for men like Sam who sucked the life out of his Indian brothers on reservations across the United States. Joseph continued by reading both men their rights and pushing their bodies into separate squad cars. The scene was over and the cars were gone in less than fifteen minutes.

Linda looked at Big Lights and started to cry. He responded with his own tears as he comforted her in a long embrace. Jake felt the need to do something. Because of the finality of the moment, however, he didn't or just couldn't. The one person he wanted to be with wasn't there, and no one else could fill the void.

After composing themselves, Big Lights put his arm around Jake and announced, "We've got an assembly to go to."

Jake smiled. "Lead on, brother."

Don Pasquesi made the opening remarks of the assembly as planned. He had no knowledge of the charges against Sam and Chase and knew only that they had been arrested. For most, the grand entry ceremony began in the traditional manner. Jake watched as hundreds of Native

American participants wearing incredibly ornate traditional costumes danced in their moccasins to the rhythm of the Native American chants and sounds from the tribal M'dewinwin drum pits. Men, women, and children danced together, keeping a continuous step, forming a circular procession around the center of the parade grounds. Their movement was slow and the beat metrical, representing the continuum of life. Jingle dresses, shawls, and bandolier bags adorned the women. Authentic feathered headdresses, war bonnets, roaches, and bustles of intricate design and artistry decorated the men. The Indian motif gave tribute to a spiritual way of life full of tradition and meaning. Seeing the young people participate in full ceremonial dress signified the commitment and progress in keeping the generations together.

The dancing and parade went on for almost an hour. As the festivities neared a natural break, Jake approached Big Lights.

"There's only one person they're going to want to hear from," he said. "And I think Linda should be standing next to you when you tell the story one more time."

"Thank you for everything, Jake. Your name will mean *friend* throughout our reservation and will be honored for all time to come." And in a flash of recollection, Big Lights realized he was ready for this moment because of Jake's insistence that he plan and practice the story that day in the cabin.

Don was happy to turn control of the assembly over to Big Lights, as he had no clue as to what was going on.

"Get their attention with the PA system," Jake told Don, "and then give the microphone to Big Lights. Forget whatever else was planned; Big Lights has a story that needs to be told."

Chief Esh-ke-bug-e-coshe undoubtedly smiled that day, as Indians attending from a cross-section of tribes all over the Midwest listened with great pride to the story Big Lights told. Trading at the vendor trailers stopped and everyone present focused on his message. Even the children stood still. The Big Bear Tribal Band of the Ojibwe Nation had found their new leader.

fifty-five

DONNA AND JAKE talked happily for a long time the next day on the phone. Donna put aside the information Warren had supplied just hours earlier so that Jake could tell his version. They felt the pressure release itself during Jake's firsthand account. She celebrated every moment of their success, proud of Jake and excited for the community.

"You know, Jake, Sam and Chase's idea of a heritage center wasn't half bad," she said. "In fact, it's pretty good."

"Yeah, but the phony connection with the casino and resort would have trivialized the center completely. It would have turned it into a tourist stop, a stereotypical Indian trading post out of the '50s."

"You're probably right."

"Right now, the thing I'm happiest about, though, is Big Lights and Linda," she said with a big smile in her voice. "They are perfect together in their new role on the reservation, aren't they?"

"You bet. Both of them are very special. Six months ago Big Lights was just a fun-loving, beer-toting drifter. Don't get me wrong, he was a good friend and always reliable, but now—my God, he's an entirely new person. It's like the assembly and all the meetings we had on the reservation telling the story were his coming-out party."

"No question. Warren told me about how everyone there yesterday focused on what he had to say. It must have been very special. He really is the rightful spiritual leader. He earned it."

"And Linda, well, I just don't know where to begin when I think of all she's been through," Jake said. "Maybe you were right when you told me after your first trip to the hospital that Linda could just as easily be my daughter. I don't know how I would feel any different if it actually were true."

After finishing their discussion about the assembly, Donna changed direction. "What's going to absolutely blow your mind, though, is the news that my boss, Jordan Barnhart, has tendered his resignation."

"What?" Jake was floored. "What happened?"

"The official word is that he is 'drawing to a close a successful career, and allocating some time off for himself and his family.' Apparently, foreign travel and more involvement for his favorite charity, the Boy Scouts of America, if you can believe that, are all in the cards.

"The insiders, though, namely our friend Warren, say otherwise. He says you can expect formal charges of fraud, gross neglect of duty, and conspiracy with various organized-crime violations will be filed soon.

"He also told me yesterday that a pattern of bribery has been established in connection with the large federally protected reservations. It seems that our friend James Wingfoot and the McMillan, Larsen & Wingfoot accounting firm functioned as the money front for at least seven other casino scams, using the Sawgrass Investment Fund as their laundering mechanism. Can you believe that it was my boss who guaranteed that these schemes never reached a level of concern in the government?"

"Unbelievable. It looks like Humpty Dumpty has fallen," he said.

"Absolutely. And one thing's clear for sure."

"What's that?"

"The rumor of an Indian Mafia is over, Jake. It's real . . . Jordan Barnhart was their political leader."

"It's just amazing what people believe they can do."

"Jake, it scares me to think that he knew everything. It's like nothing has changed in hundreds of years. Native Americans are still getting screwed out of their rightful heritage. It's no surprise he didn't want us pushing and snooping around, is it? Anyway, it's over now."

"It actually is over, isn't it?" Jake questioned rhetorically with obvious relief in his voice. "It was like a bad dream—trapped in a merry-go-round cliché with no place to get off. We're lucky that no one else got hurt. And we're damn lucky you became involved. Without your knowledge and experience the outcome would be entirely different."

"Well, we all deserve credit on this one," Donna said, twisting the phone cord.

"And I couldn't have been prouder of my team. They stood by me. What you don't know is that all of us were interrogated yesterday and today for hours. To a man, everyone supported my position as agent in charge. This story's bound to make headlines in every newspaper in America, and the president is very concerned about public opinion. With the government taking such a beating in the press lately, I totally agree that quick action was warranted. I'm sure they don't want any surprises to surface later."

"You did the right thing, every step of the way."

"Anyway, it looks like I'll have to stay in D.C. to testify for a Congressional subcommittee for several weeks. The good news is that they're going to want to talk to you very soon also."

"I can't wait," he said in a softened voice. "Do you think our government will let me stay at that nice Marriott overlooking the Potomac River again? It's difficult to forget such a good hotel, considering the great service and personal care."

Both laughed, knowing they couldn't wait to be together again.

* * *

While hanging up the phone, Jake heard a truck coming down his access road. In the time it took him to cross the kitchen and hallway, he could see the purple-blue-and-orange logo of the FedEx truck coming to a stop by the garage. He met the driver with a friendly hello, and they chatted for a few minutes on the early reports of great walleye fishing that everyone was enjoying.

After the driver left, Jake returned his attention to the envelope. The return address was from a law firm in Chicago, one that he had heard of before in connection with Alex—Harter, Faulkner & Brown LLC.

"Now what?" he said under his breath.

fifty-six

On the right Minnesota day, there was no more perfect place in the world. The robin's-egg-blue sky came to life with flourishes of clouds being pushed into every imaginable formation. June had brought excellent warm weather along with the expected smattering of early-summer visitors. The forest bloomed with growth, green growth on every tree, shrub, and groundcover known to Minnesota: cattails, berry bushes, ferns, lady slippers, maples, oaks, ash, and basswood. And the one-hundred-fifty-plus species of birds turned Jake's little piece of paradise into a living aviary. The respite from bugs the North Woods were infamous for would only last a few more days, however. Warm temperatures would certainly accelerate the various larvae hatches soon to fill the woods with insects of every size and description.

But until then, the day was made for the gods. In bathing suits, Jake and Donna slouched back into their lawn chairs in two-feet-deep water just off the lake's shoreline. The sun reflected all around them. They aimlessly dug their toes into the soft, sugar-sand lake bottom. Between them, its legs firmly stuck into the lake bottom, sat a TV tray with snacks. The cool lake water was perfect to keep the beer and wine just right. Completely chilling out had not quite made it onto their agenda over the last few months. They had a lot of catching up to do.

The warm breeze ran parallel to the shore, encouraging the seagulls to fly in a line up to Jake and Donna for breadcrumbs they tossed into the air in front of their chairs. A bird caught a morsel in mid-flight and let the wind peel its agile body backward to the end of the line. Another gull would position itself and follow in turn after catching his prize. It was an endless rotation of birds that would only end when the breadcrumbs ran out. Jake enjoyed sharing this amusing pastime with Donna. They laughed with each bird's performance.

"Where do we go from here?" Jake asked, hoping they wanted the same thing. He wasn't completely sure, however, how her career and their different living locations were going to play out.

The Congressional subcommittee hearings that immediately followed the Memorial Day arrests had lasted for two weeks. Their time together in D.C. solidified that what they had didn't come along very often. Both felt their relationship important enough to make sacrifices for, but Jake knew that was always easy to say. In reality, he thought, it could be hard to do.

"Let me answer you with a little surprise I've been saving. I didn't want to seem too pushy."

"Hard to imagine a federal government agent being too pushy," he replied, not passing up the dig. Jake acknowledged Donna's pending surprise announcement with the tip of his beer, turning the floor over to her.

"I've been reinstated to my old team, Jake. It means that I'll be here for most of the summer supervising the research on your land."

"Absolutely perfect," he said, celebrating with a clink of his beer bottle against hers.

"When you voluntarily added your land to the original investigation and gifted it to the tribe, it seemed only logical that my team should continue the work. I just found out yesterday before leaving D.C. Everyone's excited."

She paused. "What's most important, though, is how you feel about this. Are you sure you're happy?"

She knew that Jake had struggled with giving up his land. This special piece of property on Sandy Cove had been the one anchor throughout his life, from childhood through adulthood. Whenever he needed space to figure things out, the cabin was there. He loved this place and it would be difficult to let go. His gift of the property to the tribe was as gracious as any could be, but the truth remained that it wasn't his first choice. She knew that better than anyone.

"This is a good time to let you in on a little secret that I have. Maybe it will answer all of your questions as well. Before I do, though, my answer to your question is yes, I am happy. Happy about all the things that we've been thinking about and sharing from the time we first met. I am very excited about you being here for the summer and getting your team back. I can't think of anyone more qualified to head up the final investigation of Chief Flat Mouth's village. I know it will be done right. And that's important for just a whole hell of a lot of reasons."

He tipped his chair sideways, managing a kiss, no, several kisses, before continuing.

"So what's this secret you've guarded so carefully that even I didn't know?"

"Remember when I told you that Alex kept saying everything would be all right the night he died? I never could connect his comment to anything other than a wish he may have held for himself. Well, I got the real answer a week ago. I didn't want to tell you until the time was right. I think that's now."

The element of surprise and suspense Jake had created absolutely blotted out all awareness of their physical surroundings.

"You're gonna kill me if you don't tell me what it is right away," she said, her heartbeat quickening with curiosity and excitement.

"Well, right before I left for D.C. I received a FedEx from a law firm in Chicago. I knew I recognized the name on the return address as one that Alex had retained. But to keep you from exploding, I'll go directly to the point."

"Two days before Alex died he changed his will. Apparently there was no one in his family he was close to, or maybe it was because he changed how he felt about things here on the peninsula. Of course, he didn't know that his property would be removed from the sacred burial ground claim. Whatever his thinking was, I'm not sure I fully understand."

"Anyway, Donna, you're not going to believe this. He left his entire estate on Arrowhead Peninsula to me."

Donna screamed with delight and threw herself at Jake. They both tumbled off their chairs into the water. "I can't believe this happened. It's perfect, there's nobody who deserves it more. Jake, I'm so happy for you!"

They both laughed joyously.

"It just gets better," he said, trying to keep his beer from spilling into the lake as he lay on his back with Donna straddling him. "He also left a trust fund that generates $85,000 a year to use any way I see fit, as long as Tony is kept on as the caretaker at his current salary."

"Could it be any better?"

"There is one more thing—a handwritten note from Alex presented by his lawyer. It reads, 'Jake, I want my last deed to be an honorable one.' Can you believe that? The old son-of-a-bitch did have a heart after all."

"That's because you helped him find it, Jake."

"You think so?"

"How can a smart guy like you be so blind? Alex's life was filled with shady characters like Sam and Chase. They honor nothing— not the land, not their partners, not even their own ancestors. In the absence of honor, terrible things happen. Just look at all the tragedies. But in the midst of this greed, you were unselfish. You were just your-self. That's what I love so much about you."

Unable to say anything, Jake simply held Donna close for a long time. Then he pulled away slightly, fighting back tears, and said, "Here's what I'm thinking, at least for now. I don't need 375 acres. What if we take the land the old lodge is on and commit seventy-five acres or so to a state park recreating the history of the Hudson Bay and American Fur Trading Companies? I've had it checked out with some contacts at the state of Minnesota. They're very interested. We could also configure the land for the state park to adjoin a real heritage center with the sacred burial grounds. They tell me the idea represents the only integrated reconstruction of an original Indian village and trading post in the entire United States."

"This is absolutely perfect," was all that Donna could say.

"I think the tribal support will be easy to get as they've already expressed interest in rejoining the six corpses with their ancestral brothers and sisters. But I can't do the rest by myself. I'd like you to be my partner on the project to do it right. It will give us the chance to build something together, and I do mean more than a state park." Donna's shriek of joy was the response Jake had hoped for.

Their time together that day felt surreal, as if the outside world had stopped to give them the opportunity to finally celebrate their triumph.

"By the way," he said after a long period of silence and while opening up another Stenway Lite, "Remind me to trash-can all those new resume copies in the cabin for my job search. I don't think I'm going to need them anymore."

A Conversation with Jim Proebstle

I am struck by how many people are fascinated with books. Some are writing their own stories, many are involved in book clubs, and a few are part of writing groups. But for most of us, we just want to enjoy a story that takes us on an adventure in such a way that we feel a kinship or connection with the characters and their circumstances. For that reason I offer my response to a few of the questions that have been asked of me and that I experienced while writing *In the Absence of Honor.*

Q. How did you become so familiar with Minnesota's North Woods setting?

A. Both of my parents grew up in Minnesota and as a child I learned of the North Woods on family vacations. My grandfather was a switchman on the Great Northern Railway in the small Indian town featured in the book. We were told many stories of growing up near a reservation and experienced many adventures of being in the wilderness. Now, our family summer home is Sandy Cove. The beautiful setting and friendly environment seemed to just call for a story.

Q. Did you start with an outline for the story or just let it develop?

A. I did start with an outline, as I have on other writing projects, but it didn't seem to pass muster after the characters become involved. For me the outline just helps me to get started—it's my way of making a commitment to write.

Q. What is the most productive time to write?

A. It really depends on my routine and my project client involvement in Prodyne, Inc., a consulting firm I started in 1991. Early on in the book I found that 7 P.M. to 9 P.M. was perfect—typically at the local library to get out of my home office for a while. If I could get at least five pages written I felt successful. Somewhere along the line I switched to the morning—9 A.M. to noon, after a good work out. It seemed my energy was stronger and my thinking clearer.

Q. Did you find any useful techniques in getting started with actually writing the novel?

A. Yes, definitely. After the rough outline, I started to think about developing the characters. They couldn't just represent different versions of Jim Proebstle. Carole, my wife, is a psychologist and very skilled at personality profile instruments—Myers Briggs, Temperament, etc. Over the years I've also become reasonably knowledgeable of the various profiles and it occurred to me that each character should be assigned a profile. Character disorders and value systems were added, as needed. This helped me get started in thinking through the characters.

Q. Do characters really take over during the writing process?

A. I know this sounds weird, but they really do, particularly during intense scenes. I remember coming upstairs from my office after writing the rape scene. I was disgusted with the thoughts and words that were on the paper and I was drained of emotion. Carole said, "What's the matter with you? Are you alright?" Without thinking, my response was, "I can't believe what Morey's just done!" I think this comes from the character and personality development done up front. Once they become entrenched in the story they seem to have a mind of their own and won't be taken off track.

Q. Did you write the story to be published or just to tell the story?

A. In the beginning I had this vague feeling that it would be nice to just write a good story about the cabin, kind of a "to do" on the check list of life, but I was kidding myself. Anyone who works hard at something takes pride in what they do, and I'm no different. The goal of getting the book published became a very strong motivation of improving my craft to a point where it would be commercially acceptable.

Q. What were your biggest learning points is writing *In the Absence of Honor*?

A. First, editing, and more editing. I actually thought I was good at writing. I had no idea how many mistakes I would make. It was humbling to see the red lines. It also took me a while to learn not to worry about the mistakes, as correcting them is what a professional editor does—the best of all novelists have editors who are critical to the writer's success. Second, every writer has to learn how to use dialogue to communicate action and the content of the story's plot. I am amazed as to how good the really talented writers are. In my case I worked at it quite a bit. I think that this is at the core of good writing and will be a continuing education effort.

Q. What are you writing at present?

A. I am very excited about the novel I'm working on, although it doesn't have a title yet. It's inspired by the real circumstances of my uncle, Curly, and the devastating plane crash he piloted during WW II. All nineteen passengers and crew were lost on an unnamed mountain at 11,000 feet in Alaska—never to be found! To this day, the plane and the passengers are buried in a glacier slowly moving down the mountain. Curly's children were too young to have met their father. One of them said recently, "I may see my father for the first time and he'll be half my age," referring to the possibility that a cryogenically preserved corpse is likely to appear soon. I hope that my telling of this story has the excitement of a novel while maintaining the respect for the men who suffered on that day in 1944.

Q. How are you staying in contact with readers interested in your work?

A. Two ways primarily: First, the website www.InTheAbsenceOf-Honor.com will provide updates regarding the progress of the book. I'll make a commitment to respond to questions readers may have about the book or future writing endeavors. Second, I plan to make myself available via conference call to book clubs and reading groups that choose *In the Absence of Honor* as their book selection. I would be happy to answer your questions about the characters, the story, or the writing experience itself. Please go to www.InTheAbsenceOf-Honor.com for details. The feedback will help me become a better writer, and I look forward to bringing something new to your event.

Questions for Discussion

Question: Who is your favorite character in the story? Did any characters grow more than others as a result of their experiences in the story?

Question: The two working titles for the book were *Arrowhead* and *Sandy Cove*. *In the Absence of Honor* was suggested by Linnea Schlobohm after her involvement in an early editorial stage. Which title do you prefer and why?

Question: The story reflects several major transitions involving various characters. Which are the most significant from your perspective? Which involved the most courage?

Question: Which character did you enjoy the most? Which character did you absolutely despise?

Question: Did the book provide you with any new insights to Native American history and/or reservation life?

Question: Since the story is fictional, are there any scenes that didn't seem believable?

Question: How did you feel about the developing relationship between Jake and Donna? Between Big Lights and Linda?

Question: How would you rate this book as a first-time novel?

Question: Having read the novel, are you more or less likely to visit northern Minnesota?

There are many more questions of course, but I hope you find these interesting.

acknowledgments

I always knew writing a novel would be an adventure—an accomplishment in which I would take great pride. What I experienced and learned, however, came through the hard work of writing and rewriting. And at times, I felt that I couldn't contribute anything at all to the story. It's the support and feedback that I received throughout this process that was essential to my motivation to press on. For that I am forever grateful to a few who tirelessly stuck with me to the story's conclusion. Among those are the following:

- Carole Proebstle, my life's partner of forty-two years, for her gentle reminders and encouragement that I can accomplish whatever I choose.
- My family for their shared love of the Sandy Cove property and their insightful feedback to the story.
- Mary Norris for her devotion in untold hours of reading, critiquing, and offering suggestions that helped me grow as a writer.
- Wonderful friends who listened with interest to the many turns in the road involving the progress and development of *In the Absence of Honor.*

As I look forward to the completion of the next novel, I do so with the same expectation of adventure and pride. But I realize that while writing is a solitary activity, it is never done alone.